D1428886

PRAISE FOR KATHLEEN B. JONES'S
CITIES OF WOMEN

"With a scholar's commitment to accurate detail, and the heart of a lover of beauty, Kathleen B. Jones's engaging and well-crafted parallel story brings to light female creativity in medieval France. Jones's writing is as colorful and lucid as the illuminated manuscripts at the center of her novel, and the unforgettable story makes *Cities of Women* a must read for anyone interested in finding and honoring the forgotten women of western art." —**Laurel Corona, author of *The Mapmaker's Daughter***

"At its heart, *Cities of Women* is both a detective story about the search for, and love letter to, the women who worked on the beautiful illuminated manuscripts of the medieval era. The novel is both sensitive and well researched, an accomplished debut which marks Jones out as one to watch." —**Laura Shepperson, author of *Phaedra***

"Kathleen B. Jones' great talent is her ability to slide through history showing how the past is inextricably alive inside of every present moment. With witty dialogue and lovingly rendered descriptions of beauty, *Cities of Women* is both a page turning mystery and an intricate tapestry that entwines academic research, medieval history, art, love, and most importantly, the enduring friendships of women." —**Karen Osborn, author of *The Music Book***

"*Cities of Women* is a vivid and absorbing dual-timeline novel following a 21st century historian as she uncovers the life of a forgotten medieval female artist. Illuminating and smart, it reads like a love letter to curiosity and creativity. This is an empowering tale of two women separated by the centuries, but united in their determination to pursue their passions at all costs." —**Nikki Marmery, author of *On Wilder Seas* and the forthcoming *Lilith***

CITIES
OF
WOMEN

ALSO BY
KATHLEEN B. JONES

Diving for Pearls:
A Thinking Journey with Hannah Arendt

Living Between Danger & Love:
The Limits of Choice

CITIES
OF
WOMEN

A NOVEL

KATHLEEN B.
JONES

KEYLIGHT
BOOKS
AN IMPRINT
OF TURNER
PUBLISHING

KEYLIGHT BOOKS
AN IMPRINT OF TURNER PUBLISHING COMPANY
Nashville, Tennessee
www.turnerpublishing.com

Cities of Women

Copyright © 2023 by Kathleen B. Jones. All rights reserved.

This book or any part thereof may not be reproduced or transmitted in any form or by any means, electronic or mechanical, including photocopying, recording, or by any information storage and retrieval system, without permission in writing from the publisher. This is a work of fiction. All the characters and events portrayed in this book are either products of the author's imagination or are used fictitiously.

Excerpts from *The Selected Writings of Christine de Pizan, A Norton Critical Edition* by Christine de Pizan, Renate Blumenfeld-Kosinski, ed, translated by Renata Blumenfeld-Kosinski. Copyright © 1997 by W. W. Norton & Company, Inc. Used by permission of W. W. Norton & Company, Inc.

Cover design by Faceout Studio
Book design by William Ruoto

Library of Congress Cataloging-in-Publication Data
Names: Jones, Kathleen B., 1949- author.
   Title: Cities of women : a novel / Kathleen B. Jones.
   Description: Nashville, Tennessee : Keylight Books, [2023]
   Identifiers: LCCN 2022049194 (print) | LCCN 2022049195 (ebook) | ISBN
     9781684429998 (hardcover) | ISBN 9781684420322 (paperback) | ISBN
     9781684420339 (epub)
   Subjects: LCSH: Christine, de Pisan, approximately 1364-approximately
     1431--Fiction. | Women history teachers--Fiction. | Literary
     historians—Fiction. | Illuminators—Fiction. | Illumination of books
     and manuscripts—Fiction. | Manuscripts, Medieval—Fiction. | LCGFT:
     Biographical fiction. | Novels.
   Classification: LCC PS3610.O62624 C58 2023 (print) | LCC PS3610.O62624
     (ebook) | DDC 813/.6—dc23/eng/20221206
   LC record available at https://lccn.loc.gov/2022049194
LC ebook record available at https://lccn.loc.gov/2022049195

Printed in the United States of America

For all the women artists who've been made invisible.

But when from a long-distant past nothing subsists, after the people are dead, after the things are broken and scattered, taste and smell alone, more fragile but more enduring, more unsubstantial, more persistent, more faithful, remain poised a long time, like souls, remembering, waiting, hoping, amid the ruins of all the rest.

—PROUST

"Beauty is truth, truth beauty"—that is all
Ye know on earth, and all ye need to know.

—KEATS

CONTENTS

CITIES
OF
WOMEN

PROLOGUE

Long fingers of dawn's light crept across the tiled floor of the *atelier* on rue Erembourg de Brie, casting a warm amber glow onto a wooden pallet where an old woman lay asleep. The bells of the cathedral nearby tolled Prime, announcing the birth of a new day. Stirred from the filaments of a dream whose textures had cradled and comforted her through a feverish night, the woman rose, wrapped a woolen blanket around her shoulders, and walked to the stone hearth to stir the still-glowing embers into flame. It was time to finish what she'd begun.

She crossed the room to a workbench that stood like a patient wooden horse beside a grated window. On it rested the raised platform at which she had worked for more than half her life, coaxing colors of vermilion and ultramarine into the empty, cramped spaces and framed compartments scribes left vacant on folios of parchment for her to illuminate texts with painted miniatures and decorated puzzle initials. Hour after hour, year after year, she'd labored swirls of paint into the shapes of angels and animals and, in her last and boldest design, conjured a vision of three crowned ladies of great nobility, harbingers of reason, rectitude, and justice, architects of the City of Ladies.

Today, the wordless, unblemished parchment lay still on her desk, awaiting her touch. She had powdered, pumiced, and folded the vellum herself; readying the creamy granular front side to receive the image that had burst into her dream like a golden moon shining in a clear indigo sky. She felt the hearth's warmth and began to unfurl her gnarled fingers, racked with age, and reached for the quill she'd salvaged from the wreckage of a past, whose melancholic traces still lingered in the filtered light of every dawn. She dipped the point of the quill in ink, and with the faintest of strokes drew the outlines of two female figures in the foreground of a field encircled by hills, bending their heads toward each other as if they were sharing a whispered prayer. Against a narrowing perspective, she sketched a moon, drew its mirror image floating in a waterscape, and then polished the outlines of what she'd drawn with a bit of broken tooth.

On the left of her desk, near the window, were her brushes and paint pots filled with flamboyant colors. She pulled back her gray hair and tied it with a faded green ribbon, lest any hairs fall on wet paint, and set to work. She poured blue paint the color of lapis lazuli into a horn and fastened it into a hole in the desk. With a knife in her right hand, she held the parchment down to prevent it from curling, and, with her left hand, dipped a brush into the thick blue liquid, eddying the color in long strokes down the right side of the page, clothing the figure of one of the women in elegant drapery. Then she lightened the blue by dipping the brush in a shell filled with water to shade the fabric's folds, adding a few strokes of white with another brush to heighten the effect. On the front of the woman's gown, and around her waist, she painted a saffron girdle. Then she began the drapery for the woman on the left, decorating her gown in bright madder and gracing her shoulders with a blue cape. Behind the two women she swirled a dusky sky filled with cumulus in washes of deep violet and magenta, as if the colors of the women's costumes had leached into the heavens.

Hours passed. Day faded unnoticed to dusk. The old woman's energy ebbed. She looked at the painting. Nearly done; only the faces to finish. Time for that tomorrow, she thought, as she extinguished the lamp. She damped the embers, grated the hearth, and climbed into her bed.

Soon another dream floated into her sleep, a dream of her mother, carrying her in her womb and pushing her into the world. In the dream, she walked along a long pathway toward a verdant field blossoming with lilies and primrose and forget-me-nots. She saw the tip of a ladder emerge from the firmament and descend to the earth. The ladder was made not of wood nor of metal nor of rope but of some ethereal substance as light as the wings of a butterfly yet as strong as the stones of a castle and as eternal as beauty itself.

Outside, the cathedral bells tolled Matins, calling the faithful to midnight prayer. The hearth embers had turned ashen. The room quieted to the moment before silence enveloped the night.

She heard her mother call to her.

"Now, daughter, take hold of this ladder; I will go first and lead the way. Climb up, embrace the beauty you will see, for you go now to a new country."

1

WISDOM BEGINS IN
WONDER, FALL 2018

VERITY

Verity Frazier sat alone in her office at Monterey College, holding a letter in her hand. April had proved the cruelest month, delivering twin blows—Pauline's departure, abruptly ending their four-year love affair, followed by the letter's arrival, threatening to end Verity's career. Summer had brought temporary relief when her sister whisked her away for a beach holiday. Then came September, and California turned into an angry inferno as if the whole world was about to explode. She stared out the window at the faded tangerine orb in the sky, darkened into premature dusk by smoke billowing down the coast from fires blazing a hundred and fifty miles to the north. Clouds of ash loomed on the horizon. An acrid smell wafted in through a ceiling vent. Her life was a looming disaster.

In the far corner stood a four-drawer filing cabinet. Cascading down its front were dozens of photos of the revolutionary women of the Paris Commune of 1871 she'd spent her graduate-school years researching. She turned her head and glimpsed the face of Elisabeth Dmitrieff, the

twenty-year-old Russian émigré who'd summoned the women of Paris
to vanquish the enemies of revolution or die trying. In the dim light of
the gray day, Dmitrieff's mouth seemed to twist into a grimace, accusing
Verity of negligence or, worse still, lost faith.

"You would make peace with Versailles at any price! You would accept the generosity of cowardly assassins! No, it is not peace, but all-out
war that the working women of Paris demand!"

Verity hadn't yet capitulated to the powers-that-be, but the single-spaced
declaration of doom she'd received from the faculty promotions committee made clear that giving in was the only way to salvage her
career.

"Since this is your last review before being considered for tenure, the
committee considers it imperative that you complete the scholarly monograph that was promised when you were hired. Failure to do so by next
year's review will result in your being given a terminal year."

As for her love life, nothing could resurrect that. Pauline had declared Verity hopelessly despondent and slammed the door on any possible recovery. That was that.

She walked over to the cabinet and opened the top drawer with a
violent tug, as much to disturb Dmitrieff's stare as to retrieve the file
holding the comments that reviewers of her book had sent to the editor at Cambridge University Press. "As it stands now," Reviewer A had
written, "Prof. Frazier's manuscript reads more like a novel than a scholarly monograph." The editor was satisfied enough with the manuscript's
potential to offer Verity a contract, and told her to follow Reviewer A's
advice.

She turned on her computer and clicked on the desktop folder containing the manuscript she'd tried a million times to revise, watching a
series of chapters fan out of the folder like a magician's deck of cards. It
was neat and tidy and well-ordered—so neat and tidy and orderly that
Verity felt sick to her stomach every time she read it, as if she'd captured
and categorized the French women's lives like some lepidopterist pinning
butterflies to a board for display.

She leaned back in her chair and sighed. All she had to do was write a
new conclusion in the same lackluster style as the rest of the manuscript,

and the editor would publish it. Verity would have a book and make everyone happy—everyone, that is, except herself. Out of desperation, she reached for the phone and dialed her best friend's number.

Regina taught international security studies at UCLA. They'd met in New York in their last year of graduate school, commiserated about the experience they'd both had of having weathered a failed marriage to a psychologist unable to analyze himself, and decided to share an East Village apartment, and then a bed, until their odd-couple temperaments drove them as far apart as the subjects they studied. Getting academic positions in cities too distant to be commutable was the excuse they'd used to end their moribund affair. In the five years since, Verity's career and love life had floundered while Regina's had soared. Despite everything, they'd remained good friends.

"I don't know why you're making this so difficult," Regina said. "You wrote a dissertation. You've published articles in good journals. You can finish a book."

"I know I *can*; it's just—I'm not sure I want to."

"Are we actually having this conversation? Are you actually saying you don't want to get tenure?" Regina sounded more angry than perplexed.

"I hate what I've written. I've erased all the color out of these women's lives," Verity said.

"You're not supposed to be writing a novel."

"You sound like one of the reviewers. My writing should do justice to their stories."

"And I suppose they'll get more justice if you're fired?"

"You don't understand." A deep sigh escaped from her lungs. "I feel like a fraud. Like I'm pretending to be something I'm not."

"You're a professor, Verity. Isn't that what you wanted to be?"

"I wanted to be a dancer."

"And I wanted to be a firefighter. And then we both grew up and realized we were smart women."

"Don't be such a snob, Regina. I'm serious."

"Look, I get it. You're worried about compromising your feminist values. But you have to conform to academic standards, like I have, or your work won't be published. Then your women won't be colorless—they'll be invisible."

"I know. But how much conformity is too much?"

"You can decide that for yourself *after* promotion."

"Like you did?"

"What do you mean?"

"Nothing. Forget it."

"We've had this argument too many times. It's boring. I couldn't prove the positive impact of the nuclear non-proliferation treaty on international stability without hard data. It's not anti-feminist to use statistical analysis to prove a feminist point about peace."

"When I read what I've written, I get nauseous."

"Just because you've put those women's stories into tables of correlations doesn't mean you're a traitor. It's facts, not fables, that convince people about the truth."

"You know how I felt when I first discovered these women? It gave me chills to imagine how brave they were—"

"And you can put all that in the book's introduction."

"—I got so excited, I couldn't sleep."

"Are you sleeping now?"

"What?"

"I asked if you were sleeping now."

"I'm not talking about sleeping."

"But I am. You've been depressed since Pauline left and you got that letter in April. You need a break."

"I know, but—"

"But nothing. You've got a funded fellowship that gives you the term off. Go to New York. Stay in my place. Meet with your old adviser at the New School. He's always supported your work. And then go back to those dingy European archives. I'm sure the dusty smell of those files will return you to sanity. Anyway, do it for friendship's sake."

"You mean we won't be friends if I refuse?"

"That's not what I meant. But what kind of friend wouldn't try to persuade you to save your career? You want me to give you a push."

"I don't want a push; I want a spark."

"Just finish the book, Verity. I'll order fireworks for the book party."

They said goodbye, and Verity hung up the phone. It was early evening now. She looked out toward the Pacific Ocean. The smoke-filled coastal fog that had rolled in low and wide across the Monterey Peninsula had finally lifted its gray mantle, trailing small wisps around the edges of the horseshoe-shaped coast. The setting sun pierced the high clouds with rays of apricot and tangerine, painting a shimmering path across the water. For a moment, everything looked different in that golden light. Maybe Regina was right. She should finish the damn book and save her career. That would show Pauline, wouldn't it? No, she ought to do this for herself, prove she wasn't chronically despondent. Or a failure. At least that's how she thought about it as she emailed her Cambridge editor, requested an extension to the contract deadline, and wrote to Professor Berman, her thesis adviser, suggesting they meet to discuss her manuscript.

Two weeks later, she was on a plane headed for New York.

Verity arrived at JFK on a red-eye flight and took the AirTrain to Howard Beach, where she got the subway to West Fourth Street. After an hour's ride and a short walk, she found herself standing in front of the building on East Eighth Street in the East Village neighborhood where she and Regina had lived. A hefty divorce settlement had allowed Regina to hold on to it all these years since, even after the building went co-op.

The place looked nothing like when they'd lived there. It had undergone a magnificent facelift. The brick structure was power-washed back to its original warm speckled red, and the windows now sported high-end, noise-mitigating double-paned glass. There was even a virtual door attendant, a panel that trained a security camera on whoever tried to enter the building. Who could afford to live here? Certainly not the starving artists and graduate students who'd populated the building years ago.

Using the fob Regina had mailed, Verity opened the heavy security door and entered a marble-tiled reception area that sparkled with gentrified pride. She crossed the lobby to the elevator, converted from the old freight lift only the super had used, and pressed the button for the third floor. The same fob opened the door to Regina's apartment, which seemed brighter than Verity remembered.

The once brown-and-beige-wallpapered living-room walls were painted chalky white, making the high-ceilinged room look double the size etched in her memory. The overstuffed couch she'd salvaged from a mound of old furniture dumped outside the building, which Regina had considered an eyesore, had been replaced by a sleek chocolate brown leather sofa. Two lime green velvet chairs stood opposite the sofa at an inviting conversational angle.

She looked around the room for a television. None was in sight. Had Regina finally given up the habit of watching late-night shows while grading student papers, like she'd done when they were graduate teaching assistants? It always bugged Verity that Regina could laugh at all the comedian's jokes and still get through twenty papers in the time Verity marked five.

"It's your own fault," Regina would say, "for assigning all those essays. Multiple choice and short answers are easier to grade."

"That might work in international politics, but not in social history."

"Every field has a set of facts you can test. Even history. You can verify events with evidence just as easily as I can document the impact of a nuclear weapon on a population of a certain density."

"Maybe, but what counts as a fact is open to question. That's what I want my students to see."

"Good luck with that."

On the windows facing the street, the clunky aluminum blinds that always squeaked or got stuck were gone. The windows were left uncovered, which seemed odd for someone like Regina, who guarded her privacy as carefully as national security secrets. Verity noticed a switch between the two window casements and pushed it, watching in amazement as the window glass turned opaque, as if Regina intended to tantalize gawkers with a fading glimpse of some unfinished scene, whose climax they'd regret having missed.

Clever Regina. Clever, controlling Regina.

The once-dreary galley kitchen had undergone a complete makeover. No more grease-covered, cockroach-infested, yellow-painted cabinets or outdated appliances. In their place were a scaled-down Sub-Zero refrigerator, a small Viking stove, and a deep stainless-steel double sink surrounded by polished concrete countertops. Verity ran her hand across the counter's smooth, spotless surface, recalling the weekend she'd spent replacing the old orange Formica with butcher block she'd salvaged from a nearby restaurant undergoing renovation. She'd spent an entire Sunday sanding and finishing the grain into a satiny sheen to surprise Regina, who returned from a research trip to Washington, D.C., and promptly spilled red wine all over the newly treated wood.

"Well, at least it was free," Regina said, while Verity mopped up the mess.

God, she could be so insensitive, Verity thought, and exited the kitchen, turning down the hallway toward the small room that had become hers when they'd stopped being lovers. She was taken aback by how upset she became to discover Regina had converted the room into a study, and even more shaken to realize she'd actually hoped to find some trace of herself lingering in that room, some part not replaced, some memory still cherished. What a mistake it had been to come here.

A sudden urge to get out of the apartment overtook her. It started to rain, so she grabbed an umbrella, stuffed her notebook and fountain pen, along with her cell phone and wallet, into her book satchel, and hurried into the hallway, raced down the stairs, exited the building, heading toward Tompkins Square Park. The air smelled of wet, oily pavement mixed with the faint whiff of marijuana. A wave of nausea—the result of a noxious mixture of jet lag and too many bad memories—made her duck into a nearby Starbucks to find a restroom. Leaning over the basin, she splashed water on her face and stood up to check her appearance in the mirror. Behind her on a bulletin board she caught sight of a colorful poster and turned around for a closer look.

The poster advertised an exhibition of rare pages from medieval illuminated manuscripts opening that day at the Morgan Library. Verity remembered her mother had once taken her to the Grand Army Plaza library in Brooklyn for a special program organized for schoolchildren by the Morgan. The suggestion itself had come as a shock, since her mother's preferred outings tended toward trips to Coney Island more than visits to the library. When they arrived, her mother had wandered off while Verity was directed to the library classroom, where staff had arranged a few illuminated manuscripts on a long table. There had been a short talk about the making of ancient books, nothing of which she now recalled. What had stuck with her was how it felt to touch those old, yellowed pages. She'd run her fingers around the decorated borders and the curlicued letters of script and felt a jolt course through her, as if she'd absorbed the words and images through the pores of her skin, and they wound their mysteries through her bloodstream and into her heart and made their way to her brain. Even now, the memory made her hands tremble.

Still shaking, she took out her cell phone, looked up directions to the Morgan, and then left a message for Professor Berman, postponing their meeting to tomorrow.

Twenty minutes later, Verity stood outside the Madison Avenue entrance to the Morgan Library. She entered and walked toward the reception area, inquiring about the manuscript exhibition from the young woman seated at a desk in front of a wood-paneled wall.

After purchasing a ticket, she checked her coat and satchel, walked across the hall to the atrium café, and took a seat for a minute at an empty table next to a tall glass wall of red, blue, and yellow panels. The rain had stopped, and light streamed through the three-story-high apertures, splashing rainbows of color across the floor. Verity felt as if she were inside a sanctuary and fell into a daydream, imagining she heard a choir sweeping her up in the prayerful arms of song. The sound of metal chairs scraping the stone floor broke the spell. She stood up and walked toward the exhibition room down a hallway on the left.

At the doorway, she froze, stunned by the lavish images filling the room's four walls with jewel-toned colors edged in gold. The manuscript pages were so intricately designed, they looked like the unacknowledged medieval forerunners of graphic novels, although depicting more somber religious scenes. A dozen or so people wandered from one image to another until a tall, gray-haired gentleman carrying a clipboard motioned the group to gather around.

The man was dressed in a dark suit and a crisp white shirt. He wore an unusually long tie designed with horizontally stacked, multi-colored dashes that looked like how Mondrian might have painted the scales of a Gregorian chant turned on its side. He spoke in reverent tones about the exhibition, every now and then pushing a pair of horn-rimmed glasses back up the bridge of his narrow nose. Verity had happened upon a special lecture for medievalists by the library's lead manuscript curator; she sidled over to listen.

"Welcome to this exhibition of single leaves, or orphaned leaves, as I'm sure you know they're called." Two tweed-coated women near the front nodded assent.

"These were culled from the magnificent collection amassed by Pierpont Morgan. Besides acquiring whole manuscripts, Mr. Morgan became enamored of these single pages, sixty of which—some from donors other than Morgan—are included in this exhibition, several for the first time. Some, like the magnificent leaf from the Winchester Bible you see in the center, date from the twelfth century; others, like the one depicting the *Adoration of the Magi* from an Italian manuscript, are from the sixteenth. We've even included three impostor pages, fakes produced in the early twentieth century by that rascal now known as the Spanish forger. We know they're forgeries because, although the artist used genuine vellum, he painted with a pigment not available before the early 1800s."

While the curator continued his lecture, Verity meandered toward the rear wall and approached one of the paintings, tantalized by its central image: a large initial *C* decorated in the brightest blue she'd ever seen. The initial was fitted inside a square illuminated in glittering gold, while out of its edges tumbled tendrils of vines and other flora in red and green, with gold-flecked flourishes. In the middle of the *C*, the artist had painted a scene of *The Last Supper.* A golden-haloed Christ sat at the apex of the table, surrounded by his twelve apostles. At the table's nadir sat Judas, his head encircled in black, clutching a blood-red purse at his waist containing the infamous thirty pieces of silver he'd received for his betrayal.

Verity stared at the painting; the longer she stared, the more it seemed as if the gold-embossed letters, tendrils, and halos were some kind of multidimensional time machine: incandescent, ethereal, and luminous, transporting meaning beyond the ordinary boundary of understanding. It was like seeing dust burst into flames.

She took out her notebook and wrote one word: *Beauty*. When she looked up, she noticed that the two women in tweed were standing next to her.

"Extraordinary, isn't it?" one of them said.

Verity mumbled agreement.

"By the length of time you've contemplated this one, I surmise you favor the Italians of the fifteenth century," the other one said.

"I—I don't know why it caught my attention. I'm actually a political historian."

"Not much politics here," the first one said. Her companion giggled.

"It's like learning to see all over again," Verity said, and walked toward the next image.

It depicted a woman outfitted in a blue gown and a white horned headdress. She was seated at an angled wooden desk next to a grated window in a room inside an ancient stone castle. On the wall behind her hung an elaborate maroon tapestry decorated with inverted gold hearts bursting into curlicues. She held a red pointer in one hand, a silver quill in the other. Next to the open manuscript on her desk stood a silver ink-well. A little white dog sat patiently at her feet.

"She's writing a book," Verity exclaimed, caressing her notebook.

"That's the fifteenth-century author, Christine de Pizan," the second tweed-clad woman said, who'd moved next to Verity to admire the painting. "The image is the frontispiece from a presentation copy of her manuscripts produced for wealthy French patrons of the arts. It's from her earliest poetry collection, *Cents Balades*."

"One Hundred Ballads," Verity translated. "A woman writer. In the fifteenth century. I've heard of her but never seen a painting of her close up. It's remarkable."

"Since you're interested in political history, you might want to read her *Book of the City of Ladies*. Quite risqué for its time. Filled with images of women building a city. I believe they have a copy in the library bookstore."

"Who painted the portraits in her books?" Verity asked, unable to take her eyes off the woman.

"Oh, my dear, no one really knows. He's identified merely as the Master of the City of Ladies."

"He?"

"Well, naturally, one assumes it was a man."

The two women walked away, chatting together, leaving Verity transfixed by the portrait. She fell into an infinite regress, pulled back to the point where beauty began, before there was a before. A woman writing alone in her room, as if nothing in the world were more important than the story she was crafting, as if every letter were sacred, and every stroke of the pen were holy. Only someone who knew Christine well could have created a scene of such intimacy with so much care.

It suddenly seemed obvious to Verity how wrong everyone had been. Amplified by years studying revolutionary women, her instincts told her a medieval woman with the temerity to overcome every roadblock—and there were surely many—in the pathway of her aspiration to become a writer would want an ally of her sex for a collaborator. Another woman had to have painted this portrait, a woman still hidden from history, waiting patiently through centuries of misapprehension for someone to grasp her existence in the shape and shimmer of the brushstrokes she'd left behind.

Electrified by the possibility of finding clues to the identity of this artist in Christine's writing, Verity hurried to the library bookstore and bought a copy of *The Book of the City of Ladies*—an English translation from the medieval French, including reproductions of images from the original manuscript along with a biographical essay. She began reading the biography on the subway downtown and was so enthralled by Christine's life that she missed the Astor Place stop. By the time she arrived at Regina's apartment, it was dusk.

She fumbled for the key fob, entered the lobby, and raced up the three flights of stairs. Still grasping the book in her hand, she ran down the hall to the study, sat down at the desk in front of the window, and turned on a lamp.

In the warm amber light, Christine's portrait inside the book's cover took on an ethereal glow. Bordering the walls of the writer's study, the artist had painted garlands of flowers in vermilion and cerulean flecked with filigrees of gold. Verity reached for the switch to darken the window and caught a glimpse of herself in the glass. Behind her, on a shelf, she saw a vase full of colorful glass flowers glimmer to light, washing streams of blue and crimson light across the pages of the book as she read:

"I know a woman today, named Anastasia, who is so learned and skilled in painting manuscript borders and miniature backgrounds that one cannot find an artisan in all the city of Paris who can surpass her."

At the sight of that name, an astonished cry escaped Verity's lips, while, on the cabinet back in her office, Elisabeth Dmitrieff's grimace turned into a smile.

2

NEAR AVIGNON,
FRANCE, 1355

I n that frost-filled first winter after my parents fled Flanders for France, I, Béatrice Tapis, slipped free of my mother's warm womb and entered the cold world of Crécy three days before the feast of Epiphany and ten years before sickness and death blackened the earth. In those ten years before death shaded my vision with sorrow and wreathed my soul in the desiccating flowers of woe, I had thought of myself as beauty's apprentice.

My father, Gilbert Tapis, was a weaver by trade. His delicate, intricate patterns woven into the finest fabrics of silk or wool brought him the honor—or misfortune, depending on one's perspective—of being chosen master of furnishings for the great house of Louis de Nevers, then Count of Flanders. There he met my mother, Jeanne, an exquisite fair-haired young woman who served as handmaid to Countess Margaret. In my mother's blue eyes, and in her impish giggle, my father must have been beguiled by the twin charms of passion and humor. After only a fortnight of courting, they married in Count Louis's grand hall, surrounded by walls filled with my father's luxurious tapestries, woven scenes of bucolic delight.

They lived contentedly on Louis's lands until the burghers of Ghent allied with the English king to force Count Louis from Flanders, sending my parents fleeing to Crécy, soon to be joined by myself.

As my mother tells—after her tongue has been loosed with a few pints at L'Auberge Rose—the seven years of my youth spent in Crécy were joyful ones. They were filled with games of hide-and-seek, spinning tops, and dressing up poppets, though mother says I preferred running and jumping to costuming dolls. I was a clever child, she says, a wild thing, even as an infant, able to charm all and sundry. And when she reminisces about how I walked and talked earlier than any child she has ever known, she still laughs a little and reminds me how, at the tender age of three, I began to follow my father into his workshop, bothering him for instruction in all manner of things, from treadle loom to spinning wheel.

Now, at age fifteen, I cannot say if all this is true, but I remember the workshop.

It occupied the uppermost level of the high tower, cresting to a red-tiled point on the chateau's southwest wall, which bordered the glittering green beech woods of the Crécy forest. To reach it, one climbed a narrow circular stone staircase that uncoiled like a snake from our rooms below to the floor where my father's low warp loom stood against the far wall, looking like a wooden chair big enough for a giant. Mother says I first mounted those steps by crawling on hands and knees from one to the next, slapping each cold stone as if to announce my approach, until my father, worried I'd slip, fastened a rope low enough along the tower's wall for me to grip and climb faster and faster. By the time I was five, I ran up those stairs as fast as a hare.

When I close my eyes now, I can still see the treasures inside that room. Sketches cover the walls with his latest ideas for tapestry designs, some populated with flora and fauna, and one that featured an elegant lady dressed in a cerulean gown that fell to the floor, enveloping her in waves of blue while she played the lyre. Skeins and skeins of yarn, balls of silver and gold thread, and jars of indigo, saffron, and madder dye shimmer in the setting sun's glow; their filaments and colors pull me into that sacred, dangerous space of beauty's embrace.

In that room, I watched my father stretch the warp threads across the horizontal planes of the loom's limbs, fixing the threads tightly and in careful symmetry to one of two bars, even-number threads on one and odd numbers on the other, each bar attached to a treadle pedal that would cause the bar of pinned threads to rise at the gentle pressure of his foot, creating a space through which he passed the shuttle carrying the weft threads to begin to weave his imagination into being. Over one, under two, over three, under four, right foot, left foot, right foot, left foot, the wool danced to the *whoosh-whoosh* of the pedals, in time with the shuttle's whispering glide, until Father reached the end of one color he was working, tied off the thread, and began again on the same line with the next in his palette. When he reached the end of the row, he pressed the weft threads down to touch the warp and made one seamless line of the complicated image he held in his mind's eye, the reverse of the webbed threads lying before him. This image remained obscured, sometimes as long as the season of Lent, until he pulled the final weft thread into place and turned the fabric over to admire his work.

One day, a few months before my fifth birthday, I crawled under the loom, wiggling into a corner to watch a field of azure flowers slowly materialize above me. Underneath the loom, the earth was upside down and I floated somewhere in the sky above the bright blue field. I drifted and drifted until the slow, steady *whoosh-whoosh* of the treadle lulled me to sleep, and I dreamed of a unicorn dancing with me in that field, like the one Father had drawn on my wall and promised to weave into a cover for my bed. When the shuttle stopped, Father wrapped me in a brown wool blanket and carried me downstairs, where Mother had prepared our evening meal of oxtail soup.

Seated at the table, our prayers being said, Father asked me to tell Mother what I had seen.

"A unicorn was dancing with me in a field of flowers," I said.

Mother laughed.

"Silly girl," Father said. "You aren't in the tapestry."

"But I saw myself."

"You imagined yourself into the scene," Father said. "Use that powerful gift wisely, my precious one."

"May I watch you work again tomorrow, Father?"

"Tomorrow is a special day. I'm placing you under the tutelage of another artist. Gilles d'Orléans, the master *enlumineur*, illustrator of some of Count Louis's rarest manuscripts, has agreed to teach you his craft."

I must have been shaking with excitement at the thought of being instructed by this master, because Father touched my shoulder to calm me, and smiled.

"Come now," Mother said. "You must be well rested for tomorrow's visit."

That night, I lay awake thinking about the times when Mother had been working in the countess's chambers and Father required solitude to complete an unusually ornate weaving. I was allowed to wander down the hall and into the Count's library, an enormous wood-paneled room filled almost to the coffered ceiling with shelves and shelves of books of every size and shape, many with the imprint of *Maître de Nevers*, as Gilles came to be known. There were miniature prayer books one could carry in a pocket nestled against leather-bound Bibles and grand manuscripts of lyric poetry covered in the most exquisite red silks and embroidered in gold with the Count's signature lion, helmed and crested, and bearing the arms of Flanders.

I could read not a word but found pleasure sitting on the tapestry-covered library bench, holding a book in my lap. I'd bring to mind stories Mother had told me of knights, fairies, and angels, and pretend those were the same tales drawn with letters and paintings on the pages before me.

I fell asleep thinking I might bring such beauty into the world one day and conjure with the stroke of a brush a battalion of knights in shining armor slaying dragons, or a coterie of ladies elegantly dressed for a festival, or a panoply of saints arrayed like celestial bodies, luminous in the night sky.

When I awoke the following day, the feast day of Mary's Candlemas, one of the other chambermaids in Countess Margaret's service brought me to Gilles's *atelier*. Unlike my father's workshop, it was on the ground floor of a manor house adjacent to the main chateau. That icy winter day, I entered his studio and felt warmed as much by the gentle manner of the man I met as by the fire burning brightly in the large stone fireplace.

Gilles was seated on a tall-backed wooden chair, working on a manuscript positioned on a slanted, triangulated platform atop a trundle desk. When he heard us enter, he put down his quill, wiped his hands on a cloth, and stood to greet us. I noticed that his saffron robes were belted with a woven fabric and recognized my father's handiwork. Gilles held out a hand to welcome me, and I saw a smile take shape on his kind face, a smile so gracious that the whole room full of scattered books and paints brightened.

For the next three years, Gilles instructed me in every facet of the painstaking work of manuscript making. From him I learned how to fold the oblong sheets of parchment into bifolia and assemble them into gatherings or quires of eight leaves, or sometimes twelve, if a calendar was wanted. He taught me how to prepare the surface of the parchment for writing, rubbing it with chalk and then ruling the smoothed vellum carefully in thin red lines with a plummet, readying it for the copyist's writing, leaving ample space for the illuminator's designs.

Oh, those designs Gilles taught me to make! Beautiful arabesques of puzzle initials finished with flourishes in cinnabar and ultramarine spilling down the page and around the edges of stories the scribes had already copied. Through Gilles's patient instruction I learned how to cherish what lay below the images as much as the glistening metal gilding the surfaces, calling attention to itself by catching the light from so many angles.

First, I'd select an image from the store of pattern books Gilles kept in his workshop, and draw a rough draft of the picture on the vellum with a metalpoint plummet before outlining the picture with a thin line of gall ink. Gilles had made the ink himself, by crushing the nut found inside an oak gall and adding vinegar, iron shavings, and gum arabic, turning the mixture into a black liquid the color of midnight. Next, I'd polish the dried lines with the tooth I had lost a few months earlier so the colored paint could hold fast on top. Only after I'd created this dark and

delicate scaffolding would Gilles apply the gesso to build a sticky platform the thickness of a shell. My preparatory work took an entire day,
and on the next day I watched Gilles add gold leaf to the raised platform
he had built with gesso. The gold floated onto the sticky surface and
hugged it like a moth drawn to the heat of a fire. When he later added
red and blue and other colors around the gold, the whole picture began
to shimmer as if the sun itself were shining out of the page.

I don't know why, but the process mesmerized me even more than
my father's weaving. Perhaps it had something to do with the tactile
pleasure of conjuring with brush and pen, layering tones of light and
dark, dark and light, with the delicate twist of my wrist and the slow
movement of my steadied finger until a magnificent image would seem
to float above the page, as if the letter had been given breath and the
book a beating heart.

"If we do not preserve these masterpieces," Gilles told me, "we would
lose the wisdom of centuries. Not only sacred texts, but also poetry and
philosophy, medical works, and accounts of great voyages; all these texts
our work safeguards for generations to come. Remember, Béatrice, stories keep us alive. Without stories to console us, the world would be
impossibly bleak."

"If I practice, might I become an artist one day, Master Gilles?"

"Why, little one, you already are!" And then he handed me one of
his finest quills, setting me to work gilding the edges for the large lapis-
colored *B* he had planned to grace the left corner of the page.

"One day, perhaps I will have my own *atelier*."

"Anything's possible, dear child. You may keep that quill and use it
on your first commission."

My twin sisters were born two years after I began my apprenticeship,
when I turned seven. They soon delighted in the squiggles and lines I drew
for them on parchment scraps Gilles allowed me to keep, and that I fashioned
into colorful whirligigs, which Father hung above their cradles.

Gilles d'Orléans. Though it has been eight years since those days in
Crécy, Gilles's wisdom sometimes still echoes inside my head. His patience and kindness filled me with reservoirs of resilience that comforted
me for a while until the memory of all the beauty he had shown me how

to create with brushes and quills couldn't salve the wounds of loss that festered in those later bleak years, and fester still.

"One day. . . ," I had said. How far away that day seems now.

Fortune's wheel turned when brave Count Louis rode forth to do battle against the English king in 1347 and never returned. His defeat left the countess no choice but to divide her lands, and my family no choice but to leave Crécy that same year. We wandered along the River Oise until we settled on a small plot of land in Picardy, in the shadow of that marvelous and much-feared castle, Coucy. The palatial estate was home to one of the most powerful families of the realm, the rich descendants of Enguerrand II, who, I've been told, willed the castle to completion in the short space of seven years.

Its four magnificent corner towers stood like massive sentries surrounding a thick-walled castle keep twice the size of its other towers, a *donjon* of monumental proportion that thrust itself one hundred eighty feet into the sky, making it visible for miles across the great green valley of the Oise. A wide moat separated the outer bailey—where the servants lived—from the castle itself. Beyond the bailey were clusters of scattered houses and huts of wattle and daub where my family made its humble home for three years. Within the first year, Father traded two goats for a loom and began weaving fabrics again, though none were as elaborate as those he'd designed for Count Louis's court.

The castle seemed a fortress capable of vanquishing, almost by the sight of it, any infidel who dared cast his eyes upon it in longing. Townsmen who lived just outside the thick walls of the compound, and with whom my father traded fabrics for tools and foodstuffs, bragged that the citadel could hold more than a thousand knights readied for battle. Yet even a thousand-thousand could not stop the great wave of horror that cut a swath through the region of Picardy and infested our home the summer of my eleventh year, taking half our town and all my innocence in its pestilential wake. I fear I will forever be transfixed by the memory of that terrible night when death came to our doorstep and crept into our humble abode.

Father had returned from several days' visit to the castle grounds with melancholic news of the demise of the grand seigneur's mother,

Dame Catherine of Coucy. He said she had awoken with a pain in her belly and, the next day, a protuberance the size of an egg had appeared. Purple blotches soon covered her chest and back, and she emitted a foul stench as putrid-smelling as a barrel of rotting fish. In little more than a day, she met her demise, but not before half the household had fallen ill with fevers and sweats, overtaken themselves with this black malady. Children were felled in less than a day. The disease slithered from household to household, as if an army of vipers had joined forces to drive us all from this earthly garden.

I remember his hands shook, his face flushed, and his breathing quickened as he recounted how bells of mourning tolled incessantly while some villagers he'd passed along the route had danced and drummed as if their happy music could keep death at bay. Mother and I were astonished when he told of the dead being piled into pits, one on top of another, like sacks of flour.

Then, unable to bear the weight of his own news, he ran to my sisters, scooped them into his arms, and covered their faces with wet kisses and watery tears. He took the twins, still half-dazed by the suddenness of his affection, down the hall to the bedchamber. Father looked so weary and worried; it pained me to see him tremble so.

"Let them rest," Mother said, lighting the hearth candles. "We must prepare baskets of bath oils and fragrances for the Feast of the Assumption. We will pray and make offerings to the Blessed Virgin at tomorrow's mass. Mother Mary will protect us from harm."

We sat together at the table. Bits of dried lavender and waxy scraps of amber soap carpeted the table's rough wood in soft violet and yellow hues of perfumed debris, and I drew my finger through the crumbles and raised it to my nose, the pungent aroma tickling and taunting me. We worked in silence until the hour just before dawn. Mother looked up and smiled as she fastened a bouquet of garnet ribbons shaped into roses onto the last basket.

Whenever this memory spoils my mind, what troubles me most is how I can still smell that table, still see the shape of my mother's hands. Those fragrant colors, my mother's once-graceful fingers, bring tears to my eyes.

What mocking God allows such beauty in the world on the same night as so much ugliness and pain? Will I ever again look upon beauty and not be reminded of death?

We went outside to pack our baskets into our cart, readying to drive to the church and distribute them to the parishioners. The air was heavy with a stinking mist. As it lifted, I saw a group of barefoot penitents walking toward us. Some wore sackcloth and ashes; others were naked to the waist, beating themselves with whips, calling to the heavens for mercy. Mother pointed in horror as one member of the group fell to the ground, writhing in pain. Another bent over to help, but he, too, soon began to wail in agony. Grabbing my hand, Mother pulled me back into the hut and bolted the door.

"We must check on your father and sisters," she said.

Taking the pewter lamp, Mother walked slowly to the end of the hall toward the bedchamber. I followed. Reaching the doorway, she froze. Her lamp cast a sallow slant of light across the room. We saw her babies, flesh of her flesh, lying on one side of the bed, their bodies covered in blackened blotches; blood leaked from their noses and ears. Her dear Gilbert, my father, lay next to them, his swollen arms wrapped tightly around the twins.

He turned toward us, his eyes bulging, his arms encircling my sisters like a vise. He was shivering with torment and fear. Mother screamed and moved to step forward, but the terrified look on Father's face and the violent shake of his head held her in place. I watched Father close his eyes and turn away from us, holding on to my sisters. I heard a strange sucking sound and stared at the three of them in terror. They were writhing and wriggling and sinking into a deep, oozing pit. The air thickened and swelled into a cloud of putrid foulness, massive and impenetrable, and I saw something rise up out of the darkness. Not the bodies of our beloved, but ugly, unrecognizable, monstrous shapes.

Terror engulfed me and held me steady in its grip and gave me an uncanny strength to whisper in Mother's ear.

"Do not enter the room," I said, touching her arm and pulling gently at her sleeve. "We must stay back, or we too will be doomed." She turned to me and touched my face. "My beauty," she said. "My beauty." In her eyes I saw that fear had already given way to denial.

With a determination that pushed me past remorse, I reached around my mother and closed the door to the bedchamber and walked her back down the hall. I sat her at the table and wrapped a shawl around her shoulders. She said not a word.

I opened the door to fetch the baskets we'd put in the cart and brought them back into the house. I moved around the hut as if it were no longer our home, but the house of a stranger. I gathered provisions, putting bread, cheese, preserved fruits, and salted fish into a basket. Into another, I packed two blankets and some pots. Mother did not stir or speak. In the cupboard I found bolts of fabric. As I removed them from the shelf, something fell onto the dusty floor. I saw it was one of the whirligigs I had made for my sisters, and I shook with violent longing and fear until Mother's arms hushed me into an embrace.

"Take your satchel of quills and brushes," she whispered.

I clutched at those talismans as if they had the power to blot out all sorrow and pain. Then we left the hut and climbed into the cart. Mother struck the mule, and I turned to glance one last time at the church steeple. As I did, I caught sight of a pack of dogs, snarling and fighting over something in the road. They had descended on the bodies of the dead penitents. We fled from the town, abandoning the dying as if they were strangers.

All that summer, the pestilence spread north. By a stroke of luck, Mother and I moved south, traveling wherever and however we could. Sometimes, if we happened upon an abandoned house once owned by a wealthy family, we lived sumptuously for a week or even a month, until a larger pack of wanderers found their way to the same village and claimed the house as their own.

We drifted from village to village, farther and farther from anything we once knew as home. We traveled on foot, or were towed in a stranger's cart, or climbed on the broad back of some horse we had pilfered and galloped for miles. Along the way, we exchanged what we looted for a bit of food and shelter. We stayed alive one more day, one more week, and then one more month, until fortune landed us in the village of Villeneuve lez Avignon, on All Hallow's Eve.

There, in the market square where I now ply a rough trade, I bartered our last plundered goods for a plow, a mule, two pigs, and some sticks of furniture. We set up home in this tiny cottage where we have lived for five years. Mother sleeps fitfully on a straw mat in the corner, while I sit at this table near the window, watching the setting sun bathe the fields in strands of rosy gold, searching in those glinting angles for some ray of hope to cut this grief that has tightened each year like a charmed snake around my heart.

Mother gambled at the L'Auberge Rose last night and lost our best mule. I would have been beside myself with worry if she had not been sober enough by the time she got home to remember every detail of a most remarkable story.

She had run into Gregory Lemoille, the pastor's secretary, at the Inn. They shared a few pints of brew and talked about the increased tithe due soon in the bishopric. With only three Wednesdays left before it was owed, mother told him she worried we'd never trade enough to pay the debt. Worse still, the squire who rents us the miserable hillock we till and graze had threatened to send his best men to collect the rent before the tithe.

Lemoille had laughed and said that would mean I'd have to fight off Jeremiah once again.

I've seen how that nit Jeremiah expects every damsel to swoon at the mere sight of him. He is nothing more than a buffoon, nothing more than a slimy snail in a clanking shell. When he's not wearing his belt and spurs, he preens and parades around in checkered fabrics as if he were a real *gentilhomme*, when everyone knows he is a mere few vassals and hunting dogs away from landing right back in the lowly estate of his birth.

Mother thought we were on the brink of disaster.

Everyone may be threatened, Lemoille said. Except Father Baron.

Mother said she understood the parish supported the pastor and that he was a talented orator who could drum the fear of damnation into any quivering soul to replenish the church's coffers with the sale of indulgences.

Lemoille laughed and said Father Baron's sermons would amount to far less without the extra eyes he rented around the village—and without Lemoille's skill with numbers. He explained how Father Baron employed a coterie of well-placed spies to gather news of parishioners' transgressions, and used what he learned to modify his weekly sermon so as to increase the likelihood of profiting from the most tantalizing scandals his spies brought to his attention.

Lemoille kept two ledgers of all the pastor's transactions.

We all knew about the spies; these days, everyone is fearful. Mother wanted to ask Lemoille to explain the ledgers when his wife tapped him on the shoulder and said it was time to leave. But I already understood Father Baron's scheme.

My father once told me a story about Artevelde, the scheming money-grubber who had led the burghers of Ghent against Count Louis of Flanders. Artevelde disliked the Count's loyalty to Philip, the French king; he wanted the Count to support Edward, the English king, whose country supplied the Ghent weavers with wool.

Father said Artevelde kept two books of accounts, one falsely recording the revenues he had raised from the burghers to finance the war against Philip, and the other with the full sums, including those he had skimmed from the Flanders merchants and intended to keep for himself. When the merchants discovered his trickery, they mobbed his house, demanding he return what he'd stolen from them. When he refused, they slaughtered him on the spot.

I hadn't grasped the meaning of the tale at the time, but its import became clear to me now. I suspected Lemoille had devised the same deceptive technique to record in one ledger the penance donations Father Baron garnered from fear-filled sinners, and in another kept a secret accounting of the real amounts, including the portion the priest hoarded for himself.

And I remembered something else. Without realizing it at the time, I had witnessed Father Baron's manipulation of Scripture in action. Last Sunday, the readings were from John, chapter ten. At verses nine to eleven, Father Baron's voice had risen: "The thief comes only to steal and kill and destroy; I have come that they may have life, and have it to the full." Then he had added his own gloss on the passage and swept his right arm across the heads of the assembled to bellow, "The thief steals from the fullness of life promised us by our Savior, the Lord Jesus."

As his voice reached its crescendo, he curled three fingers and his thumb slowly inward and pointed one long, bony digit toward Pierre, startling the unsuspecting publican seated three rows from the altar.

"Woe to any among you who deny the fullness of things to my brethren."

I remembered seeing poor Pierre quake in his seat at hearing those words. As the congregation rose to leave, he ran to the lectern and begged Father Baron to meet with him that very afternoon. At the time, I thought Pierre had simply been moved by the sermon. Now I knew why.

More than once, Mother had complained that the brew at the Inn seemed weak, but I had thought her complaints were merely excuses for having drunk more than she ought. Now I surmised that one of Father Baron's spies had seen Pierre watering down ale at the Inn, and the priest knew how to profit from that news.

A cold, black rain fell all night, flooding the rutted roads to market, making travel more difficult than usual; but the wet does not daunt my determination. I must go to the village square and set up my wares. I expect Father Baron will make his usual way through the market a few minutes before the bells toll Prime. When he passes my stall this time, I won't refuse his attention. Our trials have given me an eye for sales and an ear for slander; and with the tale mother told me last night, I should have no trouble at all connecting the two.

I've waited too long for this chance. My brushes and paints taunt me daily with the memory of my craft. I've prayed to whatever remains of the sacred in this cruel world to show me a way, no matter how canny, to escape this village and make my way to Paris.

I look out the window and see it is the darkest hour before dawn. Mother is asleep. I quietly sweep the floor and stoke the coals in the fire to keep her warm. The loom stands in a corner with a half-done tapestry. It is a simple pattern of red, white, and flax-colored flowers woven into an azure background, nothing like the elaborate designs of my father's. Still, I have no time for weaving until after market. When Mother wakes, perhaps she will work it while I am gone. I gather the few smaller fabrics she finished last month, along with skeins of wool, some cloth, and the looming spindles I bartered from an itinerant weaver who passed through town, and tie them into a linen cloth.

The lesser of our mules is tethered to the fence. I take the collar and bridle from the hook on the wall and carry them outside to hitch the mule to our wooden cart, nearly falling in mud rising almost to the top step in front of our door. I slip the collar over the mule's head, slide the bridle over his snout, fit the bit in his mouth, and pull the bridle over the top of his head, making sure the animal's ears are clear of the side straps before I clip the bridle to the collar. The harness in the back of the cart is heavy and Mother usually helps me lift it to attach to the bridle. Today I do it myself.

I go back to the cottage for the rest of my things. The room feels warmer already. Mother has not stirred, and that is good. She rarely sleeps well these days, and will need to be rested for the trip we will make if my plan proves successful. I am determined to get us to Paris and establish a workshop in the arts for which Gilles prepared me all those years ago.

I take the items for trade, along with some dried fruit and nuts. The mule looks at me as if he cannot believe we will brave these roads, but I climb into the cart and slap the reins. He moves, slowly at first, and then quickens his pace after we crest the hill leading from our plot to the road.

The rain slows to a mist. Before me, the woodsy pathway breaks into a clearing and then continues in a straight line all the way to Villeneuve lez Avignon. The rutted road makes the journey take longer than usual. It is sunrise when I arrive at the square. The carpenter is arranging his finely turned wooden bowls and goblets in his stall. And there is the blacksmith with his cutlery and swords. It remains a mystery how he managed to cart his heavy wares through this muck. The widow Harriet's stall is crowded with cauliflower and cabbages. Bunched and basketed, they look like the decapitated remains of last week's executions of thieves.

My stand is next to the butcher's, near the lane leading to the church steps. On one corner of his table the butcher has positioned a leg of mutton. Links of sausages hang from the canopy overhead. We exchange nods as I busy myself with arranging my wares.

Two dogs are chasing each other's tails, kicking up clumps of dirt into my fabrics. As I shoo them away, I notice a vaguely disheveled Father Baron crossing the market. He is rearranging and smoothing his alb, mumbling to himself as he rushes to get to chapel before his assistant. He slows his pace when he notices me. Despite the weather, I've worn my best yellow muslin skirt and braided my auburn hair with a silken green ribbon that matches the color of my eyes. I smooth my skirt and sweep my braid over my shoulder to dangle it close to my breast, and angle my head coyly toward my shoulder, trying to look temptingly innocent. I know a few things Father Baron would rather keep secret. From the laundress who washes his clothes, I learned about those nasty, sticky stains she removes from his garments, as well as the name of the young maiden in Villeneuve who helped put them there. I have harbored this gossip for the right moment to use it. Adding this salacious tale to the one my mother told last night makes me certain the right moment has come.

Gilles had taught me how to make images dazzle by layering gold leaf onto a raised gesso platform, hiding from view the darker forms lying below the glittering surface. I paint on my sweetest smile as Father Baron approaches my stall.

He fingers the texture of wools I have on display and then leans in to whisper in my ear. The butcher cranes his neck in interest, so I giggle to muffle the priest's words.

"I love to touch your things," the priest says.

"You are too kind, Father," I say. "Yes, I will bring the wool to you in the rectory after Mass today."

I'll bring more than that. Father Baron has profited from selling indulgences by stoking sinners' fears, swelling his coffers with the wages of sin. There may be worse ways to take people's money than promising salvation for a few measly *sou*. Bribery is one. I have the evidence to accuse him of that. And if I, too, will be guilty of that transgression, I care not. I plan to pry from his hands the ill-gotten gains of a gout-riddled priest and use them to change the lives of Mother and myself. He cannot shame me into silence with the threat of God's condemnation. God forgave me by allowing me to live. I know I will honor God by the work he has called me to do in this life, and, with the strength I've found to push past the ugliness of this corrupt world, I will make beauty burst into it like a bright light.

3

ALL ROADS LEAD TO LONDON

VERITY

O utside Regina's study window, Verity noticed that the city's roar had quieted to a low murmur, pierced occasionally by the rumble of garbage trucks making nightly rounds. She looked at her watch. It was two in the morning. She'd been reading about Christine de Pizan's life for hours, drunk with an excitement she hadn't felt in years.

I will tell you how I who
Speaks to you, became from a woman to a man
Through Fortune who wanted it thus;
She transformed my body and my will
Into a perfect natural man.

The assumption everyone made that the master artists of medieval manuscripts were men seemed as unfounded as the prejudices Christine had castigated with her prose. As if men were the only architects of beauty, as if vision had only one sex.

I have long wondered about the reasons why so many different men,

learned and nonlearned, have been and are so ready to say and write in their
treatises so many evil and reproachful things about women.

Verity opened her journal to make notes.

A fifteenth-century woman, widowed at the age of twenty-five, with three
children and a mother dependent on her, had had the temerity and sheer
persistence to reinvent herself as a writer. Yes, she'd been privileged: she was
educated and enjoyed royal connections through her father's association with
Charles V. But those circumstances didn't seem enough to explain her defiance. To become a writer, to become "from a woman to a man," someone
must have helped her fight against ridicule and against accusations like the
claim that other men—clerks or monks—had written her books.

At the end of these jottings, Verity wrote one more word, followed
by a question mark.

Anastasia?

Then she turned off the light, walked down the hall to the bedroom,
and fell into a deep sleep filled with images of women building a city
fortified with crenellated walls.

By late morning, Verity's excitement had tempered, forcing her to face
the sobering fact that her conviction about the illuminator's female identity remained as unfounded as the assumption she wanted to debunk.

She made herself a coffee and stood next to the living room window
to consider what to do next. Where could she find proof that Anastasia—if that was her real name—was the artist who'd decorated Christine's books? She had no idea where to begin. She pushed the button
between the window casements, and the glass turned from opaque to
clear. Across the street, a florist was arranging bunches of sunflowers in
a display case, their bright yellow petals bursting out of muddy brown
centers like the rays of the sun. She called Professor Berman and asked
to meet him that afternoon.

———————————

Verity arrived at the New School at precisely four o'clock, walked to the
second floor, and knocked on Professor Berman's door.

"Come in," the old familiar voice called. "It's open." Professor

Berman rose to welcome her with a broad smile and a hug. As he took her coat and hung it on a rack in the corner, she noticed that his hands shook slightly and his gait had slowed, signs of age belied by his still-lively spirit.

"It's great to see you, Verity." He gestured to a seat, and then sat down in an oak chair, swiveling to face her.

"Thanks for rearranging the appointment. Sorry I had to cancel yesterday." Verity looked around the room. Nothing had changed. The same bookshelves overflowed with manuscripts and scholarly journals, the same uneven stacks of papers were piled on the desk and the floor, and the same poster on the wall displayed red Phrygian-capped Marianne, brazenly bare-breasted symbol of the French Revolution, proudly hoisting the Republic's tricolor in her right hand.

"No trouble at all; I had plenty to do. Putting the final touches on a paper for the American Historical Association meetings in a couple of months. Even an old guy like me still has a few things to say." He laughed. "You'll be pleased to know I'm citing your research."

"Really?" Verity said nervously.

"Of course! Why does that surprise you? You know how highly I think of your work."

"I'm—I'm honored."

"Elizabeth tells me your book will be out next year. You must be excited."

Hearing the name of the Cambridge University Press editor made Verity cringe.

"I don't think so," Verity said. "In fact, I don't think it'll be published at all."

"What? Why not? I thought you'd finished the revisions."

"I couldn't complete them. I missed the deadline."

Professor Berman gripped the arms of his chair and leaned forward. "I've known Elizabeth for more than twenty years. She's an understanding editor; I'm sure she'd give you an extension."

"That's not the problem. She already agreed. But I can't publish the book the reviewers want." As she spilled those words into the room, Verity felt a great weight lifting off her shoulders, as if, for the first time, she understood what those nineteenth-century rebels had taught her. Integrity mattered. Without it, the whole world looked murky and dull.

Professor Berman sat back in his seat and stared at her for several seconds in silence, clearing a space for her to explain.

"I can't stand what I've written. So I came to New York because I knew you could persuade me to publish the book. Then, yesterday, something happened. I canceled our meeting and went to the Morgan Library and saw something so extraordinary, I felt, I don't know, like that time I was in the social history archives in Amsterdam. The files were a mess; none of them had been catalogued with anything more than a name. All I knew was I'd been given a box that contained things from Louise Michel. I reached in and my hand touched something woolen and scratchy. I lifted it out and held this worn, brown satchel in my hand and knew immediately I was holding the satchel Louise Michel had carried through the streets of Paris during the Commune—"

"I remember you told me about that—"

"It felt like I'd crossed some kind of invisible threshold between the past and the present, like I was in those streets with those women in 1871. I could hear them shouting '*Citoyennes de Paris, aux barricades!*' They were laughing and singing. I wanted to write about that experience, how it felt to touch the texture of the past, but I couldn't—or, anyway, I didn't. And I've regretted it ever since. But yesterday I was given a second chance. I know it sounds crazy, but I want to see where it takes me."

Professor Berman let out a deep, long breath. "Verity, please tell me what happened."

She paused, trying to muster courage. He was such a serious scholar; how would he understand? In the lengthening pause, the gentle look on Professor Berman's face bolstered Verity's resolve.

"In all the years I lived in New York, I never visited the Morgan Library. The robber-baron wealth behind Morgan's collection turned me off. But yesterday I saw this poster for an exhibition called 'Pages of Gold' and remembered my mother taking me to the Grand Army Plaza Library in Brooklyn a long time ago. I got to touch those books— pages that had survived five hundred years. It was sacred, as if the light reflected in those paintings emanated from some otherworldly, ancient source, animated by touch."

She told Professor Berman about reading *The Book of the City of Ladies* all night, about learning the name of an artist named Anastasia. By the time she finished, the look on Professor Berman's kind face had turned into a wide grin.

"And now I have a story to tell you, Verity. I've been a professor of French history for most of the forty years of my career. I say most, because I didn't start out in this field. I began my studies in diplomatic history."

Verity's eyes widened. "I had no idea," she said.

Professor Berman laughed. "I never talk about the book I was supposed to write, the one I never published. It was based on my dissertation on Sino-Soviet relations in the period following Mao's Great Leap Forward. While I was finishing the book, I spent a year in Paris, researching in the National Archives for a chapter on the role of China in the Vietnamese war. It turned into a year of being distracted by the conflicts in the streets. I'm not sure 'distracted' is the right word to describe 1968. I was twenty-five, a *wunderkind* set on the fast track toward success in a field I suddenly realized I no longer wanted to pursue. You see, I'd fallen in love with France, a subject I knew nothing about. So I decided to start over. I stayed in Paris five more years, tracking the roots of the sixties movement in France's Revolutionary past. The rest, as they say, is history."

Verity was dumbfounded, as much by the confidence in her he'd displayed by the gift of his story as by the confession itself.

"I don't know what to say," she mumbled. "I guess all I can say is 'Thanks'."

"No, it's you who deserves the thanks."

"I don't understand. What for?"

"For the greatest compliment a teacher can receive. To have a former student become so fired up, so overtaken by wanting to pursue something, no matter the danger or risk, that she's willing to chart her own course. That's an experience every teacher fantasizes about. It makes you feel as if something ineffable, something holy, has been exchanged in the learning."

Professor Berman looked as dapper and composed as ever in his corduroy jacket. Only the twinkle in his mushroom-colored eyes suggested the daring that must have propelled him all those years ago. That twinkle turned into a spark in Verity's brain and gave her the strangest sensation, like the weightlessness she used to feel performing a *grand jeté* across the dance studio floor in her younger days, never once worrying about being watched.

"I can't guarantee you'll find what you're searching for, but I understand why you want to try," he said. "As I learned a long time ago in Paris, be humbled by your obsession; there's wisdom in the journey."

"Do you think you can help me figure out how to find Anastasia?"

"I don't know much about medieval manuscripts, but I know who can advise you. An old friend of mine teaches medieval history at Columbia. Her name is Priscilla Millard. She's studied the subject for decades. I'll give her a call and tell her you'll contact her this week." He reached for the phone.

It was hard to believe what was happening. She'd expected to be chastised by her mentor for abandoning the Commune women. Instead, he'd encouraged her. "You know, I never understood what that phrase 'embarrassment of riches' meant until now. I thought you'd be hard on me. Instead, I'm embarrassed at how little I understood, until now, what a great teacher really is. Thank you."

Leaving the New School, Verity headed down Fifth Avenue toward Washington Square, turning east a few blocks above the square, heading back to Regina's apartment. Regina had been right after all about Professor Berman, but for the wrong reason. For a moment, she considered calling to tell Regina the story he'd shared. But the moment passed as quickly as it came. His story had been like a portal she'd slipped through, crossing a threshold from one place in her life into another, one where she no longer needed Regina's approval.

When she got back to the apartment, she called Professor Millard's office and made an appointment to meet at her Columbia office in two days. Then she went into the study to be with Christine de Pizan.

Then I closed my doors, that is, my senses, so that they would not wander toward exterior things and snatched up these beautiful books and volumes of tales so that I could make up for some of my past losses.

The stately red brick and stone buildings of Columbia University's campus in Morningside Heights were arrayed in a rectangle around a campus green edging toward an expansive plaza where dozens of students raced between classes or gathered on the broad flight of stairs that led up to Low Library, which now housed the university's administrative offices. Professor Millard had left a voicemail, directing Verity to that building.

"Impossible to miss, given its faux Roman Pantheon lines, complete with Ionic columns and grand rotunda, not to mention busts of Zeus, Apollo, and Pallas Athena. Nevertheless, it's neither low nor a library. My office is a short walk on a path to the right of the grand steps. You'll find me in Fayerweather Hall—614 Fay, as I'm instructed to call it, though I prefer the multisyllabic moniker. We'll meet at four thirty, just before Minerva's owl takes flight."

From the high pitch and accent of the voice and the wry sense of humor reflected in her references to classical architecture and the owl in Hegel's theory of history, Verity guessed the professor was older, Oxford-trained, and British. The meeting would be entertaining, if nothing else.

Exiting the 116th Street subway station, Verity walked west toward Morningside Park and entered a middle gate, meandering toward Morningside Drive along a serpentine route lined with magnolias and shrubs. The Harlem park had been completely refurbished in the last decade. Once a dangerous hangout, it was now a delightful oasis. The new playground was filled with young families, and assorted groups populated picnic areas and sporting fields dotting the park's perimeter. Verity remembered reading about the 1968 Columbia protests and smiled. If Professor Berman hadn't been in Paris, he probably would have joined that action, preventing his alma mater from taking over the park as space for a gym. Verity shook her head. How different things might have been if he hadn't told her that story; how different they were becoming because of it.

She left the park, crossed Amsterdam Avenue, and followed College Walk toward the steps of Low Library. Along a path on the right, she found Fayerweather Hall and took the elevator to the sixth floor. Professor Millard's office was near the end of the corridor. She knocked on the door.

"Coming, coming. In two shakes," an older woman's voice called.

When the door opened, Verity's jaw dropped. Before her stood a small-framed woman in a green tweed suit, the same talkative woman who'd introduced her to Christine de Pizan at the Morgan. Professor Millard put her hand out to greet Verity, a smile of recognition sweeping across her face. "What a delightful surprise! I'd no idea we'd meet again. Do come in." She ushered her into a high-ceilinged office, and gestured her toward a comfy upholstered chair in the corner. Nonplussed, Verity sat without saying a word.

"Would you like a sherry, dear? It's an old habit of mine from my Oxford days. The professor always offered a sherry at private conferences. I suppose nowadays that might be misconstrued. Never mind, you and I are peers. Shall I pour?"

Verity nodded and thanked Professor Millard when she handed her a tiny crystal glass full of amber liquid, refilling her own.

"Please, please call me Priscilla," she said with a dismissive flick of her hand. "My good friend, James Berman, speaks highly of you. He tells me you've recently become enamored with medieval manuscripts, particularly those authored by Christine de Pizan. Of course, having seen how long you lingered at her portrait at the Morgan, I know why," she said with a wink, taking a sip from her glass.

Verity shifted in her seat, eager to hear any suggestions this engaging woman would make.

"The Italians of the fifteenth century are my specialty. However, given how much borrowing and cross-fertilization occurred among medieval scribes and artists, one can hardly regard the arbitrary geopolitical boundaries of an era as a limit to the scope of one's scholarly research. I also dabbled in the French. Now, how can I help?"

While Priscilla spoke, Verity tried to figure out how to explain her interest in Anastasia to the same woman who'd informed her so assuredly that the master illuminators were men. "I'm interested in learning more about the *Maître de Cité des Dames*," she said, using the French title to signal some familiarity with the subject. "I spent the last two days in the Fifth Avenue Library, developing a bibliography on Christine's life and the production of her manuscripts. But I don't really know where to begin."

"Begin at the beginning, and go on till you come to the end; then stop," Priscilla said, quoting Lewis Carroll.

"Excuse me?"

"Oh, my dear, I didn't mean to be so coy. It must be the sherry. Makes me a little cheeky. What I mean is, all roads lead to London. To the British Library and Harley 4431, *The Queen's Book.*"

Verity squirmed. "I don't know what that is."

"Ah, but you soon will. It's a collection of Christine's manuscripts, which she presented to Queen Isabeau, wife of Charles VI and regent during those times the king was beset by disabling bouts of madness. Schizophrenia, one supposes. Though with all the violence of the Orléanist-Burgundian feud dappling the radiance of his rule with the shadows of chicanery and intrigue, one wonders whether poison might not have triggered the king's attacks."

Verity looked at Priscilla blankly.

"Forgive me, dear, for wandering into speculation. The Harley manuscripts were acquired by the British Library long ago, the crown jewels in their collection of medieval books."

"So, you're saying I should go to London?"

"Well, Harley 4431 *has* been digitized. Still, I always say, there's no substitute for a close perusal of the original to get a real feel for the artist's technique. The truth of the touch, I call it. Of course, you must familiarize yourself with paleographic methods of manuscript assessment. In my opinion, Ouy and Reno's masterful *Album Christine de Pizan* is an indispensable point of departure. The result of thirty years of work among a group of historians and medievalists, it's the most comprehensive examination of her oeuvre and the artists associated with it."

Verity took copious notes as Priscilla continued.

"I must say, you have your work cut out for you, dear. But I confess, I'm a little jealous."

Verity looked up from her notebook, wondering if she were being mocked. But Priscilla's face wore an expression of bittersweet delight.

"From the rising color in your cheeks, I sense you can barely contain your excitement. The thrill of it all! To stand on the threshold of discovery, why, it makes your heart race, doesn't it? I remember when I first saw those magnificent books, those golden flourishes, those intertwined garlands still shimmering in colors that resisted centuries of decay and dereliction, my heart fluttered like a thousand butterflies were beating their wings inside my chest." Priscilla turned toward the window. She took a sip of her sherry and sighed. "How familiarity and routine can dampen passion, *n'est-ce pas*?"

Verity said nothing, waiting for Priscilla's mood to shift. She was surprised by how quickly it did.

"By the way, I have a cousin in London who lets her Clerkenwell flat to visiting scholars. I'm sure she'd be delighted to have you as a tenant. Shall I give you her contacts?"

It felt awkward to refer to this venerable scholar by her first name, but since she'd been invited to the familiarity, Verity set aside her own self-consciousness and accepted the generosity. "Yes, thank you. That's so thoughtful, Priscilla."

"No trouble at all, Verity, dear." Professor Millard took a sheet from a pad of paper on her desk, wrote down a few lines, and handed it to Verity.

Verity read the name and looked quizzically at Priscilla. "Your cousin's name is Mrs. Fairweather?"

Priscilla's impish grin made its way from one corner of her mouth to the other. "Amusing, isn't it? *Fairweather. Neither wet nor stormy.* Odd name for a Brit, I suppose. But at least she spells it the proper English way and not the bowdlerized variation used by the wealthy family of that Connecticut Yankee shoe manufacturer, Daniel B. Fayerweather, after whom this building was named." Priscilla refilled her own glass. "I've always wondered what motivated him to bequeath the balance of his fortune to a set of colleges, this one included, in which he had no personal interest, instead of to his wife. Even after a lengthy court battle, his poor widow was left only with a meager allowance. Come to think of it, something similar happened to our Christine. The Crown reclaimed her husband's property after his death in 1390 and she spent years—fourteen, I think—battling to be released from the obligation to pay rent on a house she no longer occupied. Poetic justice, I say, when those rebellious students occupied this building in '68. Too bad such rabble-rousers weren't around in Christine's time. More sherry?"

Verity declined. As much as the conversation was stimulating, it was getting late and she was eager to return to Regina's, review her notes, and plan her trip to London. She needed to make a plane reservation, secure Mrs. Fairweather's apartment, and go to The Strand Bookstore to find whatever other de Pizan works might be available in the used section.

"I'd better be going," she said, putting her notebook into her satchel and folding the paper Priscilla had handed her into her pocket.

"Of course," Priscilla said, standing up. "You're welcome back any time." With a wistful look in her eyes, she held out her hand. When Verity took it, the older woman covered both their hands with her other one. "May Almethea, the wise Cumaean Sibyl who guided Christine on her long study, lead you along verdant pathways."

"Thank you," Verity said, confused.

"Oh, my dear, I only meant to say good luck. Goodbye, for now."

It was early evening when Verity left Fayerweather Hall. A few stars dotted the autumn sky. She pulled out the slip of paper and noticed Priscilla had written something else on the reverse side.

"It is not presumption that leads you . . . it is your great desire to see beautiful things" (de Pizan, Chemin de Long Étude*). Good luck! Yours, Priscilla.*

4

A BARGAIN

BÉATRICE

The rain stopped, and a shard of sunlight lanced the clouds with a sharp arrow of light. Not wanting to raise the butcher's curiosity any further about my arrangement with Father Baron, I exchanged pleasantries while he packed his meats and sausages, and I packed my wools and bolts of fabric.

I do not pretend to innocence. Innocence is for those who never question whether the pain we suffered through the plague and all the years of misery that followed was the product of some mysterious, divine plan, or a meaningless catastrophe: nothing more than a simple turn of Fortune's wheel. I've opened my mind to that question, and it will never again be shut. I know what I saw, and what I saw wasn't the work of God but of man. Man betrayed man. I speak not only of those terrible, terrible things many who survived the pestilence did to live, but also of what was done by those whose spiritual guidance was the sustenance we needed most in the moment when fear gripped us like a wild boar sinking its teeth into our souls.

When we needed consolation, the priests abandoned us. When we needed the sacraments, they charged more for their services. I watched the church's coffers swell to excess with the practice of selling indulgences in the year of the plague and all the years since. I watched Father Baron enrich himself and become fattened with gluttony and pride. I saw bishops who visited our parish collect large sums from the faithful to build lavish cathedrals and palaces no one in our village will ever set eyes upon. I listened to the clergy preach humility and watched them become puffed up and pompous. I listened to them preach poverty and self-contentment, only to become the most avaricious of men. I listened to them preach chastity and watched every man of the cloth satisfy his lusts. About this mendacity I have remained silent too long. I know now silence is not golden but the dark death knell of the soul.

No, I do not pretend innocence. I admit I have woven treacherous threads into the warp of the fabric of a story I will bring to Father Baron today, along with the wool—and everything else—he so covets. I pray seduction will be my salvation and deliver me into the future I now crave with every fiber of my being.

At last, the butcher covered his cart with a tarp, climbed in, and slapped the reins, awakening his mule to an unsteady gait. When he was safely out of sight, I removed the green silk ribbon from my hair. Grabbing a bolt of my finest wool, I wrapped it in paper. I'd brought a small vial of rosewater Mother prepared to scent our clothes until she could launder them again in the stream. I sprinkled a few drops on the ribbon, dabbed the perfume behind my ears to sweeten temptation, and bound the package with the ribbon. Then I loaded the remainder of goods from my stall into my cart and headed the mule down the lane leading to the church steps. The flow of people ambling toward the square told me mass had ended. I tied the mule's reins to a post outside the rectory entrance and gave him a bag of hay to occupy him while I tended to business with the priest.

Before I knocked on the rectory door, I checked my appearance in the glass window. I tightened the leather belt around the waist of my skirt, to highlight the shape of my figure, and hid a small knife in a secret pocket. Then I bit my lips to rouge them and shook my loosened hair until it cascaded around my shoulders in curls that looked like maddened snakes coiled and ready to strike.

Madame Clermont, Father Baron's housekeeper, opened the door to my entreaty.

"Please come in, Béatrice. Father Baron is expecting you." Her smirk told me she knew full well the character of her employer. I wondered what reward she garnered for her discretion.

"The rain was so unrelenting, I worried these fabrics would mold. I'm lucky I had paper and ribbon to bind them," I said.

"Follow me; I will take you to his study."

We walked down a long hallway to the rear of the building. She opened one door and then another until we reached the end of the corridor and she turned to face me, pointing to a closed door on her left. I hesitated a moment, adjusting my shawl, feigning nervousness. We were two actors in a scene that had played out here before; we knew our parts well.

"He's waiting," she said, with an impatient shake of her head.

I knocked.

"Enter, in the name of the Lord," Father Baron called.

He was seated behind a large wooden desk. Madame Clermont led me into the room toward a chair where the alb I'd seen him wearing earlier that morning was strewn. She picked up the soiled garment and draped it over her arm without comment, indicating for me to sit.

"Shall I bring refreshment?" she asked the priest.

"Béatrice and I have some business to conduct first," Father Baron said, eyeing me. "Perhaps later; I'll signal when we've finished."

"Very well." She turned to leave, adjusted a small jeweled cross that hung above the lintel, and exited, closing the door behind her.

The room was larger than the whole of our cottage. To the left of the chair in which I was seated, a stone hearth warmed the room. Above it, a large crucifix was mounted, and another was affixed to the wall behind Father Baron. I noticed a third between two small curtained windows on the right. I nearly laughed at the spectacle of Christ's effigy surrounding us in a room where all sorts of perfidious acts must have occurred. I kept my composure and unwrapped the package of wool, placing the green scented ribbon on Father Baron's desk. He reached for the ribbon, grazing my hand with the tips of his fingers.

"Lovely to touch," he said.

"I have a proposition to make," I said.

"You are a saucier wench than I imagined." He winked.

"Perhaps you should listen before making judgments."

He leaned back in his chair and clasped his hands together in a gesture of faux prayer. He bowed his head and brought his fingertips to his nose and then down his puckered lips, parting them in a menacing way that gave me pause. For a moment, I worried I'd gotten myself into a more dangerous situation than I could handle. My father's words came back to me then, fortifying my will:

The best advice I can give you to carry you through this vale of tears is this: use the strength of your imagination against the weakness of others' character, and you will survive.

I stood and circled the desk to sit on the edge, dangling my leg close enough to Father Baron that he quivered.

"I understand the bishop's agents are due in the parish next week to collect the tithe," I said, removing my shawl.

"Yes, as is usual." The puzzled look on his face told me I'd caught him off guard.

Emboldened, I continued. "I've been wondering why the provinces sacrifice so much for the sake of the center."

"When the bishop's collectors come for the sums, I'm obliged to turn over the funds; it's for them to decide what to do with those monies. But what has that to do with your visit today?"

I moved a little closer. "Shouldn't the shepherd be more concerned with the welfare of his own flock than with the comforts of those far away?" I allowed my foot to rub against his leg.

"Are you feeling neglected by your shepherd, my dear?" He brought my foot to rest in his lap, and I shivered with revulsion. "I live to tend those in my care." He removed my clog and massaged my foot. I felt his member swell.

"You seem to care more for some than for others," I said with a coy turn of my head.

"Envy is one of the deadliest of sins." He slid his hand up my skirt.

"As is lust!" I pulled away from him so suddenly that he fell to the floor from his chair. He looked up at me with such astonishment that I could barely contain my delight.

"Vicious strumpet! What kind of game are we playing?"

"Blind man's buff, except you didn't know you were blinded."

"Insolent girl!" Father Baron stood and motioned toward the door. "Get out. Get out at once!"

"As you wish, Father. But I wonder why you haven't asked me."

"Asked you what?"

"How I came upon such an idea."

"No need. You have the imagination of a guttersnipe." He smoothed his garments.

I laughed. "You've forgotten, haven't you, Father Baron?"

"'Forgotten'?"

"My mother frequents L'Auberge Rose almost every evening. As does your secretary, Gregory Lemoille. It doesn't take a guttersnipe to imagine what conversation occurs between those two after several pints."

"Your mother is a drunk," he said with disgust.

"I do not deny it. But she is no liar."

Father Baron sat back in his chair. The look on his face was a mixture of curiosity and pique, like an animal sensing a trap yet unable to resist trying to defeat the hunter who has set it.

"The night before last, my mother and Lemoille got to talking about business; she was lamenting the increased tithe. Lemoille asked how she kept her books. The usual way, she replied. You've not heard of the technique of two ledgers, he retorted. His wife interrupted their conversation before he could explain. But when my mother told me this conversation, I understood immediately. Now, Father, wouldn't you like to hear my proposal?"

As I spoke, the expression on his face changed from anger to alarm to calculation. He nodded for me to continue.

"When the bishop's men come to collect the parish earnings, you'll turn over the usual portion, providing records accounting for total parish sales. The balance you'll give to me."

"And why would I do that?" he asked, smirking at me as if I couldn't possibly have an answer.

I grabbed the ribbon from his desk, tied back my hair, and rearranged my skirts. "You have your spies and I have mine. The laundress, to whom Madame Clermont has by now delivered your soiled alb, told me about Marianne, your village mistress. You really should consider paying more for cleaning services in the future. Last week I noticed Marianne was looking poorly and went to visit her. She was touched when I offered to weave her a special garment to hide her condition. She told me everything." I put on my clog and stood tall.

Father Baron's smirk dissolved into a grimace. A few seconds of silence passed between us. Then his face brightened.

"No one would believe such an accusation. And even if it were true, no one would dare speak out against me. I know too many secrets."

"Perhaps you are right about Marianne. So many priests' children: Who can keep count? But can you be certain Lemoille will guard your secret ledger at all costs? I wager the safer bet would be to pay me what I demand."

"You expect me to trust you? That's absurd. Bribery, like greed, knows no end."

I'd anticipated this response. "No need to trust me if you condemn me as a trollop in that special way you have to shame a sinner."

He looked at me as if I were mad. "You're asking me to preach against you?"

"Not exactly. To stage a scene, invent a fabricated infraction embedded in one of your homilies. I desire to leave this miserable place, but I lack the means. The amount I demand is enough to allow my mother and me to travel north. I have no interest in exposing your history of theft, unless you refuse my proposal. If you agree to my terms, I'll pretend to be shamed into exile and leave Villeneuve forever. Your enterprise can continue as before."

Father Baron sat for some moments, ruminating over my proposal. Then he rose and neared me. He stroked my hair and pulled me close. I felt his hot breath on my neck and nearly gagged. I touched the knife in my pocket, prepared to use it if he tried to grope me, but he only whispered in my ear: "You strike an excellent bargain, you tempting whore."

I wanted to slap him, but there was no need. He released his hold and walked back to his desk. We'd both gotten what we wanted. I would play the penitent begging for forgiveness after Sunday's sermon. He'd invite me to the sacristy to hear my confession and pay me. "Thank you for the compliment," I said, relieved I'd had no need to use the knife.

As I left his study, I ran into Madame Clermont in the hallway.

"Leaving without refreshment?" she asked in a sardonic tone.

"I've had all the refreshment I need," I said and scurried down the hallway, out into the cool morning air.

The mule was lazily chewing his way through the last of the hay. I bridled him, returned the knife to the box where I kept my tools, climbed into the cart, and headed out of town toward home. The long ride gave me time to consider how to prepare for our journey. I knew Mother would not object to leaving Villeneuve, but I worried she would tremble with fear of another long journey when I told her our destination was Paris. I needed to find a way to buoy her spirits.

At the start of the narrow lane that led to our cottage, the mule halted the cart with a jerk so sudden that it nearly threw me into the muck. I recovered my balance and slapped the reins, but he refused to budge. I descended from the cart to check on the animal and found its front leg trapped in a cluster of thorny vines. He began to bray. I grabbed my knife from the toolbox and freed him. Luckily, the wounds were not deep. I rested him a few moments longer, then slapped the reins. He moved, gingerly at first, and then continued steadily forward.

How I wished Mother hadn't lost our best mule! Suddenly an idea came to me. If Mother could win the mule back, it would be a boon for us both. I felt certain her spirits would soar high enough to distract her from worry about the journey I'd planned. I'd use the day's market earnings to throw the game in her favor. I turned the cart back around and headed toward L'Auberge Rose to set my plan in motion.

It was early evening by the time I returned to our cottage. The trek back from the Inn had taken me on a circuitous route. Smoke curled from our chimney in languorous gray ribbons like the graceful moves of dancers I remembered seeing in my youth in Count Louis's great hall, swirling to a gentle melody. I missed those halcyon days so terribly that sometimes it felt as if my heart might forget to beat. Most of all, I missed the beauty I'd learned to create with Master Gilles.

One day, perhaps I will have my own atelier.

Anything's possible, dear child.

As I unbridled the mule and unpacked the cart, I began to imagine the possible reshaping itself into the real. I was confident that Father Baron would do as I had asked; he wouldn't risk sacrificing the future of his enterprise for the small price I'd demanded. As for Mother, I'd arranged a special game for her at the Inn. The innkeeper, Pierre, assured me that she'd be feted and jollied all night with her winnings.

I was lost in thought when Mother opened the door and greeted me with a broad smile and a bowl of mutton stew. She was dressed in a clean skirt and blouse and had coiffed her hair. I entered the cottage and noticed that the patterned fabric on the loom was nearly complete. A look of bewilderment washed over my face. Mother laughed.

"Did you expect me to sleep all day?"

"I thought you needed to rest," I said, taking the bowl to the candlelit table, which she'd covered in a linen cloth we saved for special occasions.

"I will have all of eternity to rest," she said. "And, right now, eternity feels far, far away."

I couldn't account for the change in her mood. It was as if she had shed years of sorrows in the short span of a day.

"I'm gladdened by how cheerful you seem. May I ask what we're celebrating?" I gestured to the elegant table.

"Didn't you notice who's returned?"

I looked around the room.

"I see no one here but us, Mother," I said. A tremor of terror traveled from the back of my neck down my spine. Had madness finally overtaken her?

"No, silly girl, not *here*. There." She pointed out the window.

I turned, and our best mule stared back at me through the opening.

"But that's impossible," I said, nearly choking on my words.

"You're not the only one with friends in this village. Pierre and I have grown close over the years. And he has a horse that travels faster and over narrower trails than a mule-drawn cart. He brought our animal back after repaying my debt. And he returned the monies you gave him. Now, dear daughter, I think you have some explaining to do," she said with a look of feigned anger.

I drew the outlines of the arrangement I'd made with Father Baron in broad strokes, leaving out the finer lines of trickery I'd used on the priest. Mother listened intently and nodded. But at the mention of Paris, her brow furrowed in worry.

"A trip of more than three hundred miles. How will we provision? Where will we stay?"

"I've learned of a pilgrimage that will pass through a town not far from here as it makes its way back north. We can join them. The town is perhaps a few days' drive from here. We'll find supplies of food and accommodation in monasteries and convents along the route."

"There's been talk at the Inn of soldiers, desperate and wearied from battle, attacking the religious houses," she said, covering her eyes with worry.

I took her hand from her face and lifted her chin. In her eyes, fear had eddied like a river in turbulent flow. I knew she was thinking of that other journey, that other time we abandoned all that we loved.

"Whatever hazards we may meet can hardly be worse than those we've already faced," I said. "And not knowing what we may meet is not reason enough to stay in this miserable place where tomorrow is guaranteed to repeat yesterday."

"When you talk like that, I know you are your father's child," she said with a deep sigh.

"I am my mother's child too. May I remind you that I get my feistiness from you," I said, tickling her ear.

Mother laughed a little. "But, thank heavens, not my bad habits."

If she'd known what wiles I'd employed to trap Father Baron, she might have had a different judgment of me. I intended to keep that part of the story to myself. I'd find a way to ensure that mother wouldn't be in our regular pew, or indeed anywhere near town, when Father Baron gave his sermon three days from now.

Not wanting to jeopardize our plans, Mother avoided L'Auberge Rose for the rest of the week. Instead, she finished weaving the flower-patterned fabric and made an inventory of our stores. We had supplies of salted meat and pickled herring and jars of preserved fruits and vegetables harvested at the season's end. While mother baked three loaves of rye bread in the hearth, I packed our provisions into a wooden crate, cushioning the jars with linens and clothing. Then I scoured the garden for potatoes and onions, finding enough to last several weeks. We supped on bread and cheese. When we finished eating, I covered the remainder of the cheese in cloth; the colder autumn evenings would preserve it on the journey ahead.

"What about the loom?" Mother asked as I was packing plates and cups into a basket.

"We must leave it behind. It's too cumbersome to carry with us."

"Perhaps Pierre would take it in trade for some beer. Then he could sell it."

"Why not ask him tomorrow? I'll take you to the Inn on my way to church. I've arranged with Father Baron to collect the amount we agreed after his sermon. It's best if you're not with me for that event," I said, relieved that she'd created her own distraction from a scene I had no desire she witness.

That night I slept fitfully, anxious for the day to arrive and as anxious for it to end. I rose before first light and watched the enveloping darkness give way to a majestic procession of magenta, amber, and gold hues that slowly awakened the firmament to the sun's full embrace. But daylight hadn't driven out my apprehension. I walked to the cupboard where I'd hidden the quills and brushes I'd saved from death's grasp. I'd not touched them since, but felt the need to hold them now as if they had the power to ward off evil itself, for I sensed evil lurking like some rough beast waiting to pounce.

Father Baron ascended to the pulpit and intoned the benediction. "May God be with you."

"And with your spirit," we responded in unison.

"Today's first passages are drawn from Numbers five, where God commands Moses to tell the Israelites they must pay for their sins.

When a man or woman shall commit any sin that men commit to do a trespass against the Lord, and that person be guilty, then they shall confess their sin which they have done. And he shall recompense his trespass with the principal thereof, and add unto it a fifth part thereof, and give it unto him against whom he hath trespassed."

My heart began to pound in my chest. I braced myself for the part I was expected to play.

"As the scriptures tell us," Father Baron continued, "the sinner must recompense for trespasses. But against whom has the sinner trespassed? The Lord himself! And who represents the Lord on this earth? The Church. I hear some among you have questioned the practice of collecting monies for atonement. I have even heard accusations that the Church has put these funds to ill use."

The crowd murmured and mumbled. Neighbors looked askance at each other. I felt myself stiffen with anger as Father Baron gazed directly at me.

"We are one in Christ's earthly body, the Church. That is why, as the scriptures instruct, the Church is the proper coffer for making recompense. *And every offering of all the holy things of the children of Israel, which they bring unto the priest, shall be his.* These belong to the priest, not in his own person, but as Christ's earthly representative, as guardian of your spiritual welfare; shepherd of your souls."

I understood immediately what he was saying. He had no intention to keep our bargain. I sprang from my seat in a state of such fury, I could hardly breathe. I pushed past the others in the pew and ran outside to my cart. Driving the mule hard, I reached L'Auberge Rose in less than an hour. I tethered the mule and entered the Inn. Mother was seated at a table with Pierre, laughing.

"Béatrice, come join us," she called. "Pierre has agreed to take the loom for a generous trade."

"How kind," I said, scarcely able to force words from my mouth.

"You look poorly, dear. Pierre, bring her some ale," she said. Pierre left to fetch drink and she turned to me. "Has something gone wrong?"

"I've been played the fool." I pounded the table with my fists.

"You're no fool, Béatrice," she said in a voice I hadn't heard express such conviction in many a year. "Tell me what happened."

"Later," I said, as Pierre set the drink before me.

"Pierre is our friend; tell me now," she said, unfurling my clenched hands.

Her words fell on my ears like an invitation, not a command. I took a draft of the ale, then I told the whole story—about the priest crossing the square every market day, disheveled and readjusting his garments; about the laundress coming to my stall, seeking advice about washing wool, complaining about her wages and letting slip her suspicions about Marianne; about the spies, including the butcher, on the lookout for scandal, bearing news to the priest about any infractions; about Lemoille's tale of the two ledgers and how I'd known what that meant; about my visit to the priest to trap him with his own vices; about our bargain; about his betrayal; about the death of our dreams.

"Enough," Pierre said, slapping the table. "I've heard enough. Enough of this thieving devil; I know of others who've paid him to garner forgiveness for sins amplified by his devious sermons. Even the butcher," he said with a frown. "I will arrange a meeting here at the Inn. Now, go home and rest."

A tinge of hope tickled my heart. I hugged Pierre and took my mother's hand, and we headed home.

Three days later, Pierre led a group of aggrieved villagers toward the rectory door. As we passed through the streets, the crowd swelled to number half the town. The grumbling of parishioners sharing stories of the priest's odious acts grew into a low roar. By the time we reached the rectory, the shouts and jeers made my ears ring.

"Bring us the monster," someone shouted. "Let's be done with him."

"To the scaffold for justice," another cried out.

I stood next to Marianne at the rear of the crowd and watched a spectacle unfold such as I expected never to have seen or ever to see again. But time has taught me that the words *never* and *ever* are mere fabulations, fairy stories intended to pacify idiots or infants still suckling at their mother's breast. Etched in my memory like a sharp image outlined in metalpoint is the shape of the crowd, villagers bound together in fury, intertwined like a bundle of thorny vines. And I remember, too, the eerie quiet that enshrouded us like the seconds of silence between a thunderclap and lightning's strike when Madame Clermont finally opened the door to Pierre's incessant pounding. Then a rush of bodies pushed against her. She must have been carried forward, because she disappeared as if she'd been swallowed. When the crowd receded again, Pierre had Father Baron in tow. The priest was dressed only in his undergarments. Madame Clermont stood next to him, holding a large bag.

"There's the thieving scoundrel," someone shouted. "Let's be done with him."

"Hang him now," another yelled.

The crowd cheered and surged forward, but Pierre held them at bay.

"It's sacrilegious to murder a priest," he cautioned.

"He's no longer a priest. He's broken his vows by giving false testimony," a woman's voice shouted. I turned toward the voice and saw that those words had come from the laundress.

"The better punishment is to take back what's rightfully ours," Pierre counseled. "He will suffer more at the loss of the wealth he amassed with his treachery than being turned into a martyr at our hands."

Marianne was no longer at my side. When I looked for her, I noticed her making her way to the front. Soon she stood face-to-face with the priest, who looked like a mangy dog with his head bowed and his tail hidden between his legs. Her swollen belly was visible beneath her cloth cape. She raised his head and spat in his face and then turned to the crowd.

"He is the father of my unborn child. I wish him kept alive. I'll allow him nothing to do with my child except to provide and provide and provide."

The crowd cheered. Then, one by one, others approached the priest and demanded a fair portion of what he'd stolen. I asked for my share— fifteen silver coins, one for each year of my life. Madame Clermont reached into the bag and doled out the claim. Lemoille kept an account of it all in his ledger. When everyone had finished, Pierre released the priest, telling him to enjoy the remains.

I knew then I had seen a miracle. Not the kind portrayed in the scriptures, but the sort of uncanny apparition of a spirit that emerges between people when the things that divide us and make us bicker and scratch each other until we bleed transubstantiate into the recognition that we belong to one another and that if God exists he, or perhaps she, exists only in that belonging.

I held on to that vision, along with money the villagers gave me as reward for exposing Father Baron, and drove the cart back to our cottage, where I found Mother waiting to begin our long journey toward Paris.

5

A CABINET OF CURIOSITIES

VERITY

I n the week since her conversation with Priscilla Millard, Verity's
excitement had increased to an almost unbearable degree. She'd
contacted Mrs. Fairweather about the London flat and received an
immediate reply.

"You are most welcome to rent the *maisonette*, as I lovingly call it. It
is well situated in the Clerkenwell area of London. Priscilla tells me you
plan to spend some months researching the illuminated manuscripts in
the British Library! You'll enjoy the convenience of being within walking
distance." She explained she was a retired academic with a specialty in
the history of textile design, who rented the mostly below ground residence to other academics whenever she was on holiday, as she frequently
was. "I have attached a renter's manual for your perusal."

Proximity to the British Library had been sufficient to entice Verity
to rent the place sight unseen—save for the few odd photos its owner had
posted on a web link. One featured an oversized, somewhat dilapidated,
wooden desk sitting enticingly underneath a window she later discovered
had a less-than-enticing below ground view of a brick wall and pedes-
trian feet in the street above, splashing in puddles pooling outside on

any given London day. The apartment was quirky, but affordably priced. She wired Mrs. Fairweather money for the first month's rent and security deposit, and bought a plane ticket to depart in two weeks. In the meantime, she concentrated on designing a speed course on the art of medieval manuscripts.

Priscilla had introduced her to Geoffrey Goodman, a curator at the Morgan Library, whose lecture on medieval manuscripts Verity had overheard. She met him the following week to discuss sources for her research.

"I'm delighted to make your acquaintance, Professor Frazier."

"It's very generous of you to make time for me."

"No trouble at all. Priscilla spoke highly of your enthusiastic interest in Christine de Pizan. Although we don't have any extant copies of her illuminated manuscripts in our collection, we do have several secondary sources related to her works in our library. And, of course, a number of manuscripts from the same era that Mr. Morgan collected. To introduce you to the period, I've arranged a viewing of a French missal from the early fifteenth century and a mid-fifteenth-century French Book of Hours. Shall we go to the reading room?"

Verity nodded and followed him upstairs. They entered a large, well-lit room surrounded by stacks of reference books. The curator led her to a long wooden table. A thick book covered in red velvet rested on a V-shaped stand. He indicated a seat next to his for Verity to sit.

"I've chosen this missal from the early fifteenth century because it's an exceptionally well-crafted example of the period of Christine's books. It should give you a good idea of what to look for when you study Harley 4431."

"*The Queen's Book*," Verity added, relieved she could cover her ignorance with a little knowledge of the object of her obsession.

"The missal was written and illuminated on folio pages of vellum, as were most books of the time."

"Vellum?"

"That's the technical term for parchment or material fabricated from animal skins. The manuscript pages are referred to as folios, bound together in gatherings called quires." He opened the book to a luminous illustration depicting a crucifixion scene.

Verity gasped, as much at her proximity to the shimmering painting as at the sight of a flurry of angels encircling the dying Christ's head, three of whom were catching blood pouring from his hands and side into chalices. The scene trembled with such graphic imagery that she felt, if she touched the page, that her fingers would have been wet with blood.

"Notice the highly burnished ivy-leaf borders, the ample, elaborate drapery painted in a harmonious palette of reds and blues. We suspect at least two hands created the decorations in the missal. The less expressive one we've identified through other sources as Jehan de Nizières. He and the men in his *atelier* worked for the court of Charles the fifth. Possibly he may have illuminated some of Christine's books."

Verity felt as if her head were about to explode. Her desire to obliterate the assumption that the artists working on Christine's books were all men was in pitched battle with the realization that she would have to master an entirely new vocabulary to track Anastasia. "I'm overwhelmed."

"I have a suggestion. We're sponsoring a special workshop on medieval manuscript production for our members later this week. I can offer you special admission. It will give you hands-on experience in the art of making the medieval book."

"Thanks; that would be wonderful."

Two days before leaving for London, she found herself, along with four other subscribers, in the Thaw Conservation Center. The instructor, an assistant curator at the Morgan, welcomed everyone, directing them to a nearby table arrayed with an assortment of odd items. There were curled sheets of parchment of various shapes and tones; a ruler made out of cuttlebone; several round objects the size and shape of a shriveled tennis ball with small holes in their sides; some Petri dishes next to small bottles of unidentified liquid; a few feathers; jars filled with dusty material in saffron and blue; and a long metal tube that came to a sharp point at the end.

"In a minute, I'll show you a video about parchment-making, but I wanted you all first to feel the material."

Verity picked up a cream-colored sheet and stroked the suede-like substance, her fingers sensing the irregularity of depth across its surface. She shivered to think that this had once been living animal tissue. But then, so was paper once the living flesh of a tree. Funny what touch brings to mind.

"You'll notice one side is darker than the other. The lighter, smoother side is the flesh side; it tends to curl outward, while the darker, or grain side, where the hairs had been embedded, curls inward. You can tell how well made the parchment in a medieval manuscript was by how little it curls, as you'll see later with some of the exquisite examples we've laid out on the table behind you."

The group moved to a set of chairs arranged in front of a screen, to watch a video about a studio in Upstate New York that still manufactured parchment according to ancient methods. It took days to complete the tedious process of stretching and drying the taut skin on a frame, then scraping the surface to a thin suede before cutting it into sheets, folding them into pairs of leaves, or bifolia, and gathering those into quires, sets of pages that would be stitched together to form the codex, or turning pages, as in a modern book. Verity closed the notebook in her hand to observe its spine, startled at the realization that every modern book she'd ever held had been a descendant of this centuries-old process. Electronic books eliminated any tactile sense of this lineage.

"The medieval book trade had one of its most flourishing centers in Paris." It was a common misunderstanding, the curator explained, to think of book production centralized in a single workshop. "Each of the members of the trade worked in a separate *atelier*, devoted to his craft. The parchment maker would deliver quires to a scribe, who worked on a single gathering and then passed it to the illuminator to decorate in spaces the scribe had left vacant, according to the publisher's plan. Only after all the quires of a codex were finished would they be bound together." The curator picked up a sheet of parchment. "Remember we noted that a piece of parchment has a different texture and color on each side? All books, whether ancient or contemporary, have facing pages that match. In medieval books, flesh faces flesh, hair opposite hair. How do you think they accomplished this consistent sequencing nearly a thousand years before the printing press was invented?" No one in the room had an answer, so the curator continued. "I'm going to demonstrate what I like to call 'medieval origami.'" He placed the oblong sheet on the table horizontally, hair side up. Then he folded it in half, creasing it vertically with the cuttlebone, and repeated this action two more times until its form resembled a small book with uncut pages. He passed it to Verity. "Hold this in your hand by the crease and peek through the openings underneath. What do you notice?"

"All the facing sides match!" Verity was astonished to learn that several scribes worked on separate quires of the same manuscript, which accounted for the differences in script observed in some medieval books. "How did they know which quire followed which?"

"A scribe would place what we call a catchword on the bottom corner of a section of text, indicating the word to start on the next page. You'll see examples of this in the books on display. But before we move to those, I want to call your attention to the rest of the objects on this table." He pointed to the shrunken balls. "These are oak galls, found on shrub oaks even today. They're formed around the larva of a wasp that has laid its eggs in a young bud on the tree." He pushed his finger into the small opening on the side, and out popped a hard black nut. "Like an alchemist, a scribe crushed the nut and mixed it with a little white wine or some other acidy substance, adding iron shavings and some gum arabic, to make the black ink sticky. If he needed red ink for chapter headings, called rubrics, he would use some of this vermilion"—he pointed to the red powder—"mixed into the gum arabic and thickened with the white of an egg."

He dipped the tip of a quill in a Petri dish of ink he'd mixed and drew a thin red line across the parchment surface, steadying the line with what looked like a leaden ruler. Verity remembered a multi-chambered ballpoint pen her grandfather had given her as a child. She'd delighted at sliding the clasp down one chamber to release a stylus with red ink, then replacing it with a click with one from another chamber that held blue ink, and then with a third filled with black ink, never knowing that the history of the magic pen's purpose could be traced back to the designs of medieval scribes, whose employment of color displayed such an extraordinary integration of form with function.

"The scribe would rule the folio with this leaden instrument called a plummet to guide the text straight across a page, leaving empty spaces where the illuminator would paint miniatures."

At the end of the demonstration, the curator invited the group to view a dozen of the Morgan's most magnificent medieval manuscripts on display. Some were sealed behind the same glass enclosures Verity had seen that first day, but a few were arranged on the table, their pages held open with knotted cords to reveal elaborate illuminations.

"A little handling is good for these manuscripts," he said. "In the absence of touch, the parchment would become overly stiffened. Think of what happens to leather if it isn't massaged from time to time. A light touch reveals much more about these books through the fingers than the eyes could ever sense."

Verity touched an ancient Torah parted to a page with a hole in it and felt how the scribe, not wanting to waste the precious parchment, had simply divided the Hebrew around the empty space. It seemed a task no less monumental than the parting of the Red Sea. Her fingers caressed a Book of Hours from late fifteenth-century Bruges, produced entirely on parchment painted with carbon black. It bore an illuminated scene of the Annunciation on its cover. The brilliant lapis lazuli of Mary's gown was velvet to the touch and matched the color of the frame surrounding the scene. A burnished garland undulated around the book's edges. She pulled her hand back, feeling as if her fingers had been scorched with beauty. She raised her head. On a bare brick wall hung an oval sign written in medieval script:

'Tis on the works themselves we must chiefly and ultimately depend.

And that was how Verity felt—as if her whole life, its direction and meaning, depended on the works themselves.

She exited the library into the cool Manhattan evening and walked down Madison Avenue in a dazzled state. Words like *codex, bifolia, quire,* and *plummet* danced together in her brain. She was learning to speak in tongues.

A few days before leaving for London, Verity printed Mrs. Fairweather's renter's manual and leafed through it. It detailed every nook and cranny and explained the operation of every fixture and fitment comprising the five hundred square feet of what Verity surmised was essentially a refitted basement with sitting room and bedroom above. The manual also included a "brief history of the surrounding area" that went on for five pages of florid prose exclaiming the wonders of living, even temporarily, in Clerkenwell. It was littered with what Verity came to recognize as Mrs. Fairweather's signature punctuation.

The amateur historian will marvel at this area's long association with radicalism! Not only were the nineteenth century working class Chartists, with whom Marx collaborated, known to have lived in the borough and frequented its watering holes; the following century's Communists considered Clerkenwell a salubrious environment in which to develop their ideas and solidify their networks!

Mrs. Fairweather recommended a short walk to Clerkenwell Green to visit the Marx Memorial Library housed in a Georgian structure that once served as Lenin's newspaper-publishing headquarters (*inside the building, Lenin's original office was well preserved!*). The library housed a vast collection of Marx's works, including original copies of *Neue Rheinische Zeitung*, the newspaper Marx edited for a few years. She also advised viewing the blue and white ceramic plaque at 16 Percy Circus—*a mere two blocks from the* maisonette!—commemorating Vladimir Ilyich Ulyanov Lenin, founder of the Union of Soviet Socialist Republics (U.S.S.R.), who resided in 1905 in a former structure (*demolished in 1968!*) on the site of the new building now standing in its place.

Verity considered Mrs. Fairweather's exclamation point after the year 1968 a well-placed embellishment of irony. The building where Lenin once lived had been demolished in one of the most revolutionary years of the second half of the twentieth century. At least they'd replaced the plaque.

The only thing that dampened her enthusiasm slightly was the call she made to Regina the night before her flight, explaining that she was leaving New York for London.

"I hope you know what you're doing," Regina said. "You're taking a big risk."

"Taking a risk is exactly what I want to be doing. I'll put your key fob in the mail in the morning before I head to the airport."

"Keep it. I have extras," Regina said. "You might need it sooner than you think."

On a surprisingly sunny Friday in October, Verity's flight landed at Heathrow. She nudged the still-snoring gentleman to her right. He came to consciousness with a start, shook his bearded head, and grimaced at her, like some startled bear ready to pounce.

"Sorry, but we've just landed, and I'd like to get my bag from the overhead compartment."

"Right, right, forgot where we was for a minute," he said, stretching and then yawning. When he stood up, he removed Verity's carry-on from the overhead compartment.

"Woof, that's heavy. Carrying a load of coals to Newcastle, eh?" he asked, guffawing at his own joke.

"Thanks. Just books and papers."

The carry-on bag held her notebooks, along with her annotated copy of *The Book of the City of Ladies*; another book of Christine's, *L'Avision*, detailing the author's progress as a writer, which Priscilla Millard had sent by courier as a bon-voyage gift; and a biography of de Pizan Verity had found at The Strand bookstore. She wouldn't trust the airlines not to lose or damage her most precious things.

After collecting her luggage from the baggage carousel, she made her way to passport control. An hour and a half later, she emerged into the chaos of the arrivals reception area in Heathrow's terminal three, stopping at the Costa coffee shop for a bottle of water before consulting a piece of paper she'd zipped into the inner pocket of her jacket.

Mrs. Fairweather had sent elaborate directions. She'd instructed Verity to take the Heathrow Express to Paddington Station and then the tube (*Either the Hammersmith & City line—pink!—toward Barking or the Circle line—yellow!—toward Aldgate*) to King's Cross/St. Pancras. After exiting the station onto Euston Road, she was to head northwest until reaching Acton Street and then turn left, crossing King's Cross Road (*Advise keeping to the zebra markers as the traffic has gotten frightful!*) The street would climb to Percy Circus and, from there, into Great Percy Street, in the middle of which she would locate Mrs. Fairweather's front door, well marked by a distinctive brass knocker in the shape of a crocodile. *Its model greets everyone upon entering the hallway,* Mrs. Fairweather said.

Given the weight of her luggage, Verity ignored the directions and took a cab.

As the taxi headed up Great Percy Street, she spotted the front door among the row of Georgian houses populating both sides, its lizard-shaped brass knocker visible half a block away. "It's the green door on the right," she said, and the cabby stopped. She paid the fare.

From the bottom of her briefcase, she dug out the set of keys Mrs. Fairweather had mailed across the pond and fitted an old-fashioned silver key into the lock, opening the door into a dark hallway. Feeling along the wall on the left, she switched on a light and shrieked. Affixed to the wall above a dust-ridden bookshelf hung an immense taxidermy crocodile.

"So that's what she meant by 'greeting.' What else am I in for?"

Past the stuffed beast, Verity used a second key to unlock another door and stood on the landing above a narrow staircase. To the left was the door to the flat's ground-floor sitting room and adjacent sleep area. Verity descended the stairs to inspect below ground first.

Mrs. Fairweather had been scrupulous about everything except the accuracy of her description of the flat as "bright, airy, and furnished to the highest standards." The rooms were the antithesis of clean. In the kitchen, the counters were covered in a thick layer of grease. Opening the refrigerator, Verity found jars and jars of pickles, jams, and other condiments she couldn't even identify. At the other end of the open living area, she spotted the wooden desk from the photos online and grimaced at its brick-wall vista. Atop a wobbly chest of drawers stood an old black-and-white TV, rabbit ears poking out from behind its plastic casing. A sign had been taped to its face listing the four channels available for viewing once the renter paid a television license fee of twenty-five dollars per month.

"At least I have my books for entertainment," Verity thought.

She opened the door at the rear of the kitchen and walked up three steps into the back garden, which looked as if it hadn't been tended in a decade. One lonely apple tree occupied a far corner, its rotting fruit littering the ground below. A rickety and rusting wrought-iron table with two chairs was positioned underneath. Two metal garbage bins, filled to the brim with refuse, stood unsteadily in the opposite corner, looking as if the first strong wind would topple them.

Verity returned to the kitchen through the garden door and went upstairs to investigate the adjoining rooms designated for sitting and sleeping.

As she entered, a musty smell made her swoon, as if someone had thrown an old damp blanket over her head. But the shock to her vision was even more overwhelming. Shabby upholstered furniture assaulted Verity's eyes with a dizzying array of red and green floral patterns. Blue and brown birds, bobbing and gobbling in fields of strawberries, danced on wallpaper that covered all four walls, from ceiling to floor. A large red, yellow, and blue area rug overlaid the beige wall-to-wall carpet, probably to cover stains and tears. Thick damask curtains in a matching design hung on the two front windows. The dense repetition of patterned flowers and vines looked like a jungle of exploding foliage snaking across the room, climbing up the windows, like a reticulated python readying to strike. She felt as if the room were swallowing her.

The longer Verity stared at the swirling designs, the queasier she felt. As she sat down in an armchair in the corner, its cushion exploded in a cloud of dust that made her sneeze so forcefully that her whole body trembled with its seismic effect. She stood up to leave the room and noticed a tag stuck to the wallpaper near the light switch. Another was pinned to the rug near the door. Clever Mrs. Fairweather had labeled the fabric designs with museum tags, which identified them as the work of the nineteenth-century textile artist William Morris. The wallpaper was Morris's "Strawberry Thief," aptly named, Verity thought, for the ravenous birds loitering across it. The tag on the area rug identified it as Morris's "Snakeshead" design, although, as far as she could tell, the only snake's head in sight was the one she'd imagined.

With some trepidation about what sensorial experience awaited, she slid back the broad wooden doors separating the front sitting room from the tiny sleeping area. Its aesthetic was monastic in comparison. A bed, two bookcases, and a small nightstand with a lamp were all it contained. She sat down on the bed; it was comfortable enough. She took her shoes off, stretched out, and fell asleep. Waking three hours later, she descended downstairs to the dark, grim bathroom and showered.

The first things she found in her suitcase were a pair of jeans and an orange sweater. She pulled them on, grabbed her notebook and her well-thumbed copy of *The Book of the City of Ladies*, and went out for a walk in the lively London streets to look for a place to eat. If she didn't stay awake until at least nine, she'd never manage the jet lag.

From the flat she walked toward Amwell Street. Except for distinctively painted front doors, festooned in bright, glossy colors of sunflower yellow, British racing green, royal blue, crimson, or bootblack, the four-storied residences on Great Percy Street looked nearly identical and bespoke the upper class of their current owners. Glancing through uncovered street-level Venetian windows, she caught sight of rare antiques, floor-to-ceiling libraries, and crystal chandeliers glistening in unoccupied parlors. She turned the corner to discover an upscale boutique featuring hand-woven woolen and silk scarves, and another selling fine fabrics and draperies. Verity thought Karl Marx must be turning in his grave at the transformation of an area that had once been the denizen of artisans, artists, and social activists into a fashionable, conspicuously chic neighborhood.

Black cabs bumbled across speed bumps down Amwell Street. The delicatessen owner on the corner was closing up shop and putting trash in plastic bins down the alleyway next to his store. Outside a corner pub, groups of thirty-somethings spilled onto the street, holding pints of ale or golden cider, and laughing into the Saturday night. Verity continued down the street.

Mrs. Fairweather had recommended The Old China Hand, a gastropub nearby. Given her landlady's taste, Verity gave it a pass. She crossed the street into Exmouth Market, found Santore's, an Italian restaurant, ordered a pizza and a glass of Chianti, and opened her notebook.

Where to begin the search for Anastasia?

Before she'd left New York, she'd had a little time to study the methods art historians used to identify which artists were responsible for specific paintings in medieval manuscripts. To assign a painting to the workshop of one master or another, she learned, they evaluated the elements of composition—whether the artist had achieved depth of field, whether the palette was vivid and varied, whether the style and repetition in foliated borders was sophisticated or dull. Their techniques were similar to those used to determine if a painting was by a master or from his *atelier*. If, for example, you wanted to verify that a painting alleged to be part of the Rouen Cathedral series was a genuine Monet, you studied its brush strokes and variations of color. There was one big difference, though: records of Monet's life existed in his letters and the signatures on his work, but the only clue Verity had to the very *existence* of Anastasia was the tantalizing mention of her name in a single line in Christine's book.

On the inside cover of her notebook, Verity read a passage she'd copied from George Eliot's *Middlemarch.*

If we had a keen vision and feeling of all ordinary human life, it would be like hearing the grass grow and the squirrel's heartbeat, and we should die of that roar which lies on the other side of silence. As it is, the quickest of us walk about well wadded with stupidity.

Did she have keen enough vision to find Anastasia? She didn't know; but she remembered those lines from Christine's book that Priscilla had scribbled on the paper that led her to London:

It is not presumption that leads you . . . it is your great desire to see beautiful things.

6

OUTSIDE THE WALLS
OF PARIS, 1355–1365

BÉATRICE

I could tell a hundred stories, one for each of the hundred days it took Mother and me to journey from Villeneuve along an eastern and serpentine route to the abbey in the north of France, just outside Paris, where I found a home for a while among a group of holy women. I could tell stories of foul weather and the torment of hunger, of the weariness of traveling for nights without shelter, of robberies and deception, of slander and calumny, and of the vicious debauchery of men who violated women, whether young, like I was, or old, like my mother. None of these, especially the savagery of those men who defiled us, deserves one more jot of attention in the annals of those times. Such stories have already glutted the past with the detritus of their horrible acts so much that we let the women who suffered at their hands fall into oblivion while memorializing the names of their tormenters. The only story from that journey that I will narrate is one that gives testament to charity and kindness and the welcoming embrace of a community of women who took us into their care, even though Mother was in failing health, I was with child, and we had nothing to offer in exchange for their prayers and protection.

In late December, on the last leg of our months-long pilgrimage to Paris, we had been following a rutted road winding along the River Marne. The jiggling cart mixed with fetid smells of refuse and bodily waste thrown into the river's waters made me so nauseous that I halted the cart and hid behind a tree to vomit. Mother was still sleeping when I climbed back in and continued on our way. A few miles farther on, I caught sight of a church spire puncturing the clouds like a beacon of glad tidings, and headed toward it. We crossed frosty pastures of grazing sheep and meadows lying fallow in the winter cold. We passed rows and rows of vines whose bare branches looked like bony arms silently clutching one another with their skeletal fingers, images reminding me of the death-choked streets of Picardy five years before. A little while later, we descended into a valley and came upon a cluster of buildings surrounding a high-steepled church enclosed by low stone walls the color of thick cream. I drove the cart toward a wooden gate and tied the mule to a post.

We entered a courtyard, Mother following as best as she could—her pace had grown more halting since the attack. I noticed how labored her breathing had become. Sometimes her attention wandered so much that I had to repeat whatever I'd said several times before she comprehended my words. How frequently I'd watched a smile die on her face before it came to full expression. It seemed as if she'd aged a decade in the months since we left our village.

The yard was empty, except for a few laborers carting sacks of grain in wheelbarrows toward a silo at the far end. Then a woman wearing a long white gown with a black apron exited a small building ahead of us. The white cowl enshrouding her neck and encircling her head was crowned with a black mantle that fluttered behind her. I recognized the holy garb of the Cistercians, called "White Nuns" because of their costumes. Earlier in our journey, we had found shelter and nourishment at another abbey of theirs farther south, not far from Dijon. Perhaps we could find respite with their community again.

Spotting a bench on the side of a small building, I sat Mother down and then quickened my pace, reaching the nun before she entered an imposing three-storied building.

"Excuse me," I said. When she turned around, I saw she was my age. Her youthful face had an ethereal look that even the surprise of my presence hadn't disturbed, as if nothing could trouble the state of grace in which she existed. She folded her arms into the wide sleeves of her dress and stood still. Later I would learn the reason for her silence. Since the abbey was so close to Paris and the influence of its wealthy and powerful citizens, the nuns had been cautioned against unexpected visitors, who were not to be admitted until they had been interviewed by the Abbess. My disheveled attire, my haggard appearance, and the pleading in my eyes must have told her I meant no harm, because she didn't turn away.

"We come from a town near Avignon and have been traveling for months," I said, gesturing behind me to indicate where Mother sat. "My mother and I are weary to the bone and request but a few nights in a warm bed and enough food to strengthen us for the rest of our journey."

She nodded and, with the slightest hint of a smile, indicated I should fetch my mother and follow her.

At the entrance to the cloisters, she opened a carved wooden door onto a portico surrounding a rectangular courtyard. I held Mother against me to steady her and we followed in silence, our footsteps echoing in the corridor. Through the open arched windows, I glimpsed evergreens in each of the courtyard's four corners, gesturing heavenward. A mellow winter light streamed through the curved openings, pooling into shapes like illuminated stepping stones to guide us along the passageway. When we reached a dark door, the nun turned and whispered for us to wait while she announced our presence to the Abbess.

Mother was growing more tired, and I rested her head on my shoulder.

"Béatrice," she said, her voice weak and garbled with pain. "I wish we'd never left Villeneuve."

"Hush, Mother," I said. "We've come so far. You're tired and weak and in need of nourishment, that's all."

"I could not stop them," she said.

"We agreed to speak no more of that event," I said.

"It speaks itself in my dreams," she said.

I hadn't told Mother about missing my monthly courses, holding on to the hope that I wouldn't have to, believing the trauma of the event itself and our lack of food and the labor of our journey had interrupted my body's rhythms. The strange fluttering I felt deep inside me now shattered that hope, and foreboding crept in between the cracks.

Sister Emilia, as she introduced herself to us, returned to lead us to the Abbess's study on the second floor. I worried Mother would never manage the stairs, but she took them slowly, and with my assistance made it to the top. Emilia opened a door into a sumptuous study the likes of which I hadn't seen since our days in Count Louis's court at Crécy. Three walls were filled with hundreds of leather-bound books. On the fourth wall, a fire roared in a stone hearth, filling the room with welcoming waves of warmth. I stared in wonder at flickering tongues of light licking the spines of the books, making their gilt edges sparkle in the darkening hour.

The Abbess rose from her chair to greet us. I guessed she was a few years older than mother. Her kind eyes and gentle manner put me at ease.

"I am Agnès, Abbess of this house. You are welcome here, my daughters. Please be seated," she said and sat down again. "I know you are weary from a long journey."

Emilia brought us goblets of water and placed them beside a tray of cheeses and fruit on a small table near us. I took a goblet and gulped its contents, but Mother sat still, not taking a sip.

"You must take refreshment before we talk," Abbess Agnès said, looking directly at Mother. She moved on command, as if in a trance, and reached for a piece of cheese and a slice of apple. I realized then that the trauma we'd experienced was caused not only by the violence of events that had recently befallen us, but also by the shift in our roles whose seeds I'd sown in Picardy on the day that we abandoned our home. On our long journey, it had grown into a malady as threatening to my mother's sanity as the pestilence had been. The creature growing inside me would only fester the wounds, and I resolved to find a way to excise the scars of our past.

"I see your mother is in poor health; and by the look of it, you are worn down with worry," Agnès said.

"If you can give us shelter for a night or two, we will burden you no more, and only ask you to keep us in your prayers," I said. "We would be grateful, but we have nothing to offer in exchange."

"We are fortunate to enjoy the endowments of many prominent citizens of Paris. Their donations allow us to build chapels in their honor and plant fields of wheat and vineyards to sustain our community, but also to offer shelter to those without wealth who are willing to contribute to our community in other ways," she said. "When your health is restored, you could assist with spring plantings. We have room to house you both."

Warring thoughts racked my mind. There was wisdom in accepting her offer. Mother was too weak to continue, and a few days' rest would be insufficient to revive her. If we stayed at the abbey until spring, she could regain her strength. If we stayed, I would risk the shame of the discovery of the sinful deed I was planning; or, if it failed, the shame of the pregnancy itself. Then another thought presented itself between these two rivals.

"We have only these rags for clothes. We would not want to dishonor your order." I'd calculated that a nun's costume would disguise my condition.

"Your consideration is a sign of reverence and respect. We will provide appropriate clothing," the Abbess replied. "Sister Emilia will show you to your rooms after you gather your belongings from your cart."

"Thank you." I choked down the bile of hypocrisy that welled in my throat.

"Thank you," Mother whispered, the first words she'd uttered since we entered the Abbess's study.

I left mother waiting on a bench with Sister Emilia while I retrieved our few belongings from the cart, including my most precious possession—the quill Gilles had given me years ago, which I'd protected by sewing it into the lining of a wool cap. We'd been forced to trade my other brushes and quills for food. Thieves had stolen everything else of value we'd brought from home, except our mule and cart, which I'd protected from loss by hiding ourselves at night far from the road, deep in the forested woods. A hollowed shaft from the right feather of a bird was the last shard that remained of my craft, the merest stick of a memory of who I'd once dreamed I'd become.

Our sleeping quarters were simple rooms with a narrow bed and clean linens, luxurious compared to our months of sleeping in the cart under a copse of trees, only once finding shelter in another abbey.

Emilia brought a basin and water, some linen nightclothes, and novitiates' habits. Then she left us alone. Mother was too frail to undress herself, so I helped her change, wash, and settle into bed.

"Béatrice, I cannot go on," she said.

"We'll stay here until you heal," I said.

"I cannot go on," she repeated, turning her head toward the wall. "And you'll soon be unable to travel."

"We've promised to stay until spring. After we've repaid our debt to the Abbess, we'll both be able to leave," I said, troubled by her comment. How had she discovered my secret?

She turned back toward me, and the look of anguish distorting her face made me bury my head in my hands.

"I could not stop them," she said. "The pain racking my own body is bearable, but not the pain tormenting my heart with the knowledge of what is growing inside yours."

I fell to my knees and shook with shame into my mother's embrace. Not the shame of my desire to be rid of the child or the shame of deceiving the Abbess, but the shame of ever imagining that my mother had ever stopped mothering me.

"I will not go without you. We'll stay here until you are strong," I said.

"When the time comes, you'll know what to do. Until then, be comforted in the company of these holy women," she said, and turned back to the wall. I kissed her head and left her room.

Outside the small window of my room, a crescent moon slit the midnight blue sky like a scythe. A thousand stars punctured the darkness with a thousand specks of light. I must have gazed at the heavenly spectacle for an hour before noticing how silent the abbey had become, so quiet I could hear my own breath whisper against my linen nightdress. I touched my belly and asked the creature inside to forgive me. I begged understanding from the heavens and strength from the earth. Then sleep came and pulled me into the womb of a dream so deeply that not even the bells chiming the nuns to midnight prayers awakened me. When dawn broke, it brought news that shattered my fragile heart.

Sometimes death is a tempest battering the shore of a life, sometimes death is as quiet as a moth, sometimes death shoves itself into a body like a fist, sometimes death appears like a welcome partner in crime, and sometimes death is a whisper in a heart's ear that says: now, now is the time.

That night my mother died, I had dreamed of a garlanded table and the smell of lavender wafting into the room. Just as death had drifted into my life before on the wings of beauty, the night my father and sisters were consumed with the plague, so it had come again, disguised as a mesmerizing vision of shimmering stars and the solace of a silent night, the masquerade of a gorgeous thief stealing love from my life.

I buried my mother that February winter of 1356 in the abbey cemetery; and not long after, I confessed my condition to the Abbess. I didn't tell her I wanted to end the stirring of life inside me. I didn't need to. Agnès was a wise woman who'd seen how often women were wounded by the deeds of malicious men.

"You were brought into this world innocent of the actions of others and through the grace of our Lord. The child growing within you is no more guilty of the crime committed against you than you are guilty of it yourself," she said.

"I can't love what I never wanted to love," I said. "I don't want to burden any child with my shallow heart."

"I do not believe your heart is shallow. There are deeper reservoirs of love inside all of us than most dare to plumb, afraid of what we might learn by loving the uninvited stranger who appears at our door seeking entry."

Her words pricked my conscience with doubt, but my will wouldn't yet follow the door of uncertainty left ajar.

"You are asking me to bring forth a life at risk of abandonment," I said, fortifying my resolve.

"We will care for the child as our own if it is female; if male, our brother monks will provide a home. I set this before you, but will not be the judge. No one can judge but God," she said.

I looked in her eyes for a hint of duplicity and saw nothing but compassion in her gaze. "You will not be cast out of our care in your time of need," she added.

I thanked the Abbess and returned to my room, tormented by doubt, yet equally bedeviled by the repugnance that welled up in me at the thought of revisiting horrific events every time I looked in the face of my child. How would it ever be possible to love what had been born of hate? Then I remembered Marianne, Father Baron's pregnant mistress.

The day I'd visited Marianne, she was so touched that anyone had noticed the terrible state she was in, she wept. As if to unburden herself of an unbearable weight, she told me Father Baron had forced her to secrecy, threatening to accuse her own father of the guilty act the priest had committed if she dared expose him as the culprit. He demanded that she continue to service him like a whore, as the price of his silence. Submitting to his lecherous commands made her repulsed by every orifice of her body. She trembled when she told me she'd wanted to rip out the thing growing inside her and strangle it with her bare hands. I held her until her trembling stopped, saying not a word. When I returned the following week with the garment I'd woven to hide her condition, she seemed resigned to her fate, as if something had brought her peace, although I never asked what.

Perhaps I'd thought her weak; perhaps I imagined that I, in her place, wouldn't have been so terrified. Now that I had come to that place, I understood Marianne's courage. Even though I'd been more interested in gathering gossip than understanding her trauma, I'd unwittingly communicated empathy with my silence. No longer feeling alone, she'd confronted the priest before the whole village, knowing the village would hold her when she stood face-to-face with her demon. As I would be held by the women of the abbey when I faced mine.

A few months later, in early June, when the earth was in bloom and the vines wore the first green signs of fruit, I washed the warm body of my stillborn child, a daughter, wrapped her in linen, and buried her, entombing the scars of the past along with her. But the feel of her still warm flesh, soft like the petals of a rose, lingered on my hands, and the sweet smell of the tuft of hair crowning her head like a golden halo wafted into my room that night. I cried out to her ghost in despair. I would never learn whether I had the strength to love her, and I mourned the loss of the chance to learn.

Not wanting to take the vows of the order, I asked the Abbess to allow me to stay and work with my sisters for some time as a laywoman in the habit of a nun, as I'd learned widowed and single women from Paris had done. Although I yearned for Paris, I wanted to honor the abbey's charity. Agnès agreed and arranged a special ceremony. Sister Emilia veiled me in white and Agnès anointed my forehead with holy oil, giving me the name Anastasia to confirm my birth into a new life.

That new life was still in its infancy when I learned that the abbey had a manuscript workshop and chanced upon it one day in late August after finishing my daily chores. My fingers tingled with excitement at the scene unfolding in silent reverie before me. Gilles had worked alone in his study on texts scribes delivered to him. In the abbey, the arrangement was different. Nuns who were scribes prepared parchment leaves their sisters had acquired in Paris. I watched them size and gather bifolia into quires for books of hours, or liturgical calendars, or psalters such as I'd seen in Abbess Agnès's library. Nearby, other nuns worked at tables filled with pigments and pots, quills and brushes, illuminating pages of text.

How I longed to flourish pages of parchment with colorful bouquets like the ones decorating the chapel altar, or paint a miniature scene of the Epiphany as I'd seen in the Book of Hours the Abbess used for prayer.

That fall, whenever I tilled the soil into long rows, I imagined the thin lines scribes draw before laying down text on parchment. And when I harvested plump grapes from vines, I furled their shapes around my basket like the foliated borders Gilles had taught me to make, and dreamed that I'd again hold a brush in my hands instead of a plow or a vine clipper.

After winter's lull and the weather warmed into spring, we began to prepare the abbey for the grand procession that would be held on the grounds at the end of Lent. By luck, I was assigned to clean the manuscript workshop. One afternoon, as I swept up the scraps of parchment that had fluttered to the floor, I stuffed a few into my pockets, including one larger piece the size of an unfolded napkin. I found two discarded pots, one of lapis lazuli and the other of madder, and a brush made from the barrel of a feather with only a few animal hairs left attached in its hollow. I took these treasures back to my room like the holiest of relics. If I could create something to impress the Abbess, I hoped she'd introduce me to the patrons who'd commissioned the manuscripts on which the nuns had been working.

Later that night, after Matins prayers, I assembled the precious objects on my desk. From under my mattress, I removed the cap I'd salvaged from our journey, and disinterred my precious quill from the woolen tomb into which I'd sewn it, placing it next to the others on what felt like an altar to art. Before me lay implements and materials able to transform line and color into the miracle of story. I looked at my hands, calloused and dirty from laboring in the fields, and prayed that they would remember how to move delicately, whispering the quill across the parchment. I felt as a priest must feel, humbled at being called to bless the bread and wine, awed by the power of ritual to transubstantiate ordinary things into something sacred.

I picked up the quill, placing it under my forefinger and middle finger, trying to still it with my thumb. It rested awkwardly in my hand. Having grown so used to gripping heavier instruments, my fingers rebelled at the lightness of touch I invited them to perform. Then, like the plow needs a field, I realized the quill needed a stage on which to glide. I set the quill aside and smoothed a piece of parchment with a small white stone I had found in the garden, pinning it to the desktop with two tiny metal points that had held the mantel to the cowl of my habit. Holding the quill again, I grazed the surface of the vellum with the dry tip. A rhythmic movement returned to my hand. I watched my fingers repeat the graceful dance they'd learned all those years ago, feeling them perform the delicate gestures Gilles had taught me to decorate with circles and loops inside the hollows the puzzle initials left between the angles of lines that made their shapes.

How unthinkingly I carried out these methods of preparation, as if the trauma of the years since I had practiced my art were not enough to warp my skills or dull my senses. Before me lay a tiny canvas of parchment the size of an oak leaf. Beside me, the paint I'd liquefied with a few drops of water and some egg yolk—the latter a gift from one of the hens in the yard—pooled in colorful pots. I dipped my quill in one with azure liquid and held my breath as I drew a thin line down from the top of the parchment at a middle point, angling the line toward the far left at the bottom of the parchment. Then I exhaled and drew in my breath again to form another line, starting at the same middle point, but angling away from the first line by tiny degrees until I stopped at the bottom, a little to the right of the first line, leaving enough space in between the two lines to add a wash of color. I exhaled into that space, joining them at the bottom with a horizontal slash. Then I repeated the same process, this time with two lines angled to the right. Across the top of both sets of lines, I drew a horizontal line to create a wide-legged inverted triangular shape, swirling a line at the middle to connect them. I trembled when I saw that I had drawn a map of my future, drawn myself back into the shape of life I'd thought all but lost. I had drawn the letter *A*, for *artiste*, for Anastasia, *l'enlumineuse*.

Those few strokes of paint on a fragment of parchment made with a treasured long-hidden quill rekindled my determination to bring beauty to life. But they also instructed me to practice patience and be guided by the virtue of humility as I repeated the ritual many more times before I felt confident enough to seek another audience with the Abbess.

I spent the next three months in the darkest hours before dawn painting three miniatures on the remaining pieces of salvaged parchment. One was a rectangular frame of intertwined flowers and birds swirling around the edges of the page. I made a red dragon emerge from an elongated tendril at the top. Another was a red-and-blue puzzle initial, inside which I added a flourish of red vines.

My most elaborate effort was a nativity scene, which I used the largest piece of parchment to create. I had only managed to sketch it with a plummet, and crisp it up with ink, but it demonstrated my understanding of perspective by the angled walls and roof of the manger.

At the end of those months, in early July, when the warm winds across our fields blossomed the flowers into full bloom, and the vines were luscious with fruit, as if imitating the designs of my paintings, I requested an audience with the Abbess.

Although I saw her every day at our prayers, and shared a table with her and the other sisters at meals, I hadn't visited her study since my mother's death. Agnès greeted me with her familiar, welcoming smile.

"Please be seated, Anastasia," she said.

"Before I sit, may I show you something?" I asked.

"Of course. What is it?"

I handed her the paintings and sat down.

"Where did you find these? Were they misplaced in the manuscript workshop? They are some of the finest I've ever seen," she said.

I smiled at her unwitting compliment. "I made them," I said.

She looked at me with such open-mouthed disbelief, I could not contain a laugh.

"You are jesting. Now, tell me where you found these," she said.

"Dear Abbess, I'm telling the truth. I painted these," I said.

As I said, Abbess Agnès knew the ways of the world. It took her but a few minutes to transform her disbelief into curiosity.

"I've never asked you the story of your life before Avignon. But your age tells me you survived that horrible pestilence that took so many nearly a decade ago. Perhaps you weren't always the poor peasant girl who arrived at our door three years ago. Please tell where you learned to create such beautiful images," she said.

For the next hour, I recounted the years of my youth in Crécy. I told her about Father's magnificent tapestries, and about Gilles, the master, who taught me the art of illumination. About the deaths of my father and sisters I remained silent, knowing she already grasped that part of the story.

After I finished, Agnès stood and walked to the chair next to me and sat down. "Perhaps you are eager to leave our community and head to Paris," she said, taking my hand in hers.

"I am," I said.

"I have a proposition to make. Stay with us a while longer. I will apprentice you to our best illuminator, Sister Héloïse. You're talented, but under her tutelage, you may become extraordinary, perhaps even a master one day," she said.

Had I been younger, I might have been too impetuous and fool-hardy to recognize the generosity of her offer. But I was eighteen, and my recklessness had been tempered by time and experience. I accepted the scheme and began working under Héloïse's instruction.

Héloïse was twenty-four years older than I was when my apprentice-ship began. She was the only child of an illuminator and had lived with her parents in a narrow house in Paris on rue Erembourg de Brie on the Left Bank of the Seine, where, she told me, most of the artists who painted manuscript folios still resided. Her father had instructed her in the art of illumination as soon as she could hold a brush, teaching her to craft images from exemplars he kept in his *atelier* until she learned to make miniatures and borders more elaborate and innovative than any before. At the age of fifteen, the same age I was when I arrived, she was sent to the abbey, along with a bequest her father had made of his house and possessions. Recently widowed, he was too tormented with grief at the loss of his beloved wife to work or care for his daughter. The Abbess now rented the house to another illuminator's family, and earnings from the property supplied the abbey's manuscript workshop.

"So, you see, Anastasia, each time I pick up a quill or a brush to layer paint on parchment, I feel as if my father's hands are still guiding my practice," she said. "And now, by instructing you, I continue his legacy."

The abbey workshop produced some of the finest manuscripts for Parisian clientele, who, undeterred by the ordinary Cistercian opposition to the use of gold in manuscript ornamentation, supplied the Abbess—herself undeterred by rules that would limit her community's acquisitions—with sufficient funds to burnish gold leaf onto the page. Her wealthiest clients provided the abbey with some of its most valuable benefactions. She was unwilling not only to forgo their largesse but to disappoint their desires. And, as I learned later, when she gave me permission to browse her library, she had a taste for the most ostentatious designs, having come from a wealthy family herself.

Several months into my apprenticeship, Héloïse handed me a quire of parchment prepared for a Book of Hours commissioned by one of the wealthiest patrons in Paris. The scribe had completed the text, leaving a small box in the upper left corner on the front of the first folio, where an illuminator was to paint the Annunciation scene next to the prayers for Matins. Near that blank box, Héloïse had sketched a tiny image as a guide for me to use. I had yet to work a manuscript. My doodles and drawings, though accomplished, had not been intended for a commissioned work, much less one for a Parisian client. I looked at the blank box and trembled at the consequence of making a stroke in ink. If my lines were not well drawn, if the angles were skewed, I worried that the page would be ruined.

"If you make a mistake, it is of no great consequence," Héloïse said, sensing my nervousness. "We can redraw a line and cover the mistake with color. Try to reproduce the model as best you can. Then I will prepare the gesso and build a platform for the gold of the Angel Gabriel's halo."

After judging my outline an excellent reproduction, Héloïse took a covered clay pot from a shelf and scraped some flakes of plaster from it into the bottom of a pestle, grinding in a much smaller bit of white lead. When the mixture had turned into a chalky crumble, she added a tiny lump of red clay and ground it again, and then added a pinch of sugar.

"Why did you add color if you'll only cover it with gold leaf?" I asked.

"Can you not imagine why?" she replied, pointing to the milky white parchment with a humorous glint in her eye. "It is a trick my father taught me and is as old as centuries."

"To make the area to cover more visible for the artist to see where the gold should lay!" I was astonished at the brilliance of a technique invented so long ago.

"You're a smart one, Anastasia," she said. "And, although you didn't ask, the sugar is for moisture. The gesso must be wet and smooth, and not too thin, or it will spread beyond the area I want to build for the gold leaf."

With her quill she dropped an amount of the sticky liquid the size of a pea into the center of the space I had outlined for the halo and began to spread it around with the gentlest of strokes, careful not to scratch the vellum. Soon a smooth, raised area, the thickness and color of a pale pink rose petal, surfaced on the page around the angel's head.

"We must let it dry for a day. Let us practice some other techniques," she said, handing me a brush. "To make the finest of strokes, you must clean the tip of the brush in your mouth, like this." She inserted the feathery tip and licked it to a fine, thin point, no wider than a pin. When she smiled, I noticed that her teeth bore the faintest traces of blue.

Over time, everything Héloïse taught me in those years of instruction became as automatic and indispensable as breathing, and as inseparable from my memories of her as the beauty of a thing is inseparable from the thing itself. Even now, when I pick up a piece of gold leaf with my gilder's tip and see it tremble in the gentle evening air, I remember how she taught me to moisten the gesso platform with my breath so the leaf would leap to the page like a lover into a warm embrace. After that, I would shine the gold with my burnishing tool to make it sparkle as brightly as the sun at midday, finally adding lapis lazuli in overlapping layers in spaces surrounding the gold, lightening and darkening the color with other shades until the folds of a dress appeared on the page, transforming a flat surface into an evocation of a world of depth and shimmering beauty.

Ten years had passed since I first entered the abbey courtyard. I yearned for Paris. My illuminations had drawn the attention of some of the finest collectors of manuscripts there. Agnès wanted me to continue my work in the abbey, but I could no longer contain my desire to see the majestic walled city, with its fabled streets of artisans and scholars, where I hoped to establish a workshop of my own. From various couriers visiting the abbey, and from the nuns who were permitted into the city to collect rents on abbey properties or to purchase goods from Parisian merchants, I'd heard about the burgeoning urban landscape and learned of the king's support for the arts and sciences. It was said that Charles V, who had been crowned only the year before, had built one of the greatest libraries in Europe and installed it in a building called the Louvre. I longed to have a manuscript with my illuminations among his collection. Ten years of service, seven of them in apprenticeship, had tempered my impetuousness, but not my ambition. At the first opportunity, I planned to seek permission to depart the abbey and move to Paris. As a laywoman, I could leave at any time; my request was to show respect and gratitude for the years of solace and support that Agnès and the other nuns had provided. The Abbess agreed to meet with me a few days after Easter, at the start of a new year.

"I know how long you've postponed taking the final steps of the journey you began when you left Villeneuve a decade ago. Or perhaps I should say, a journey whose origin is to be found in the encouraging words of a gentle artist you knew in Crécy," Agnès said, smiling when I started at the precision of her memory. "If you wish to leave us now, I'll arrange for you to stay in a house we own in Paris. I do not wish to dissuade you from your decision, but to add to the artistic tools at your disposal another kind of implement, a useful tool to bring certain kinds of impressions into focus."

The confused expression on my face must have told her to be more direct.

"I speak of the need for you to have the instrument of political insight at your disposal. You'll be entering a city at the center of power," she said. "You may be commissioned to illuminate works very different from those religious texts you've painted here. Choose your patrons wisely."

Her words shocked me out of the cocoon in which I had lived for a decade. So content had I been with the narrow scope of my concerns in the workshop—how to draw accurate outlines, how to prepare paint, how to create images appropriate for sacred works—I had nearly forgotten the wiles of the wicked and the powerful, whose influence would be wider in Paris than in the narrow parameters of Villeneuve, and whose calculations could cause greater damage than swelling the coffers of a rapacious priest.

I sat for a moment in bewildered silence.

"Anastasia, I have confidence in your strength, or I would do everything in my power to keep you here," she said, and came from around her desk. She took a small vial of holy oil from her robes, and I knelt before her to receive her blessing. "I anoint you with myrrh to purify and protect you for the rest of your journey, and will pray to the Virgin Mother to guard you and keep you from harm."

"Thank you," I said. "I promise to honor your confidence and heed your words." Then I stood and, for the last time, kissed the hand of the woman who had become like a second mother to me, a woman who had nursed me through sorrows and rekindled the flames of my vision.

7

INSIDE HARLEY 4431

VERITY

By the end of her second week in rainy London, Verity began to think the city wore its weather like an ageless woman, habitually dressed in dreary tones. Some days she chose owl gray. On others she donned the gray of freshwater pearls. At least once a week she lumbered along in dusty charcoal, wearing dark clouds on her head, the telltale signs of thunderstorms approaching from the West Country. On most days, when Verity pulled back the thick draperies covering the parlor window, the silvery, shadowless gray of Lady London's fashion made one hour look indistinguishable from another. It could be four in the afternoon or six in the morning, who could tell?

Today, the large hand on the mantel clock touched the uppermost number, tripping a switch that loosed sonorous chimes, which rang seven times. With a low rumble, a truck rolled down the arched alleyway behind the terraced houses on Great Percy Street, followed by the banging of refuse bins. The noisy ruckus startled Verity out of a troubling dream about the devouring birds on the parlor wallpaper. She dreamed that the birds were swooping around the room, pecking on the bedroom door, taunting Verity with high-pitched caws that sounded strangely like the lyrics from an absurd Beatles song.

Verity threw on her robe and slid back the bedroom door. The birds were attached to their branches. The strawberries were intact. She retrieved the newspaper from the mail slot in the front door and went downstairs to the kitchen to make coffee.

Mrs. Fairweather's silver bullet-shaped electric teakettle took pride of place on the counter. Verity pushed the button, and the kettle rumbled and roared to a rapid boil. She poured water over grounds nestled in the bottom of a glass carafe and watched the brew turn the dark-brown color of mud before plunging the strainer to the bottom. The smell of the coffee as much as its taste swept away the residue of the dream clinging to her mind like a cobweb. It was Monday morning, two and a half hours before the great gates of the British library would open their arms to welcome amateur genealogists, free Wi-Fi seekers, unemployed actors, artists, accidental tourists, and assorted scholars like Verity into its hallowed, overheated, and frequently overcrowded halls.

Carrying a steaming mug, Verity sat at the wooden desk by the window. After two weeks in the flat, she no longer minded the prospect of the brick wall. In fact, the wall had become a reliable and weirdly comforting companion. From the outside looking in, she imagined the wall had a view of the dreary landscape of her basement study, while she, looking out, had a view of the wall made equally shabby by the absence of vines or any other flourishes on its surface. It was as if, through their mutual experience of an anti-aesthetic, she and the wall had bonded.

The Guardian was filled with the usual news about the fallout from the Brexit vote. There were reports of increased incidences of anti-Muslim hostility in England, while on the Continent nationalist parties were on the rise. She deliberately skipped news about American politics and turned to the arts section to see what was playing at Sadler's Wells. This week's performance featured a new dance by an Indian choreographer called *Bayadère—The Ninth Life*. It would be amusing to see someone trained in classical Indian dance turn Marius Petipa's nineteenth-century ballet, *La Bayadère*, on its head, and Verity certainly needed amusement. After spending every day of the week, except Sunday, in the library she'd learned nothing about Anastasia.

Setting aside the newspaper, she opened her notebook to scan the history she'd copied of the ownership of Harley 4431, or *The Queen's Book*, adding a few commentaries of her own. The narrative read like the story of the generations of descendants of Adam in Genesis 5, modified by an occasional snide remark from the scribe.

In 1414, Christine, doubtless on an upswing in her career, had presented the collection of books as a gift to Queen Isabeau of Bavaria, regent to Charles VI, the mad-as-a-hatter, probably schizophrenic king of France. After the king's death, John of Lancaster, the Duke of Bedford, purchased Charles's entire library, thereby twisting the proverbial English knife in the cultural back of France during a rough patch in the Hundred Years' War. Jaquetta, the duke's second wife, got her hands on the manuscript and inscribed it with her favorite and flagrantly arrogant motto, "*sur tous autres*," a phrase loosely translated into English as "above all others!" to which the scribe—aka Verity—had added an appropriate Mrs. Fairweather flourish. Sometime in the 1460s, Jaquetta's eldest son from her second marriage, the knight and self-described bibliophile, Anthony Woodville, prized the book from his mother's courtly claws. By what means, one can only hazard a guess. The lover of books branded a folio leaf with his own paradoxical motto—"*Nulle la vaul*": "Nothing is worth it"—still decipherable even in the digital version at which the scribe had stared all week until her eyes felt drier than six-hundred-year-old parchment. Anthony's signature phrase proved predictive, as few mottos ever do. In 1472, King Edward IV of England took the book out of Anthony's grubby hands and handed it to Louis of Bruges, the Earl of Winchester, as thanks for his service.

For another twenty years, the book lived happily among other medieval books in the vast princely collection of Louis's library. After 1492, and for nearly two hundred years, its whereabouts were unknown until it turned up in the collection of Henry Cavendish, Duke of Newcastle, who declared that the book belonged to him on the first folio page: "Henry Duke of Newcastle his booke 1676." Finally, in the eighteenth century, Edward Harley, collector and patron of the arts, purchased *The Queen's Book*. Harley bequeathed it to his widow and his daughter, the Countess Henrietta and the Duchess Margaret, who sold it to the British nation in 1753 for whatever the market would bear. An Act of Parliament deposited the gold-tooled, green leather–bound vellum-filled codex in an airtight vault in the British Museum until the Museum's collection of books became the new British Library.

Verity had written the satirical account to distract herself from the nagging thought that it would take an Act of Parliament to get what she wanted—a chance to hold *The Queen's Book* in her hands. To consult the original manuscript, the library required a letter of introduction. Professor Berman had obliged with an enthusiastic endorsement of Verity's scholarship. Even that wouldn't unlock the vault unless she convinced the archivist of why the digital version was inadequate to her project. Digital perusal was as limited a method for identifying a phantom artist as looking for a needle in a haystack through a one-way mirror.

Since that visit to the Morgan Library, Verity had become a missionary on a tactile pilgrimage for truth; on such a journey, eyes were insufficient to the cause. The trouble was that she couldn't explain to the archivist in any recognizably scholarly terms that the alchemy of imagination had set her on her path, guiding her with its invisible light. She couldn't put into ordinary academic language how the glittering glass-encased paintings she'd seen in the exhibition, or the ones she'd touched at the Morgan, had made her tingle with the sensation that images were leaping off the page and under her skin. She couldn't translate into scientific parlance how caressing the folio pages, grazing the parchment, and tracing the illuminations' outlines was necessary to her project. Because what you see is not what you get. The residue of an artist's story could be sedimented on the page and resurrected through touch, like dust bursting into flames.

Verity wrote none of this in her application to the rare books and manuscripts' archivist. If she'd told the archivist how shimmering light, absorbed through the skin, transmitted what the body remembered about beauty to the brain, she'd probably have been banished to some padded room for academic miscreants and assorted crazies. Only the brick wall, which never rebuked her wildest fancies, understood.

With a sigh, Verity closed the notebook and went upstairs to assemble herself into the shape of an ordinary scholar preparing for another ordinary day in the archives. An hour later, Professor Frazier, dressed in sensible shoes and comfortable attire, stood across the street from the library.

Clad inside and out in handmade red brick, the imposing structure of the British Library imitated in architectural material St. Pancras Station and Hotel, which stood to the immediate east of it on Euston Road. Although they resembled each other in color, the modern building distinguished itself from its grand, recently refurbished Victorian neighbor through an absence of elaborate spires and arched windows, favoring right angles and squares over the curves and flourishes of Romantic excess. Today, in the rain, the library looked particularly austere.

She crossed Euston Road and climbed three steps to reach the ornate portico, where a high, rectangular wrought-iron gateway spelled BRITISH LIBRARY eight times in sixteen alternating rows of one word each. The lower five rows swung open onto a broad brick-and-stone plaza featuring a gigantic bronze effigy of Sir Isaac Newton. His looming presence made it impossible to walk past without at least a glance in his general direction.

That immortal scientist was seated on a square bronze bench, prominently positioned on a raised plinth to the left of the stairs leading to the main entrance. Hunched over, he was focused on his drawing and held a compass in his left hand. An elongated finger of his right hand pointed to the sketch; he was indifferent to everything and everyone else. His posture and gesture seemed to say, to anyone entering the library, "Here is instrument and order, here is calibration and precision, here is measurement and method; use these to tally the limits of the real."

Verity noticed a blue-and-white plaque attached to the base of the statue. *Hear Isaac here*, it read, followed by a number. Bizarre, she thought, and typed the number into her mobile phone.

A few minutes later, Sir Isaac Newton called her.

"Look up; I'm the giant, towering above you. Isaac Newton. You may think I'm not interested in you because you see me bent over with a divider in my hands. But everything you do interests me. And most of the things you're doing now, like listening to me on your mobile phone, can only be done because of my discoveries. Come closer. Now stand still.

What keeps your feet on the ground? Gravity. Before me, you would have been given all kinds of false explanations. I calculated the force of gravity. Now look up. Can you see the moon? Do you wonder why the moon doesn't fall down . . ." Newton droned on.

Before me, you would have been given all kinds of false explanations. That phrase stuck in Verity's craw. She knew Newton's discoveries had been magisterial. His calculations helped make the world a more managed, predictable place. She thanked Sir Isaac every time she stepped on an airplane. But his speech sounded pompous, as if his swirl of protractor and thrust of ruler hadn't left anything out of the picture.

Looking up at this gargantuan, wide-eyed, yet oblivious Newton, Verity recognized the statue's resemblance to William Blake's watercolor print of the mathematician she'd seen in the Tate British Gallery last week. Blake's Newton was less gigantic, though no less self-involved. The artist had depicted the scientist like some blond-ringletted, entitled Adonis. Perched on an algae-covered rock mottled in colors of aqua and rust, he was mesmerized by the geometry of triangle and circle, as if nothing could disturb the serenity and balance of his vision—not poetry, not the immaterial stuff of spirit, not even siren song.

She turned away from Newton and walked through the sliding glass entrance doors into the library lobby, where a guard checked her briefcase for dangerous objects. "The pen is mightier," Verity murmured and descended a flight of stairs to the researchers' lockers.

From her briefcase she removed her laptop, some pencils, a sharpener, a notebook, a small red leather purse, and her well-worn copy of *The Book of the City of Ladies* and put them into a recyclable plastic bag. After entering a code to open a locker, she secured the rest of her personal things inside, then walked into the corridor leading to the staircase to the second floor, where the manuscript reading room was situated in the wing opposite to the one containing the reading room for science.

Mondays were usually busy, but only a dozen or so people were spread around the well-lit room, seated at desks in one of four rows, heads bowed into old books. The rear rows were reserved for readers of unbound manuscripts or special collections. Verity chose the corner desk in the second row facing the entrance, near the book distribution station.

She took out her notebook and pencils and opened her laptop, pressing the button to turn it on. In the high-ceilinged, hushed room, the deep *bong* the computer made whirring to life sounded louder than usual. She'd forgotten to turn off the sound. Embarrassed, she looked around. No one had budged.

For the next three hours, Verity's eyes scanned the digitized version of *The Queen's Book*. She made detailed lists of every folio page containing a large or small miniature or decorated borders, adding secondary sources to her bibliography like a Girl Scout earning points for a Medieval Scholar badge. It was tedious work, and it only temporarily distracted Verity's itchy fingers from wanting to touch what even her eyes were forced to glimpse mediated by pixels on a computer screen.

She clicked through pages with painted miniatures, one after the other, and then clicked through them again. On the dedication page, a kneeling Christine presented a heavy red-leather, gold-edged book to the queen. Verity zoomed the image until it grew as large as the machine allowed, and then shrank it again, repeating the action—out-in, out-in, out-in—until the red, white, and gold baubles on the queen's netted headdress bounced, the lapis lazuli flowers in the painting's garlanded border blossomed, and the strawberries protruding from vines ripened to a juicy, ruby red. She brought her nose close to the screen to smell them. Faces hidden on the underside of acanthus petals smiled. The book Christine held in her hand flew through time, and Verity tried to catch it until Newton, pompous as ever, interrupted to remind her that gravity still held her feet on the ground.

After a lunch of a nondescript soup in the overcrowded cafeteria, Verity returned to her lists. In a monumental bibliography on *The Queen's Book*, she spotted a title she thought must be some kind of cruel joke: "The Influence of Medieval Illuminated Manuscripts on the Pre-Raphaelites and the Early Poetry of William Morris." Curiosity transformed disbelief into frenzy as she searched the online catalogue for *The Journal of William Morris Studies* for a copy of the essay.

It turned out that in the 1850s, William Morris—yes, the very same William Morris of Mrs. Fairweather's decorative obsession—had explored the Harley collection to find inspiration for his designs. Wires crossed in

Verity's head, and she tumbled down a wormhole into the nineteenth century. There was Morris, wheezing and coughing at a desk in the poorly ventilated sixth reading room of the British Museum, blowing his prodigious nose into an equally gigantic handkerchief and then holding the bound manuscript in his hands, turning its vibrant pages while copying the colorful, repeating motifs from decorated borders in *The Queen's Book* into his shabby brown notebook. Nearby, Karl Marx sat at another desk, unperturbed by Morris's self-ministrations, intent on reading Adam Smith's *Wealth of Nations* and scribbling joke-laced notes for a caricature about Mr. Moneybags he'd later write into a chapter on value in *Das Kapital*. Morris and Marx, art and revolution, side by side in the same room. Verity blinked a few times and shook her head, and returned her attention to the article.

The author identified Morris's "Daisies" pattern as an especially instructive example of his work. Verity's eyes traveled the wide world of the web and found "Daisies" listed in an online collection of Morris memorabilia. A picture opened on her screen into an epiphany of red, white, and flax-colored flowers stitched onto a woolen sea of blue like a daisy chain pulling the past into the present. In a state of feigned calm threatened by the tremble now building in the deepest recesses of her body, she recognized the pattern. It was the same floral configuration decorating the bedspread at Great Percy Street, a replica of the bouquets swirled around the edges of a page Morris had copied from *The Queen's Book*.

Verity walked through the looking glass. Dizzying images scrolled past her until her fingers, operating on the same Newtonian principles that glued her feet to the ground, screeched the scrolling to a stop at a photograph of a colorful box shaped like a medieval reliquary. A tag identified the box as a gift from the pre-Raphaelite artist, Elizabeth Siddal, to Jane Burden on the occasion of her marriage to William Morris. Siddal had decorated the box with painted reproductions of miniatures from Christine de Pizan's *The Queen's Book*.

On a split-screen of the computer, the digital pages of Harley 4431 unfolded before her like a Kabuki fan. At folio 128 *verso*, she identified "The Judgment of Paris" from Christine's *L'Épître Othéa* as the model for the image in the box's left front panel. A few hundred pages later, at folio 376, the illustration of a lover and his lady in *Cent Ballades D'Amant et*

De Dame revealed itself as the admired inspiration for Siddal's painting in the box's center panel. But the image in the right front panel of the Morris box intrigued her the most. It remained without exemplar.

The right panel portrayed two women in medieval dress standing very close to each other. The woman dressed in blue bowed her head toward the woman in red, as if toward a kiss. In the painting's background, a pale moon shone in an evening sky, casting a mellow lemon glow across a languorous green lake. The sky was smudged with purple and red clouds, enveloping the women in a haze, making their faces indistinguishable. Whether they'd been rubbed out or deliberately disguised, Verity couldn't tell. She needed a closer look and knew exactly how to get it. Sitting on a table in the upstairs front parlor in Mrs. Fairweather's flat, covered in a thick layer of dust and surrounded by other knickknacks, was a box shaped exactly like the Morris original.

She packed up her computer and notebook, raced down the stairs to the lockers, and then out of the library like a marathon runner heading for the finish line. Reaching the bottom of Acton Street in record time, she bounded through Percy Circus. Five breathless minutes later, she opened the front door of the flat and dropped her briefcase in the hallway. She flew down the stairs to retrieve a rag from the broom closet where Mrs. Fairweather stashed cleaning supplies, then galloped back up to the parlor to inspect the box. A few good wipes of the surface brought Siddal's reproductions of *The Queen's Book* miniatures into view.

The right-panel image was clearer now than in the photograph. Now she could see that the two women were holding hands like intimate friends sharing a secret. Their faces remained indecipherable. She'd come across no image like it in any archives of Christine's books. But why would Elizabeth Siddal have chosen some other source for this one painting, when the other two reproductions were so obviously from *The Queen's Book*? Mesmerized by this tantalizing ghost of a portrait, Verity wondered what connection, if any, this had to Anastasia.

She picked up the box and turned it over. A sticker on the bottom confirmed what she'd suspected. Mrs. Fairweather had purchased the reproduction in the gift shop at Kelmscott Manor, Morris's Cotswold retreat, which was now a museum.

Opening the lid, she discovered an odd assortment of flotsam—broken pens, discarded batteries, expired London Tube passes, matchbooks from The Old China Hand, and a membership card identifying Mrs. Fairweather as a Friend of Kelmscott Manor. Verity had the eerie sensation that she was living inside an illuminated manuscript.

To break the spell, she picked up a book she'd brought with her from New York and spent the rest of the night combing through Christine's biography for any clues she might have missed that could help her solve the mystery of Anastasia.

8

BETWEEN SCIENCE AND ART: THE LIFE OF CHRISTINE DE PIZAN, 1365–1380

CHRISTINE

Not far from the Church of St. Pol on the Right Bank of the Seine stood an impressive group of buildings, the private hôtels that comprised the palace of Charles V and served as the favored residence of the Valois king and his family in Paris. The royal apartments contained a large number of rooms—reception halls and dining rooms, salons for meetings with the Grand Council and honored dignitaries, chapels for prayer and private mass, chambers furnished with canopied beds, and, in the king's hôtel, two studies: evidence of his devotion to scholarship and the arts. On the apartment walls hung oil paintings and elaborate tapestries depicting the adventures of Charlemagne and scenes from the legend of the Knight of the Swan, blending the earthly with the mythical into a visual pageantry of monarchical splendor. Around a courtyard on the ground floor, a long corridor connected the king's and queen's accommodations with other buildings. The stone passageway surrounded a luxurious array of gardens—topiary clipped into fanciful shapes and geometric designs, and orchards bountiful with cherries. The walls on the queen's side were decorated with paintings of flowering plants and trees whose branches reached toward a blue-and-white sky painted in the ceiling, creating the illusion of walking on a summer's day through the royal forest at Vincennes, an illusion broken upon reaching the menagerie of lions and boars and nightingales and other exotic animals the king had installed in another garden at his end of the corridor.

Visitors welcomed to the royal residence entered from rue St. Pol through a portal decorated with carved stone lions. It opened into an enormous courtyard, where games were held for royal entertainment. The king particularly enjoyed hosting poetic competitions. One day, a young woman would become a writer and gain entry to these courtly debates during the contentious reign of the king's afflicted successor, his son, Charles VI. There, before assembled dignitaries and doubting critics, she would successfully plead her defense of women's capacity to aid the pursuit of peace, spurning the devastation of violence wrought by the divisiveness of factions and feuds that racked the country for decades after Charles V's death. Later still, she would build a monumental city of ladies with the architecture of her allegorical prose. Her name was Christine de Pizan, daughter of Lucia da Mondino and Thomas de Pizan, formerly Tommaso da Pizzano, late of Venice and now astrologer to the French king.

Christine and her family lived in a sumptuous house, quite close to the king's residence. Only once had she heard her mother complain that their home was neither as elegant nor as grand as their *palazzo* in Venice. She'd made this complaint in the fall month of the birth of Aghinolfo, her younger brother, when her mood soured, as it had four years earlier, after Paolo, Christine's other brother, was born. Her father laughed at Lucia's remark and said it only seemed smaller because there were five of them now living in the same number of rooms as they'd had in Venice. If she hadn't enjoyed her father's encouragement of learning and the availability of the king's library to quench her thirst for knowledge, Christine would have complained herself, and far more than once, about being bound to the house and the domestic scope of her mother's life.

"Daughter, put down that book and come help me prepare the fibers for the spindle," Lucia called from her chambers.

"I will come as soon as I finish my lessons for Father. He asked me to study this treatise on the movement of the stars and another on ancient history, and be prepared to summarize what I've learned when he returns from his meetings at court this evening," Christine said, never raising her eyes from the pages before her.

"You'll have time enough for that later. Right now, I'm schooling you in the skills every woman needs to prove a worthy wife. Spinning is a talent designed to please a husband with a wife's delicacy more than lessons on stars and events long past and better forgotten," Lucia said. "It teaches patience and humility, characteristics more endearing in a woman than learning how to argue from books."

Christine sighed. How often her mother—a dour woman not given to conversation about much more than the household accounts or the proper supervision of domestic servants or the latest fashions on the ladies at court—would interrupt her studies. Her father believed that if one learned to read the stars, one could predict anything—when crops would best grow, when children would be born healthy, and, perhaps most importantly, what conditions regulated the four humors. Christine hoped her astrological talent would allow her to avoid the melancholia that clouded her mother's temperament from time to time. Still, being an obedient daughter, she tried to conform to her mother's requests even if she silently questioned their merits.

"Yes, *Maman*." She put down her book and went to her mother's side.

"Today I will instruct you in the proper way to thread a spindle for drop spinning. First you need a large-whorled spindle. Then you take a piece of yarn and double it, like this, creating a loop at one end. Next you wrap the doubled threads around the spindle and draw them through the loop, cinching the threads at the top, near the whorl, for your leader . . ."

The lesson went on and on. Christine tried to concentrate but was distracted by the arithmetic of the process—how many times you pinched the fibers before twisting the spindle, how many times you twirled the spindle, how many times you repeated the movements— adding the numbers in her head until she forgot all about the spindle and the yarn so that when her mother handed her the spindle and asked her to repeat what she'd learned, Christine couldn't execute even one step of the process.

With an exasperated motion, Lucia grabbed the spindle from her daughter's hand and, glaring angrily at Christine, started the lesson again. After the third try, she gave up. Nurse had brought Aghinolfo to be fed.

"I suppose that was your intention all along, to waste the small amount of free time I have in a day. My patience is wearing thin, Christine. If you don't try harder tomorrow, I'll ask your father to forbid you to visit the library of the king," she said.

Christine looked at her mother in horror. The king's library was her sovereign comfort. She'd first set eyes on that magnificent collection of books when her father brought her and her mother to the Louvre several years before, soon after their arrival in Paris in 1368, to be presented to the king in the chambers of his second residence. After they were introduced, the king noticed Christine carrying a small Book of Hours in her hand.

"Can you read, my child?" he asked.

Christine, astonished at being addressed directly by the monarch, could only manage a nod.

Perhaps thinking of his own small daughters, whom he'd recently lost to early deaths, the king told Thomas he wished to show young Christine the library he'd installed in the falconry tower. He took her hand and escorted her, while her parents followed a few steps behind. They descended four flights down the great stone spiral staircase that led from the royal apartments to the ground floor and crossed a wide court-yard to enter the other tower. The king described how he'd ordered the architect to decorate the library walls with rare woods from Ireland and to inlay the coffered ceiling with cypress. Light filtered through windows grated in iron. When Christine asked why they were grated, the king explained it was to prevent wily birds from nesting among the more than a thousand volumes in his precious collection of the most notable works of theology, philosophy, literature, poetry, and—he added with a wink—astrology. Christine sat down at a bench, overcome with awe. It was a tabernacle of books, an homage to learning, a reverent place.

"Why do you have so many books?" Christine asked.

"As long as knowledge is honored in this country, so long will it prosper," the king said. "Perhaps you will help France prosper, Christine. You're welcome to visit these manuscripts whenever you wish."

"Christine, did you hear me?" Hearing her mother's voice returned Christine to the present. "You'll be forbidden to visit the king's library."

"I'm sorry, Mother. I'll be more attentive, I promise," she said.

"Then leave the book with me and take this spindle to your room to practice," Lucia said.

"Yes, Mother." She curtsied and went to her room.

When Christine had left, Lucia gave the book to Nurse and told her to hide it.

Later that evening, Christine joined her parents and her brother Paolo at table for the evening meal. She noticed that her father was in an excited state after his consultation with the king. Charles V, a thin, rather sickly man, frequently sought the advice of his astrologer for remedies to treat various ailments from which he perennially suffered. From the look of consternation on her father's face, Christine worried that the king's condition might be grave.

"Did you find His Majesty in good humor, Father?" Christine asked after the meal had ended and the servant had cleared the table.

"He responded well to the treatment I prescribed and listened intently to my preliminary discourse on the stars," Thomas answered. "I hope my guidance will serve the plan he's decided to undertake."

Thinking her father must be referring to some new building project of the king's—Charles was well known for the great perimeter walls he had added to Parisian defenses as well as the marvelous architectural expansion of the Louvre—Christine pressed him for details.

"Don't trouble your father with pestering questions, Christine," her mother said. "Fetch the wool you worked today. He'll be pleased to see your progress."

Christine rose from her chair, but Thomas motioned for her to be seated again.

"It is important that she learn about worldly matters as well as womanly crafts," he said, turning to Lucia. "What I heard today concerns us all, even women."

Christine listened intently as her father told how the king had recently gained the advantage in the never-ending war with the English, recovering territories ceded under his own father's reign, and had negotiated a year's truce to begin in early summer. Yet what troubled the king now, and why he had sent for his astrologer, was news he'd received that brigands, bands of armed and well-equipped warriors, who'd joined forces with French knights to defeat the English, were now threatening the country from within. With the enemy becalmed, these military men of no country but that of their own greed were without purpose or means of support and had set about plundering the territories they'd only recently protected. Charles feared they might be mobilized to pillage Paris itself, creating outbreaks of violence in the capital such as the king had experienced in his youth.

The king's two closest advisers, Bureau de la Rivière and Jean le Mercier, his chamberlain and treasurer, suggested Charles devise a campaign to distract the marauders into a foreign war, and put the knight from the region of Picardy, Enguerrand VII de Coucy, in charge of an attack on territories held by the Hapsburg Dukes in Austria. Wary of undertaking any risky endeavor without consulting his astrologer, Charles had summoned Thomas to determine whether the alignment of the planets was auspicious for his success.

"And so I spent all afternoon consulting certain astrological works I had recently sent from Bologna to include in the king's library. To give him the most reliable reading, I must return tomorrow to continue my work," her father said.

Filled as it was with the terminology of war and politics, much of what her father recounted confused Christine. But bewilderment gave way to excitement with the next sentence he uttered.

"You may come with me, Christine, and continue your study of Latin translation in the king's library while I work," he said.

"She hasn't finished the spinning project I gave her to complete," Lucia interjected.

"There will be time enough for that later. The king himself requested Christine's presence tomorrow. He said it gives him great pleasure to see a young girl with such a bottomless appetite for knowledge."

In the following months, Christine added Boccacio's *Decameron* and the writing of Aristotle and Augustine—translated into the French vernacular by order of the king—to her studies, along with Arthurian romances, the poetry of Ovid, and illuminated manuscripts of Holy Scripture, culling from these varied sources threads of insight about the myriad weaknesses and temptations besetting mortals and beginning to spin these into poetry and prose when the housewifely spinning she'd learned from her mother proved insufficient to save her from boredom.

In the December days of 1377, the whole of Paris was caught up in a frenzy of planning. Having displaced the threat of marauders and recovered lands from the English—thanks, no doubt, to his astrologer's wise counsel—the king had invited his uncle, the Holy Roman Emperor Charles IV, to visit Paris. As the king's prized adviser, Thomas de Pizan and his family were to be guests of high rank at the grand banquet planned for the night of the Feast of Epiphany to celebrate the emperor. For the occasion, Lucia had ordered forty meters of red silk in two different shades from the finest silk merchants in Paris, and also hired the best dressmaker—one recommended by Queen Jeanne herself—to fashion their attire. Since her mother was usually more conservative in taste, Christine was surprised to see her making such a fuss over finery.

"I suppose you were so lost in your books, you forgot how carefully we must prepare for the emperor's forthcoming visit," her mother snapped.

Christine, of course, knew about the visit. When she'd visited the library earlier that day, she'd observed the king's stewards and butlers preparing the Louvre for the festivities. She'd heard the chefs discussing elaborate dishes of all manner of fish, fowl, and hoofed animal. She'd seen goldsmiths bringing jeweled goblets and swords that the king intended to gift the emperor on the occasion. She'd even helped the king select two Books of Hours from his library to offer as a parting gesture of thanks for an alliance he hoped to secure with the emperor. What hadn't registered was any other purposeful way she might be involved, besides as an unofficial chronicler.

For the last three years, Christine's father had overseen the schedule of his daughter's education. While he encouraged her instruction in the womanly crafts of spinning, sewing, flower arranging, planning for a feast, and all the other necessary skills a young wife would need to provide for a husband's comfort and pleasure, he insisted that time be set aside every day for more scholarly pursuits, including at least one day a week for Christine to visit the king's library.

"Since you've been distracted elsewhere, I've had to shoulder all the arrangements for ensuring our proper attire and comportment without your assistance," her mother added.

"I'm sorry if I've failed in my daughterly duties, Mother," Christine said. "Tell me how I might relieve your burden."

"It will be a very special occasion, more so because the king gave your father permission to invite a young gentleman to be your escort. He is the educated son of a court official, now deceased, whom your father met some years ago. Your appearance and manners must be impeccable," her mother said.

The mention of a gentleman escort piqued fourteen-year-old Christine's curiosity. Several suitors already had sought her father's approval, but he'd deemed none of the petitioners worthy, judging them more interested in currying his favor for influence at court than caring and providing for his daughter. That her father had asked the king's consent to invite a gentleman to accompany her to a feast of such renown must mean that he considered the young man suitable. She'd have to comply with her father's decision, no matter whom he chose for her to wed, but trusted him not to marry her to a man she would find most disagreeable—a man who refused to consider a woman his equal. While her mother continued to describe plans for her attire and comportment, Christine weighed how to devise her own test of the gentleman's worthiness, and how to signal approval or distaste to her father without compromising her duty as a daughter.

"I've made arrangements for the dressmaker to attend to a fitting tomorrow and requested that one of the royal maids recommend an adviser on protocol to tutor you. You will set aside any other plans and make yourself available for the rest of the week," Lucia continued.

"Yes, *Maman*." Christine looked forward more to exercising her wits than the arts of coquetry, but she was dutiful.

Word that the emperor had left the Abbey of St. Denis rippled through the streets of Paris. Parisians of every class had assembled to view the pageantry. Because the emperor suffered from an illness that caused him great pain, the king had sent a litter to carry him. The litter was drawn by two beautiful black horses draped in blue velvet blankets stitched with gold *fleurs-de-lis*. Harnesses bearing the French coat of arms attached the horses to the carrier. The litter paused at the royal chapel, just before the meeting point with the king. Two footmen helped the ailing emperor to mount the dark brown horse the king had sent as a gift. Then the emperor continued on horseback to the edge of the old Palace courtyard, where the provost of Paris awaited his arrival, flanked by some four thousand Parisian citizens, all mounted on horseback and dressed in their finest multicolored livery of purple and white.

"We, the officers of the king at Paris, the provost of the merchants and bourgeois of Charles's beautiful city, wish to pay you reverence and to please you, as the king, our lord, has commanded."

Christine stood next to her mother near the front, marveling at the spectacle of regal authority emerging in layers of sound and color until the majesty of Charles V's rule over France was on grandiose display. A low murmur moved through the assembled crowd and then died to the faintest of whispers as the royal procession approached.

The king's trumpeters announced the monarch's impending arrival with regal blasts from their silver instruments. His brothers, the Dukes of Burgundy and Bourbon, led the procession, followed by nobles, prelates, and other officials of the crown, arrayed by rank and dressed in color-coded finery that reported their station, from the red of royalty to the dove gray of valets and the muddied brown of stewards, as if each rank of service were a rung on the ladder of monarchy that led from the lowliest to the divinely ordained one at the top. Christine saw her father riding among the royal ranks, wearing the red silks of his station. And then came the king, mounted on a large white palfrey, his scarlet, ermine-lined robes flowing around him. On his head he wore a pointed hat covered in pearls, which he removed to welcome the emperor. The emperor removed his hat as well. They shook hands and then led the procession back to the palace, where they would meet in private to discuss secrets of state.

The crowd began to disperse. Christine and her brothers followed their mother along a winding path that led to the grand hall where all the luminaries of Paris, more than eight hundred in all, were assembled to wine and dine the visiting dignitaries. Her father had arrived before them and waited near the entryway, accompanied by a young man who was nervously adjusting an embroidered belt at his waist.

"May I present Étienne de Castel," her father said.

He was a broad-shouldered man, whose small frame was disguised by the multi-layered folds of his red velvet surcoat. A few sandy curls peeked out from the edge of his cap, making Christine think he'd donned it hurriedly. He turned toward her, removed the cap, and, with a sweeping gesture that went wide of its mark, bowed, not noticing that the feathers in his cap had tickled her face on their rapid descent toward the ballroom floor. When he rose, she was laughing.

"You'd better practice next time," Christine said.

"Forgive me if I offended you, Mademoiselle," Étienne said, confusion furrowing his brow.

"*You* have done nothing to offend me, but your unruly plumes had a mind of their own." She picked a small feather from the tip of her nose and dropped it onto the floor.

"I apologize on behalf of the feathers," he said, adding, with a smile, "I will scold the rude beasts in private after the festivities have ended."

He held out his arm to escort her into the great hall. She was pleased he made no trite comment about her magnificent red dress, slender figure, delicate hands, or sparkling blue eyes, though she saw an approving look wash over his face. Neither crude nor humorless, Christine thought, taking his arm. It pleased her even more when, after they were seated next to her parents, he inquired about her work in the king's library.

"Your father tells me you've had the honor of viewing the king's magnificent collection. I hear he's commissioned some of the finest scribes and illuminators to translate ancient classics into the vernacular French," he said. "Tell me, has he any copies of Aristotle's *Ethics*? I studied that treatise in Latin at the University of Paris."

"Yes, and also his *Politics*, as well as Augustine's *City of God*," she said.

"You're more learned than I, if you've read those difficult works," he said.

Christine glanced at him suspiciously, as if he might be mocking her. Finding neither taunt nor envy, nor even sarcasm, but only kindness on his face, she allowed a coy smile to appear, and decided to test him further.

"With my father's blessing and thanks to the king's largesse, I have garnered wisdom from science. And also from poetry. Or perhaps you share my father's doubt that rhyming couplets have any use for the ills of the world?"

Before Étienne could answer, Thomas interjected. "Scribbling lines might distract from personal worries, but only science can salve an ailing heart or heal a failing liver. Even Petrarch proved unable to stave off the putrid misery that befell so many thousands in the years of pestilential outbreak."

"I doubt even a man of science, or the most talented physician, could have foretold the speed with which death spread like thick black smoke around the corners of Europe," Étienne said.

"Perhaps not," Thomas replied. "But surely you agree that the movement of the stars alters the balance of elements and explains the course of events better than poetry can?"

"I agree that the influence of the stars is paramount. Yet poetry has another kind of force," Étienne said, casting a sideways glance at Christine.

"Its power can console us in times of misery, and buoy us in moments of joy." His willingness to engage in verbal jousting with her father pleased her so much that she averted her gaze to suppress the giggle tickling her throat. What a companion this suitor would prove to be!

"A power no doubt affected by the conjunction of Jupiter and Saturn," Thomas continued. "Ptolemy, after all, taught us about the relationship between planetary movements and musical tones in his masterful work, *The Harmonics*."

"Ah, yes, Ptolemy." Étienne smiled. "'There is geometry in the humming of the strings, there is music in the spacing of the spheres.' But that's poetry!"

"As my daughter has protested to me every day since she learned to read," Thomas said, standing to raise his glass in a toast. "And will surely remind you, should you ever betray her devotion to words."

A year later, in 1379, Christine was betrothed to Étienne de Castel, and they married the following February.

Thanks to Thomas's influence at court, Étienne was employed as a royal secretary. Often, after her studies in the king's library, Christine met her husband on the grounds of St. Pol before walking the short distance to their home. Today, her father joined her in a promenade around the king's gardens, while they waited for Étienne to finish preparing an ordinance for the king's signature. It was some months after the wedding, and the young couple had been invited to dine that evening with Christine's parents and brothers.

"You're looking well, daughter. Are you content?" her father asked.

"I'm full of happiness," she said. "I couldn't have wished for a husband more wise, prudent, handsome, and good."

Étienne soon joined them. They exited the castle grounds and headed toward the de Pizan residence, adjacent to which the young couple now had a house of their own.

"It's such a beautiful evening. May we not take a short walk toward the river?" Christine pleaded.

Before Thomas could object that it would delay supper, Étienne took his young wife's hand, and they dashed toward the Seine. It was a clear June evening, not yet dusk. Haymakers were working the fields on the plains on the Left Bank of the river. A group of revelers floated past on a *barque*, laughing, singing, and toasting one another. Standing next to her husband before this tableau of growth and vitality, Christine felt as if peace had finally settled on France in the same way it had settled in her heart. Then the bells of the churches all across Paris began to chime the hour in synchronicity. *Gong, gong, gong* . . . until Christine counted seven, not knowing seven was the number of months before she would give birth to a daughter; seven, the number of years before her father's death; and seven, the number of years after the death of her beloved Étienne when her first-born child would choose a path against her mother's wishes and enter a convent at Poissy to take up the religious life.

9

THURSDAY'S CHILD
HAS FAR TO GO

VERITY

Another week of laboring in the library's haystacks, another lengthening of lists of arcane information, another layering of the labyrinthine bibliography about Christine's manuscripts and their makers. The entire process felt like some weird reenactment of the nine circles of academic hell. Begin in the limbo of ignorance. When desire has aroused curiosity, enter bastion of knowledge and overindulge the appetite for every factual crumb. Hoard discoveries in notebooks like precious jewels locked in a safe that only its owner can open. When every answer leads to another question, fire up the engines of anger. With no end in sight, fabricate lies and present them as truths—or, better yet, burn everything and pretend to expertise. Finally, betray the whole enterprise by giving up.

At least thinking about Dante helped Verity ignore William Morris for a while.

For the rest of the week, she lost herself in the forest of aesthetic objects described in the arcane source Professor Millard had recommended—*Album*

Christine de Pizan. She wandered through the underbrush of script to admire the branches of ornamental design and sprays of blooming miniatures. She marveled at the playful, exuberant handwriting of X, likely Christine herself, compared to which the script associated with the scribal hand known as P was tame to an anesthetized degree. The large blue-and-red puzzle initials ornamentalists drew to announce the first line of a chapter befuddled Verity with their complexity. Cocooned between the legs of a letter *A*, tiny circles and loops of alternating colors slept in quiet companionship like unscrambled eggs. Sometimes a vine of three-petaled flowers erupted from the back of a letter *T* and sprouted along the edge of an entire page. But oh, those illuminated miniatures! They illustrated stories of an imagined world of castles and queens, interwoven with allegories of Reason, Rectitude, and Justice. Christine's codex was an archaic graphic novel conceived by a woman who ordered a portrait of herself as the writer to be painted into the beating heart of the narrative.

The illustrations amplified the text, and the written words reverberated in the paintings, creating something close to sound. Such sensual harmony was only achieved because Christine had overseen its design, the authors of the *Album* declared, adding the caveat that what remained more difficult to grasp was how the writer communicated her thoughts to the illuminator. Perhaps exemplars were passed from one workshop to another. Maybe a guidebook of preferred samples once existed. Sometimes instructions wrongly copied onto a page by a scribe, who mistook them for a line of text, suggested general ideas for illustrations, leaving room for the artist's interpretation. One unmentioned possibility established itself as fact to Verity—the collaboration between writer and artist depended on a close relationship of trust. Or love.

The only artist Christine mentioned by name among those associated with her books was Anastasia, and she was the only artist identified by name in the *Album*. All the others were indicated by titles, such as Master of the City of Ladies or Master of the Duke of Bedford. Although their given names were unknown, the use of the masculine noun, *Maître*, in their titles and the masculine pronoun, *il*, in sentences describing their works was enough to tell Verity that everyone assumed the masters were men. Lacking records of Anastasia's life, she couldn't prove otherwise. With a sense of dismay, she began to feel Newton's compass encircling her again.

On Friday, when she received an email response to her request to view the original manuscript of *The Queen's Book*, dismay morphed into despair.

Dear Dr. Frazier,

Thank you for your application to examine the manuscript. As you can appreciate, this is one of our highest-grade manuscripts. For conservation reasons, access to it is strictly limited. It is only available for research questions that cannot be answered from the digital surrogate, which does not appear to be the case here.

I can appreciate that you would like to see the original. I regret, however, that I cannot grant permission.

You indicate your interest in the identity of the artist(s) who created the illustrations. In the nineteenth century, Birch and Jenner (see their *Early Drawings and Illuminations: An Introduction to the Study of Illustrated Manuscripts* (London: Bagster and Sons, 1879)) provided the original scholarly evidence about medieval French manuscript workshops; it was supplemented by further studies. I am sure you are aware of the early twentieth-century research of Léopold Delisle and, more recently, the exhaustive studies of Millard Meiss on the subject of Christine's *enlumineurs*. Together, this research has identified those artists responsible for the paintings in Harley 4431, known as *The Queen's Book* (c. 1410–c. 1414), definitively attributing the work to the Master of the Cité des Dames and workshop and to the Master of the Duke of Bedford.

For your purposes, might I suggest you consult another copy of de Pizan's work in the Harley collection? Harley 219, 4410, 838, or 4605 may be of interest to you.

With best wishes,

Dr. Caitlyn O'Toole

Lead Curator, Illuminated Manuscripts

Verity wanted to touch those paintings, wanted to feel the artist's hand in the swirl of the brush stroke or the squiggle of the quill, wanted to graze the raised platform of gold leaf that made images shimmer with someone else's touch. Whether Newton's descendants decided between light's being a particle or a wave didn't matter. To Verity, light was a tactile emissary. It could carry a message across the centuries. She had felt the first inkling of light's report in the Morgan Library, when a rainbow had led her to a sanctuary where a chorus of light materialized into a woman writing a book in a room of her own.

Then an ancient memory emerged from the recesses of Verity's temporal lobe. Once, she had been lost in a small boat in a foggy sea without a compass and smelled land before she could see it and knew where to steer to safety. When one sense was dulled, another could compensate. If she couldn't touch, she could smell her way to Anastasia, could listen for word of her existence, and maybe even taste Anastasia's essence in something as evocative as *petites madeleines* were for Proust. She trusted that her senses would guide her to some forgotten corner of the past where Anastasia might have hidden. Without knowing where it was, she felt its presence mounting and deleted the archivist's email.

Half an hour past noon, Verity presented her reader's card to the librarian to see if other books she'd ordered had arrived.

"Frazier. Hold on a minute, I think we have yours," the librarian said, retrieving three large bound volumes from the shelves behind her and handing them to her.

Verity noticed an odd title among them. *Spiritual Economies: Female Monasticism in Late Medieval England.* "This one's not mine," she said, about to hand the book back to the librarian.

"I'm sorry; there's more than one Frazier in the reading room today," the librarian apologized. "I believe the other one is sitting there." She nodded toward an attractive, dark-haired woman about the same age as Verity, who was seated at one of the restricted desks, her head buried in some ancient text mounted on a book holder in front of her.

"I'll take it to her," Verity said, holding the book in her hand like she'd just received an invitation to a celebrity party.

"I think this one is yours," she said a moment later, handing the book to the woman.

"If it's about convents, it's mine," the woman said. "Thanks." She looked up at Verity, extended her hand, and introduced herself: "Anastasia Frazier." The woman had the most extraordinary thick-lashed blue-gray eyes. Her dark auburn hair was drawn back from her long, oval face in an elaborate chignon that made her look like she'd stepped out of another era.

"Did you say Anastasia?" Verity had to stop herself from giggling like a schoolgirl.

"Yes. I know, an unusual name for this century. Mother was a frightfully unusual woman, inexplicably fascinated with mischievous geniuses, especially if they were Russian and female. And you are?"

"Oh, sorry. Verity Frazier. Your, um, name distracted me. Anastasia happens to be the name of a woman I've been trying to research, an artist from the fifteenth century."

"What a delightful coincidence, to meet another Frazier fascinated with women of the medieval persuasion."

Verity watched the corners of the woman's mouth curl into a smile as mischievous and enigmatic as the Cheshire cat's, and an unexpected shiver of attraction coursed through her while an alarm bell tinkled in her head ever so gently. The man seated next to Anastasia cleared his throat a couple of times, so Verity lowered her voice to a whisper. "I was about to grab a bite in the cafeteria. Care to join me?"

"If you give me a few minutes to finish my notes," Anastasia said, glancing at her neighbor with an imperious look. "Then we can have a proper conversation."

"Sure," Verity said. "Stop by my desk when you're ready." Grateful for those minutes, she plotted how to mine the treasure of meeting this accidental partner in medieval sleuthing, weighing whether to acknowledge her ignorance or cover her naiveté with small talk, while trying to manage the not-unwelcome sensation that the woman she'd just met had been flirting with her. Before she could decide, Anastasia stood at her side.

"Whatever gems you're about to discover in those files can wait. I'm famished," she said, wrapping a long purple paisley scarf around her neck.

The first floor was packed with people. All the tables around the perimeter were populated with folks who had brought lunch and were either still eating or had camped out at the tables, working on laptops. An overflow of visitors spilled down the marble stairs all the way to the ground level. Scores sat on the cold steps, sipping coffee and swiping their mobile phones. Verity and Anastasia walked into the Terrace Restaurant. Every seat there was also taken. Verity was about to give up when Anastasia made a beeline for a small table in the corner where two people were having an animated conversation. She leaned over the couple and whispered something. They nodded, looked in Verity's direction, pushed their seats back, and left. Then she draped her scarf across the tabletop, dropped her notebook on top of it, and gestured with a fluttering hand for Verity to get in line to order food. A minute later, she joined Verity in the queue.

"How did you know they were getting ready to leave?" Verity asked.

"They weren't. I simply hurried them along," Anastasia said, looking at the whiteboard menu.

"What did you say to them?" Verity asked, a little nonplussed by Anastasia's audacity.

"I told them you had to catch a train in less than an hour," Anastasia said, not taking her eyes off the menù.

"But that's not true," Verity said.

"It's plausible enough. Besides, I want to get back to my work in less than an hour. Don't you?"

"Well, yes, but—"

"As for those two, they're here every day, same time, same table. You'd think it was embossed with their names. I never see them in any of the research rooms. They needed a nudge. We needed a table. Voila!" Anastasia raised her right hand in a flippant gesture and touched her left to her heart. Then she ordered the soup for them both.

"I hope you don't mind that I ordered for you," she said.

Verity shook her head, bemused at how easily she'd acquiesced. This woman was nothing like Pauline. Or Regina. Was that why she felt so attracted to her? Or was what she took for attraction actually nothing more than curiosity, or merely temptation resulting from an extended period of loneliness bubbling up in a familiar, still dangerous way? The same mistake in a different disguise. The alarm bell inside her tinkled a little louder but she ignored it.

"Not very British of me, I suppose," Anastasia continued. "But then, I am an unusually good judge of taste. And how British is that?" She laughed and gave Verity a sly look.

"Besides the professor at Columbia who urged me to pursue my research here, I don't know many British people," Verity said.

"On the whole, I'd say we're a stodgy bunch. Stiff upper lip is only the half of it." Anastasia picked up the tray of their food. "Grab a couple of serviettes and some cutlery, would you?"

Verity picked up the napkins and utensils and followed Anastasia back to the table.

"I do find it terribly annoying that some people come here simply for the free Wi-Fi, don't you?" Anastasia said as she finished her soup. She wiped her mouth with a napkin and reached into a small leather pouch for a lipstick, applying the bright red color and checking the glamorizing effect in a tiny mirror affixed to the tube's end. "They monopolize tables for hours, reading email and their ridiculous social-media feeds."

"It is a public space, after all. I think it's exciting to see so many different sorts visiting a library. But yes, sometimes I can't find a place to sit to eat," Verity said. "How was your soup?" she asked, wanting to change the subject.

"Boring, but adequate."

"I can never tell the difference between one cream of whatever flavor they're serving and another," Verity said.

"The secret's in the color." Anastasia gestured to the orange-tinged residue in her bowl. "Probably carrot. Definitely not mushroom. Now I suppose you think I'm just being a snooty British person."

"About the soup?"

Anastasia laughed. "No, not the soup. Wanting readers to have priority seating. It's just, I think those of us who are here for serious work ought to be given preference over others mindlessly surfing the internet. The library doesn't have that policy, so I carry out my own, as it were."

"The staff work here too; I don't think they have special seating." Verity nodded to a table of librarians next to them.

"Point taken," Anastasia said, casually leaning forward, elbows on the table, chin resting coquettishly atop her clasped hands, lips pursed. "Now, tell me about your research. Fifteenth century, you said?"

"Yes, I'm trying to identify who decorated the illuminated manuscripts of Christine de Pizan. I believe it was a woman named Anastasia. She's mentioned in *The Book of the City of Ladies*, where Christine lauded women and complained that their accomplishments had been ignored by men." Anastasia had changed the subject so unexpectedly, Verity had to scramble to sound like she knew what she was talking about.

"Such an extraordinary period," said Anastasia, sitting back in her seat and rearranging her scarf around her shoulders to dramatic effect. "Chock-full of catastrophe and intrigue and grand displays of corruption and opulence. And what powerful women! As you've probably surmised, I'm a medievalist too. Researching English medieval nunneries in their heyday, the three centuries before the Dissolution, for a monograph I'm writing. My university's generous with research funds, especially for a book under contract."

"The Dissolution?" The words flew out of Verity's mouth as if they had a mind of their own.

"Are you such a Francophile that you don't remember?" Anastasia furrowed her brow. "The Dissolution. From 1536 to 1540. When Henry VIII destroyed the English monasteries and convents."

Verity felt her cheeks flush. Caught in the act of her ignorance. "I really can't call myself a medievalist, Francophile or otherwise," she stuttered. "It's sort of a newer interest of mine. Until now, I've worked mostly on nineteenth-century French women's history."

"Another neophyte dabbling in the treasure troves of the Middle Ages. I do admire your audacity." Anastasia smirked.

Verity gave her a wounded look. "I'm going to get a cup of tea; would you like one?"

"Can't stand the stuff. I'd take an espresso, though. I do so want to hear more about my fifteenth-century eponym."

A few minutes later, Verity returned to the table with their drinks. Anastasia was scribbling with a beautiful black fountain pen in a leather-tooled notebook. "Thanks," she said, not looking up. "Just a minute while I finish this note. There," she said, screwing the pen into its top with a flourish and returning it to a special holder that matched the notebook. "I'm ready now for the big reveal about my ancestral moniker's unrecognized enterprise."

"Actually, I haven't discovered much about the . . . other Anastasia. In fact, I haven't found anything more than I already knew," Verity said. Not wanting to appear like a dilettante, she left out what she'd learned about the William Morris connection. For all she knew, this Anastasia hated the decorative arts. They seemed to Verity to be an acquired taste. But what wasn't? "I've been wading through art historians' accounts of the composition of Christine's books. There aren't any real names, only generic titles for the artists associated with her work."

"How unfortunate. Have you tried searching the French national records for the period?"

"Well, of course. I'm familiar with those archives from my nineteenth-century work. But it's quite difficult to read medieval French script in the *Archives Nationale*'s digital copies of official records." Verity tried to salvage a modicum of self-respect from the pyre of embarrassment erecting itself around her. Neither Anastasia was being particularly cooperative in coming to her rescue.

"I sympathize with the challenges of deciphering medieval French script. I find Latin an equally petulant opponent." Anastasia looked at her watch and stood up. "Shall we get back to our respective albatrosses, then?"

"Sure," Verity said, saddened that she'd been unable to redeem herself before the conversation ended.

A few hours later, Verity was packing her things and heading toward the readers' lockers when Anastasia tapped her on the shoulder.

"I'm leaving early too. Care to join me in a drink? I know a cheeky little place in Bloomsbury. It's called the Noble Rot Wine Bar. Serves Franglaise food; it should suit both our tastes."

Verity sensed an oblique apology in the invitation. It would be nice to have someone else to talk to besides the wall, she thought.

"I'd love to, but I can't. I have a ticket for a dance performance at Sadler's Wells tonight," Verity said.

"Rain check, then?" Anastasia asked.

"Sure," Verity said with a smile. "Around here, that's something you'll be able to redeem as early as tomorrow."

"Except I'm not an American; I don't work on the weekends like you lot."

"Monday, then?"

"Monday," Anastasia said, smiling. "Rain or shine."

Outside, the sky was surprisingly clear. The damp London streets bustled with excitement about the end of the workday and the allure of sharing a pint at the local pub with one's mates. Despite her disappointment at the archivist's decision not to allow her to see the Harley manuscripts, Verity felt surprisingly elated. She decided to treat herself to dinner and joined the jostling crowd heading into the evening light.

An hour later, she sat at a table by the window in a restaurant on Roseberry Avenue next to Sadler's Wells and ordered a glass of Chardonnay. The street seemed busier than usual for a Friday night. Several double-decker buses whizzed by, filled to the brim with revelers headed toward pubs and cafes on the Islington High Street. A group of girls in matching school uniforms, sharing bags of candy and taking selfies, nearly collided with an elderly British gentleman walking a tiny white terrier. The girls giggled and apologized, and one of them knelt down to pet the terrier, defusing the tension. Verity had seen the man and the dog walking in her neighborhood before, but hadn't noticed until now how much the dog resembled the one at Christine's feet in her *Queen's Book* portrait. *I need a break. I've spent too much time with Harley 4431.*

A trio of elegant women dressed in bright saris strolled past, heading for the Sadler's Wells show, snapping Verity back into the twenty-first century. She decided on a dish and signaled the waiter.

"Seems busier than usual tonight," Verity said, gesturing to the crowded street after ordering a light meal.

"Monday's a holiday," said the waiter. "I'll be back with your food shortly."

She'd forgotten about the bank holiday.

An elegantly dressed woman walked past and then turned and walked back, stopping in front of the window by Verity's table. The woman waved. At first, Verity didn't recognize her, distracted as she was by the gaudy spray of peacock feathers wrapped around the woman's head and fastened over one ear with a blue-and-green-glass beaded ornament. Then the woman smiled. It was Anastasia. She gestured toward Verity's table, and Verity nodded yes.

Anastasia entered the restaurant, removed her coat, and hung it on the hooks near the door. She was wearing a short, forest-green suede skirt and a lilac silk blouse with mother-of-pearl buttons. A green leather belt cinctured the outfit tightly around her waist and matched in color and quality the pair of high-heeled green leather boots that came up to the top of her knees. A diamond-and-emerald cluster studded each ear. She looked gorgeous. Verity felt like a frump in her simple black linen dress.

"What a surprise to see you in this neighborhood," Verity said, after Anastasia joined her at the table, taking off the feathered headdress and freeing her hair from its pinned binding at the nape of her neck.

Until this moment, Verity hadn't noticed how much Anastasia resembled the pictures of William Morris's wife, Jane, that she'd seen in the Great Percy Street flat. The dark, curly auburn hair billowing around her shoulders, the elongated face with its pouty cherry-hued mouth, the aquiline nose, the smoky gray-blue eyes. Those same features had enthralled the pre-Raphaelite painter, Dante Gabriel Rossetti, so much that he'd anointed Jane his muse and she became his lover, despite her marriage to Morris. The striking resemblance flustered Verity, and she took a sip of her wine, amplifying the tingle of attraction whispering through her veins and coloring her cheeks two shades short of vermilion.

"I hope you don't mind," Anastasia said, touching Verity's hand. "I decided to get a ticket to that performance you mentioned. Besides, I'd forgotten, Monday's a bank holiday. I didn't want to wait until Tuesday for our rain-check drink. And to tell you how truly sorry I am."

Verity gave her a quizzical look.

"I shouldn't have mocked. I truly am interested in your research; perhaps I might even be able to help."

"I appreciate that, but . . . what's with the feathers?" Verity had to say something to break the spell.

"Feathers? Oh, you mean my fascinator," Anastasia said, waving the bejeweled decoration and sending the feathers into a sensuous dance. "A gift from my eccentric mother. Hardly ever wear it. Bit too garish for my taste, but I thought it suited the artsy occasion."

"Well, it's certainly a conversation piece. A little out of context for what we're about to see," Verity said, and explained the revisionist history of the ballet *Bayadère—The Ninth Life*.

"I guess it's my turn to be embarrassed. I'm not terribly sure I think a few feathers necessarily signal loyalty to the aristocracy and its colonialist past, though I do appreciate the advice," Anastasia said, fanning herself with the decoration. "It's a bit warm in this place, don't you think?"

"Let's just agree that it might obstruct someone's view." They both laughed.

"I noticed you brought your library satchel with you. Could you possibly hold this for me until after the show?" Anastasia tickled Verity's hand with the feathers. "And I promise to keep my comments about the performance to myself until we've shared a glass of champagne," she said with a wink.

The audience was bubbling with excitement when Verity and Anastasia exited the theater. Anastasia was uncharacteristically quiet.

"Well, what did you think?" Verity asked, handing Anastasia her feathers.

"I promised not to speak without champagne." Anastasia put the feathers back in her hair. "But that was just about the most weirdly sensual and utterly uncomfortable thing I've ever seen. I mean, a male temple dancer, and other men and women pawing all over his body like he was a piece of meat," Anastasia said.

Verity laughed. "I think that was the choreographer's point. Changing the gender of the dancer changes what we see and how we feel about what we see."

"If I was supposed to feel uncomfortable at the gender-bending, what was I supposed to feel about the fellow on stage with the iPad, messaging his friend about seeing the classical version of the same ballet?" Anastasia asked.

"I think it was a clever device to indicate how the same old scripts continue to be repeated, even in the twenty-first century, reproducing the same old story—remember how he texted his friend that the classical plot was right out of a Bollywood movie?"

"That made everyone laugh, including me," Anastasia said.

"The choreographer was trying to break out of the mold of that plot," Verity said.

"Well, it certainly broke out of the mold for me. Then again, I'm an iconoclast myself when it comes to medieval monasteries and nunneries. Lots of untold stories behind those walls," Anastasia said with a devilish smile. "A glass of champagne might prompt me to share one or two of my more salacious findings," she whispered into Verity's ear.

Verity looked at her watch. It was only half past nine. She remembered that the wine shop near Exmouth Market stayed open until ten, and suggested they buy a bottle and walk the few blocks back to her flat.

"A smashing idea," Anastasia said. "My treat."

"What is that monstrosity!?" Anastasia nearly dropped the bottle of champagne when Verity turned on the light in the hallway.

"That's Cecil, the stuffed crocodile. My landlady's bizarre idea of a mascot. The pink party hat is my own addition. Gives him a rakish look, don't you think?"

"I would have added more than a hat to that fiendish spectacle," Anastasia said.

Verity opened the door to the parlor and turned on the light.

"Egads!" Anastasia exclaimed. "What hideous surprises await around the next corner?"

"The rest of the flat is perfectly ordinary, if a bit drab. I've come to think of this parlor as an outsized nineteenth-century diorama."

Anastasia looked around the room. "I'm getting a headache from the whirling-dervish designs, and I haven't even had any champagne." She sat down in an armchair. Luckily, Verity had vacuumed it the day before.

"I've gotten used to it. The patterns are by William Morris," Verity said. "The owner of the flat is a fan."

"More fanatic than fan, I'd say."

"I'll get the glasses and be back in a minute."

"And not a moment longer, or I fear I shall have disappeared into the wallpaper like that woman in Charlotte Perkins Gilman's novel."

Verity descended to the kitchen and returned with two champagne flutes to find Anastasia absorbed in a book.

"So that old socialist gadfly was an admirer of the medieval period," she said, holding up a catalog of an old exhibition of Morris's works. "Sitting in this room and looking at these images plastered across the walls and floor, one can't help but notice the family resemblance."

"I knew nothing about the connection until I came across a reference to Morris and medievalism in the British Library, and I'd been living in this museum for almost a month." Verity uncorked the bottle and poured some bubbly into Anastasia's glass and then into her own. "I found that catalog at a used bookstore earlier this week, on my way home from the library. I was looking for clues about the model for this image."

Verity showed Anastasia the box from Kelmscott Manor.

"What a horrendous object. It looks positively funereal," Anastasia said.

Verity laughed. "It's a reproduction of a wedding gift the pre-Raphaelite artist Elizabeth Siddal gave to Jane Burden when she married William Morris. The original is at Kelmscott Manor in the Cotswolds. I've identified two images Siddal painted with illustrations from *The Queen's Book*. But I can't find a prototype for this third one of the two women in any of the collections of Christine de Pizan's works." She pointed to the image on the right. "Although the colors and composition are like others created for her books."

"Maybe that one sprang from Lizzie Siddal's vivid, albeit odd, imagination," Anastasia said as she sipped her champagne. "I remember studying her at university and thinking she was, well, strange, even for the pre-Raphaelite circle."

"Possibly she invented it without a model. But Morris and his friends took inspiration from the illuminated manuscripts for their art. They even collected medieval memorabilia and decorated Kelmscott with their designs," Verity said.

"A medieval scavenger hunt. Count me in!" Anastasia's eyes sparkled with impish delight.

Verity was getting used to her new friend's sense of humor and figured Anastasia was joking.

"You think I'm teasing," Anastasia said, as if reading Verity's mind. "I'm serious. It will do us a world of good to get out of that stuffy reading room and head into the countryside for a weekend of *je ne sais qua*. We've been sitting in that library, each in her same spot, all week long. Besides, I've postponed visiting the nearby medieval convent, Lacock Abbey, far too long. We'll start in Wiltshire and then head to the Cotswolds and—"

"Wait a minute. How did you know I've been there all week? We only met today," Verity said.

"Oops." Anastasia gave her a sheepish look. "Caught in the act. I'm very clever at looking without being seen," Anastasia said. "Although it helps to have spies."

"Spies?"

"Monica, who distributes the books in the rare-manuscript room. She's a friend. When I expressed an interest in meeting you, she helped me concoct the book ploy. Being British means disguising one's curiosity with the cover of discretion, feigning disinterest in the service of desire. My real name's not Frazier, it's Griffin."

"You mean you lied to me?" Verity felt a little sick to her stomach. "What about calling yourself Anastasia?" Verity asked as if the wrong answer would make the woman she'd found so intriguing disappear, replaced by some menacing doppelganger.

"Truly, serendipitously, 'tis my name. Now, what do you say to a little road trip?"

"I can't. I have too much work to do, and only a few months left to complete it."

"Oh, don't be so predictably American. Where's your sense of adventure?" Anastasia crossed her legs, causing her suede skirt to inch a little higher and reveal a hint of lilac lace near the top of her thigh. Then she hid her mouth behind her fascinator, rustling the feathers with her breath. "I'm offering to whisk you away on an Oxfordshire holiday, and you prefer the faded luster and muteness of old books to a weekend *avec moi*?"

Maybe the champagne had gone to her head, or maybe she'd become intoxicated with a newfound delight in spontaneity, or mesmerized by the flutter of those flamboyant feathers, tempting her like a fly before a plant called Venus; but whatever the reason, Verity heard herself agree to Anastasia's plan and say she'd be ready to leave in the morning.

10

UNE FEMME SEULE À PARIS, 1365–1390

BÉATRICE

In those first years of my new life as *une femme seule*, a single woman, living in Paris, I resided with the family of the celebrated *libraire*, Monsieur Guy Bonhomme, in a house the Abbess rented to them on Île de la Cité. The house stood in pride of place on rue Neuve-Notre-Dame, adjacent to the cathedral, the jewel of Paris, an apt location for someone so prominent in the production of luxurious books. There I had privileged access to the throbbing heart of the city and to the much-revered bookseller who became my new mentor, a kind and gentle man as devoted to Dominique, his ailing wife, as he was to the art of the book and the business of its production. Since his two sons had disdained the book trade, preferring the clang and clatter of knightly armor in battle to the scratch of quill on vellum, and his wife was too ill to take on the work, Monsieur Bonhomme welcomed me into his home, taking me under his wing and treating me like a long-lost daughter as he tutored me in all aspects of the trade. His wise and generous manner reminded me so much of my own father, now long deceased, that I came to feel as if I were honoring his memory by honoring Monsieur Bonho-mme with service to art.

The house was a narrow, half-timbered structure that rose three sto-ries above a stone-and-mortar foundation, cresting at its pinnacle into a triangulated tiled roof shaped like an arrow pointing heavenward. A small window poked its tiny face out from my room nearly hidden under the eaves. The day I arrived, I climbed the exterior stairs at the back of the house to this attic chamber that served as my bedroom and studio. After arranging my quills and brushes on the wooden table next to the window, I sat for hours staring through the bird's-eye portal, mesmer-ized by the endless bustle of Parisians of every station, from nobility to peasant, thronging the square. I engorged myself on the cacophony of sounds and panoply of sights like a starved pilgrim of the senses who had finally arrived at a banquet of sumptuous delights.

Traders carried baskets brimming with herbs and vegetables and cut flowers the likes of which I had only seen in the Abbey chapel on feast days. Others bore wooden boxes of squawking fowl. Two women pulled a cart filled with loaves of bread. Behind them, a young peasant girl carried trays of cheeses. A man dressed like a jester led a small brown bear across the square. A group of patricians, elegantly outfitted in coats of bright red silk and tapestried brocades with fur collars, hurried in the direction of the cathedral, while from the opposite corner of the square a bevy of young scholars engaged in animated conversation unwittingly rushed toward them. The near-collision of nobles and scholars jostled an artisan standing in the middle of the square, dislodging rolls of parch-ment bundled in his arms. Only the swift response of a woman in a bright green dress saved the precious vellum from being trampled in the dusty street. The artisan doffed his cap, the woman curtsied, and Paris continued its riotous, unruly display.

Before my eyes, the swoosh and swirl of gesture and movement dissolved into vibrating washes of vermilion and gold and emerald, as if the colors of the miniatures I'd painted in the convent's manuscript workshop had leaped off the page and into the streets of Paris, daring me to corral them into new shapes on pages of parchment. I grabbed my sketchbook, quill, and a pot of ink from my satchel and drew the outlines of the stunning pageantry unfolding below me. As I did, I endeavored to paint it into an exemplar of Parisian life, perhaps even fit for a book for the king.

In those happy first weeks in Paris, eager as I was to learn every aspect of the trade, I accompanied Monsieur Bonhomme on his visits to the *ateliers* of all the best artists of the book, from *parcheminier* to bookbinder, mapping in my mind their locations in the labyrinthine streets of the city. My apprenticeship in the convent had taught me the work of scribes and illuminators, but I knew nothing about the *parcheminiers*, who produced the raw materials for books, nor about the *relieurs*, who bound them.

On the Left Bank of the Seine, the parchment-makers were clustered along rue aux Écrivains, near the church of St. Severin. Halfway down the cobblestoned street, Monsieur Bonhomme halted at the entrance to an *atelier* and rang a small brass bell beside the front door. Soon an old man no taller than a small boy opened the door. At the sight of Monsieur Bonhomme, his wrinkled face broadened into a wide smile. He pulled Monsieur down to his height, kissing him three times as if they were old friends.

"Monsieur Jean, may I present Mademoiselle Anastasia, *enlumineuse*." Monsieur Bonhomme gestured me forward.

"Delighted to meet you, Mademoiselle." Jean bowed his head to me.

"The pleasure is mine." I curtsied, embarrassed by the lofty introduction.

"Your timing is as perfect as ever, Bonhomme. We're preparing a new batch of skins." Jean led us through a small antechamber toward the rear courtyard. The acrid odor of the skins of cow and sheep soaking in vats of lime permeated the air. I covered my nose and mouth with my shawl to dull the burning sensation welling in my throat. Jean noticed my discomfort and pointed to a bench in the far corner.

"Perhaps you'd be more comfortable watching from across the yard," he said.

"I withstood worse in the years of the pestilence," I said, not wanting to appear delicate. "I am honored to witness the process of your craft."

With a long pole, Jean fished one of the calfskins from a vat and slapped it onto a wooden board. Bending over it with a curved knife, he began to scrape off the remnants of animal hair, until every last follicle had fallen into a mound on the earthen floor. Then he turned the skin over and continued scraping, removing globules of fat stuck to the inner skin of the once-living animal until what remained was a damp, quivering mass. Next, he stretched and pegged the skin onto a frame, tightening and pulling it into a rectangular shape. I could still see striations in the skin and tiny points where hair had protruded from the animal's hide, the ineradicable markings of life, telltale signs that a book begins as flesh. I reached over to touch a stack of vellum that was cut, shaped, and readied for the imprint of quill or brush. As I did, I whispered a silent prayer to the spirit of the animal that gave its life, praying that my touch would honor it, and that some trace of my hand would linger on the parchment, connecting the touch of one creature to another.

We left Jean's shop and crossed to the Right Bank of the Seine to visit an *atelier* near rue St. Antoine owned by Monsieur Henri, a scribe reputed to be among the most accomplished in Paris. While Monsieur Bonhomme explained the project he'd been commissioned to produce—an elaborate Book of Hours intended for the king's new daughter—I marveled at the samples of Henri's script displayed on the walls of the studio. The manuscripts I'd worked in the convent contained texts of angular, regimented lettering—a conventional format favored by more traditional patrons. Monsieur Henri's hand was like a magician's, fashioning curlicued letters with the flip of his wrist, spinning and twirling an author's thoughts to life on the page, conjuring meaning with the sleight of his hands. Never again would I see words as mere frames for my paintings.

Monsieur Bonhomme continued his rounds, introducing me to the artisans who'd made Paris the center of the book trade. I could hardly contain my excitement as we approached the Petit-Pont, across which he'd told me we'd find the illuminators' *quartier*. But instead of crossing the bridge, we turned down a narrow street. A disappointed sigh escaped from my mouth.

"I know you're eager to meet those of your own *métier*, Anastasia, but what you will learn in the next studio we'll visit is the most important lesson of all," Monsieur Bonhomme said.

His words struck me oddly, but I trusted his judgment. Then, down the street, I caught sight of an odd wooden sign hanging above a doorway. As we walked closer, I saw that it depicted a woman seated atop a stack of books. In one hand she held a long, threaded needle, while her other hand balanced a pile of quires in her lap. Next to her on a shelf stood a few elegantly bound books. I guessed we'd reached the *atelier* of a *relieur*, but couldn't imagine anything of use I might learn at a simple bookbinder's studio. In the convent, once I completed my paintings, the folios were delivered to binders in Paris, whose work I never saw, but was regarded as menial and, I thought then, of little relevance to my craft.

"This is the *atelier* of Madame Lescaux, the most talented bookbinder in Paris," Monsieur Bonhomme said. The way he entered the studio as if entering a sacristy piqued my curiosity.

Inside the pristine room, I saw an array of tools hung on the far wall, arranged by size and within easy reach of the woman seated below them at a long wooden table. Undisturbed from her task by our presence, she continued her work. When she finished the task at hand, she rose and turned to greet us. I saw she was about the same age as me.

"Monsieur Bonhomme, it's always an honor to welcome you," she said. "Is this the talented young artist you told me about?"

"May I present Anastasia. Her skills are considerable but would remain unappreciated, perhaps even unknown, without the fine art of your finishing touch. Might you demonstrate your craft for her?"

Madame Lescaux took my hand and guided me toward her worktable. Set on either side of what I now recognized as quires or gatherings of manuscript pages were two thin wooden boards with channels grooved into their surface. The quires were attached at their spines to six leather ribbons, equally spaced and arrayed horizontally like six pairs of outstretched miniature arms. I guessed she'd been sewing the quires onto the bands of leather when we entered her *atelier*, but their purpose bewildered me. She must have sensed my confusion, because she continued her instruction.

"These are called cords." She pointed to the bands. "I use them to fasten the manuscript into its cocoon."

"Cocoon?" I was befuddled by her use of the word.

"The book's cover," she replied with a smile. "Like a cocoon when opened, the casing releases into the world a creation as beautiful as a butterfly."

She sat down at the table. Picking up an end of the top leather band, she began to thread it into the uppermost grooved channel of the board on the left and then flipped the assembly to thread the other end of the band onto the board on her right. Her long, delicate fingers worked the leather into the wood. She breathed onto the strips from time to time, warming them, coaxing them gently forward along the tight channel.

"How long does it take to bind a Book of Hours?" I asked, my cheeks reddening with embarrassment at my own ignorance of a book's construction. In all my years in the convent, I'd been so focused on the dance of word with image that I'd given little thought to the work of those architects who designed and assembled the structure in which the dance would take place.

"A fortnight, sometimes longer," she said. "Once I've completed the threading, I cover the boards in leather, or silk, depending on the commission, and tool them or embroider them in gold. Then my work's done, and the precious art inside will be protected from the wrath of the elements for years to come."

I swore an oath to myself to remember the lesson in humility I'd learned that day in Madame Lescaux's *atelier*. How wrong I'd been to consider the *relieur* a lesser star in the constellation of artists of the book. Without the bookbinder's painstaking labor, whose art remained mostly hidden, the work of ages would flutter away like orphaned leaves, detached from the stories bound together at the spine of a book like branches on the trunk of a tree, distorting the wisdom of centuries.

Several weeks passed before Monsieur Henri brought the first sections of the Book of Hours to Monsieur Bonhomme. It was the day I'd longed for—when we'd deliver the scribes' pages to the artists who would paint puzzle initials, illuminate miniatures, and decorate borders around the handwritten text. My whole body tingled when I heard the bell ring in the *atelier*. The buzz of the men's conversation reached my attic chamber. I grabbed my shawl, a pencil, and my sketchbook and ran downstairs to wait outside to take the short walk across the Petit-Pont to the *quartier* on the Left Bank, where the *ateliers* of the most famous *enlumineurs* were housed. Today, Monsieur Bonhomme had promised I'd witness one of the master illuminators transform the manuscript into an object of multidimensional delight.

The air was warm with summer and sweet with the smell of jasmine climbing a trellis on a nearby wall. The sky was awash in a dazzling color of blue, without even the tiniest wisp of a cloud whooshing across it. It was an unblemished blue that should have filled me with joy, but surprised me with a jolt of sorrow as an uninvited thought pierced my brain—blue had been the color of my mother's eyes and might have been the color of my daughter's eyes, had she lived. Suddenly, in the cerulean firmament, a parade of ghostly memories and images of what might have been took shape, despoiling my vision with taunting reminders of everyone and everything fate had pulled from my life in its ever-widening gyre. How I might have loved that child, taught her to dream and to illuminate those dreams, as Gilles and Héloïse had taught me. How Mother and Father might have loved her, as they had loved me. How my twin sisters might have intrigued her with games. Mocked by this heavenly blue evocation of death's capricious appearance in life, I returned to my attic chamber and wept.

When he did not find me outside, Monsieur Bonhomme sent the servant girl to fetch me. Feigning illness, I asked her to beg forgiveness for my absence, and turned toward the wall, hoping sleep would ease my grief. A little later came a knock on my door. With a worried look on his face, Monsieur Bonhomme entered the room, setting a tray of bread, cheese, and mulled wine on the table beside me.

"I've sent Monsieur Henri along with the quires to the illuminator's *atelier* with instructions to begin only the simplest borders. We will observe the more elaborate miniatures being painted when you are well," he said.

"I'm sorry to have caused a delay in the manuscript's completion," I said.

"The king will be untroubled by the change of timing. Even an infant daughter of royalty cannot yet read." He forced a smile to cover his concern.

At the mention of the king's daughter, my eyes welled again with tears.

"What saddens you, Anastasia?" His smile disappeared into a frown.

I hesitated to speak of the source of my grief, or admit to being overwhelmed by its mad force in a moment of immeasurable beauty. Were I still living among the community of women in the convent, I wouldn't have felt such reluctance. At that thought, I sunk deeper into a well of loneliness.

"I'm weary, that's all," I said, hoping he wouldn't press me further.

"I'll leave you to rest, then," he said. "Perhaps tomorrow we'll venture across the bridge."

When he'd left, I took a few sips of the wine and drifted into a fitful sleep, awakened a few hours later by another knock on my door. I was surprised to see Dominique, Monsieur's wife, enter my room. Since I'd arrived weeks earlier, my days had been so consumed with manuscript-making, I'd exchanged not more than a few words with her, idle chatter about the weather and such. I knew little about her, except that she was ill and walked stoop-shouldered and with a limp. She took a seat by my bedside and spoke to me in a quiet voice.

"My husband is sick with worry. He fears he's done something to make you unhappy," she said.

"Nothing could be further from the truth," I said, alarmed that I'd upset him.

"Perhaps you couldn't speak to a man about what's bothering you," she said.

Her words caught me off guard and I felt my cheeks redden.

"Anastasia, whatever you wish to share, I'll keep in confidence. I only ask if the cause of your unhappiness is something I can remedy, that you give me the chance to do so. I say this as much out of concern for my husband as for you."

I looked at her askance. She saw my confusion and continued. "The book business has been in Monsieur Bonhomme's family for more than a century. Our sons' departure last year on a knightly expedition left no one to carry on the trade. Lacking an heir to carry on his legacy pushed Monsieur Bonhomme into despair. He couldn't even bear to look at any manuscripts. It was as if their beauty somehow mocked him. His best patrons complained that their commissions were delayed and threatened to withdraw their contracts. I could do nothing to help. Out of desperation, I conveyed my worry to the Abbess. In her wisdom, she arranged for you to reside with us. So, you see, your arrival has been a gift, more than you could have known."

"It is I who have received the gift of your generosity," I said. "I worry I'm now more of a burden."

"Burden? No, Anastasia, you are a miracle. You're the age the daughter I lost in childbirth would have been, had she lived. To have her returned to us at this time in the form of a talented artist is a miracle. Let me shoulder whatever troubles you now. I wish to repay you for the life you've breathed into our household again."

I hadn't talked of my own daughter since that June day I buried her a decade ago. Now, I pulled the story of her stillbirth out of the deep soil of my soul and wept as I shared the memory of the feel of her flesh with another woman, a stranger who was strangely familiar, who understood beyond words why sometimes I cried at the color of a blue sky, and sometimes I painted it with joy in my heart. As she held me gently in her embrace, I trembled with gratitude at the chance I'd been given to live again in the company of women.

A week later, on a warm summer morning, I accompanied Monsieur Bonhomme to the *atelier* of Maître Jehan de Nizières, whose masterful paintings illuminated several books in the King's grand library. The artist's studio stood on the Left Bank of the Seine among a row of half-timbered structures along rue Erembourg de Brie. In every way except one, they resembled the house I now called home. But instead of a small, shuttered window on the ground floor, each of these houses was fitted with a large grated opening to encourage ample light to wash across the desks of the painters, whose bowed heads bent over their work I glimpsed through every portal we passed along the street. When we reached the last house, Monsieur Bonhomme pulled a velvet cord to ring a bell, signaling our arrival. Moments later, Jehan opened the door. The sight of his belted saffron robes and the graciousness of his welcoming smile made me start, as if I were seeing a reincarnation of Gilles d'Orléans standing before me. Despite the warmth of the day, I shivered at the resemblance.

"My dear colleague, Monsieur Bonhomme! And this must be Anastasia, the fabled young woman whose artistry you've lauded. Please, come in. I'm working on a new commission for the king." He led us toward his desk. "It's for a book of ancient poetry. Can you guess what it is?"

On the desk before me lay a piece of parchment the size of two outstretched hands. No words appeared on the folio, only a painting. At the center was a dense, tangled mass of lines and swirls that reminded me of the motions of whirligigs. Rays of golden light and streams of pale green air and waves of cerulean water unfurled from this center with such vitality, it seemed as if the image would lift off and take flight. Though I'd seen nothing as astonishing as this in all my time in the convent, it seemed holy to me, as if Jehan had captured the moment of creation itself, when the world was birthed into beauty, when everything was formed and named, each was given its place, and all was harmony. I shook my head in speechless wonder.

"It is the beginning of time, before there was a before." Jehan invited me to touch the parchment.

I caressed the painting. My fingertips swelled with heat. My hand tingled, and a current of warmth traveled up my arm and around my shoulder, wrapping me in an invisible shawl. The last shiver of a disorientating memory left me. Becalmed, I asked Jehan to explain.

"King Charles has commissioned me to illuminate a French translation of Ovid's *Metamorphoses*."

The quizzical look on my face urged him to continue.

"A poem of transformation and change. Its first lines describe the world's beginning out of Chaos, when God wrought the discordant mass into balance."

I touched the image again and felt the air swell and the waters rise and shimmer.

"The poem sings of things changed into new forms, of people transformed into animals and insects, and of others changed by their avarice and greed into murderous scoundrels; it tells how we are blinded, by fear of death, from the fact that every moment is an occasion for renewal. Shall I show you my drawings for those stories?"

I nodded. He removed a quire of parchment from a shelf and spread it open. Outlines of creatures wondrous and strange spilled across the folios. A woman's head emerged atop the body of a spider. Another depicted a woman transformed into a cow; and in a third, a woman stared into a pool and saw herself reflected as a bear. I knew nothing of the stories captured in these pictures and asked what transgressions the women had committed to be so doomed. He told me of Arachne, defeated in a weaving contest with Pallas Athena, who turned her into a spider; of Io, changed into a cow by Jupiter to conceal his defilement of her from his wife, Juno; and of Callisto—another target of Jupiter's lust—who was transformed into a bear by Diana, the goddess of the hunt, who'd once favored the young nymph.

I stared at the images. Magnificent though they were in detail and composition, I couldn't help wondering what the women might have told of their punishments, had their contorted bodies been allowed to speak in different gestures. Would Arachne have demonstrated her defiance, accepting the risk she took in agreeing to Athena's challenge? Lacking words, would Io have found another way to communicate her pain? And would the hunter Callisto have shown how she avoided becoming the hunted again?

Jehan interrupted my ruminations. "Perhaps you'd like to sketch a miniature of one of these scenes yourself?"

"I'd be honored but am inadequate to the task. Although I was schooled in Latin in my youth, and illustrated many sacred books in that ancient language in my days in the abbey, Ovid remains unknown to me. Not wanting to misrepresent his poems, I'd need further study."

"You're wise to be cautious. I've known too many artists who misconstrue the meaning of words, only to make silly mistakes. Our task is not to supplant the text but to translate the ephemeral meaning of an allegory or a myth into an image, modulating tones to express with light what the mind reads as sound."

I thanked Jehan for his time and accepted his offer to return to his *atelier* for further guidance as I began preparations to establish my own *atelier*. I was determined to use the skill of my hand and the strength of my imagination, forged as it has been on the anvil of so many experiences of human folly and debauchery, to craft images that would alter what we know of women's suffering.

―――――――――――

Within a year of my arrival in Paris, I had a space for my *atelier*. Lacking heirs, the widow of an *enlumineur* on the Left Bank had bequeathed all her property—the house, workshop, and all its contents—to the Abbey in exchange for recitation of anniversary masses to guarantee her husband's heavenly rest and secure permission for her continued residence in several rooms on the upper floors. Abbess Agnès arranged for me to take over the workshop on the ground floor of the building but a stone's throw from Monsieur Jehan's *atelier*.

The first day I entered the room, I was astonished by the cornucopia in the airy space. Shelves overflowed with book after book of exemplars of the most elaborate miniatures, puzzle initials, and borders for manuscript illumination. In another cabinet I found jars of material for mixing paints of various colors and drawers of tools of all sorts—dozens of quills for both hands, plummets, and burnishing implements. Next to a grated window stood an enormous wooden desk with a matching high-backed cushioned chair upholstered in velvet. The sheer scope of treasure overwhelmed me.

I opened one of the pattern books to find human faces spilling out of ivy leaf borders intertwined with animals, dragons, and other grotesques. In another, the ornamental flourishes of decorative initials cascaded down and around an entire page. In a third, I recognized a scene of the Annunciation for a Book of Hours. Except for the elaborate parade of angels interwoven into the border, it resembled paintings I'd made during my years in the abbey. It was common practice for illuminators to reproduce images from exemplars, yet I yearned to add innovation to my paintings. How far would my imagination be allowed to stretch composition to reveal things not yet known about women's lives? I decided to test the limits, if Fortune would but present me with the opportunity, and set to work arranging the *atelier* to my liking.

Hours later, I returned home to find the Bonhommes in animated conversation.

"Come in, dear Anastasia. Join us for an aperitif before dinner," Madame said. "Did you find the *atelier* suitable?" She handed me a crystal glass of *pastis*.

I mixed in a little cold water from a jug to dilute it, turning the color from amber to milky yellow. "It's a magnificent space. Well-stocked with treasures any illuminator would covet."

"And now, all yours." Monsieur Bonhomme raised his glass. "A toast to the future *enlumineuse* to the king."

"You're too kind." I took a sip of the licorice-tinged liqueur. "I'm far from achieving such a title."

"Perhaps much closer than you think," Madame Bonhomme said with a wink. "Guy, shall we tell her our plans?"

"Anastasia, as you know, our sons have been joined in the king's war for some time. Since they'd declined to take over the family business, I'd been troubled with worry. Your arrival changed everything. It breathed new life into my work. My commissions have multiplied. As a show of gratitude, I've decided to make you an heir and have assigned a portion of my estate to you. I recorded the executed document with the *prévôt* of Paris today."

My hand betrayed the shock coursing through me, and the aperitif glass crashed to the floor. Madame came to my side at once.

"Dear Anastasia, you're shaking. We meant to bring joy with this announcement, not worry."

Monsieur called for the servant to clean the mess and then joined his wife to reassure me.

"Even without this extraordinary announcement," I said, "my ears can hardly believe what I've heard. You've both brought me more joy than I ever thought possible." Tears welled in my eyes. "I fear I'll never repay your kindness."

He touched my shoulder. "Ah, dear daughter—for we've come to think of you as our own—you've done that already. Now let us enjoy our dinner."

Five years passed, during which I benefited as much from Jehan's counsel as from the Bonhommes' generosity. Under Jehan's careful tutelage, I advanced my skills. My reputation circulated around Paris. Soon scribes who'd been selected to work on commissions from the nobles of the French court, including one from the king himself, sought my *atelier*. All those years ago I'd wished for the day my illuminations would find their way into Charles's library, and now it had finally arrived. Or so I thought. When I learned of its contents, the Abbess's warning to choose my patrons wisely rang in my ears. The manuscript was to be an enormous collection of writings such as I had never before seen—manuals to give guidance to princes, along with works of philosophy and ethics. Years before, when Jehan had invited me to take on a miniature for the book of poetry, I'd hesitated out of caution. I was now familiar with the requirements for poetic works. But a guidebook for royal authority? Might that not catch me up in the sort of political intrigue that the Abbess had cautioned me about?

Around the city I'd heard grumbling about the costs of the endless war being shouldered by ordinary citizens through burdensome taxes. When I returned home that evening, I learned that even Madame Bonhomme had grown anxious.

"I understand we must guard our borders from the marauding English and our towns from the mercenaries who pillage the residents once a battle's been won. But I worry the king and his family may be threatened if they don't restrain more lavish spending." She'd been arranging flowers to decorate our home for a special processional the king had planned to celebrate a royal birth—the first son born to the king's brother, Philip of Burgundy and his wife, Margaret of Flanders—and had called me into the room to assist.

Monsieur Bonhomme sighed. "Would you have me decline the king's requests? The commissions I've received from the royal household keep us in comfort."

"Of course not! And not because of our comfort. Those works are the world's treasures. But I worry we'll be engulfed in the conflict," she said.

"You shouldn't fret, dear wife. My position as a university-sworn bookseller exempts me from having to serve as a civilian guard on the walls and at the gates of the city. King Charles is a wise ruler. In his magnificent library, he's amassed the wisdom of ages, which he consults to guide his decisions. And he's surrounded himself with knowledgeable men, not only clever military advisers, but a physician and astrologer of the highest reputation—Thomas de Pizan, former counsel to the Venetian doge."

At that, I made my entry into the conversation. "I was approached today by one of the king's scribes to contribute some illustrations for his latest project. I seek your advice about whether to undertake it. It is a collection of manuals for princes."

"Anastasia, that is wonderful news." Monsieur smiled.

"I worry that I lack adequate knowledge to do it justice." I fiddled with the flowers.

"Worry not. The king's scribe will give you elaborate instructions for the designs. He'll provide detailed chapter rubrics with descriptions to indicate what images should accompany the text and where. There will be little leeway for any errors of judgment. Since this is your first royal commission, I'm certain you'll share the task with other illuminators."

"I've been told so."

"As I expected. Now, let's celebrate your good fortune and ignore idle chatter that could cloud this glorious day."

The political winds blew in Charles's favor in 1372, the year I worked on the king's magnificent book. My miniatures and borders graced but a few quires. In the most elaborate one—the frontispiece introducing a book on ethics and morals—I portrayed the author of that book, Jean de Vignay, offering his book to a prince, painting the prince to resemble Charles V dressed in cerulean robes decorated with fleurs-de-lis. Around the image of the learned monarch, I illuminated a frame in burnished gold surrounded by red and blue garlands. Though I'd never met the king, having witnessed parades he'd led through the streets of Paris etched in my mind the shape of his thin frame, the thrust of his prominent nose, and the sheen of his sandy hair as vividly as if I'd had a private audience.

My paintings were celebrated, and my stature grew among the community of artisans, as did my confidence. Yet, twelve months later, Dame Fortune's mysterious wheel turned again, bringing discord into my life with the death of Monsieur Bonhomme and the return of Pierre, the elder of the Bonhommes' sons, one dark November night made darker still by his appearance.

Madame had received disturbing news of the death of her younger son, Robert. He'd been felled during a campaign in southern France, though not by the sword but by the return of the same pestilence that had claimed the lives of my father and sisters more than two decades earlier. Her only consolation was Pierre's survival. She busied herself with preparations for a great feast in his honor, while I decorated the front door with a banner to welcome him home. I soon learned that I needn't have bothered; before entering the house, he'd pulled the banner off the door and ripped it to pieces.

"The only thing that would make me feel welcome is seeing this one gone," he bellowed in a gruff voice, pointing to me with his thumb. "I've come back to claim my inheritance. She has no right to any of it."

He was a swarthy man, only a few years older than I, with a countenance contorted into a permanent grimace—and, I suspected, a sullied soul to match. Perhaps I should have run at the sight of him, but I stood still and said not a word.

"You must be tired from such a long journey," Madame said. "I'll have the servant draw a bath."

He turned to me then. "You'll pack your things and be gone tonight."

Madame interjected: "I've prepared your favorite meal, Pierre. Wash and rest. Then we'll talk."

He bolted across the room and grabbed her by the arm.

"Have you forgotten your place? I'm head of this household now. And I say she's gone!"

"Pierre, you're hurting me." The fear in his mother's face must have startled him back into his senses, because he let go of his grip, pulled her into his arms, and wept.

"Hush, son," she said, motioning for me to leave the room. "You've seen horrors worse than anyone should be asked to bear."

I climbed the stairs to my room and packed my things, not wanting to risk further outbursts of his rage. As for my share of the property, I expected the contract that Monsieur had recorded would protect it. I'd no sooner concede defeat to this brutish man than to any other, and resolved to appeal to the court if he challenged my claim.

How I'd underestimated the chicanery of a man tormented by memories of ruthless war and bereft for so many years of any companionship besides murderous, pillaging louts and their destitute victims! For seven years we battled in court, long after Madame's death, until Parliament ruled in Pierre's favor, declaring him sole direct heir of the entire estate. I'd hoped Fortune would give me the chance to use my art to reveal the breadth and depth of women's experiences. Those years of struggle against Pierre enshrouded my hope in robes of sorrow until, more than a decade after the wise King Charles's death in 1380, that chance presented itself in the form of another woman's grief and her account of the solace she'd found reconfiguring Ovid's ancient, rhythmic verses to serve the needs of mourning in her own years of despair.

11

FORTUNE'S TRANSFORMATIONS, CHRISTINE DE PIZAN, 1390–1399

CHRISTINE

Fortune, that perverse trickster, destroyed the happiness Christine de Pizan had enjoyed during the decade of her marriage, crushing the joy she'd felt in Étienne's companionship like a desiccated flower. While on a royal mission in 1390, sudden illness befell her dear husband, robbing him of his life and stealing from hers the one whom she loved more than anything in this mortal world. She'd scarcely recovered from earlier wounds—her father's death three years after King Charles's death—when the loss of her beloved nearly drowned her in a pool of sadness, which her tears only deepened. She closed herself into her study to lament alone with her books, and reeled at life's bittersweet paradox—all we love on this earth is transitory and must die.

One October evening, two months into her mourning, she heard her mother's footsteps reverberate down the corridor. She damped the candle, pretending to sleep.

Her mother stopped outside her door. "Christine, I've prepared a soup for our supper. You must eat something, dear daughter."

Christine kept silent until her mother walked away with a sigh. Then she lit the candle again and opened a ledger on her desk to inspect their accounts. Columns of diminishing sums mocked her with the bitter arithmetic of loss. Her husband's wages from his work for the king had yet to be collected. What was left of her father's estate in France wouldn't carry them through the year. Paolo and Aghinolfo, her two brothers, had returned to Bologna soon after Thomas's death to claim farmlands in the *contado*, outside the city, along with the family home in the parish of San Mamolo, where Christine had lived with her mother for three years before they joined her father in Paris. After her brothers sold the land and the house, they'd bought another, larger house for themselves in the same parish. She'd learned of the sale of her childhood home in a letter they'd sent, enclosing a small amount of money to be set aside "for *Maman* in her later years."

Memories of that home, where her father had been born, flooded her thoughts—the dance of shimmering rays of heat rising from the tiled roof on sultry summer afternoons, the sound of the maid's metal pail scratching across the tiled floor as she washed the corridors, the aroma of bread baking in the hearth, the view of the stream from her bedroom window, the feel of her mother's touch on her forehead lulling her to sleep in her cot. Her brothers had discarded it as if it were nothing more than a tattered box. How cruel were the ways of the world!

She didn't blame her father for following the law by leaving his property in Italy to his sons, although such a law was unjust to any female heir. What disturbed her was his failure otherwise to secure his widow's welfare, and not only because Étienne's death had now transformed Lucia into her own daughter's ward. More burdensome than shouldering responsibility for her mother was the weight of her father's damaged reputation, a topic she forbade herself to discuss with her mother.

Ugly rumors had circulated soon after Thomas's death, innuendo that he'd defeated himself by fabricating a dangerous potion for the young king. Étienne had assured her that the gossip was nothing but the work of jealous competitors he'd heard complain at Court about her father's influence. She'd settled into that belief until last week, when she was searching for evidence of further investments to add to their dwindling finances, and found among her father's papers a manuscript from another alchemist to whom he'd turned for advice. The man had cautioned her father against the recipe he'd concocted, accusing him of miscalculations bordering on treason. Now, alone in her study and filled with grief, doubt insinuated its vicious acid into the recesses of Christine's thoughts. And where doubt wallowed, self-doubt would soon follow.

How could a man as wise as her father have been so feckless as to assume that young Charles VI, or his guardians, would continue to provide for his widow after his demise? Kings can be fickle, especially when their own house is divided. Shouldn't his witnessing the machinations at court immediately after Charles V's death have cautioned him into securing his estate? She remembered the day, not long after the royal funeral, when her father had rushed to her side, enraged with news that the dead king's brothers—Philip, Duke of Burgundy, and Louis, Duke of Anjou—were engaged in pitched battle over control of the regency.

"The arguments before the *Parlement de Paris* about the royal ordinance that Charles the Wise signed before his death have not yet concluded, but Philip will brook no opposition to his plan to deny Louis the regency and place himself at the head of a council to rule in the name of the Dauphin." Her father shouted these words of impending disaster without taking a breath.

Christine shook her head in disbelief. "Surely none of the lords will agree to such a violation. They witnessed the public proclamation of the king's intention. They're duty-bound!"

"I fear Philip has the upper hand." He reached for a table to steady himself. "He's secured the support of Charles's chancellor, who claims the king wished to revoke his regency ordinance just before he died and wanted his young son crowned immediately following his death, putting Philip in charge of his care."

"That's preposterous." Christine was certain the king would never have abrogated rank by favoring his younger brother as protector of his successor. "Étienne showed me the ordinance his own father had copied, and that Charles had signed. The Dauphin was to assume the throne not before the age of fourteen, and Louis was to supervise until then."

"None of that matters now. Philip's knights have breached the city walls to force the issue. He's cudgeled the barons with the specter of violence into siding with him against Louis. To avoid carnage, Louis has left Paris, conceding governing authority to Philip."

Startled at this announcement of Louis's abandonment of the city, Christine raised her voice in alarm. "How could he abandon his duty to the king's wishes? And what of the king's counselors, Bureau de la Rivière and Jean le Mercier? Surely they'll testify against Philip's usurpation of power and stop this madness!"

"Disappeared." Thomas collapsed into a chair, holding his head in his hands. "What's done is done; I shall offer my support to Philip. He is regent now and will reward loyalty."

Worry furrowed Christine's brow. "A man who would breach a royal ordinance. I mean no disrespect, Father, but should you trust such a man to honor any oath he may swear? We've both witnessed the ruthlessness of ambitious men."

"Even an ambitious man requires wise counsel, if only to restrain his appetite for political gain until the time is auspicious for victory. The Duke of Burgundy has observed how I aided Charles V to secure his power. He'll want me to consult the stars to stabilize his regency."

Poring over her ledger in her rooms now, Christine flushed with anger at the recollection of the scene and the ruination of her father that came in its wake. Had arrogance blinded him to the whims of avaricious men? Or pride? Tempted by the promise of a generous sum, her father had agreed to stay at Court advising Philip. No sooner had he let his guard down than Philip dismissed him, reducing his pension to a pittance and plunging him into an illness from which he never recovered. To make matters worse, after his death the house near the Tour Barbeau that Charles V had given her parents reverted to the crown, forcing her mother to seek shelter in the de Castel household.

Étienne had welcomed the old woman into their home. "It will cheer her to be with the children. And relieve you of some of the burdens of the household."

Christine was guarded at first, concerned that her mother would interfere with her plans for the education of her daughter, Marie. But when she saw how much her three children buoyed the old woman's spirits, she rebuked herself for lacking compassion. Lucia was no longer the same dour woman who'd been torn apart by bad moods after the birth of each of her own children. Age and the wearying work of mourning had softened her rough edges and deepened her devotion to prayer. "I'll take care of the little one while you set Marie and Jean to work on their studies so you can continue with your own. You've blessed me with the renewal of love in this time of despair."

"Thank you, Mother." The surprise of her mother's support had opened her heart and given her strength to forbear whatever Fortune had in store for them, until now, when the paltry sums in her ledger announced the precariousness of their situation in the bleakest of terms. A wave of anger swelled up inside her again. As hard as she tried, she could hold back no longer and cried out in rage.

"Father, why were you so stubborn? You looked to the stars for guidance about matters of state. You gazed heavenward for signs, worrying not about the humble struggles women must manage on earth. Husband, how could you leave me with three children and a widowed mother in such a penurious state! Abandoned to a life of destitution and struggle without records of your financial affairs. How did you think we'd manage?" Picking up a document, she waved it in fury. "This notice announces our doom. Shall I read it to you now?"

The sum of one hundred francs is due in rent on lands owned by M. Étienne de Castel in the region of Picardy, now reverted to the Crown. The debt must be paid within six months.

"I owe rent on property the Crown has reclaimed, property about which I remained ignorant. Did you think me stupid or imprudent? Is that why you kept your finances secret? Or had you taken a lover? Because your thoughtlessness astounds me. You claimed we were equals. But then, my own father declared his belief that a woman's capacity was equal to a man's, and he too proved as unconcerned about the mundane business of daily survival with which women are consumed. The pigheadedness of men causes widows incalculable pain! All your soft words mean nothing to me now. They won't keep me warm, feed us, or protect us from ruin when the last sou of what's left in our accounts has been spent."

Christine's head throbbed to think what misery lay ahead. "If only I'd been born a man."

The cathedral bell sounded the call to midnight prayers. She snuffed the candle and went to her bedchamber, falling into a fitful sleep.

Hours later, on the threshold of sleep, Christine heard a voice. She rose from her bed, lit a candle, and tiptoed into the corridor. No light appeared from under her mother's bedchamber door, nor was there a glimmer from the children's room. She turned back toward her room when the voice started again.

"Christine, I've heard your tribulations and have come to appease your concerns."

Was she mad? Had anger polluted her reason so much that she'd lost control of her senses?

"Fear not, dear daughter. Come closer that I might help heal your sorrows and show you the path forward."

Who was speaking? Nurse had been dismissed for lack of resources to retain her. Had a stranger entered an unlocked door? Worried for her family's safety, she let curiosity conquer her fear, felt her way down the hall toward the study, from which the voice had clearly spoken, and slowly opened the door.

An apparition shimmered before her in the form of a woman. She was neither young nor old, but ageless. She was not comely, but dignified. Dressed in a wide tunic the color of a robin's egg, such as Christine had seen depicted in some of the king's oldest manuscripts, she carried herself like a lady of great stature. On her head she wore a simple white veil, and on her face a gentle, dignified smile. She extended her hand in welcome, gesturing for Christine to be seated at her desk.

"Daughter, may God grant your soul peace and untrouble your mind and allow you to remain devoted to your love of learning. I wish to impart a portion of my knowledge to you. If you retain even a little, your powers will be greatly extended, and your name will be resplendent long after your death."

Christine sat speechless before the mesmerizing vision.

"I am Almathea, the Sibyl born in the city of Cumae, come to guide you to another, more perfect world, where you can learn better than in this one about the things that are truly important."

She gestured toward the wall, where Christine kept her most cherished books. As if powered by an unseen force, two volumes flew from the shelf and opened themselves before her—Boethius's *On Consolation*, and the *Metamorphoses* by Ovid. The Cumaean Sibyl continued her discourse.

"A little while ago, you were plunged into despair at the world's wicked injustices. Find consolation here, in Boethius's philosophy. Study his teaching and learn, through his example, how to bear misfortune and be undefeated by your enemies. Understand, as he did, that although Lady Fortune controls the ebb and flow of material riches, she lacks the power to influence that other wealth that flows from virtue. Be truly virtuous and your sorrows will turn into joys. And look here, in Ovid's poetry, to find the means to strengthen your will. There you will learn how forms can be changed into new bodies, just as you will be changed from a woman into a man."

Those last words shocked Christine so much, she started from her chair. But the Sybil's gentle look calmed her back into her seat.

"Be not alarmed. One word will help you understand my meaning." Christine felt a whisper of sound against her ear. "Imagination." A quizzical look came over her, so the Sybil continued. "Along imagination's pathway you will walk one day. For now, I will lead you along another road—the path of long study that lies ahead."

Consoled by those words, Christine rose to adjust the belt around her long skirts so she could walk more easily. "Please proceed; I will follow," she said and turned toward the far wall of her study. Before her eyes, the dimensions of her study altered themselves to open onto a lush field

bursting with violets, lilies, flowering herbs, and all manner of medici-
nal plants. To add to the visual delights, the air filled with the warbling
sounds of songbirds. Steadied by the Sybil's guiding hand, she followed
her along a wide route that climbed high into mountains rippled with
babbling brooks.

"Here the princes of learning once lived. Aristotle, Socrates, Plato,
Democritus, and Diogenes all gathered around these waters to fill themselves with knowledge," the Sybil explained. Onward they trekked,
across many climes and terrains, past marvelous sights until they reached
the height of the firmament. In this celestial world, where all beauty is
revealed, they met another grand lady seated on a high throne. The Sybil
stepped forward to greet her and introduce Christine.

"Lady Reason, I come before you to propose someone to be your
good messenger. She will not fail you, for she is a handmaiden of our
school. She lives in France and will serve well your efforts to end the
conflicts besetting those lands." Christine blushed and bowed her head
to hide her embarrassment. Then Reason spoke.

"Christine, dear friend who loves knowledge, report before the
world's sovereign assembly what you've learned. Take this parchment
and quill to write down everything you've discovered on this path of
study, leaving out no detail. In that way, Wisdom will govern the world."
Then the Sybil touched Christine's shoulder and signaled that it was
time to return along the same path back to her study. The ghostly presence vanished from sight, as Christine heard the mother who'd carried
her in her womb call to her and enter the room.

"Christine, why aren't you yet awake?" Lucia walked over to the table
and touched one of the still-open books. "It's nearly midday: Have you
been reading all night?" Christine raised her head from her desk and
nodded. "I worry for your health," Lucia said, embracing Christine and
brushing her cheek with a kiss.

"I wish not to distress you, Mother. But when desolation besieges my
soul, the wisdom in these books consoles." Christine returned the kiss.
"Almost as much as your loving devotion."

Her mother smiled and, in a gesture that nearly took Christine's
breath away with its tenderness, cupped her daughter's face in her hands

and kissed her eyes. "I bless these organs of vision, windows to the soul and source of our family's salvation," she said, and left Christine to her books.

Alone again in her study, Christine ruminated on the vision. Had she truly been chosen to serve as Reason's messenger? The weightiness of that burden made her tremble until she recalled the Sybil's words. *I will lead you along the path of long study.* Strengthened by the Sybil's guidance and the force of her mother's love, Christine took up her quill to scribble a rhyme in the pages of her notebook. Weeks later, she stunned an assembly of nobles by reading the pleading ballad at a royal poetry competition:

Worthy and valiant men, put your virtues
On alert, or widows are destined for great harm;
Help them with a happy heart and put faith in what I
Say: For I see no one who is friendly toward them,
Nor do princes deign to listen to them.

Before the year was out, she'd secured commissions as a scribe.

Three years later, misfortune struck yet again. While Christine was at court arguing to defeat a debt claim against her, her youngest child succumbed to a fever. The news plunged her once more into a river of sorrow and doubt. In her mother's arms, she wept. "This death must be God's punishment for abandoning my motherly duties!"

"My love, you're not to blame for his death. Time will heal the pain of his loss. Remember, your devotion to learning pleased your father as it pleases God. The Lord wants to be served by people in all ranks and stations. It's not the occupation chosen that leads to damnation, but whether the person employs it wisely, as you have."

"What wisdom have I shown? We're tormented by further claims I may never stanch. God has punished my arrogance. I'm but a weak woman pretending to the strength of a man."

"Grief clouds your vision. I understand how the loss of a child can rupture a mother's heart and befuddle her reason."

Christine looked at her mother in alarm. "You lost a child?"

Her mother nodded. "Before you were born, a son."

"Why have you never told me?"

"Any mention of it aloud would've been your father's ruin. His mourning had been so grievous, I set aside my own pain to console him. Your birth brought him out of despair. You see, you resembled him so much, in body and mind, that he poured all his hopes for his firstborn son into you, his daughter, and erased the memory of that son from his heart. I never spoke of the child again."

"How you must have suffered." Christine brushed away tears on her mother's face.

"As any mother would. A mother's body reminds her of what she once carried. Even when another child has occupied that space. It's as if the ghost of the dead child haunts her insides. She feels his spirit struggling against being replaced and finds no way to tell him how special he always was, always will be. As special as you've been to your father and me."

They sat for a moment in silence. Then her mother rose to receive visitors who'd brought food to their house of mourning. "Remember, Christine, without your efforts to secure our finances, we would have foundered on the treacherous rocks endangering us in the sea of troubles in which we've sailed since the deaths of your father and your dear Étienne. You've steered us to safe shores with the treasure trove of insight and learning you've accumulated, a treasure more valuable than gold. Use those gifts wisely and you will confound any liar who tries to claim what is not rightfully his. You will bring honor to France and the memories of all our dead."

Her mother's consoling words made her berate herself for ever doubting her father's wisdom. No matter how learned, no one could have predicted which way the temptations of power and the wiles of men would take them. After all, hadn't Louis of Anjou departed for Naples to conquer those lands when he'd been denied the regency? Had he not died in battle, he might've returned to Paris to reclaim his position and tumbled them all into chaos again. And what if her father had lived to see that bright coronation day in 1388 when Charles VI assumed the throne in his own right, installing his own brother, Louis of Orléans, as his closest adviser the following year? He might've been returned to favored status, only to see his position disrupted again by the madness that afflicted the king a mere three years later, and continues to afflict him still. He'd have watched in dismay as Philip regained ascendancy. Who could know whether France would ever be rid of these dangerous factions dividing the country and again experience peace? Only someone in possession of the philosopher's stone could foretell the mysterious turns of Fortune's wheel. To aim for perfect knowledge was a fault as fatal as Icarus's fantasy that he could fly as high as the sun without melting his waxen wings.

And Étienne? How could she have blamed her dear one when his management of their accounts during their marriage had freed her to pursue the path of learning that was her calling? To derogate the affection he'd showered on her with his soft words was but evidence of how much she missed his voice whispering to her during their lovemaking, testimony to how much she longed for his tender embrace and soothing countenance.

Christine knelt in prayer. "I beg forgiveness from my father's spirit and that of my beloved Étienne for ever doubting their care. May I be imbued with valor and discretion in the face of extremity. May I be granted the power to recollect whatever I observe or hear or taste or smell or touch in a day. May I be granted the power of memory to perceive what has lain hidden in the past and use it to heal the wounds of the present wrought in my heart and in the heart of my beloved, adopted country—Lady France."

Women's stories of woe and achievement never figured much in the annals of history. Of the inequity accompanying the birth of a daughter, of the treachery hidden between false lovers' words, of the tribulations of women abandoned for the thrill of battle, of the depredations besetting the downtrodden poor, of the loneliness and penury of widows, of the discourses of scorn heaped on women, and of their valiant accomplishments—had such tales from even one woman's life been told in fullness, the whole world would have split open with grief. And so, Christine took up her quill again to write:

I'm like a turtledove without its mate,
Who turns away from greenery and heads
Toward aridity; or like a lamb the wolf
attempts to kill, which panics when its
shepherd leaves. Thus, I am left in
great distress by my lover, which gives
me so much pain that I will always weep
for his death.

Between the lines of her morbid poetry, Christine encoded her worries for France and cast her lot and that of the French kingdom with Pallas Athena, the Goddess of Wisdom, beseeching her to undo all wrongs and procure all good things.

The poetic muses to whom she'd turned for comfort in the years death trampled her heart made her voice loud enough now to attract the attention of Louis of Orléans, brother and adviser to Charles the Mad, to whom she'd sent gifts of her poems in the late autumn months of 1397, spreading her reputation among princes. She soon dazzled audiences of men and women in the courtyard of Louis's residence near the Louvre, where she joined royal contests of poetry. And so it was that Christine de Pizan began to craft stories on parchment with quills and inks, and, with the help of artists who illuminated her works, maneuvered among those Ladies of Fortune and Reason controlling her fate to curry the favor of princes and heal her heart's wounds, along with those of France.

12

NOTHING IS OURS,
EXCEPT TIME

VERITY

Saturday it rained, and Verity waited by the window in the upstairs parlor for Anastasia to arrive. She was supposed to pick her up at nine in the morning, so they could get an early start. By nine-thirty, Anastasia hadn't shown or phoned, texted, or even emailed to say why she'd been delayed. Verity sent several messages to her, by every modern means possible, asking when she should expect her. There was no reply. After another half-hour ticked by, she messaged Anastasia again. Nothing. At eleven, she left a note for her tacked to the front door of the flat saying she'd gone to the library to get some work done while she waited for Anastasia to turn up or call to explain where she was.

The library closed at five and Verity headed back to the flat to find her note still tacked to the front door. She phoned Anastasia again and sent another email, but got no answer, so she took herself to dinner.

A few hours after she returned to the flat, Verity's cell phone buzzed, and she answered immediately.

"Hello?" she said.

"Hello, Verity. I'm not interrupting your work, am I?" It was Regina.

"No." Verity sighed, disappointed it wasn't Anastasia calling to explain her absence. "I just got in from dinner."

"You sound a little down in the dumps," Regina said.

"Just tired, that's all," Verity said with a sigh. "It's been a long week."

"Really? I thought being with those musty old books excited you. Haven't found what you're looking for?"

"Not exactly," Verity said.

"Ready to come home, then?"

"You know me better than that, Regina. I don't give up that quickly."

"That's true. You stuck with me even after I threw you out of my bed." She laughed.

"I'd say that was a process of mutual removal. But then, you always claimed you'd won, no matter what game we were playing."

"Don't be so bitter. Are you still upset about Pauline?"

"No, I'm over her. In fact, she did me a favor by leaving."

"She probably feels the same way, now that she got her promotion."

Verity winced. "Good for her. Why did you call, Regina?"

"Just wanted to check in. From the sound of it, I'd say you're not doing too well. It can't simply be a research dead-end that's put you in such a foul mood. Tell me what's really bothering you."

Verity hesitated before answering. She didn't want another lecture from Regina. On the other hand, despite having to endure her friend's prickly prodding, it usually helped her clarify her own feelings, especially when those feelings were clouded by fear of making a mistake.

"I met someone. We were supposed to take a trip to the country today. She never showed. Or called to explain."

"You met someone? Who is she?" Regina asked with a little too much eagerness.

"She's a medieval historian," Verity said, smarting from the sting of Regina's judgmental remark. "We met in the library, and she offered to help with my research."

"And I suppose a ride in the country was . . . research? Is she British?"

"Yes," Verity said.

"Well, that explains her failure to turn up. The British are notoriously bad with intimacy. Especially with Americans. Or have you already forgotten my former husband's emotional shortcoming, his psychoanalytic training notwithstanding?" Regina asked.

"I haven't forgotten. But Richard was clinically depressed. Anastasia isn't like that; in fact, she's exactly the opposite," Verity said defensively.

"Anastasia." Regina stretched out the multiple symbols of the name for effect. "That's an unusual name for a Brit."

"I know. She told me her mother was fascinated by the Russians," Verity said, keeping to herself why the name had tantalized her so much.

"And you believed her," Regina said in a tone not intended as a question.

"Why shouldn't I?"

"Because, Verity, you've always been a little too gullible, especially when it comes to attractive women."

"You and Pauline finally cured me of that," Verity said. "Anyway, I never said she was attractive. All I said was she's an historian."

"To throw me off the scent, I imagine. Well, is she?"

There was a long pause as Verity considered whether to simply hang up and give Regina another victory or acknowledge the obvious. "Yes, in an exotic sort of way, I suppose."

"The worst sort. Be careful, Verity," Regina said. "The woman could be bluffing and really is Russian, in which case beware a mercurial personality. Or, even worse, she's another pretender to the throne, like that crazy woman in Germany a century ago who insisted she was a Romanov princess so she could claim the throne."

"And what throne would this contemporary Anastasia be trying to claim, and why?" Verity asked, regretting having told Regina anything about her new friend, or even having answered the phone.

"The throne of your heart, Verity. Some people have an uncanny ability to sniff out vulnerability and take advantage of it. As for why, I guess that's what you'll have to figure out."

"Stop being melodramatic, Regina. She probably got sick and couldn't make it. That's all," Verity said. "I'm sure I'll hear from her when she's feeling better."

"Maybe," Regina said. "But you have to admit, you've been a little too eager lately to throw caution to the wind."

"Thanks for the vote of confidence, Regina."

"All I'm saying is, be careful. I'm your friend. I worry about you."

"Right. Well, thanks for the concern. I have to go now; it's late."

They said their goodbyes and Verity hung up. But the conversation lingered with her the rest of the night. It certainly was strange that Anastasia hadn't sent even a text to say she couldn't make it. Verity would have understood if their plans had to change. Or had something Verity said or did scared her off? No, Anastasia had been eager to take the trip. In fact, it had been her idea.

She went downstairs to the kitchen to make a cup of tea, refusing to let Regina's cynicism overtake her common sense. There had to be a simple explanation for Anastasia's absence. Before heading to bed, she left another message on Anastasia's phone, changed into her nightgown, and fell asleep with the phone next to her on the pillow.

In the morning, sunlight streamed through the windows of Verity's bedroom, waking her earlier than usual. She got up, pulled aside the doors separating the sleeping area from the sitting room, walked to the front window, opened the curtains, and let out a cry. Anastasia was standing next to a vintage green MG sports car outside her flat, beaming and waving. Verity raised her arms as if to say what the heck, grabbed her coat off the hook in the hallway, and went outside.

"What are you doing here? I waited for you all day yesterday and you never turned up. What happened?" she asked, her anger somewhat dampened by the sight of the car and the driver, who was dressed in a camel-colored leather jacket and pants and a matching driving cap, looking like she belonged on a movie set for a 1960s James Bond film.

"I had a terrible migraine. Started Friday night. Must have been the champagne. Couldn't get out of bed all day Saturday. Woke up this morning like a new woman." Anastasia did a poor imitation of a pirouette. "Ready to head out now on our little adventure?" She tilted her head coyly, gave Verity a winning smile, and leaned over to beep the horn.

Verity crossed her arms, unwilling to brush off the incident so easily. "I called and called, sent you texts, emails. You never replied," she said.

"I know, darling." She pouted. "Had to turn off the phone, couldn't bear even to touch the computer. Got all your lovely messages this morning and thought the only proper apology for being so rude would be to whisk you off to the countryside forthwith. Now, hurry up and get your overnight bag. We still have plenty of time to explore our treasured haunts."

Verity shook her head.

"Oh, don't be daft. I promise it won't happen again."

"You promise you won't get another migraine?"

"No, silly, of course I can't promise that. But I do promise to send a message if I'm ever stricken again. By carrier pigeon, if necessary," Anastasia said. "Now, please, go get your bag."

Verity hesitated. She could hear Regina's voice rattling around in her head. *Oh, shut up. Like Professor Berman said, there's wisdom to be had on the journey.* She moved closer and removed Anastasia's cap, freeing her mane of curly hair, which tumbled around her shoulders in a glistening mass of red swirls, and kissed her on the cheek. "Apology accepted," she said. "But now you'll have to be patient while I pack."

"I'll be stretched out on tenterhooks until your return." Anastasia extended her arms out in either direction and closed her eyes.

"What am I getting myself into?" Verity asked, laughing.

"A rare jewel of a twentieth-century time machine operated by an even rarer and cleverer medievalist," Anastasia said, patting the car. "Now hurry up before a plague of hesitation slithers up Great Perry Street, wraps itself around us both, and ruins our day."

"So much for patience," Verity said and went into the flat for her things. Twenty minutes later, she came back outside.

"Pop your bag in the boot of the little green dragon and hop in, darling. It's such a scrumptiously warm, sunny day, I thought we'd ride *al fresco*," Anastasia said. "There's an extra leather driving cap in the glovie."

Verity watched Anastasia tuck her hair back under her cap, and despite knowing it would have been dangerous, felt a tiny twinge of regret that those gorgeous auburn locks wouldn't be hanging loose, flying in the wind. She fastened her seat belt, and they took off with a jolt.

Light traffic on the ring road around London allowed them to reach the entrance to the M4 in record time.

"Are you sure this car is safe for the highway?" Verity asked.

"Guaranteed by MG—Morris Garages—and yours truly!"

"You had to have a car with that name," Verity said and laughed.

"The perfect chariot for heading deep into Morris's country lair," Anastasia said.

Verity relaxed into the rhythm of Anastasia's agile maneuvering. Just past the last exit to Heathrow, lush fields dotted with grazing sheep replaced the suburbs. It was hard to believe how green the fields were, greener than any green Verity had ever seen, as if some mad artist had crushed emeralds, added oil, and painted the landscape with the mixture. If the sky in California achieved best in show for blue, England won the contest in green.

"You were right," Verity said loudly over the engine noise.

"I know. I'm an excellent driver," Anastasia said.

"I meant about getting out of the library. I feel much better already. I'm inhaling countryside green and exhaling London gray."

"Wait until we get to Wiltshire. Absolute bucolic delight. Or, as the National Trust puts it, *An Area of Outstanding Natural Beauty.*"

"I'll take all the beauty I can get," Verity said, touching Anastasia's hand.

"And there's so much you haven't seen or even imagined yet," Anastasia said with her Cheshire-cat smile.

As they motored along, Verity watched layers of English history intertwine in the countryside. Billboards advertising new housing developments were scattered among sprawling fields littered with large bales of hay covered in white plastic. Every now and then, out of the low, rolling hills, the spire of a medieval country church popped up with five or six houses nestled around it looking like the surprised remnants of the Hundred Years' War. A few miles later, a nuclear plant appeared on the horizon to whiplash Verity back into modernity, only to be replaced by a crumbling stone marker on the side of the road that sent her spinning back to Saxon times.

"Windsor Castle," Verity shouted, as they approached a sign announcing the exit for the ancient castle.

"Yes, and bloody Legoland Windsor Resort at the other end of the town," Anastasia said with a disapproving shake of her head.

"You're kidding." Verity was half intrigued by the idea of seeing a replica of the castle founded by William the Conqueror miniaturized in plastic. "Castle, moat, dragons, and all?"

"Naturally. Verisimilitude is the *trompe l'oeil* that keeps capitalism churning, *n'est-ce pas*? Though I must say, having that appalling kitsch near their weekend retreat serves the royals right. Come to think of it, I bet they earn rent on Legoland too."

"I didn't take you for a left-leaning anti-royalist."

"A woman on the trail of someone who may only be a figment of her imagination ought to know how to look below the surface of things," Anastasia said as she smiled slyly. "You shouldn't be fooled by a bit of finery and an antique car. When we get back to London, I'll introduce you to the best secondhand shops in the city. I borrowed this car from my cousin."

"You're full of surprises," Verity said.

"There's a lot about me you've yet to discover." Anastasia squeezed Verity's knee, sending a tremor that rumbled all the way to her unmanaged heart.

They stopped for a late lunch at a pub overlooking the River Avon in Chippenham, a few miles north of Lacock Abbey. While Anastasia went to the restroom, the server showed Verity to a table with an unobstructed view of the river. Reflections of maples dappled the water in an autumnal palette of bright red, burnt orange, and lemon yellow, as if the shards of a stained-glass window had been scattered across the water's surface. A small houseboat floated past, rippling the colors into new shapes like a kaleidoscope. Distracted by the picturesque scenery, Verity didn't notice the carpet until she sat down.

"I suppose this is your idea of a joke," Verity said in an annoyed voice as Anastasia approached the table.

"Whatever do you mean? This is a perfectly ordinary British pub."

"And that is perfectly ordinary, wall-to-wall William Morris," Verity said, pointing to the carpet. "Pineapple design."

Anastasia looked at the carpet and laughed so hard that the couple seated two tables over began to stare. "My dear, I assure you, the pineapples are nothing more than an amusing coincidence. But I should've warned you. In the Cotswolds, sentimentality reigns. Lacock Village positively reeks of nostalgia—timber-framed houses, a medieval tithe barn, the lot. We might even run into the ghost of an ancient mill worker or two. Now, what shall we eat?"

After lunch, Anastasia headed the little green dragon south on Cantax Hill toward the village of Lacock. Given the narrow, winding road, Verity was grateful they were riding in a sports car. Four miles later, they crossed into another century. Apart from the external pipe work for indoor plumbing, modern glazed windows, and tourist shops, it looked as if little had changed in the tiny village since Henry V defeated the French at the Battle of Agincourt in 1415. Yellowed stone-and-mortar-houses with pointy slate roofs were joined cheek by jowl down the length of West Street. Here and there, bits of modern masonry shored up a crumbling wall. A few weathered wooden lintels hung so low above doorways that no one taller than five feet could enter without stooping.

"Cotswold taste on full display," Anastasia pointed to a sign on a little shop in the ground floor of an old stone house that announced itself as "Quintessentially English." "Nostalgia embedded in smelly soaps and soy candles. An imitation medieval apothecary."

"Christine's father dabbled in herbalism. I read about some of his failed experiments in potion-making, including one that led to accusations he'd tried to poison the king. I wouldn't mind stopping in later," Verity said.

"Why not, if it serves research? But first we have to check in to our lodgings and visit the abbey," Anastasia said. "I booked us at The Sign of the Angel Inn on Church Street. You'll simply adore sleeping within its historic walls."

"So you assumed I'd come with you, even after you stood me up the day before?" Verity asked, a little annoyed that Anastasia had taken her agreement for granted.

"Oh, don't be cross with me again. I didn't stand you up, darling. I told you, I had the most incapacitating migraine. I made the reservation after you agreed to the trip, while you were packing your bag," Anastasia said, touching Verity's cheek.

Verity had the sneaking suspicion Anastasia wasn't telling her the truth. "And if I'd changed my mind, would you have come here anyway, without me?"

"Of course. I'd want to drown my sorrow within its historic walls," Anastasia said, sweeping the back of her hand to her forehead with melodramatic excess.

"Sentimental, are you?" Verity asked with a teasing grin.

"Only about all things medieval," Anastasia said. "And their admirers," she added. "And also frugal. I wouldn't have wanted to lose the deposit I put down for the room."

"The truth comes out in the end," Verity said.

Anastasia smiled at her. "When it's coaxed out of the closet."

The inn was a little gem of fifteenth-century architecture. The two-storied, timber-framed structure had witnessed the Hundred Years' War. On the ground floor, an alcove led to an ancient, arched wooden door that creaked open into a long, low-ceilinged, whitewashed hallway paved in red stone. To the right, Verity spied a dining room with a massive carved-stone hearth. She half-expected to find someone dressed in medieval garb stirring a cauldron of stew. Instead, a cheerful young woman with short white hair spiked to form a stunning pink coronet around the crown of her head bounded down the hall to welcome them.

"Professor Griffin, how nice to see you again," she said. "I have you and your guest in a superior suite with two beds. Your room isn't ready yet, but leave your luggage and enjoy a glass of Prosecco while you're waiting."

"Always a pleasure to be back in the comforting arms of the Angel," Anastasia said. "I like the crescendo of color on your royal coif, Marianne."

"Just trying to liven things up a bit. Gets a bit stodgy around here. Shall I bring your drinks to the garden?"

"I think we'll wait on the bubbly until after our tour of the abbey. My colleague, Professor Frazier, has never visited Lacock, and I've arranged a special viewing in the cloisters."

"That's a smashing idea. Will you be joining us for dinner?"

Anastasia turned toward Verity, who signaled her approval with a vigorous nod of her head.

"We wouldn't miss Chef's cornucopia of delights for all the pasties in Cornwall," Anastasia said. "Book us for an eight o'clock seating, please."

"Excellent. Enjoy your visit to the abbey." Marianne smiled at them both.

"I take it you're a regular at the Angel," Verity said as they left the inn.

"Yes, I come here quite often. It's the perfect atmosphere to ruminate on all things medieval," Anastasia led the way down East Street toward the abbey. "As well as being owned by a distant cousin of mine."

"How many cousins do you have?" Verity asked.

"Five, counting Emily, the owner. She isn't really a cousin. Just a dear, dear friend I've known from childhood. We went to the same primary school."

"You grew up in Lacock?" Verity asked.

Anastasia laughed. "I'm from Swindon, not far from here. We whizzed by it on the M4."

"Maybe we can stop by on our way back to London," Verity said.

Anastasia scrunched her face. "Not worth the bother. Nothing much to see in Swindon. Certainly nothing as picturesque as this," she said, pointing to a line of half-timbered houses they were approaching at the village square.

Verity caught sight of a large carved stone cross atop a pedestal in the middle of the square. "I know I've never been here before but something about this place feels eerily familiar," she said.

"Probably because of Lacock's frequent appearance in film. Notice the absence of ugly TV antennae or above ground electrical wiring. We're walking through the set of *Pride and Prejudice* and episodes of *Downton Abbey*," Anastasia said.

"That's it!" Verity exclaimed. "The last season of *Downton Abbey*."

"Filmed here. And the cloisters we're about to enter were used for the exterior of the Seymour family home in the production of *Wolf Hall*, the BBC's adaptation of that marvelous Hillary Mantel novel," Anastasia said.

"Haven't seen it," Verity said. "I worried any film would ruin how richly imagined and gorgeously textured Mantel had layered those times in prose."

"It chuffs me to think how perfect it was for the producers to choose a thirteenth-century Augustinian convent founded by a woman—Ela, the Countess of Salisbury—as the set for a film based on a book lambasting Henry's absolutely treacherous treatment of women," Anastasia said. "Despite his dissolution order, the convent survived."

"How did this one escape demolition?"

"Henry sold the place to one of his courtiers, Sir William Sharington, who simply couldn't be bothered to tear it all down. Instead, he converted the upper floors into his home and left the cloisters, the nun's quarters, and other assorted rooms, including the kitchen and sacristy, as he found them. And we are the lucky beneficiaries of his preservation, as you'll soon see."

Anastasia completed her mini history lesson just as they reached an enormous stone building off High Street. The renovated sixteenth-century barn now served as entrance to the abbey and its grounds and also housed a museum dedicated to the photographic work of William Fox Talbot, whose ancestors had inherited the property in the eighteenth century, according to the brochure Verity browsed while Anastasia got their tickets.

"I never expected to find a museum of photography inside a medieval abbey. The brochure says Fox Talbot invented the art," Verity said.

"Right here, at Lacock Abbey in 1833," Anastasia said, looking at her watch. "We've enough time for a quick look around before the surprise I've planned in the abbey."

"I'm beginning to worry about your surprises. Not the bones of one of the nuns encased in a gaudy monstrance, I hope," Verity said.

"Nothing so macabre. But first we'll take in the photography exhibition. Let the other lookie-loos see the abbey first," Anastasia said, gesturing to the half-dozen other visitors heading out of the building ahead of them. "It's best to wander the cloisters as empty of gawking tourists as possible."

Verity headed over to a display case filled with sepia photographs of statues and other architectural ornaments, a still-life series imprinted by light on pages now faded with age. Fox Talbot appeared to have transformed his domestic surroundings into a laboratory, capturing moments in time through a technique he invented to apply light to a treated page. A fluttering curtain through an open window on the side of a building, the protrusion of an oriel window above an arched doorway as if spying on unsuspecting guests. Without quill or brush, he'd used what he called the pencil of nature to capture these moments of time in lines and swirls and traces of objects, creating images in the blink of an eye that artists centuries before had labored for months, or even years, to produce.

The next display case held photographs with some of the sources that had inspired them. There was a picture of a statue next to a photograph of a woman posed in the same posture as the statue. Adjacent to a print of a painted group portrait was a photograph of a group of people arrayed in the same pose as the painting. But it was an image of two women standing close to each other in a garden that caught Verity's attention. Their long gowns, the way one woman bent toward the other, as if sharing a secret, looked uncannily familiar.

"Does this remind you of anything?" Verity asked Anastasia as she came to stand next to her.

"It reminds me of the cloister gardens we're about to see," Anastasia said. "We really must be going, Verity."

"I don't mean the background. Look closely. The way the two women are standing. The composition is just like that unidentified third image Siddal painted on the Morris box," Verity said.

Anastasia leaned in for a closer look. "In a vague way, I suppose. But this photograph couldn't possibly have anything to do with that painting of two women you think is associated with Christine. The photo wasn't produced until about four centuries later," Anastasia said.

"I know the photo's modern. But look at the others in this case. Fox Talbot imitated archaic artistic compositions in many of his works. I guess my mind just made an associative leap from this one to the painting on the Morris box."

"More like a dissociative leap, I'd say," Anastasia said. "Some fresh air will clear your overwrought mind of repetition compulsion."

"So, you think I'm crazy?" Verity asked, annoyed.

"Don't be so sensitive. I was only making a joke." Anastasia leaned in to kiss her cheek, but Verity pulled away. "Guess I hit a nerve," Anastasia said and backed off.

"That kind of joke isn't funny, it's hurtful," Verity said, walking away in a huff. Anastasia followed her, catching her by the arm.

"I didn't mean to upset you. I was only trying to—

"Never mind. Forget about it."

"No. You're upset, and I want to understand why," Anastasia said. "Please, tell me."

Verity sighed and looked away. "The short version of an answer is that I was once married to a psychologist, a man, who used to throw around his considerable bank of diagnostic labels all the time. He was really good at analyzing everyone. Just not himself."

"Oh, I see. An advanced case of physician, heal thyself?" Anastasia asked.

"Pretty much incurable," Verity said. "Which is why I left him—I was in graduate school at the time—and moved in with Regina, who'd had a similar experience to mine."

A museum attendant walked up to them. "Ladies, I'm so sorry to interrupt, but the exhibition is closing; if you want to visit the Abbey, the last entry is in ten minutes." He ushered them toward the exit.

"Thanks," Anastasia said to him. "We'll make our way outside."

They exited the museum and walked along a pathway under a canopy of ancient oaks and maples between fields carpeted with sheep. A few steps later, an immense structure rose out of the wooded landscape.

"Wow," Verity said, relieved to shift the conversation away from her failed love life. "I wasn't expecting anything so elaborate."

"Ela was quite wealthy and a bit of a spendthrift when it came to creature comforts," Anastasia explained. "Quite magnificent, don't you think, if a bit haunted."

"Haunted?"

Anastasia raised an eyebrow. "You don't believe in ghosts?"

"I'm not taking the bait. I'm sure you don't believe in ghosts either," Verity said.

"Oh, but I do, my dear. Apparitions of all sorts are the stock-in-trade of medieval historians. Since much of the material record of that period was either destroyed or simply never preserved, we must rely on other senses to uncover stories otherwise hidden. Like you've been doing with your artist, Anastasia."

Verity remembered staring at those digital images in Harley 4431, leaning in to smell the flowers, lick the strawberries. Had Anastasia been watching her that day? She pushed the thought out of her mind as too bizarre a coincidence.

They entered a wide courtyard through an opening in the wall surrounding the property, turned left at the corner of the building, and headed toward a sign pointing to the cloisters beyond.

"So, tell me more about Regina," Anastasia said as they neared the archway.

"She's a good friend," Verity said, a little unnerved by Anastasia's returning to an uncomfortable subject. "We met in graduate school."

"I take it you were once more than friends?" Anastasia asked.

"Yes, but our affair, if you can call it that, didn't last long. Turns out mutual hostility to ex-husbands isn't exactly the kind of glue that can keep an amorous relationship from falling apart."

"Same with ex-girlfriends," Anastasia said. "Different sex, same sort of repeti—"

"Stop," Verity said, mock-punching Anastasia in her side and laughing. "You're incorrigible."

"Lightened your mood, though, didn't I?"

"Okay, I didn't mean to spoil it with the sad history of my love life. But you asked."

"Well, darling, we all have our sad stories to tell."

"Even you?" Verity asked.

"Especially me," Anastasia said, rolling her eyes. "But, as you say, let's not spoil the mood by washing dirty laundry."

"Fine with me. I don't really like doing laundry, anyway."

Anastasia laughed. "Neither do I. So much more boring than the surprise I have in store for you."

Verity smiled and took Anastasia's hand. "Can't wait," she said, even though she was feeling a twinge of trepidation about whatever her unpredictable companion might have arranged.

It was nearly four in the afternoon when they entered the cloisters. The descending sun cast a mellow light across the floor of the corridor through the open arched windows surrounding an interior courtyard. Graceful fluted columns reached their arms up like frozen golden-hued fountains to support a high curved ceiling. As she wandered along the corridor, Verity imagined hearing women's voices echoing along the walls in chanted song. She turned to face a shadowy stone wall, and, like a *camera obscura*, the memory of an image superimposed itself on the surface before her—the portrait in the Morgan Library of Christine, writing in her study, in front of the same kind of arched windows as the cloister's. Had the medieval Anastasia once wandered similar corridors and used their architecture as a model for Christine's sacred writing space?

"Verity, did you hear me?" Anastasia asked.

Verity turned away from the wall, startled out of her trance. "Sorry. What did you say?"

"I said it's time to meet the curator," Anastasia said in an irritated voice. "The abbey closes in half an hour."

Anastasia hurried down the hallway toward a door. Verity trailed a few paces behind her, wondering if she'd just seen a ghost.

They entered a long room. In the center was a narrow wooden table with a bench next to it. A glass-covered cabinet stood at the far end of the room. A middle-aged bespectacled sandy-haired man in a tweed jacket was standing in front of the cabinet. Anastasia walked over to greet him.

"Peter, this is my colleague, Professor Verity Frazier, from America, a recent aficionado of all things medieval, especially rare manuscripts."

"Pleased to meet you, Professor Frazier," he said. "Welcome to Lacock."

"Thank you," Verity said.

"As an admirer of books, you'll appreciate knowing the abbey once housed a library. Although we can't be certain how many or what kinds of books were collected, the nuns who lived here were quite literate. They came from wealthy, local families and brought with them all sorts of endowments, including manuscripts. What I'm about to show you is our most prized artifact, one of three remaining books from the abbey library."

Peter stepped aside to reveal an ancient Sleeping Beauty of parchment and leather resting inside the glass cabinet.

"This is a fourteenth-century copy of William Brito's *Bible Dictionary*, explaining passages from Scripture. It's handwritten in Latin script with a few colorful, if somewhat primitive, puzzle initials on a few pages. Although not richly decorated, it's an important example of a distinctive script found in the English book trade. In its binding we found scraps of parchment from early abbey accounts, indicating that the nuns participated in the wool trade."

"Did the abbey collect other illuminated manuscripts? Perhaps the nuns had a book workshop," Verity asked, her mind racing in too many directions at once.

"It's likely that the library held many books. We know of one psalter identified with the abbey now held in the Bodleian Library at Oxford. Whatever other books the abbey might have held would have been seized by Henry's soldiers during the dissolution and either destroyed or disbursed into other collections. Lord Sharington appears to have had no interest in manuscripts, only the house and grounds. As for a workshop, no evidence remains of its existence."

Peter unlocked the glass, removing the delicate object to the wooden table. He motioned for Verity to sit next to him on the bench and opened the book to a decorated page.

"I can touch the book?" Verity's voice shook with excitement.

"With care," Peter said, handing her a pair of white gloves and something that looked like a plastic lollipop. "Put these on, and use this paddle to turn the page."

She donned the gloves, trembling as she turned the page. A red puzzle initial drew her attention. She traced its outline and felt a jolt of heat travel like lightning through her gloved finger to her brain; she snatched her hand back, as if the letter were a flame leaping across seven centuries to scorch her.

"*Resurréxi, et adhuc tecum sum*," Verity read aloud. "Can you translate?" she asked Anastasia.

"What a ghostly coincidence to land on that page," Anastasia said with a mischievous expression. "It means *I am resurrected and with you always*. Resurrection, otherwise known as anastasis, happens to be the ancient derivative of my name and that of your phantom artist."

Verity dropped the paddle and crossed her arms. "So that's what you meant by 'surprise.' I suppose you're going to deny that you arranged for me to land on this exact page, just like you denied the pineapples."

"Guilty as charged of this bit of chicanery. But innocent of the sudden profusion of pineapples. Those were entirely an accidental tourist's discovery."

"Pineapples?" Peter asked.

"Long story from another century," Anastasia said. "Thank you, Peter, for your medieval wizardry."

"'Twas but a trice of planning," Peter said. "I rather enjoyed playing the sorcerer's apprentice."

"Ready for that glass of Prosecco, Verity?" Anastasia asked.

Verity wanted to be angry at Anastasia for tricking her. But how could she be mad at someone who'd arranged for her to touch such a rare and ancient manuscript and feel time itself course through her like a sensuous river, as if there had been an unintentional slip in the interlocking wheels of human illusion that keep the past from leaking into the now, enabling Verity to travel to the moment before there was a before?

"I deserve more than one glass, don't you think? But only after that promised stop at the medieval apothecary we spied on our way into town," Verity said. "I'm in the market for a little philosopher's stone." She returned the gloves to Peter, thanked him, and took Anastasia's hand. "Ready if you are, Mr. DeMille."

"And for pudding, I'll have the spotted dick," Anastasia said to the waiter at the Angel Inn.

"Spotted dick?" Verity looked down at the menu and found the item listed among the desserts.

"A delightful concoction invented in the nineteenth century by adding currants to a rather thick pastry—hence, spotted." Anastasia handed her menu back to the waiter. After he left with their orders, she continued. "As for the dick, well, etymologists have scratched their heads in wonder before settling on the polite explanation that some Cockney-accented Londoner, not unlike Eliza Doolittle in Shaw's *Pygmalion*, mispronounced pudding as pud*dick*, and then dropped the first syllable to scandalous effect."

"I'm beginning to think the Victorians have been misrepresented in history." Verity raised her glass. "Perhaps they weren't as prudish as we've been led to think."

"Much like the women in that other Victorian circle we're tracking tomorrow to their Kelmscott lair, among whom are your Lizzie Siddal and her mysterious box. Here's to paying more attention to women." Anastasia clinked her glass against Verity's, allowing her fingers to graze her friend's hand. "I do hope our trip to Kelmscott will correct the inequity."

Verity took a sip of wine. "I believe Lacock already has. By the way, are you sure this wine won't give you another headache? I don't want you to disappear on me again."

"No worries. I remembered to take my medication this time."

"That's a relief. Now, tell me those stories you promised to share about the antics of your medieval nuns."

"I thought you'd never ask," Anastasia said, taking another sip of wine. "Actually, I've found little evidence from Lacock—the extant abbey records are too sparse—but I've speculated that there must have been stories among the many women who took refuge here like the well-documented example of Benedetta Carlini, an Italian Renaissance nun in the seventeenth century. She was accused of having carnal knowledge of another woman in the same convent where she was Abbess."

Verity covered her mouth in an expression of mock surprise.

"The charges against her may have been trumped up to undermine her burgeoning power. She enthralled the other nuns with stories of her ecstatic visions. But at the inquisition, her lover,

Bartolomea Crivelli, testified against her. She said Carlini seduced her and kissed her 'like a man' until they both were stirred into a state of 'corruption.' In the end, Carlini confessed, and blamed her lasciviousness on the devil."

"What led you to assume that there were similar stories at Lacock?"

The waiter brought their first course. Verity took a bite of the salad.

"Well, in the case of convents, we know many widows and unmarried women of considerable wealth sought the solidarity and privacy of walled communities to escape the predations of men, including our dear Ela of Lacock, who'd rejected several suitors after her husband's death." Anastasia dipped into her soup. "Mmm, delicious *potage des legumes*, each of its components visible and in harmony with the others, unlike that indistinguishable concoction the BL serves up as creme de whatever. Pour me another glass, would you?"

"But that doesn't prove they were having sex with each other," Verity said, filling Anastasia's glass.

"Whose side are you on, my darling? Please pass the salt; I wish to throw some more on my wounds."

Verity laughed. "Don't be so melodramatic. I'm trying to figure out how to support a conclusion without much data."

"You've got to know where to look for evidence. Sometimes it's hiding in plain sight. Have you forgotten how little attention was paid to women, much less to their sexual behavior, until recent history?"

"Of course I know that." Verity picked up her spoon and scooped a taste of Anastasia's vegetable soup. "That's excellent!" She went back to eating her salad.

Anastasia leaned closer to whisper: "In some ways, I suppose, being ignored can be an advantage." She took Verity's salad fork from her hand. It held a plump tomato. "One can't condemn what one can't even imagine." She bit the ripe fruit, letting moisture drip down her chin. "Much less record it in history." Then she fed the rest to Verity.

Verity wiped the juice from Anastasia's face with her thumb and licked it. "I see what you mean." She waved to the waiter. "We've decided to finish dinner in our room."

"Very good, Madame. I'll send up a tray."

"Cheeky maneuver." Anastasia sipped the last of the wine in her glass. "You're a quick study, my dear."

"I've learned to expect the unexpected." Verity rose from her chair and held her hand out to Anastasia. "As should you."

After, they lay intertwined in silence. Through the open window, each time a light breeze parted the curtains, the moon spilled slivers of cool light on their naked bodies. Bits of conversation floated up from the street as the pubs and restaurants emptied of people. Anastasia's breathing had stilled to the whisper of sleep. The aroma of musk lingered in the rumpled bed. Verity licked her lips and tasted the remnants of tangy kisses, absorbing every sensual residue.

Anastasia stirred. Verity turned toward her and brushed her curly hair away from her face. "Happy?"

"Mmmm. Gobsmacked with ecstasy—and desperate for a pee." Anastasia hopped out of bed and headed for the bathroom. "Get dressed. I've another surprise. We're going out."

"But it's late and I'm tired. Come back to bed."

"It's the perfect hour. Trust me."

"That's what Benedetta must have said to Bartolomea, and look where that got her," Verity teased.

"Ah, but, my darling, there's no doubt who played the role of Benedetta in this room an hour ago. Back in a jiffy."

Verity pulled on a sweater and a pair of loose jeans and waited to use the bathroom. Then, while Anastasia dressed, she washed and brushed her teeth.

"Where are you taking me?" Verity asked, once they were outside.

"Back to the abbey, of course. I want to show you something."

"But it's closed." Verity gave her a suspicious look.

"Only to the uninitiated." Anastasia reached for her hand.

The moonlit night made it easy to navigate the uneven pavement. They walked quickly down High Street and reached the tall wooden gate of the abbey grounds just as the village church bells tolled midnight.

Wrapped across the top of the gate's center posts was a large padlocked chain.

"Definitely locked." Verity crossed her arms. "And I'm not climbing over that gate."

"You won't have to." Anastasia walked toward it, raised the chain from one of the posts, placed it over the other, and pushed the gate open. "Illusion deters all but the most intrepid of explorers. They never lock it properly until the end of the season. Follow me." She took a small flashlight from her jacket pocket and turned it on. "We need a little more light than the moon's reflection provides along the woodsy path. Once we're inside, Lady Selene will suffice to guide us."

Verity took Anastasia's arm. "You must've been a Girl Scout."

"Hardly. Just a determined Romantic."

They entered the cloisters. Anastasia turned left and led them down the long corridor, stopping at the end. "This door was the main entrance to the abbey chapel. The nuns were called to prayer two times a night and once just before dawn—Matins at midnight, Lauds a few hours later, and Prime near dawn. They'd descend in a candlelight processional from their dormitory down the night stairs, a circular staircase that once stood in this archway." She beamed her light to illuminate the corner. "Straight from bed to prayer."

"You didn't bring me here from bed to pray, did you?"

"Don't be silly. You asked me what led me to speculate about the sexual proclivities of these women. Well, here's the answer." Anastasia pointed her flashlight up at the ceiling. At the apex, a series of stone beams formed an octagonal shape, buttressing the structure. Carved into the joint between two beams was a long-haired bare-breasted mermaid, her nipples prominently protruding. In one hand she held a mirror, and in the other a large comb.

"I didn't expect to see such an erotic carving in these hallowed halls." Verity imagined flickers of candlelight dancing across the mermaid's naked torso as the nuns processed below.

"My colleagues would say you're misreading the past with modern eyes. They'd inform you it wasn't uncommon to find mermaids in medieval churches to warn sinners of the dangers of lust. Yet they'd also have to admit, in those days, lust between women was unthinkable." Anastasia wrapped her arms around Verity and pulled her close. "So, I asked myself, why would such a warning be needed in an abbey filled with women? Can you guess?"

"It's not a warning!" The stones echoed Verity's words along the walls of the corridor as if cackling their confirmation.

"Precisely. As that ballet we saw in London so ably demonstrated, a symbol's meaning can change, or be changed, from one time or context to another. I believe the mermaid signals acceptance, not condemnation."

"That's a provocative idea. Have you presented it to your colleagues?"

"Call me foolish, but to stir the pot, I gave a paper at an international conference last year. I risked being thrown out of the profession for lacking standard documentary evidence like we have for Benedetta—abbey records, court cases, etcetera—but I wanted to shake things up. Several people accused me of idle speculation, but they couldn't disprove my interpretation. I think you should develop a theory about Anastasia based on what you've already discovered."

Verity sighed. "You want me to go out on a limb like you did? I haven't enough clues to hazard a theory like yours about Anastasia, much less present it in public."

"All you'd need is a few more suggestive dots and a leap of faith to connect them in imaginative ways."

"Taking that leap is what worries me most," Verity said.

"But, darling, you already have. Who else but another madwoman in the attic of academia would've been willing to take a trip with me to Lacock, much less come out at midnight to indulge my story about the nuns being called from their post-coital beds to prayer."

"I have to admit you've made it impossible for me ever to hear Shakespeare's Hamlet tell Ophelia to 'get thee to a nunnery' in the same way again."

Anastasia burst into laughter. "That line's been misheard for centuries. In Shakespeare's time, 'nunnery' was slang for 'brothel.'"

"Shall we go back?" Verity asked.

"Not until I introduce you to the pleasures of convent life," Anastasia said and clicked off the flashlight.

They stood facing each other in the dark for several moments, listening to the steady drip, drip, drip of water falling like a benediction from the mermaids' moist mouths onto their heads. Then Anastasia reached under Verity's sweater and caressed the warm, soft flesh of her breasts. Verity's breath quickened, and she felt an accumulating wetness between her legs. Anastasia kissed her lips, and then knelt before her and caressed the dark valley between her other two lips.

The next morning, they awoke late, exhausted from their nighttime adventures. Verity picked up some sandwiches and fruit from the bakery nearby, while Anastasia checked out of the Inn. She returned with their picnic to find the little green dragon revved up and ready to go.

"I've planned a scenic route. Not exactly the way Morris and Company would've traveled—they'd have come by boat from London along the canals of the Thames—but clever enough to get us in the right mood for conjuring their spirits."

"From the look of that sly grin on your face, it seems that you're already in the right mood."

"Of course, darling. Sex and adventure always boost one's spirits. Put on your driving cap. I plan to test little greenie's mettle on the curving road to Pre-Raphaelite *Shangri-la*."

On the outskirts of Lacock they joined a small country road bordered on both sides with massive hedges more than eight feet high. It looked like they were speeding through an endless green tunnel. As the road narrowed, hedges gave way to stands of oak and ash and elm so ancient that Verity half expected King Arthur and his knights to come bounding out of the woods.

"What is this place?" Verity asked.

"Fyfield Nature Preserve. Among the oldest woods in England. Beautiful, isn't it?"

"Almost primeval."

A little further, they rounded a curve. Anastasia slowed the car to a halt at the edge of a village. A procession of enormous boulders loomed before them. Sheep grazed, unmoved by the towering rocks. A few people wandered among the stones, ignoring the sheep. Verity was stupefied.

"And where are we now?"

"A half hour from the Angel Inn and thousands of years before it was built. Welcome to neolithic Britain and the henge monument of Avebury, site of a ceremonial theater constructed more than two millennia before the common era. I thought you'd be amused to see how the folks of ancient Avebury carved their runes into earth and stone long before your manuscript-makers scratched their poems onto parchment."

Verity stared at the extraordinary scene. It was like being ricocheted through time. If the earth were a book and the monuments to human habitation were chapters recounting stories of the ages of humanity, then the endurance of trees and the persistence of rocks mocked the idea that those stories were the only tales that earth-book could tell. Like the garlanded borders decorating *The Queen's Book*, trees and stones paid homage to nature's immortality, testaments to the eternally repeating cycle of a deathless universe, defying rectilinear time.

"Hold on to your hat. In half an hour, we'll be returned to the nineteenth century." Anastasia restarted the engine.

"That'll feel like *terra firma* to me," Verity said.

Twenty miles farther, the road thinned to a single lane and Anastasia had to pull the sports car off to the side to allow an enormous tractor to belch past. They crossed a bridge over a river tributary, as a small barge of revelers floated downstream on the sparkling Thames. In the late morning light, Verity had the uncanny sensation she'd seen Dante Gabriel Rossetti and Jane Morris among them. "Maybe we should've traveled to Kelmscott by boat," she said.

"Another day, we'll rent a houseboat and float blissfully along in the current's embrace while I feed you grapes and cheese all the way from London to Bath. It'll put you in the mood of Roman times."

Verity caught Anastasia's gaze and saw affection in her eyes, along with something else—the slightly worried look of a woman with a previously wounded heart trying a little too hard not to appear vulnerable. "Behind all that bravado, you're just a softie at heart." She kissed

Anastasia's blushing cheek. "Your secret's safe with me," she said, wondering when she'd find out what that secret really was.

They turned down a lane toward the Kelmscott Manor car park and then walked along a footpath to the main entrance. After buying tickets to the exhibitions, Anastasia pointed to a bench by a stream. "There's a lovely spot for our picnic. I'm starved."

After lunch, they wandered around the Manor House gardens to avoid entering the building with a large group that had just arrived in a van. Arched trellises of intricately intertwined vines covered some of the pebbled pathways. In the springtime, Verity imagined hundreds of tulips, poppies, and hollyhocks blooming as effusively as they figured in Morris's print designs. In one corner, an enormous mulberry tree outstretched its bare arms to the sky. In another, a profusion of fruit trees laden with ripe apples and pears sheltered a nearby wooden bench. She was stunned at how carefully the landscape recreated the setting of a medieval garden. They walked toward the house, entered a narrow hallway, and turned right.

At the sight of the fabric covering the walls, Verity gasped. "Morris's *Strawberry Thief*! Those birds, pecking at strawberries, they're going to haunt me forever."

"Never mind the birds. We're after that box."

The next room was filled with sketches and paintings of Jane Morris, including one of her posed in a stunning blue silk dress. Anastasia walked over to the large canvas. "Whoever painted that portrait certainly had a feeling for the subject, and I do mean in the most lascivious way."

"It's a portrait of Jane Morris by Rossetti," Verity said.

"Wasn't he married to Lizzie Siddal?" Anastasia asked.

"Yes, but he became Jane's lover. He often stayed at Kelmscott with the Morrises; sometimes when Jane was here alone," Verity explained.

"Well, that puts a delicious gloss on the goings-on in this place!"

Verity asked a docent to direct them to the room where the Siddal box could be found, and they climbed the stairs to reach Jane Morris's bedroom. Against one wall stood a four-poster bed surrounded by willow-patterned linen curtains. The same design was duplicated on all four wallpapered walls. Verity's gaze wandered through the willows until she spotted the sought-after jewelry case atop a cabinet opposite the bed. "There it is." She grabbed Anastasia's hand and bounded past several startled tourists for a closer look.

The box was nestled inside a protective plastic casket. She leaned closer to see if the mysterious image on the front was sharper on the original than on the replica in Mrs. Fairweather's flat and was disappointed to discover it was as blurry as the one on the souvenir.

"That was a wedding gift from Elizabeth Siddal to Jane Burden after Jane's marriage to William Morris," a woman standing next to her said.

"I know," Verity said. "I've identified two of the images on the front with Harley 4431; but the third remains a mystery to me."

"You've certainly done your homework. You're correct about the connection to the manuscripts of Christine de Pizan. As I'm sure you know, William Morris was fascinated with all things medieval, and his wife came to share in his passion. Lucinda Faucet, docent." The woman extended her hand.

"Verity Frazier." They shook hands. "And my friend Anastasia Griffin." Anastasia nodded.

"This unusual item was used as a jewelry box," Lucinda said. "I had the good fortune to assist the lead curator cleaning it. When we opened it, we discovered little trinkets inside, probably items belonging to May Morris, who lived here at Kelmscott long after her parents had died."

"I'm most interested in the image on the far-right front panel," Verity said.

"Unfortunately, we've been unable to locate the model for that one, although it does bear a striking resemblance to the composition of other paintings in Christine's manuscripts."

"I thought so too."

"Possibly it was based on another, lesser-known painting by the same artist. Morris was a great collector and traveler, acquiring old manuscripts on his trips, including a journey he took to Paris just before marrying Jane. Perhaps an exemplar for the unidentified image was in his collection, which Siddal may have seen. She visited the Morrises at their home in Kent in 1860 during the time she worked on the box. Mere speculation, of course."

Anastasia elbowed Verity.

"Is there an inventory of his collection?" Verity could hardly contain her excitement.

"Nothing that could remotely be considered comprehensive. Morris sold some of his acquisitions in the mid-1860s, when he suffered financial woes. I believe Jane dispersed other items to supplement monies she'd inherited after Morris's death in 1898. The London Societies of Antiquaries at Burlington House may have records of those transactions."

"Thank you. You've been most helpful." Verity felt her excitement dwindle. It seemed hopeless to think she'd ever locate the inspiration for the mysterious painting, much less connect it to the medieval Anastasia.

"My pleasure. Enjoy the rest of your visit."

"Back to London we go," Anastasia said as they left the room. "But not before exploring the rest of this mausoleum to the Arts and Crafts Movement. I find I'm growing rather fond of tapestries and frenzied wallpaper."

"I appreciate your good humor, but I feel pretty defeated at the moment," Verity sighed. "Even if I found some oblique reference to a painting resembling the one on that box, how will I ever prove Anastasia painted it?"

"Ghosts always leave traces behind. Anyway, don't worry about that yet." Anastasia's eyes sparkled with mischievous delight. "In the meantime, think of the thrill of simply finding the source for the design!"

"I suppose it can't hurt to try," Verity said.

"Besides, I'm up for a visit to the RA," Anastasia added.

"The RA?"

"There's me falling into London-speak again. Forgive me, darling." Anastasia pretended to slap her own cheek. "RA. The Royal Academy of Arts. It shares space at Burlington House with the Antiquaries Society. While you're mining their archives for all things Morris, I'll delight my senses in the galleries nearby. You can join me when you're finished— my membership admits two—and we'll celebrate your sleuthing over cocktails and charcuterie in their elegant Senate Room overlooking the gardens."

"You make it all sound so appealing. But I've spent weeks in the BL—"

"See? You're catching on—"

"and I've found nothing, really."

"Do you consider me nothing, then?" Anastasia feigned offense, but Verity heard a note of worry underneath the pretense.

"That was more you finding me, I'd say." Verity couldn't help laughing. "But I'm not complaining."

"I shouldn't think so, not after last night." Anastasia brushed Verity's lips with a kiss. "Then it's settled. 'The game's afoot: follow your spirit and upon this charge cry God for Anastasia, France, and Saint Christine!'"

An accident delayed traffic on the M4 for over an hour. Anastasia drummed her fingers on the steering wheel. "What a load of bollocks," she said. "Why can't this country build roads for the twenty-first century? I'll never make it in time."

"Make it where, and in time for what?" Verity asked, surprised by how suddenly Anastasia's mood had soured.

"Cousin George insisted I return the car this evening, and I have to drop you off first, which will make me even later."

"Then I'll come with you, spend the night at your place," Verity said.

"Not a good idea," Anastasia said.

"If it saves you time, why not?" Verity asked, a little surprised by Anastasia's response.

Anastasia didn't answer right away, as if trying to come up with some excuse for not accepting Verity's obvious solution to the problem. Then she shook her head and smiled at Verity. "Because I have an early-morning appointment with the chair of my department, and I'm afraid spending another night with you isn't the best way to prepare for that," she said and pinched Verity's cheek.

Verity was disappointed but understanding. "Then I'll see you at the BL tomorrow, after your meeting."

Anastasia shook her head again. "Afraid not. Doctor's appointment." The traffic began to move. "It's about time," Anastasia said. "Do you mind, darling, if I drop you at King's Cross? It's easier than having to maneuver through Islington."

"Sure," Verity said, "if that helps."

They reached King's Cross half an hour later and said their goodbyes. Verity walked home, unable to shake the feeling that Anastasia was hiding something from her.

13

COLLABORATION, 1395–1397

BÉATRICE

After three decades in the Parisian book trade, I'd earned the praise of the most prominent booksellers for the delicacy and proficiency of my work. *Libraires*, who commanded the talents of the finest scribes, chose my workshop to illuminate their most important commissions. I worked with distinguished copyists, such as the *écrivain de roi*, Jean Lavenant, collaborating on several devotional works for the royal collection. My clients included other nobles and university men, who required the best manuscripts and were willing to pay the highest price. The tormented years of my youth and the loss of my inheritance seemed like chapters from some ill-fated storybook of another person's life. I lived alone, but was never lonely. My days were spent in work, and my nights in gratitude for those who'd enabled me to live by my brush, and for the joy of aiding two other women who'd apprenticed themselves to my workshop—Perrette and Ghislaine.

Perrette's husband, Matthieu, had been an accomplished illuminator himself. When I had more work than I could manage, I sent quires to him for painting. His style matched my own—we both favored precision of expression; elaborate, exacting designs for borders; and amply flourished historiated initials. Perrette assisted him, preparing inks and quills, but had not tried her hand at painting until Matthieu was felled in the plague that had swept the land again, four years before. Taking up his trade was the only means of support left for her and her infant daughter. I agreed to provide her with further instruction in the art of foliated borders. Her cousin, Ghislaine, accompanied her every day to my *atelier* to care for the child. A fifteen-year-old full of verve to equal her beauty, Ghislaine proved an enchanting addition, charming everyone with her quick wit and clever banter. She soon became fascinated by the art of illumination, and once her charge was old enough to amuse herself with poppets and games, asked to be apprenticed as well.

We three worked in happy companionship in the larger *atelier* I now occupied in a house I'd rented on Île de la Cité, not far from where I'd first lived in Paris. Heavily populated with booksellers' shops, the location positioned me at the nexus of the trade, between the university on the Left Bank of the Seine, which regulated it, and the houses of noble personages on the Right Bank, whose commissions supported it. It was also located in close proximity to the poets and orators who competed across the city and at court, and who later employed me to transform their ballads and fanciful arguments into precious books. Ghislaine had recently attended one such royal competition and returned ablaze with news of a woman poet who'd mesmerized the grand assembly of citizens with her erudition, admonishing the city leaders to abandon petty conflicts engendered by envy and fulfill their duties to the crown.

One day, early in 1395, I looked out the window above my desk to see a small-framed woman crossing the cathedral square and walking with purpose in the direction of my *atelier*. She was dressed in a threadbare yet elegantly proportioned crimson cape with a fur collar and wore a white, horned headdress with a tattered silk veil that fluttered in the wintry wind. Her gait and attire bespoke of nobility roughened by woes, while her comportment communicated a dignity unperturbed by whatever misfortune her worn costume betrayed. She held her head down against the force of snowy winds and soon rapped on my door. I opened it to find a woman about half my age. Under one arm, she clutched a large leather satchel, while her other hand grasped at her cape.

"Madame, please come in from the cold." I ushered her into the room. "Anastasia Tapis, at your service, along with my assistants, Perrette and Ghislaine."

"*Enchanté*. I am Madame de Castel." She shivered the words out through clattering teeth.

"Ghislaine, please bring some mulled wine for Madame." Ghislaine disappeared into the back kitchen, while I gestured Madame toward a table and chairs near the fire. Perrette returned to work at her desk.

"How may I help?"

"Praise has circulated around your name at court." She struggled to remove her cape. I hesitated to assist, sensing that she preferred to do battle with the weathered garment herself. "I have come with a commission."

"I am honored." I bowed my head and raised my hand to my heart. "Do you have a retainer from the king?"

"No, but I'm supported by my connections at court. My late husband served both Charles the Wise and his successor, as my father had before him. Perhaps you knew my father, the king's astrologer, Thomas de Pizan?"

"Only by reputation." I kept to myself the strange rumors I'd heard that his concoctions had threatened the life of the king.

"He was a dedicated scholar. Untroubled by customs limiting women's opportunities, he encouraged my learning."

"In that we have much in common." I smiled.

Ghislaine returned with the wine. Christine nodded thanks, wrapped her hands around the cup to warm them, and took a small sip. "While my father served Charles, it was my good fortune to have access to the king's collection of beautiful books in his library. Even as a young girl, my father allowed me to be tutored in both Latin and French script. In due course, I became skilled in reading and writing." From her leather satchel, she withdrew a large package wrapped in embroidered green silk and placed it on the table between us. "I'm here to commission you to decorate an edition of poetry as a gift for Louis, Duke of Orléans." Undoing the gold satin ribbon binding it, she removed a few pages from a large sheaf and passed them to me.

The poems were copied on luxurious vellum in a script more expressive and ostentatious than I'd seen in other secular works, where tradition could give way to experiment. I didn't recognize the hand of the scribe. "Whose hand copied these?"

"I did," she replied. "Of necessity, I've relied on the craft of transcription in the recent years of my widowhood, or debt would have dragged me into penury's ruinous pit."

"You've an elegant hand." I turned my attention from admiring the shape of the letters to reading the words. The boldness of the subject astonished me even more than the beauty of her script. In a plaintive voice, the poems spoke of the melancholy multiplication of loss upon loss. What suffering had driven their author into such sadness, I could only imagine. "And who authored these poems?"

"I did so, under the name of Christine de Pizan."

"Madame Tapis," Ghislaine interrupted excitedly, "this must be the woman I told you about, the poet who transfixed the audience at the royal competition a few weeks ago. I was standing too far back in the crowd to see her face clearly. But I remember the name I heard on everyone's lips: Christine de Pizan. What an honor, what an honor."

Christine bowed her head, perhaps embarrassed by Ghislaine's sudden outburst. But when she looked up, I saw only gratitude in her eyes and a smile bursting on her face like the sun at dawn. "Madame, we'd be privileged to assist you," I said, mirroring her happy countenance. "You've earned a stature that neither noble lineage nor the acquaintance of royalty has ever guaranteed to a woman." I stood to retrieve a book of exemplars from my shelves.

"I have very particular ideas about the illustrations I require."

"Of course. Your poems are—unusual in content. Provide me with notes on the rubrics and I'll accommodate your needs." I thought perhaps she didn't understand normal practice. "Let me show you some designs, and we can modify as you wish."

"I'm grateful you are literate. My poems are intended to awaken sympathy, not only for a poor widow's plight, but also for the woes besetting our dear lady, France. I've seen mistakes illiterates have made, muddying the meaning of a word with an ill-suited image."

"Like you, I've benefited from education, both in my childhood and in later years, in an abbey not far from here, where I advanced my craft." The mention of the abbey seemed to discomfort her.

"You were in the convent at Poissy?" she asked.

"No. For a decade before coming to Paris, I lived as a laywoman at another abbey to the east of the city. But the women at Poissy are also skilled manuscript-makers."

"So I'm told," she said. "I prefer to supervise all aspects of the production, from selection of vellum to binding." She removed a small book from her satchel. "May I count on you to work under these conditions and to maintain the strictest secrecy?"

In all my years in Paris, I'd come to know many artists, but never an author who acted as publisher of his own works. The frail woman seated next to me, whose poems bespoke anguish and worry, transformed before my eyes, as if the mantle of mourning she'd donned in prose were merely the self-deprecating dependency expected of our sex, a clever disguise enabling her to mount a campaign of words against those arbitrary, capricious forces waging war against women. With a nod, I accepted her terms with the enthusiasm of one who has waited too long for a comrade in arms.

"Since we are in agreement, would you please sign this contract?" She passed the notebook to me, indicated where to make my mark, and occupied herself with my exemplars.

I stared at the book in stupefied horror. The wastrel Pierre Bonhomme had scratched his name on a line as provisioner of vellum! Since defeating me in court, he'd inherited his father's business, and, with the help of my former patron's stellar reputation, had had himself installed as a bookseller. He cared nothing about art. The title and control of his father's estate gave him access to the best parchment-makers in Paris, along with the means to feed his avarice. I'd heard from more than one scribe that he hoarded materials and then sold them at prices far in excess of what he'd paid. Worse still, some complained that he switched the better vellum displayed in his *atelier* for an inferior grade before dispersing the quires. Christine would have been no match against his guileful ways. I suspected that the duplicitous tongue of that wily snake had tricked her into wasting precious funds, but covered my worry with an indifferent expression. "I see Pierre Bonhomme has agreed to provide you with parchment."

"His supplies are reputed to be the best in all of Paris," Christine said. "I purchased those quires from him." She pointed to the pages I'd set aside on the table.

"Have you agreed to a further purchase for the new manuscript?"

"When I saw the exquisite vellum in his workshop—velvety smooth and without blemish—I subscribed immediately, even though the price was higher than I'd wanted to pay. It will delight the eye to have miniatures illuminated on such gossamer pages."

Her tone was filled with such pride that I smarted at the idea of diminishing her pleasure by revealing my suspicions. I decided to confront Pierre myself. It would satisfy me to take something back from a man who'd stolen from me and so many others. "I'm sure you made a wise choice. As it turns out, I've an appointment for Ghislaine to deliver exemplars to him for another commission." I glanced in Ghislaine's direction to ensure that she wouldn't contradict me. "To save you trouble, I shall have her retrieve your order and deliver it to you."

"How kind of you." She gathered her manuscript pages, preparing to leave. "We can discuss my ideas for the illuminations after I've received the vellum."

"Of course," I said, already hatching a plot to entrap the brute who would steal from a widow. "I'm eager to secure your vision."

———

I'd learned early in my life how a vain and violent man could bribe his way to victory by trafficking in fear. Father Baron had counted on the complicity of those he'd threatened to cover the truth with lies, and on the unwillingness of others to launch a campaign against him lest they become his next target, never imagining that his vanity—the enemy he'd created himself—would be his undoing. Arrogance pushed him to court disaster when he confronted an opponent he'd once thought defeated and assumed he'd conquer again. I'd seen that vainglorious man betrayed by implements of his own fabrication and vowed to see another undone.

Three days after Christine's visit, I sent Ghislaine to collect samples of vellum from Pierre, instructing her not to tell him that she worked for me. "Take this purse. You're to pose as a messenger sent by Raoulet d'Orléans to obtain quires for a manuscript for the king. Pierre will give you his best vellum. He wouldn't dare cross a scribe of such prominence as Master d'Orléans. Be sure he signs this paper, then bring the parchment to me." I handed her a double-paged invoice on which I'd forged the mark of Raoulet d'Orléans and explained the reason for the ruse. "You must do this, or Christine de Pizan will have lost a large sum for inferior goods."

Without hesitation, Ghislaine agreed to the plan. "Her poetry has emboldened me. I want no harm to come to her."

"As if you needed emboldening," I laughed. "I'm sure your charms will distract him from any suspicions he might otherwise have."

"I'll wear my finest gown and most fascinating smile," she said.

Two hours later, Ghislaine returned to my *atelier* laden with treasures—four thick quires of the rarest vellum, each of ten folios. "I thought you'd distract him; I didn't expect he'd be driven mad," I said, stroking the smooth texture of parchment fabricated from the skins of calves.

Ghislaine blinked her eyes and brought her fingers to her lips in mock surprise. "Like any other man of a certain age, he was taken in by the implication of an assignation," she said. "I feigned interest, or he wouldn't have signed the invoice."

I groaned at the thought of her playing the coquette to that horrible man. "I hope you haven't done something that you'll regret."

She bent over with laughter. "He asked if he could walk me home. I told him I had another appointment today, adding that when I chanced in his neighborhood again, I'd be delighted to accept his offer. That cheered him enough to sign." She handed me the document.

"Clever girl." Ghislaine watched with interest as I took it to my desk.

"Shall I prepare the parchment to deliver to Madame?" she asked.

"No. Put it in the storage cabinet in the back room." Ghislaine looked at me with a perplexed expression, but followed my order. I removed the second page of the document, placed a thin piece of paper over it, and rubbed it carefully with a bit of charred wood until the outline of Pierre's signature appeared, the dark shape I'd use to seal his doom. Next, I prepared another invoice with my insignia to replace the original, and with a hand steadied by the force of revenge, blackened the lines of his name into their evil form. I retrieved a sheaf of damaged parchment I'd saved to use for exemplars. Now I would put it in service to a higher cause. "Please wrap this sheaf," I told Ghislaine when she'd returned from storing the fine vellum. "You're to take it to Madame this afternoon."

"I don't understand; these are blemished folios." She shook her head in disbelief.

"Precisely. As would have been the ones Pierre intended to deliver to Madame had we not intervened. He is an arrogant scoundrel who preys on the vulnerable." As I explained his tricks, her eyes widened in horror. "Already defeated by others who've schemed against her, Madame would never have had the energy to prove his duplicity. But now we have the means to beat him. You must follow my instructions precisely." I handed her the wrapped parchment. "Take these to her and say you came straight from his *atelier*. Show her the signed invoice. Be prepared. She will be shocked when she opens the package. If she asks why you didn't inspect the material before leaving his shop, tell her he handed the package to you already wrapped and you wouldn't have thought to distrust him."

Not an hour had passed when I heard a commotion outside my *atelier*. I opened the door to find a distraught Christine de Pizan clutching the bundled parchment as if she were holding fast to the last, tattered fragments of her life.

"I've been robbed of my savings. I am defeated."

Ghislaine guided the shaking woman to a chair by the fire.

I felt a pang of guilt at having added to her pain, but it quickly passed into determination to conquer the real source of her consternation. There would be time later to explain why I'd concocted such a devious plan even at the risk of losing her trust, though losing the trust of this woman had become more important to me than losing her custom. "What's happened? Did Pierre not provide the parchment you ordered?"

"He sent inferior folios." She let the package slip to the floor. "See for yourself. I am ruined."

I faked a horrified look at the inferior parchment. "This is disgraceful. His treachery must be exposed. Demand an inquiry from the *prevôt* at once."

"He has the prestige of being a university bookseller behind him. I haven't even my honor left to defend me. Ever since my appearance in the poetry competition, rumors have passed from mouth to mouth that I only gained entry by taking a lover from among the nobles at court." She held her head in her hands and wept.

"Nonsense. None but the idle or the insane would believe such jealous prattle. In the meantime, you must continue work on your manuscript for the duke."

"With what? I have no materials. And no means of replacing what I've lost."

"I'll provide the parchment." I signaled to Ghislaine to bring the parchment she'd stored earlier. "When you prove the scoundrel's guilt, your accounts will be replenished, although I require no more repayment than to illuminate your work."

"Prove? With what evidence? My word is insufficient to defeat his prestige."

"Ghislaine, didn't you obtain a receipt from Pierre for the parchment, as I instructed?"

"Yes. But in the confusion, I neglected to show it to Madame." She handed the invoice to Christine now, who regarded it in stunned silence.

"If he denies the accusations levied against him, you'll have more than your word to prove his guilt." I touched her gently on the shoulder. "I'll accompany you to the office of the *prevôt* to file your case."

We spent the next months, before the case was heard, elaborating plans for Christine's book of poetry. The work kept her distracted from worry and me occupied with the task of designing a miniature of the author presenting her manuscript to the duke. I'd visited her *atelier* on rue St. Antoine several times—the same one, though now much changed, where I'd met another master scribe in my earliest days in Paris. In the fleurs-de-lis drapery around her window, in the gentle green tones painted on the walls, in the soft red woolen fabric that covered her desk, in the silver inkwell and pointer, and in the little white dog who sat at her feet in admiration every hour of her writing day, I saw the marks of a woman's touch and worked these details into sketches that delighted her with the precision of my reproduction of creativity's stage.

By the time the day arrived for her to appear for the trial, she was so elated by all we'd accomplished that she danced around the room with a joy that surprised me to tears.

"Now who's the mournful one?" she teased.

"I weep from happiness," I laughed, wiping my eyes with the edge of my painting smock.

"I know the duke will be pleased with this book. Your support has been a motherly blessing to me." She grabbed my hand and kissed it. "Had I burdened my own aged mother with any more troubles, her heart would have broken."

Not wanting to dampen her happiness with any lingering worry of my own, I whispered my thanks and returned home to prepare for my appearance in court. I was to be called as a witness, as was Ghislaine. I needed to summon every fiber of my being to restrain my temper at the full force of accusations I expected Pierre to hurl.

"That woman is a strumpet and a liar." Pierre's eyes throbbed like orbs of hate. He pointed an accusatory finger at Ghislaine. "She appeared before me with an invoice from the scriptorium of Raoulet d'Orléans. I provided her with perfect vellum. I am accused of a theft I never committed. I demand you call Monsieur d'Orléans to testify!"

"Calm yourself, Monsieur Bonhomme. We've no need of additional testimony. The invoice the witness provided is evidence enough of your guilt. Do you deny your signature?" The judge ordered the bailiff to show the papers to Pierre.

"It is a forgery! I signed a document authenticating an order prepared for Raoulet d'Orléans."

"And where is that document, sir?"

"I gave it back to her, along with the vellum required. Where either are now, I can only imagine." He was sweating profusely, despite the chill in the room. He turned toward me and shouted. "Anastasia Tapis, you're behind this! Your greed knows no limit. You sent that young woman to cheat me." He rose from his seat as if to attack me, but the bailiff restrained him. "Ask her what happened to the paper I signed." His face reddened with rage. "I am being falsely accused." The bailiff led him from the dock to a bench in a far corner of the room.

"Madame Tapis, please come forward." The magistrate summoned me to the stand. I suppressed the laughter bubbling inside me and assumed a calm expression as I mounted the steps and took the witness's seat.

"Is Ghislaine Pucelle in your employ?"

"She is an apprentice illuminator in my workshop, yes."

"She admits she sent the woman to cheat me!" Pierre shouted.

"You'll remain silent, sir," the magistrate instructed, "or I'll remove you from this chamber."

"Did you send Mademoiselle Pucelle on an errand to fetch goods from Monsieur Bonhomme?"

"Yes, on behalf of Madame de Castel, who was otherwise occupied with another legal matter and could not retrieve the material herself. I asked Ghislaine to be sure Monsieur Bonhomme signed the receipt so there'd be no misunderstanding."

"And did she deliver the goods to Madame de Castel?"

"She took the unopened parcel immediately to Madame, who then discovered she'd been tricked into a purchase of damaged parchment." Ghislaine nodded her head in agreement, providing cover for my dissembling.

"Liar, liar!" Pierre's furious shouts reached a fever pitch. "It is I who was tricked. I provisioned that young woman with my finest vellum."

"Bailiff, remove this man to the antechamber while I continue this inquiry."

While Pierre was escorted from the room, the magistrate invited Christine's testimony. "Madame de Castel, if you please."

Christine approached the stand, carrying the spoiled parchment under her arm as if it were the Holy Grail. Her air of dignified self-assurance was as evident in her visage as in the calm tone in which she recounted the story of Pierre's transgression. The weeks of work we'd accomplished together had boosted her confidence.

"Did you secure the services of Monsieur Bonhomme?" the magistrate asked.

"Yes, I have here the notebook I asked him to sign as a contract and assurance that his materials were of the finest quality. This is what he delivered." She brandished the mottled parchment with a majestic gesture of disgust. I knew then that Christine had understood my ploy and endorsed the subterfuge. "If that man impugns my testimony, his own signature is witness against him."

Later, when we celebrated her victory—Pierre was forced to give her adequate compensation and was banned from the profession—Christine confessed she'd been shocked at first, realizing I'd proffered a forged document as evidence.

"Then why did you conform to the plan?" I asked.

"When a woman falls into widowhood, she learns that death has taken away much more than her beloved. Her anguish is multiplied by troubles tearing at her from all sides. Everywhere she turns for relief, she finds only inconsideration and the withdrawal of friendship. Assaulted by lawsuits and malicious claims against her person and property, she must arm herself against these plagues, defend herself against those who would beat her down. Avoid them if she can, destroy them if she must. I drew strength from your wisdom and steady support. Until this world treats us with equal respect, a woman cannot survive if she does not take on the heart of a man."

14

THE COLLECTOR AND THE COLLECTED

VERITY

About a week after Verity's application to access the London Society of Antiquaries' archives was approved, she stood outside the building, mouth agape, looking up at the image carved into the keystone above its portico. The comely female face was half-concealed behind a curtain of translucent stone that fell across the left eye like a wave frozen in time. Unlike Newton, this sculpture remained stoically mute, a silent invitation to explore whatever secrets the hallowed halls behind her held about the forces of medieval magnetism that had attracted the circle of artists at Kelmscott Manor into whose center Verity had been thrust on her peripatetic journey to find evidence of the medieval Anastasia.

"That's called *The Veil of Time*, in case you're wondering," the Anastasia whom Verity already had found offered without prompting. "Amuse yourself among Morris memorabilia until the cocktail hour, when you have an appointment with me in the Senate Room at 5 p.m. Sharp." She kissed Verity on the cheek and hurried across the courtyard toward the art museum.

Verity pushed open the heavy wood-and-glass doors below the portico and entered an opulent corridor. Its ostentatious evocation of Victorian grandeur made the modern lines of the British Library seem austere in comparison. Past a wide marble staircase carpeted in bright royal red, she entered the main reading room. Light spilled from windows in the coffered ceiling onto the nimble fingers of a few dedicated researchers seated thirty feet below, silently combing through assorted books, manuscripts, and other arcana at a long table, each searching for a needle in the haystack of the library's holdings of artifacts of material culture. She approached the staff librarian and presented her approved research forms to a young woman staffing the desk.

"Ah, Professor Frazier. Welcome!" The young woman looked up at her and smiled. "I've been expecting you. Daphne Witherspoon at your service. How may I help?"

"I'm researching the influence of medieval manuscripts on the development of Morris and his circle's aesthetic." Verity hesitated before disclosing the precise object of her obsession. "I recently visited the Society's Museum at Kelmscott House and became fascinated by the painted box given by Elizabeth Siddal to Jane Morris."

"Such a frightful case." Ms. Witherspoon shook her head.

Verity gave her an odd look. "Excuse me?"

"Oh, dear," she laughed, "I meant Elizabeth Siddal, not the jewelry case. They say she suffered from depression and overdosed on laudanum, to which she was addicted. Her husband, Gabriel Rossetti, was so distraught by her death that he buried a manuscript of his poems with her, a romantic gesture he soon came to regret."

Verity looked even more puzzled.

"After he became enamored with Jane Morris," the librarian's voice rose at the end of her sentence fragment, as if inviting Verity to complete it with what every pre-Raphaelite scholar knew by heart. Disappointed at the lack of response, she continued: "He exhumed the body, rescued his poems, and published the collection—revised, of course, to accommodate the worms' damaging edits—in a volume dedicated to Jane." Wearing an impish expression on her face, Ms. Witherspoon ended her discourse with a sardonic flourish. "A rather more morbid enterprise than disinterring clues about Siddal's aesthetics from our archives, I should say."

"Indeed," Verity said. "About Siddal's paintings—"

"Some say she was more ambitious than talented, more imitative than original, though doubtless that reflects the patriarchal preference for assigning genius to men, no matter how derivative their own work might have been." Ms. Witherspoon lowered her voice to a whisper. Verity leaned forward to hear. "Where, after all, would the great man himself have been without his medieval predecessors? For that matter, where would Socrates have been without Xanthippe, his wife? He sharpened his skills of argument in dialogue with her, did he not? And yet Plato effectively reduces her to a housewifely mote of a footnote in Socrates's story."

Verity managed a bewildered nod of agreement, perplexed by this sisterly outburst. As if sensing her befuddlement, the librarian detoured once more, before returning to the matter at hand.

"When I read your application, I detected a feminist impulse behind your proposed scavenger hunt among our Morrisonian artifacts. Finally, I thought, someone wants to give Lizzie her due."

"Actually, it's the artist who painted the originals that served as models for her paintings whom I'm trying to track." Verity hoped her admission wouldn't dampen Ms. Witherspoon's enthusiasm to aid her search.

"Another unacknowledged woman, I presume?" the librarian asked in eager solidarity.

"I believe they're the work of a woman, a fifteenth-century painter named Anastasia, who illuminated the manuscripts of Christine de Pizan. Two of Siddal's paintings on the jewelry box have been verified as based on paintings in the collection of Christine's books known as—

"Harley 4431. Yes, the Kelmscott curator has confirmed that."

"I'm hoping to discover the source of the third in Morris's medieval collection, a clue to lead me closer to Anastasia."

"You've certainly come to the right place." Ms. Witherspoon clapped her hands together several times, but without making a sound. "Consider me an ally on the hunt!" She winked her approval. "And please, call me Daphne."

"I appreciate your assistance, Daphne," Verity said, a little nonplussed at stumbling upon such an ardent supporter in a place where she'd least expected to find a radical firebrand. But then, she had to admit, serendipity already had made it difficult for her to hold fast to the probable when the possible kept announcing its existence so frequently and insistently.

"Morris was a Fellow here, as well as an ambitious collector of medieval manuscripts and books. A good part of his collection was dispersed after his death, some to his family. A larger portion was sold privately to Richard Bennett of Manchester, who later arranged for his holdings to be auctioned in 1898 by Sotheby's. I believe we have a copy of the auction catalog in our collection." She quickly searched the online resources and located the call number. "I can have it retrieved in an hour. In the meantime, peruse our list of Morris materials to see if anything else piques your curiosity."

Verity set herself to the task.

It turned out that the library held few manuscripts from Morris's vast medieval collection. There were interesting artifacts from his Kelmscott Press days—bookbinding implements used in an edition of Chaucer that the press produced as a medieval facsimile, and an old notebook of Morris's containing some calligraphy experiments, along with letters to his daughter, May. Verity judged neither likely to guide her to the image she sought.

Just before noon, Daphne delivered the Sotheby's catalogue, which contained an astounding list of thousands of items sold two years after Morris's death. Verity scanned the pages, stopping suddenly at two tantalizing entries near the end of the tally. One described an early fifteenth-century breviary, "possibly associated with Poissy, a medieval convent outside Paris." The other identified "four orphaned leaves with finely painted and illuminated miniatures, including a portrait of two holy women bent in prayer, found within the breviary and offered as a separate lot." Remembering that Poissy was the convent where Christine's daughter had been sent, Verity let a squeal of delight escape from her lips. Three seats down, an elderly gentleman *tsk-tsked* his disapproval of the disturbance. She mouthed an apology and sidled over to the librarian for advice.

"Is it possible to discover who bought specific items from Morris's collection?"

"Found something interesting, I take it?" Daphne's eyes widened with excitement.

"Possibly, but it's a long shot." Verity sighed. "It would be helpful if I could identify the provenance of these items more definitively, before Morris acquired them, as well as where they might be now." Verity pointed to the two entries in the catalog.

"Unfortunately, Morris's collection was very widely distributed. Henry Wellcome bought many items at the Sotheby's auction for the Wellcome library, but when space became a premium, the collection was winnowed down primarily to medical treatises, in which the library specialized. Hundreds of non-medical books Wellcome had acquired were sold. J. Pierpont Morgan purchased another large portion from the same auction for his library in New York. As for the rest, one can only speculate."

"I've been to the Morgan, but before I knew about William Morris's interest." Revelation of the literary diaspora sent forth from William Morris's library to the four corners of the earth made Verity feel a little like K in Kafka's *The Castle*, who was prompted by the sight of coattails disappearing around the corner to continue his pursuit of an ever-elusive subject.

"I'd suggest exploring the Morgan Library's online resources for further clues," Daphne continued. "And perhaps browse some more recent Sotheby's catalogues. Things have a way of turning up unexpectedly at auctions when the heirs of a collector scramble for their share of a king's ransom, or an art museum needs funds and sells off part of its holdings to raise capital. We, at the Society, have perused those with profit from time to time ourselves, on the lookout for ways to enhance our collections to better protect our cultural heritage from plunder. And do let me know if you discover any tantalizing morsel in your search."

Maybe it was foolish to continue chasing a shadow. Except Verity didn't feel either foolish or delusional. Intoxicated by the possibility that she'd discover traces of the medieval artist at the next unpredictable turn, she spent the remaining hours before the library closed in the maze of the Morgan's digital records and Sotheby catalogues.

References to breviaries and missals from the fourteenth and fifteenth centuries, a first edition of Dante, reproductions of the classical works of Aristotle, a rare edition of the poetry of Petrarch, a copy of Jean de Muen's *Roman de la Rose*, and scores of other ancient and medieval works amassed on the computer screen like a literary spider web. Her efforts yielded nothing noteworthy, unless you count the thrill of imagining that a chance encounter with the trace of a medieval artist's hand might occur at any moment. Verity laughed at herself. How she'd misunderstood Kafka. If K was a fool, he was a fool for hope, a believer in unmitigated fortitude, a devotee of perseverance, a fanatic for tenacity, an apostle of optimism, a steadfast pursuer of promise. That must have been why Kafka ended K's story mid-sentence.

"Any luck?" Daphne asked as she was tidying up before closing.

"Nothing besides those listings in the old Sotheby's catalogue of the sale of Morris's library."

"Well, I do hope you carry on with your search. I'm taking vicarious pleasure in your endeavor to uncover the model for that Siddal painting. Please keep me posted on the results," she said, handing Verity a card with her contact information. "That poor girl deserves as much credit as she can get, even if posthumously."

Verity took the card and put it in her backpack. "I'll do what I can to resuscitate her . . . reputation. Thanks for your help."

"No trouble at all."

Dusk's gray mantle enshrouded the courtyard of Burlington House as she left the library. The twin cast-iron lamps outside the Antiquaries' Society flickered with light, casting eerie shadows across the keystone sculpture as if the veil of time were being drawn across history's enigmatic face. Or drawn back, depending on how you looked at it.

Anastasia was waiting for Verity at the Royal Academy's Senate Room. She was seated at the bar near the windows, nursing a champagne cocktail, fidgeting with her cell phone. "I was just texting you. You missed a magnificent sunset, darling. I've ordered some nibbles and bubbly. Viewing art always makes me famished. Speaking of food, pick up any more breadcrumbs on the trail to my namesake?"

Without answering, Verity handed her the notes about the breviary and the orphaned pages.

"A prayer book from a medieval convent outside Paris sounds positively enticing. I've known about Poissy, of course. I'm not so much of an English snob that I turn my nose up at the dalliances of the French for what they might add to my studies in comparative erotica. But before we buy tickets on the Eurostar, tell me what makes you so interested in this place."

"I'm bursting to explain. But not without a kiss and a sip of champagne." Verity surprised her lover with an audacious smooch on the lips.

"What have they put in the water cooler at the Antiquaries Society to bring out such ferocity? You've made me blush for the second time in a week. I shudder to think what will happen if we get to the city of lovers."

"Not *if*: *when*. Now, about Poissy." In between sips of champagne, Verity recounted what she knew about Christine's connection to the convent on the western perimeter of Paris. "Christine's daughter, Marie, was a dedicated Catholic who wanted to devote herself to the religious life. After opposing the idea, Christine relented, and Marie entered the Dominican order of nuns—"

"at Poissy!" Anastasia interrupted in astonishment. "Now we're on to something."

"It feels like the best lead I've had. Marie was sent to the convent with another Marie, the young daughter of Charles VI, who brought with her a treasure trove of a dowry, including missals and prayer books from the royal library."

"Ah, so you think one of the breviaries may have belonged to Christine de Pizan, who had it produced—"

"as a special present for her daughter's use. And who better to decorate such a meaningful gift, but a close friend and accomplished artist—"

"with my ancestral moniker." Anastasia clinked her glass against Verity's. "Let's toast the devotion of nuns."

"Salud!" Verity finished her glass and poured another. "But there's more. Among those orphaned pages found inside the breviary, one sounds remarkably like the unidentified image on Siddal's box. By the way, did you know Lizzie Siddal was a drug addict?"

"As were so many in those days, my lovely." Anastasia pinched Verity's cheek. She paused for a second and sat back in her chair, drumming her fingers on the counter, and gave Verity a quizzical look. "But how did you learn about her laudanum use?"

"From Daphne, the Society librarian, who shares your opinion of men."

"So, you're on a first-name basis with the librarian." Anastasia stiffened and crossed her arms. "Trading feminist bromides with Daphne. I suppose that's why you were late?"

"Late? I wasn't late. I came as soon as the library closed."

"Just had to stay until the very last minute—with Daphne." The meanness of her tone startled Verity.

"What's gotten into you?" Verity asked. "A minute ago, you were excited about my discoveries and were planning our trip to Paris."

"A minute ago, I didn't know about Daphne."

"And all you know about her now is that she's female. Don't you think you're being a little ridiculous?"

"*I'm* being ridiculous? We're not apart for more than a few hours and you're already flirting with another woman."

"Flirting? I was having a perfectly ordinary conversation with a very knowledgeable librarian about my research."

"Very knowledgeable—and very attractive, I imagine. I should have known better than to get involved with an American."

"What's that supposed to mean?"

"You're all alike. Overpaid, undereducated, and fickle." Anastasia's lip began to quiver. She got up from her seat, but Verity grabbed her arm, wondering if she'd had too much champagne, or if something else had suddenly transformed her usually self-confident lover into a jealous mess. Whatever it was, she was determined to get it out of her. She kept her voice calm and her eyes fixed on Anastasia's, who sat down again, rigid as a marble statue.

"Anastasia, this is crazy. What's *really* bothering you?"

Anastasia bit her lip and shook her head slowly.

"Trust me; I promise we're not all alike over in the colonies."

A tiny smile wrinkled the corners of Anastasia's eyes. She let out a sigh that sounded as if she'd been holding her breath.

"Last year, I had the unfortunate experience of falling terribly fast and incautiously hard for an American woman named Daisy. After a few months of delirious fun together, she announced she was polyamorous. It was a week after I'd been humiliated at that conference where I presented my research on the Lacock nuns. I was already feeling pretty glum. So, when she told me about her . . . preferences, I said I couldn't bear playing erotic second fiddle, and she left. I swore I'd never chance anything like that again. Hearing about Daphne, well, I guess it stoked some pretty ugly memories."

Verity uncrossed Anastasia's arms and held her hands. "I'm not Daisy. I'm old school—one lover at a time, and preferably for a long time," she said. Anastasia's face visibly eased. "And despite your bravado, you're an old-school softy too. Though I have to admit, yours is a pretty clever disguise."

"Promise you won't betray my secret."

"Promise," Verity said, crossing her heart.

Then, like a comedian about to punch her audience in the guts, Anastasia's tone shifted again. "There's one tiny problem with your Poissy theory, though."

"What's that? Verity asked.

"The abbey there was almost totally destroyed during the French Revolution. I doubt we'll find any evidence of that breviary. With or without Daphne's help."

Recognizing that changing the subject was Anastasia's version of extending an olive branch, Verity brightened. "Even those anticlerical revolutionaries would've recognized the worth of those manuscripts. If they looted the treasures of Poissy, they must've stored them somewhere or sold them. How else did they wind up in libraries and collections centuries later, unless they'd been preserved? I think it's worth trying to trace them. Don't you?"

A sly look came over Anastasia. "My intrepid, indefatigable, lovable sleuth, how could I ever refuse a proposal to while away the hours in Paris with you?" She brushed her fingers across Verity's face. "If we hurry, we can catch the last train from St. Pancras and be there before midnight. I know a fabulous hotel. I'll reserve a room for us and meet you at the station in an hour."

Verity poured the last of the champagne into their glasses. "It's not presumption that leads us, but our great desire to see beautiful things. May the Cumaean Sybil guide us."

"Based on the beautiful things I've glimpsed so far, I'll drink to that."

"Now you're making *me* blush," Verity said.

As the Eurostar entered the Chunnel, Verity fell asleep on Anastasia's shoulder, awakening an hour and a half later at Gare du Nord. "I missed the evening snack," she said, yawning.

"You didn't miss much," Anastasia said. "A piece of overcooked chicken, a withered salad, and a rather disappointing glass of red wine. Not worth a Michelin asterisk, much less a star. We should have up-graded."

"Not on my budget." Verity pulled her backpack down from the shelf, put on her coat, and followed Anastasia to the front of the carriage to retrieve their suitcases. "How far is the hotel from here?"

"Far enough for a taxi. My treat." Anastasia led them outside the station. Even near midnight, Paris bustled with life. *"Rive Gauche, dix-neuf Quai Voltaire,"* Anastasia directed the driver of a waiting cab through his open window, while signaling for Verity to hop in.

The taxi sped along the crowded boulevards of the Right Bank. As if dodging obstacles on a pinball machine, mopeds weaved in and out among the cars. Long lines of revelers snaked around the corners outside late-night music venues, awaiting entry to the midnight show. On the terraces of cafés, scores of Parisians held forth in animated conversation or languished over a glass of wine as if time were nothing more than a killjoy's invention.

"A decade ago, I spent my days here in the archives, and my nights were spent cataloguing the results at a wobbly desk in a cramped little room I rented from an ex-pat American my adviser had introduced me to. I barely sampled Parisian life." Verity squeezed Anastasia's hand. "I promise not to make that mistake again."

"That, my scrumptious one, is a promise I'll hold you to," Anastasia said, adding, in a tantalizing whisper that made Verity tingle, "beginning tonight."

The taxi driver took a circuitous route, zigzagging through the many one-way streets toward Île de la Cité. As they reached the Pont Notre Dame to cross to the Left Bank of the Seine, the bells of the cathedral tolled midnight. Lit by the full moon, the river glistened like liquefied crystal. Up and down its length, the bridges of Paris sparkled like strings of luminous pearls.

"Anastasia must have walked across this bridge five centuries ago to reach the Left Bank, where the parchment-makers' *ateliers* were housed," Verity said aloud.

"Certainly not this very one. It's stone and paved in concrete," Anastasia quipped.

"Oh, don't be so literal," Verity said. "I know the old wooden bridges collapsed or were destroyed in fires. If your vivid imagination can be permitted to conjure nuns *in flagrante delicto*, then mine can be allowed to fantasize about meandering these streets with my medieval artist."

"Meander with her all you want, my love, as long as your heart gallops back to me."

Verity squeezed her arm, recognizing the sign of what she now thought of as one of Anastasia's "Daphne" moments, reminding herself that feeling vulnerable was the shadow side of falling in love.

Turning west along the Left Bank, the taxi sped past rows and rows of the locked wooden stalls of the booksellers of Paris. They lined the cobblestone sidewalks above the riverbank whose slopes had been occupied by vineyards until the thirteenth century. The color green that was painted on those stalls evoked the city's medieval agricultural heritage as much as the many antiquarian shops, filled with maps and books and drawings, along the left side of the quay recalled the work of the artists whose *ateliers* once had stood in their place. *On the shoulders of giants*, Verity mused, ceding to Newton his due in the realm of epistemology, adding a caveat. *And sometimes the giants were women.*

"*Nous sommes arrivé*," the driver said, pulling in front of a quaint hotel. A sign above the arched doorway identified the eighteenth-century limestone structure as Hotel du Quai Voltaire, while a marble plaque to the right announced that Baudelaire, Sibelius, Wagner, and Wilde had once slept there.

"A shelter for Romantics and Revolutionaries," Verity commented, "on a street named after an intellectual outlaw."

"And originally a convent. A perfect place to rest before our iconoclastic enterprise, I should think," Anastasia said. She paid the taxi driver and walked toward the lobby. "I considered another hotel near Place Vendôme, to honor your communardes toppling Bonaparte off that hideous pedestal, but it's become an overpriced tourist trap since I was last here. Besides, when you see our room, you'll understand why I chose this one."

"I can't wait." Verity masked the tiniest bit of trepidation behind a tentative smile.

"And you're not to worry about the expense; as I told you, my university awarded me a hefty travel budget." Anastasia took Verity's arm and led her inside.

Around the lobby were portraits of famous visitors. Besides Wilde and Wagner, Camille Pissaro's scraggly bearded face stared at Verity from the wall behind the reception desk. Not a rogues' gallery, but a very male assembly of the renowned, she thought. After checking in, they took an elevator to a large, high-ceilinged room on the fourth floor. Verity turned on the lights and gasped at the bright red carpet, the same color as the flying red vertical stripe on the French tricolor, the same as Marianne's Phrygian cap, iconic symbol of the Republic.

"All the rooms in the hotel are decorated in red or blue, the colors of Paris," Anastasia explained. "I picked red, the color of liberty—and passion."

"It's certainly passionately present in this room."

"That's not the only reason I chose it." Anastasia pointed toward the tall French doors on the far side of the room. "Stand there, close your eyes, and don't open them until I say."

Verity obliged. A cool breeze whispered over her. Anastasia moved behind her and wrapped her arms around her. "Now look."

What she saw astonished her to silence. Through a border of bare trees standing at attention along the boulevard like an army of ancient skeletons, the monumental structure of the Louvre shined like an illuminated painting, its magisterial image mirrored in the rippling waters of the Seine. Bands of light spilled across the river toward the Left Bank, climbed the walls of the hotel, and made Verity feel as if she were standing both in the past and on the threshold of the future. Six centuries ago, the king's library had been located in a corner of the northwest tower of the museum. She imagined a woman bent over a book, while another woman attended nearby: her uncompromising, stalwart support. And she imagined herself reaching across the centuries to pull them into the present and dignify them with the action of remembrance.

15

ON THE ROAD TO POISSY

BÉATRICE

A wearying winter entombed Paris in a dark pall of disease and destruction as the long tentacles of the Black Death once again climbed over the walled city and slithered into the households of rich and poor alike. I was spared, as I had been decades before. Yet the smell of putrefying flesh and the inconsolable cries of neighbors, shrieking in horror over the deformed bodies of their beloveds, pulled me into a catacomb of painful memories of my father and sisters' demises, making me weep over images I'd long ago buried in an unmarked grave in my mind.

Christine was away from the city when calamity struck, and returned to the heartbreaking discovery that her mother had succumbed to the pestilence. Wan and pale with sorrow, she turned to me for succor. Remembering the motherly care Madame Bonhomme had showered on me in my desperate hour of need, I offered her a quiet room in my residence above my *atelier* and nursed her as if she were my own daughter. Sharing meals and stories with equal brio strengthened the bonds of our fabricated filiation with the nourishment of food, the sinews of artistic devotion, and the mutual understanding of loss's trauma. We were motherless women, bereft of our progeny—she by her daughter's departure to a convent and her son's departure to an apprenticeship with a knight in a warring land abroad, and I by nature's mysterious turn—rediscovering in friendship's generosity a reservoir of care.

One day, as spring began to announce its arrival in the low warbles of songbirds punctuating the warming air, I was preparing my inks and quills to complete a commission when Christine entered my studio.

"I do not wish to disturb your concentration, but might I sit beside you while you work?" she asked.

"On the contrary." I turned toward her, heartened to see that a healthy rosiness finally had returned to her cheeks. "Your presence would inspire my hand to its finest achievement."

"I fear I've overburdened you with my sorrows." She bowed her head in embarrassment.

I refused to allow self-pity to pollute the well of self-confidence I knew she still harbored inside her. "A wise woman once taught me that to console another is more a gift than a burden." She looked at me with a quizzical expression. "Providing comfort repays kindnesses once shown to the comforter." The corners of her mouth arched into a forced smile. I continued: "Would you like to see the illustration I'm crafting?" Her smile broadened, crinkling her eyes. I opened the quires to a folio where I'd painted a scene of the Nativity. "It's for a breviary intended for a nobleman's daughter, who will soon enter the Dominican Abbey at Poissy."

With a delicate touch, her finger traced the outline of the Virgin's face. "Those almond eyes, those wavy brown tresses. Such a beauty. Precisely as I remember her."

"*Remember* her?" I worried grief might have wounded her mind with madness.

"My daughter, now at Poissy. You've never met her, but have evoked her image precisely."

I recalled our first meeting, a few years ago, when the mention of a convent seemed to have disturbed her. At the time, I had discounted it as nothing more than minor prejudice born of experience with the hypocrisy of clergy, such as I had once had. Now I understood that Poissy named a more personal pain. Before I could imagine a way to salve it, she'd hit upon a plan.

"I was adamant that no daughter of mine would enter the religious life. But my mother persuaded me to allow Marie to choose her own path, reminding me that a meditative life was no less worthy a vocation than my devotion to secular learning. I've not seen my daughter in the three years since she left. Your generosity has redoubled my desire to visit her and pay homage to her choice. Will you accompany me on this humbling journey?"

"I'd be honored." I rose from my desk to retrieve another set of quires from the shelves nearby. "To show our respect to the holy women she has joined, I propose that we create a breviary of the finest quality as a gift in your daughter's name."

"What flawless vellum!" she exclaimed, stroking the folios.

With a sheepish grin, I explained the source. "The last of the precious material salvaged from that scoundrel, Pierre Bonhomme, will soon grace the holy library at Poissy."

Overcome with laughter, she set to work at once with her quill and plummet, ruling the pages, readying them for scripting the psalms and liturgical prayers.

We worked tirelessly through the season of Lent. Near the start of Holy Week, Christine surprised me with a proposal to visit the library Charles V had installed decades ago in the Louvre. She had very particular ideas for the breviary and wanted to consult some manuscripts among the king's vast collection.

"There's one, in particular, I remember reading as a child. A magnificent book, which the king had inscribed in his own hand. It had elegant borders, filled with flowers and grotesques and animals dancing around the edges of the prayers, and miniatures featuring knights and virtuous ladies. I long to show it to you for inspiration."

"I'd be honored to visit and observe," I said, barely able to contain my excitement to see not only the breviary but also, nestled among the manuscripts in the tower, a few of the paintings I'd fashioned decades ago for a manuscript in the king's collection of advice manuals.

On a March day, we set out by cart for the castle. Dark clouds scurried across the horizon, portending a storm. When we arrived at the courtyard, Gilles Malet, the royal librarian whose acquaintance Christine had made in her earliest years in Paris, greeted us.

"Madame de Castel, I'm delighted to welcome you again. And how is your dear mother?"

I worried that his question would disturb the tranquility Christine had so recently found, but she answered him calmly. "She's been taken to the angels, a just reward for an exemplary life."

"Please forgive my ignorance and accept my deepest sympathies," he said, bowing before her.

"You could not be expected to have known. I appreciate the kindness of your concern." She curtsied and quickly changed the subject. "May I introduce you to Mademoiselle Anastasia Tapis, the finest illuminator in all of Paris. She is preparing paintings for a breviary for my daughter, Marie. I hoped to show her samples of the king's collection, especially the one I most admire—the prayer book Charles the Wise acquired from Jeanne de Belleville."

"I'm happy to escort you to the library, but I regret the Belleville Breviary is no longer among the king's manuscripts. When the princess Isabella was betrothed to Richard of England, it was sent as part of her dowry. It now belongs to his successor, Henry IV."

A shadow of anger as threatening as the assembling clouds crossed Christine's expression. "Must all our most precious possessions find their way to our enemy?" I understood her outburst to be as much directed against herself as at the English. Her son, Jean, served as a page in the court of the Earl of Salisbury, whom she'd befriended during his visit to Paris soon after the young Isabella's marriage. She'd hoped the position would improve his prospects, never imagining a scheming coveter would usurp the throne and threaten her son's protector. After imprisoning Richard and declaring himself king, Henry Bolingbroke had the Earl slaughtered, took Jean into his court, and demanded that the "most famous woman of letters" come to England as ransom. While Monsieur Malet led us to the library, remaining respectfully silent as if Christine's bitter words weren't still ringing in the air, I calculated how we might right this wrong, even though I knew little about English politicking.

We entered a room with shelves of manuscripts extending three stories high. I'd never seen such an extraordinary monument to learning. The Abbess's collection, overwhelming to me in my youth, would have fit into a small corner of this great room. "What an assembly of works!" I exclaimed, while the wheels of my scheming mind turned toward the outlines of a rescue plan. Perhaps books could become Christine's much-needed currency in the game of political intrigue into which her son had been unwittingly caught.

"Charles was a learned king. He intended his collection to become the provenance of all France, to guide good governance and encourage virtue. A library is supposed to be used, not simply possessed," Christine said.

Her words stimulated the plot taking root in my mind. If books were the lifeblood nurturing the world's remembrance of the wisdom of ages, then they were meant to shine brightly and be seen as widely as the stars in the celestial sky. Yet my fiery illuminations could as easily attract a posturing prince as the seeker of learning, drawing him to ruin like a moth to a flame. I had hit upon a way we might ensnare Henry Bolingbroke in the ropes of greed thrown out of his own grasping tentacles.

"I'll take you to the king's study, where I frequently read. I regret you'll not see the Belleville, but there are equally accomplished illuminations to explore." That she seemed eager to oversee the selection of drawings for her daughter's gift signaled to me that her fortitude had returned. As I'd been taught by masters I soon surpassed, so Christine had grown in independence under my tutelage. I now wanted to find my earliest paintings in the king's collection, to subject them to her critique and take the opportunity to engage her in a plot to return her son to her, unscathed.

On a shelf alongside other manuals of princely advice on the second story of the library, I located the compilation in question. Side by side, at a desk below one of the grated windows filtering light onto the folios, we pondered the strengths and weaknesses of those images of mine. I was a little taken aback at the distance between my memory of how accomplished they'd been and how primitive they appeared to me now.

"Your rendition of Charles is an extraordinary likeness, down to the bulbous nose. The depth and coloration of the presentation background is accomplished. But I'd prefer the sharper modulations of tone in your later works for this new project. The introduction of verdigris in the palette for the manger scene might add a hopeful note, don't you think?"

"You've a sharp eye, as well as a sharp wit," I teased. "Adding a touch of turmeric to an indigo base should achieve the desired effect. Speaking of hope, I've an idea about how to secure your son's return." I laid out my plan: We would send two books of her poetry, each embellished with a portrait of Christine gifting the treasures to Henry. Accompanying the gifts would be her letter requesting that Jean be returned to France to escort his mother personally across the rugged sea to an unfamiliar land, a journey I assured her she would never have to make. "The flattery of receiving autograph copies imprinted with his own likeness will be persuasive enough evidence of your seriousness of purpose to entice him to fall for the scheme."

"Your mind works along devious tracks as well as on the pathways of beauty," she said with a smile sparkling with delight.

"I have found that less straightforward routes are sometimes necessary detours toward a desired end, and absolutely essential when dealing with those whose power has made them fall for the fiction of their own invincibility, making them peculiarly vulnerable to counterattack."

"Were I ever to write a book on the art of warfare, your wisdom would be one of its tenets," she quipped.

"Delighted to add to any such manual, as long as you fashion a discourse on just war."

"In my opinion, no other kind of combat is worthy of a treatise, except one of condemnation."

We agreed to add the presentation portraits to our list of needed illuminations and spent the waning hours of daylight making notes about designs for miniatures on the breviary folios for the summer and winter prayers. Around each page of Christine's glorious script, I would fashion foliated borders with sprays of acanthus leaves and spiraling vines in ultramarine and crimson. She was amused when I suggested affixing my signature peacock—symbol of resurrection and the meaning of my name—onto pages featuring scenes of the Nativity and the Virgin's assumption heavenward. At last light, we exited the library into the air crisped to cool by the afternoon's rain. The sky was clear, and the first stars peeked out from the heavens, twinkling illuminations to guide us, two intrepid seekers on the long path of learning that still lay ahead, at least for one of us, for I was in the autumn of my years.

In early April, when crocuses poked their tiny purple and yellow heads from crevices in the thawed earth, we completed the breviary, which the *relieur* bound in red leather and tooled in gold. I packed a basket of provisions and wrapped linen around the precious object. We walked to stables along the Seine to select horses for our journey to Poissy, some twenty-five miles beyond the city walls. I picked an older gray mare, while Christine chose a dark brown palfrey, saying its color reminded her of the horse Charles V had given to the emperor as a gift on the occasion of his visit to Paris.

"That was the year of my betrothal; one of many far happier years than now, both for France and for me," she said, attaching the bridle to her horse, securing the strap on the horse's right flank to stabilize her planchette, or footstool, and, after arranging her skirt, mounting him sidesaddle with aplomb. In the recent months of our mutual labor, she'd entrusted me with her views about the political turmoil besetting the land—the discord over the proper administration of the regency between Philip, the Duke of Burgundy and uncle to the incapacitated king, and Louis, the Duke of Orléans and the king's younger brother. "I fear Philip is scheming with Isabeau, the king's wife, to wrest control from Louis, the adviser whom the king himself assigned to govern should he be unable."

"Might you not intervene, since your standing at court has increased?" Recent gifts of her books to Charles VI, Louis, and Isabeau had returned her to noble favor. Yet, as I'd come to understand, the political winds can shift with the flick of a royal wrist as easily as sand moves through an hourglass. More than once, she'd plied one faction with the promise of a manuscript, only to see the agreement undone by death or some other changed circumstance.

"In my verse, I've warned of the dangers of jealousy and plots against rank. But I must be cautious, or I'll jeopardize my own life."

My mottled past and our plot to trick Henry precluded me from discoursing against expediency's remedy. Time had taught me the hard lesson that those who stick fast to some established rule of conduct, no matter the circumstances, will be the last to judge right from wrong. "Perhaps you'll find a way to appeal to the queen's more peaceable nature," I suggested, bridling and mounting my steed. "Indirection can prove useful to the task."

"Indirection?"

"You once told me your writing was intended to awaken sympathy for women's plight as well as for that of our beloved France. Might you not plead for fealty and virtue in the realm over contention and vice through stories of your own experiences?"

Christine fell silent as we ambled along the pathway to the city's northwest gate, leaving Paris and its disarray behind for the tranquility of a sylvan setting canopied by leafy junipers and yew, and carpeted with the ivory petals of hawthorn and whitebeam. For more than an hour, the only sounds interrupting our reverie were birdsong and the steady *clop-clop* of horses' hooves. As it did more often now than in my youth, the quiet propelled me into a tunnel of memory. I wandered among shards of the past—some cheerful, others not—until I was jolted out of contemplation's passageway when Christine halted her steed, pointing to an apparition taking shape in the near distance.

A golden-haired woman wearing a flowing white gown and a fierce look on her face sat astride a white horse. She carried a bejeweled goblet in one hand and a curved staff in the other and raised it to greet us. Christine dismounted, approached the shimmering revenant, and knelt before her. I remained still, holding the horses at bay, bearing witness.

"Daughter, be not afraid, I have come to comfort you, and disarm you of the ignorance that blinds your intelligence, making you reject what you know for certain and believe what you do not know. Exchange error and mere opinion for truth and know that all the evil things said about women only hurt those who say them, and not women themselves. Recover your good sense, given to you through experience. In the place you're about to visit you will find the outlines of a well-ordered space in which justice and peace can thrive."

Now prostrate before the regal lady, Christine cried out: "Who could be sufficiently grateful for such a privilege? I accept this noble commission with great joy."

The woman responded: "Up and about now, daughter! Go without delay to the field of letters: there, the City of Ladies will be founded on flat and fertile ground."

Were I not awake, I might have sworn that I had dreamt what I saw.

Emboldened by this vision, Christine's spirit soared. She continued toward the abbey at such a remarkable pace, I was breathless by the time we reached the gate. The abbey grounds were a spectacular sight. From the spouts of magnificent fountains near the entrance, newly renovated by order of the king, waters danced and glistened like jeweled necklaces in the springtime sun. We dismounted and meandered past the chapel toward the cloister. The prioress's lodgings stood apart in a cluster of buildings housing the nuns of noble families, separated from the main dormitory by an array of gardens. Profuse with daisies, primrose, and hollyhocks, the cornucopia of colors and aromas made me swoon in sensorial delight.

Marie de Bourbon, prioress of the abbey and sister-in-law to Charles the Wise, greeted us at her lodging, while a young woman of no more than eighteen stood silently next to her, head bowed. I recognized her immediately as Christine's daughter.

Barely acknowledging the prioress's welcome, Christine rushed to her daughter's side. The young woman knelt before her mother in a gesture of humility and homage, then glanced up at her with a glorious smile and asked for her blessing. "Your visit honors me and this holy place, Mother."

"Your presence in it honors me more," Christine replied. Then, turning to the prioress, she said, "As a token of my daughter's commitment to the devotional life, I wish to present a breviary to Poissy in her name."

I removed the precious object from my satchel and handed it to Christine.

"We graciously accept your generous donation," the prioress said. "Let us retire to my chambers, better to view your gift."

The prioress's rooms were not sumptuous but were well appointed. She led us to a long table and unwrapped the manuscript from its linen encasing. "A beautifully presented celebration of prayer," she remarked. Opening to the folio of the Nativity, she marveled at the finely drawn visage of the Virgin kneeling before her child. Noticing the resemblance to Christine's Marie, she smiled and turned to Christine. "You have conveyed to the artist illuminating this masterpiece the very essence of your daughter's humility. She is, indeed, an imitation of the Virgin's willingness to serve God with the whole of her being. It is fitting that he has portrayed the Holy Mother of God in her likeness."

"Not he, she," Christine said, gesturing in my direction. "Anastasia is the painter of all the images in this breviary."

"All the more reason for us to store this masterpiece in pride of place in the abbey library, Madame de Castel."

Christine, Marie, and I supped apart from the prioress that evening, served by the lower sisters of the order, who later toured us around the grounds. I remarked that the surroundings were far more spacious and attractive than the abbey in which I'd lived for more than a decade. Christine took note. "Perhaps you're thinking of leaving Paris for the bucolic life?" she teased.

"Certainly not! At least not before I've helped you build that city you've been called to found," I whispered.

We lingered long in the company of Christine's daughter and then took our leave. Nightfall made it too late to travel all the way back to Paris. At an inn a mile from Poissy, we found shelter. After Christine retired to her room, I walked into the garden behind the building to admire the starry night. The glorious clusters sparkling in the inky sky invited my gaze to linger long enough to see animals dance with goddesses in luxurious fields while the distant chords of Orpheus's sweet music spilled an ancient song into the warm air, soothing my weary soul with a vision of peace, readying my aging body for the journey ahead.

16

A BRIDGE TO THE PAST,
A WAY TO THE FUTURE

VERITY

Verity awoke from a disorienting dream a little before dawn. In the dream, she was naked, walking along the Seine. She passed a group of peasants on the Left Bank gathering hay into bushels. A barge floated by filled with revelers, singing and dancing. The bells of all the churches in Paris began to ring in unison. On the embankment above the river, she met a woman wearing a soldier's uniform and carrying a rifle. "You look better than when I last saw you," the woman said.

"I'm naked," Verity said, curiously unashamed.

"There's a difference between being exposed and being naked. Only those well-wadded with stupidity fail to understand that. It's good you slowed down. Otherwise, you would've missed Anastasia."

She got out of bed, gently removing her lover's arm from around her waist, pulled on her robe, and walked to the window. Outside, the sun slowly crested into a golden orb above the majestic Louvre, as dawn stretched her rosy fingers across the morning sky. The sight was too beautiful for Verity to witness alone, so she returned to bed and kissed Anastasia awake.

"Mmm, what a lovely alarm clock," Anastasia whispered.

"Come see this." Verity pulled her up and wrapped her in another robe.

They stood together, framed by the open doors to the tiny balcony, in silent homage to the breaking day, to an unlikely encounter, and to the slipperiness of time, holding each other in between the ever-ticking moments of now and then.

"I hate to break the spell, my darling, but I have to pee." Anastasia dashed into the bathroom. "Back in a jiff," she said, closing the door with a bang.

Outside, the day roared at full throttle. Cars raced along the boulevard while pedestrians maneuvered around each other on the crowded sidewalks. Verity watched the booksellers opening their stalls, arranging their displays of literary wares like sacred talismans of centuries past. A street sweeper pushed his cart along the embankment, concentrating on collecting scraps of debris as if he were collecting gold. The sound of the shower broke Verity's reverie. She pulled on her jeans and a bulky sweater, grabbed her wallet from her backpack, and walked down the four flights to the lobby and out into the chill November air. At the corner café, construction workers were downing small glasses of brandy to fortify themselves for a day's labor. Verity ordered two lattés and returned to the room to find Anastasia seated in a chair, still in her robe, holding something in her hand and looking upset.

"You should've left a note," she said. "I was worried."

"Where'd you think I went?" Verity handed the frothy brew to Anastasia. "I heard the shower and figured I'd get us coffee."

"Still, a note would've been nice." Anastasia took the cup.

"You're being silly," Verity said.

"I suppose I'm being silly about this too." Anastasia threw something across the room. Verity bent to pick it up and saw it was the card Daphne, the Royal Societies' librarian, had given her.

"You went through my backpack?"

"I was looking for a pen and found that woman's phone number instead. When were you planning to see her again?"

Verity looked at Anastasia oddly, unable to shake the idea that they were about to have their first real fight. "I wasn't planning on anything. I told you she helped me with the research and asked me to let her know if—

"Or would you even have told me you were seeing her? Just string me along and drop me when I'm no longer useful." Anastasia covered her face with her hands.

Verity walked over to her, knelt down, and uncovered Anastasia's face, revealing a pained, frightened expression. "What's gotten into you?"

"You! You've gotten into me," Anastasia said, burrowing into the chair, wrapping her long hair around herself like a shield and crossing her arms. "When I came out of the bathroom and didn't see you, I panicked. I thought maybe you were annoyed, you know, that I didn't dawdle with you at the sunrise—"

"You said you had to pee."

"And then I found that card and it absolutely gutted me." Tears welled in her eyes. "The truth is, being embarrassed isn't a very British thing to admit, or we'd probably have lost the Empire sooner than we did, but I hate how I look in the morning. All puffy and ruffled, like some disheveled peacock."

"I love the way you look," Verity said, brushing a lock of Anastasia's hair away from where it had fallen across her face. Night, noon"—she opened her lover's robe to caress her—"but especially in the morning."

"You're just saying that. Daisy told me I look—"

Verity touched her fingers to Anastasia's lips. "Hush, my darling. Daisy and her chain of acolytes have long departed." She kissed Anastasia's belly. "Besides, I like your feathers best when they're ruffled."

Anastasia relaxed into Verity's embrace, falling into the rhythm of lovemaking.

Verity laid out the Paris map on the desk to check the route to Poissy. With her finger, she traced the Seine bisecting the heart of Paris before snaking around the edge of the Bois de Boulogne toward St. Denis, continuing in widening S-curves until reaching the outskirts of Paris and spilling onward all the way to the Atlantic port of Le Havre. "It must've taken all day for Christine to travel to Poissy on horseback." She finished off the last of a basket of croissants Anastasia had ordered from room service and put the map into her backpack. "It looks like we can get a fast train from Paris-Saint Lazare."

"I'm relieved to know we're not undertaking a medieval reenactment." Anastasia laced up her boots.

"You're certainly in a better mood," Verity teased.

"Your remedy worked like a charm." Anastasia grabbed Verity's hand. *"Allons-y."*

It took forty minutes to reach Poissy. They stopped for a leisurely lunch near the station and then picked up a guidebook at the tourist office on Boulevard Robespierre, heading west toward the abbey ruins.

"I know Christine lived and worked in the center of Paris, but I feel her presence in these streets," Verity said.

"I'm not at all surprised." Anastasia tugged Verity's arm and pointed across the street to a modern building in the middle of a semicircular enclave of structures. It featured a prominent sign identifying it as the *Médiathèque Christine de Pizan*.

Verity gasped. "A library dedicated to Christine! Let's take a look."

"Whither thou leadest, I'll follow, my lovely. Nothing thrills my romantic's heart more than stacks and stacks of books," Anastasia said without a jot of sarcasm.

Books weren't the only things plentiful in the library. It contained a theater for musical and dramatic performances and a screening room for films. A small half-circle of a salon down a corridor on the first floor was dedicated to storytelling gatherings for youths. The main reading room housed an immense collection of magazines, dossiers, and local artifacts for adults to browse. An array of DVDs and record albums undulated along one wall of the reception area, while a bank of computers dotted another. A bulletin board announced an upcoming poetry evening to be accompanied by a jazz band. The space was a cultural cornucopia of multimedia delight.

If Mrs. Fairweather's London flat with Morris's reproductions of medieval prints made Verity feel like she was living inside an illuminated
manuscript, then standing inside the Christine de Pizan library evoked
the sensation of having entered the architectural embodiment of an electrified Harley 4431, amplified with surround-sound, and populated by
the descendants of knights, ladies, nobles, and peasants who'd once in-
habited Christine's books. She was so overwhelmed, she didn't notice
that Anastasia had wandered over to one of the computers and was now
gesticulating for her to join her.

"Look at this." Anastasia pointed to an article on the screen from
Le Monde. "I typed 'Poissy Medieval Breviary' into Google to see what
might pop up." She scrolled back to the headline announcing that, last
year, the French Cultural Ministry had blocked an attempted sale of
a fifteenth-century breviary to a foreigner by a wealthy French family,
named Lescaux.

"I did an internet search in the Antiquaries' Society, and nothing
turned up." Verity sat down at the computer next to Anastasia. "Different search history, different algorithms, I suppose." She entered the web
address to read the article herself. By the time she reached the end, she
was shaking.

This rare, beautifully illuminated prayer book was associated with the
Abbey at Poissy. It was acquired by William Morris on a trip to Paris in
1858. Several years after Morris's death, an American family purchased the
manuscript from Henry Wellcome for their private collection. Their descen-
dants later sold it to the Lescaux family. The French state has blocked the sale
of this medieval masterpiece because, in the words of the Minister of Culture,
"such an extraordinary object belongs in the collection of the Bibliothèque
Nationale, accessible to everyone." A spokesperson for the Ministry declared
it "a light into the past, still flickering brightly after six hundred years."
Among the many extraordinarily well-preserved images found on its folios,
an unusual portrait of two women, heads bent in prayer, was found behind
the interior back binding.

"I need some air," she said. "I feel nauseous."

"Let's walk to the abbey grounds," Anastasia said. "The gardens are
refreshing, even in the fall."

"I feel so close to finding what I'm looking for, and yet so far from proving the existence of that phantom, Anastasia."

"On the cusp of discovery, it's not unusual to feel flummoxed by doubt," Anastasia said. "Think of my mermaids."

"I *am* thinking of them. Your wild-eyed theory got you laughed off the academic stage."

"Which only strengthened my conviction, my darling." Anastasia's eyes sparkled with mischievous delight. "As have you."

Verity looked at her quizzically. "I don't understand."

"A wild-eyed patience has taken us this far, as your quixotic pursuit has reminded me. If we allowed narrow-mindedness to dismiss every idea that scratched against the grain of the conventional, we'd still be stuck on the flat earth, and you'd never have dared to cross the pond."

"I could kiss you right now," Verity said.

"Plenty of time for that later. Another Anastasia begs attention."

Taking a circuitous route to avoid heavily trafficked streets, they walked hand in hand along smaller avenues of the town. Anastasia recited the names appearing on the placards. "Ursulines, Capucines—all roads lead to the cities of women who once lived here."

In the late afternoon sky, the sun made its steady descent toward the horizon, bathing the leafless trees along the avenues in a quiet, lemon light. Verity looked up at the street sign. *Honestly, either I've gone mad or she's egging me on.* A right turn had taken them onto Avenue Christine de Pizan.

"As I should've expected, we're being guided by your Cumaean Sybil," Anastasia said, as if reading Verity's mind. "That one's for sale." She pointed to a small stucco house with red shuttered windows surrounded by a serene, well-manicured garden.

"In my state of mind, you shouldn't tempt me," Verity said.

"Temptation is the unsung handmaiden of insight." Anastasia's wit had returned in full force.

The paved avenue sloped downhill and soon reached a narrower cobblestone pathway that led toward the abbey gardens. A placard affixed to a gate announced entrance to the Priory's grange, now a public park. Decorating the placard was a scene of Christine de Pizan's visit to the Dominican convent, commemorated in her own words: *Here one finds the sweetest paradise full of stunning birds and blossoming flowers.* As they continued down the pathway, Verity trailed her fingers along ancient walls enclosing modern houses built on the footprints of the cloister that had once sequestered a community of nuns. Ahead of them stood the turreted towers of the gatehouse, all that was left of the ruins.

"Would you have chosen the cloistered life if you'd been born in the fifteenth century?" Verity asked as they neared the entrance.

"I'd certainly have preferred convent life to being married to some old gizzard twice my age," Anastasia replied.

"Christine was happily married to Étienne."

"But, in the forty years after she was widowed, she never married again," Anastasia said. "What does that tell you?"

"She was devoted to her art," Verity replied.

"And to the company of women," Anastasia added.

"I don't think she was a lesbian," Verity said.

"In the words of Adrienne Rich, I'd say she was on the continuum."

Verity laughed. "I'll leave that bit out of my speculative history," Verity said. "For now."

"What about you? Convent, concubinage, or coverture?" Anastasia asked with a gleam in her eye.

"No transgendered option?"

"Joan of Arc tried, and look where that got her."

"I thought you said the Middle Ages weren't all gloom and doom."

Anastasia's expression grew more serious. "They weren't. Something beautiful emerged despite the horrors of those centuries, as you've discovered in the illuminated manuscripts. I once heard the renowned historian, Régine Peroud, give a lecture on medieval art. She said manuscript ornamentation wasn't idle decoration but a vital, emotive force enlivening the surface of things to reflect the beauty of the invisible. I thought what she said was spot on. I suppose that's what attracted me to this period of history—the idea that beauty can emerge in the middle of horror." She turned toward Verity, her eyes filled with emotion. She tried to speak, but couldn't manage a word.

Verity touched her fingers to Anastasia's lips. "You don't have to say anything; I already know."

"But you don't know, not everything," Anastasia said.

"If you're talking about your own sad story, I don't need to know more than you've already leaked until you're really ready to tell me, okay?"

Anastasia nodded and breathed a sigh of relief.

Just before dusk, they came to an open gate and walked through it into a verdant field littered with the autumn colors of fallen leaves, and sat down on a bench under a tree. The air whispered to silence. Anastasia rested her head on Verity's shoulder. Around them, the outlines of ancient cloisters drew themselves in Verity's imagination. Two veiled women approached the arched entryway to the Abbey ruins on horseback and dismounted. One of them glanced back at Verity and smiled.

"Maybe Anastasia traveled with Christine when she visited her daughter, Marie, at Poissy," Verity said. "She might have decorated that breviary as a gift for the daughter. But, if she left it at Poissy, who put the orphaned page with the painting of the two women into the back of the breviary? That's what I can't figure out. But at least I know now Siddal could have seen the original in Morris's collection."

Anastasia said nothing; she'd fallen asleep.

"Hey, sleeping beauty. We have to go," Verity said, nudging Anastasia awake. "It's getting dark, and I'm eager to return to the twenty-first century and enjoy a large glass of red wine."

A twenty-minute train ride deposited them back at the Saint-Lazare station. Fifteen minutes later, after splurging on a taxi—"courtesy of the British taxpayer," as Anastasia put it—they were sharing coq au vin and a good bottle of Burgundy in a dimly lit Left Bank café not far from the hotel.

Verity tore off a piece of baguette, dipped it into the rich sauce, and stared into the candle flickering like Scheherazade's illuminated twin. "Maybe she was buried at Poissy."

"Christine? Not likely," Anastasia said, taking a sip of wine. "The region had fallen into the grubby hands of the English-supporting Burgundians, and she was forced from Paris into exile for siding with the Orléanists, who favored the king."

Verity: "I meant Anastasia."

Anastasia: "Now I can hear my mermaids singing! More wine?" Verity nodded. "Please, speculate away," Anastasia continued.

Encouraged, Verity wove the threads of a story into a pattern that had begun to take shape in her mind over the last few days like a medieval tapestry.

"Christine gifted her manuscripts to curry favor with various nobles. Except for that breviary, which I believe she gave to the convent to honor her daughter. It would have been the one book containing Anastasia's paintings that she could have reclaimed without offending a political faction. Maybe after Anastasia died, Christine requested that her friend be buried at Poissy, and because her daughter was still there and understood the importance of the artist to the writer, Marie asked that the breviary be returned to Christine, who would have wanted to keep it as a memento of the powerful friendship that had given birth to the art."

"Then Christine put that painting inside it for safe-keeping?" Anastasia asked.

"Perhaps." Verity swirled the last of the wine in her glass. "And it stayed with Christine until her own death, when Marie might have asked for it to be returned to her at Poissy."

"An entirely plausible theory. I have one question, though." Anastasia hesitated. "Why was that painting so significant to Christine?"

Verity shrugged. "That's as mysterious as why Siddal chose to paint it on the jewelry box in the first place."

"Perhaps we should spend a day at the French National Library to see if we can uncover a clue."

Verity sighed. Returning to the place where she'd spent months researching the women of the Paris Commune filled her with dread. Then an image from her early-morning dream flashed before her—that woman with the rifle on the embankment. What had she said? Verity couldn't remember, but knew she'd felt emboldened when she woke up, as if she'd seen the sun rise for the first time. "What a great idea," she said.

Anastasia persuaded the lead curator at the *Bibliothèque Nationale* to allow them to view the recently acquired breviary. "How did you manage this?" Verity whispered as they were being escorted to a special manuscript reading room.

"My reputation preceded me," Anastasia replied. "The librarian was familiar with my work on English convents. When I told her I was undertaking a definitive comparative study of the fate of nunneries during the Hundred Years' War, co-authored with a distinguished American colleague, she agreed to a private viewing."

"I'm glad I didn't have to document your claim," Verity said, bemused by Anastasia's willful indiscretion.

"Craft a compelling tale and doors will open," Anastasia said with a naughty smile.

They followed the librarian into the reading room. After she left them with the manuscript, Verity donned the requisite white gloves and began to turn the crackling folio pages of the sacred object that lay disentombed on a red-carpeted stand. Verity's heart skipped a beat when she came to the page with an elaborately detailed miniature scene of the Nativity. The Virgin's serene expression glowed with an ethereal light as if somehow the artist had captured joy, mixed it with ink, and painted it onto a face. A pale halo shimmered around her long brown tresses. Her eyes sparkled with warmth and contentment. She was the embodiment of a soul at peace with itself, in love with the world, alive to the possibility of miracles in the midst of an embittered age. Against the imagery of narrow religious iconography, the artist had created a widening vision, luminous and sacred, inventing something familiar yet altogether unique. There, on the bottom of the page, enmeshed in a cluster of acanthus vines, a tiny, glistening, blue-and-green-feathered creature fanned out its wild-eyed plumes in gaudy display.

Verity touched the page and slipped through time, feeling another woman's fingers intertwine with her own, gently guiding her hand. She closed the manuscript so its back faced her now. The leather binding was marred by nicks and stained by the handling of centuries. As if she were exhuming a body, she opened the back cover to reveal a portrait of two women, one dressed in a gown of ultramarine, the other in scarlet, their profiles illuminated by moonlight, their faces blurred, as if the artist had been interrupted before completing the work.

17

CITIES OF WOMEN,
1401–1405

BÉATRICE

In July 1401, all Paris celebrated the return of the young Isabella, released from her short-lived queenly reign in England to the comfort of the court of her father, Charles VI. A few months later, Christine delighted in welcoming home her son, Jean. As I'd calculated, Henry Bolingbroke had fallen for our scheme. In exchange for the gifts of presentation copies of Christine's poetry and the false promise she'd made to serve the English court, he'd sent Jean back to France to escort his mother across the Channel, a trip she'd never take. I invited Christine and Jean to join Perrette, Ghislaine, and me to make merry over the success of our plan.

In the years they were parted, Christine later told me, her son had grown to resemble his father so much that it sometimes pained her to look at him, though on the night of our planned festivities it was Ghislaine whose expression augured a different kind of discomfort. Opening the door to welcome our guests, she seemed smitten the moment she met with a beguiling smile from the handsome young man with curly hair the color of butter, tantalizingly green eyes, and an air of composure that belied his sixteen years. The starry-eyed look on Ghislaine's face and the reciprocated warmth on Jean's warned me that two hearts were about to be broken. I imagined Christine's ambitions for her son would preclude his betrothal to a woman five years his senior and without a dowry in anything more than quills and ink and decided against orchestrating a match. Such was the hold of a tradition that condoned marriages between older men and younger women but frowned on the reverse, an inequity Christine had yet to critique.

Ghislaine escorted our guests to the parlor, where Perrette had prepared a plate of cheeses and meats. As Ghislaine poured wine into our glasses, we sat down to hear Christine's news.

"With the aid of Louis, Duke of Orléans, I believe I will secure a position for Jean and patronage for my work with Giangaleazzo, Duke of Milan, Louis's father-in-law. Louis promised that his ambassadors would speak favorably to the Milanese court about my son and my writing." Jean struggled to suppress the emotion threatening to erupt on his face. Oblivious to his reaction, Christine continued, "I plan to dedicate my latest work to Louis."

"Given the conflict between the Dukes of Burgundy and Orléans, can you count on Louis's fidelity?" I asked.

She rebuffed any disappointment my question implied with a flick of her hand. "He is the king's closest adviser, faithful to the proper order of the realm. To celebrate his fealty, I've written *Dit de la Rose*, a poem extolling the virtues of loyalty and humility. It will be part of the larger collection of works I described to you last week, Anastasia. I'll give it to Louis as a sign of my gratitude and continued support." She turned to Ghislaine. "I've been impressed with the progress you've made in Anastasia's workshop and hope you'll assist her and Perrette in the ornamentation of this new collection."

Ghislaine's face brightened. "I'd be honored, Madame de Castel." Any lingering hope she'd harbored about a possible liaison with Jean disappeared. Perhaps she understood the risks of love's quixotic temptations more than I'd credited.

"Then it's agreed." Christine raised her glass for a toast. "To the *atelier* of Anastasia Tapis, master illuminator of manuscripts, promoter of women's artistry!" I realized then how wrong I'd been about the source of resistance Christine might have had to a marriage between her son and Ghislaine. Her own ambitions wouldn't allow her to make a match for her son at the expense of her art.

Recently she'd expressed concern at the toll the years had taken on my health. I could no longer hide the fact that although my passion to create beauty was unwavering, my eyes were no longer as sharp nor my hands as steady as once they had been. In my life's twilight, I'd come to depend on the younger woman's talents and energy, along with Perrette's, to assist me on more ambitious projects, such as the one Christine had proposed—a collection of poems and prose of surprisingly inventive forms filled with several elaborate illuminations, scores of puzzle initials, and foliated borders. She wouldn't forgo the support Ghislaine provided to our common endeavors, even if that support came at the expense of her son's happiness. As for Ghislaine, Christine had grasped more clearly than I that the young woman's desire to make art was stronger than any appeal a life of domesticity might have held. And in that, Christine was proved right.

Scarcely had we begun the grand undertaking when Paris erupted in turmoil. Philip, Duke of Burgundy, had stormed the city with an army of knights, intent on challenging Louis's influence with the king. Only the intervention of Queen Isabeau enabled the two sides to agree to a truce, albeit short-lived. Civil strife has an uncanny way of disturbing private peace, as if the atmosphere of conflict infects the vitality of the air we breathe, rendering our bodies vulnerable to illness. Distraught with worry, Christine fell into despair and took to her bed for some weeks of rest. Not long after, we received word that the Duke of Milan had succumbed to a mysterious malady, depriving Christine of a commission and Jean of a protector. To make matters worse, Louis's frequent travels abroad and increasing hostility against the English enabled Philip's schemes against him to gain a foothold.

"Men battle and women suffer," Christine exclaimed some months after she'd recovered. We were planning ornamentation for her collected works for the duke. Ghislaine had already finished the miniatures in grisaille for the first part of the collection and had taken leave to visit family outside the city, leaving us alone to discuss ideas for illuminations she wanted me to craft for a bold work she called *The Book of the City of Ladies*. "I have decided to intervene in this madness to aid Louis and support Isabeau as peacemaker."

"You're planning a defense of women?" I asked.

Christine nodded. "I wish to counter the calumny and invective I've heard too often at court, blaming women for the ills of the world that men have birthed from their brains and pummeled into our hearts with their fists and swords and duplicitous claims of chivalry."

"I worry that you'll be dragged into the fray in ways that may damage your reputation." Jealous rumors had already circulated that Christine was not the author of works bearing her name, but had passed off the work of another poet, a man, as her own.

"You worry too much," she said. "I can withstand any attack those of lesser talent might launch against me. In any case, I refuse to be constrained in a condition of servitude that would prevent me from speaking truth according to my conscience. If one dares impugn me on account of my sex, I have an answer at the ready—it is a small matter to object to what one single man says when he's felt free to blame an entire sex for the world's suffering. I care not if I am called a fool. I'll retort that even a fool can give counsel to a sage."

Her words astonished me with the strength of her conviction. Overcome with a bittersweet mixture of pride and sadness, I rose from the table arrayed with my sketches and moved to the window. Snow dusted the narrow street outside, while a wintry wind whipped the accumulating flakes into wild white swirls. The scene brought back to mind the earliest days of our acquaintance, when uncertainty had threatened to undermine Christine's confidence at every turn of Fortune's wheel. I knew now that that woman had vanished. A stalwart woman, no longer tormented by grief or worry, had taken her place, a woman who presented herself in her prose in a self-effacing costume of humility, yet believed in the unimpeachable authority of insight she'd garnered, and would yet gather into ever-more-beautiful bouquets of learning on the path of long study before her. An arrow of sorrow pierced my heart with the knowledge carried in my aging bones—I'd never witness her reach that journey's end.

"I meant to inspire trust, not cause you distress." She stood next to me now, her hand gently resting on my shoulder. "You've counseled me like a mother, bridling my fear, emboldening my will. I've drawn strength from your strength. I am the legacy of the beauty that you've shown me exists beyond the enveloping bleakness of this world."

Unable as I was to explain the strangely familiar melancholy I felt more frequently with each passing day to one so fervently committed to the future, I was equally unwilling to unburden myself by dampening her spirits with doubt. "I'm humbled by your generous acknowledgment and moved to tears by your fortitude. I, too, meant no distress."

We returned to the consolation of our work.

"Set aside your drawings," she said after a short while. "I wish to share with you a new part of the narrative I've written about the city of ladies." She handed me a few folios from her work.

Her elegant language bespoke a vision with such erudition that I was aghast with wonder. Against the reproaches hurled at women through the ages, Christine had marshaled the defenses of three goddesses, the Ladies Reason, Rectitude, and Justice. She described how they'd instructed her to overthrow the false testimony our sex had endured to the point of distrusting ourselves, and to replace those scabrous lies with the truth—that women were accomplished in all fields of learning, had fought valiantly against adversity, and were wise enough to rule a kingdom.

Thus, fair daughter, you have been given the prerogative among women to construct the City of Ladies, for whose foundation and completion you will take and draw from the three of us fresh water, as from clear fountains, and we will give you plenty of material, stronger and more durable than marble, even if it were cemented. Your city will be incomparably beautiful and will last forever in the world.

As I read what she'd written, I remembered the woman we'd met on the forest road at the end of the millennium and the beginning of a new era in that year we'd traveled to Poissy. It was Lady Reason who'd appeared and chosen Christine, because of her superior imagination, to become the architect of fortified ramparts that would defend her city of women against slanderous attacks. Imagination is the sense that inspires us to seek the transcendent. Left idle, it atrophies, abdicating its just rule over our soul's understanding, leaving behind in empathy's abandoning wake only a hollowed shell of our capacity for judgment. Kept active, imagination becomes powerful, strong enough to forge compassion on the anvil of beauty and immortalize the City of Ladies in luminous prose.

"What a marvelous vision!" My hands flew to my quills and inks, so eager was I to amplify her words with a painting of the dazzling city. "There will be no doubt who fashioned this tale, as I will make evident with my illuminations. Above the opening sentences of your story, I'll paint a double-columned miniature." With a hand steadied by my desire to bring this fantastic city of women to light and to honor its creator, I drew a rough sketch of Christine in her study receiving the three crowned Ladies' wise teachings. Next to it, I outlined a scene of Christine, accompanied by Lady Reason, laying stones for the walls of the city. "Around the whole will be garlands of flowers. Then, near the middle of the manuscript, another miniature will depict Lady Rectitude welcoming you and the most virtuous women of France to the completed city." Together we selected brilliant shades of vermilion and lapis lazuli for their costumes, the latter of which I intended to echo in a magnificently dappled blue sky. Because the tale celebrated a community of women, instead of anointing one exceptional woman with fame, I would forgo the signature peacock I'd used to sign the breviary we'd donated to Poissy.

Delighted with my ideas, yet aware of my growing weariness, Christine suggested that we rest. "There's no need to rush. I've received another commission that must take my attention away from building our city for a while, one that will no doubt surprise you when I reveal the source."

"I see you've absorbed not only my strength, but also my passion for intrigue," I said with a curious look.

With an expression of mischievous delight, she announced the commission. "The Duke of Burgundy has agreed to pay me a large sum for a biography of the former king, Charles the Wise. In addition, Jean will be placed in his service for a year, which will give him the experience he needs to secure a position as royal secretary."

My mouth gaped open in shock. "Have you withdrawn your support of the king's brother?"

Her face erupted into a smile as wicked as any I'd managed in my youth. "A less straightforward route, as you once instructed, may be the most efficient path to victory, especially when dealing with those puffed up with pride. I intend to take the opportunity not only to praise Charles the fifth, but to secure the proper government of the realm, with Philip's unwitting support. And yes, I'm aware that he thinks he's won me as the prize in his battle against Louis. He'll be surprised when he sees what I've written." She burst into laughter.

"I shall continue my work on the frontispiece while you plot Louis's ascendancy," I said, unable to contain my own mirth at how crafty she'd become, every bit a daughter of mine.

A year later, before her biography was complete, the plague struck Philip down, sparing him the embarrassment of defeat through the clever words of a woman, however strange it may be to consider death anyone's ally. Truth be told, when I read what Christine had written about Charles, I wondered whether the subtlety of her observations about royal succession, or her praise of Isabeau as a wise regent, would have eluded Philip, who seemed to be a man more engorged with vanity than possessed of a clever mind. If Philip's death also deprived Christine of the possibility to gloat at his being tricked into his own failure, she was unbothered by it. She was consumed with conjuring the *City of Ladies* in words, a project now made even more pressing by the king's escalating bouts of madness. Challenges to the queen's authority, and the likelihood that the decapitation of its leader would prompt the Burgundian faction to intensify its attacks, as soon came to pass, motivated her further. To advance her cause, she now commissioned my workshop to produce illuminations for several copies of the *City of Ladies* as quickly as possible.

The urgency of Christine's desire to complete the architectural prose of her women's fortress was matched by an urgency of my own. Worried that my failing health would soon preclude my ability to work at the pace and with the attentiveness to detail required, I engaged Ghislaine to assist in the final stages of painting and burnishment. She took to the work with an enthusiasm that reminded me of my own eager apprenticeship under Sister Héloïse, surrounded by another community of women. I found myself repeating Héloïse's wisdom whenever Ghislaine hesitated or stumbled:

"If you make a mistake, it is of no great consequence. We can redraw a line and cover the mistake with color. To make the area where the gold should lay more visible, add a tiny bit of moistened red clay to the gesso platform on which it will float. Add color to the outlined drawing surrounding the gold only after it has been affixed for a day. Then burnish the gold to shine as brightly as the midday sun."

Ghislaine absorbed instruction with alacrity and verve, learning to translate my exemplars into a style closely resembling my own, but with subtle, distinguishing flourishes that a discerning eye would detect. She favored verdigris, adding a patch of bright grass behind the image illustrating Christine and Lady Reason building the walls of the city and fashioning Lady Rectitude's gown in a lighter shade of the same green. While I had outfitted Lady Justice in a white bodice gown of the same style Lady Reason wore in the stone-laying scene, Ghislaine chose to attire Justice in a rose-colored gown, contending a bodice should be used to distinguish the manual labor Reason performed while building the walls from her philosophical work. In place of the dappled sky, she chose a diapered, or patterned, geometric background, such as those in which the older Perrette had specialized, which she much admired.

As Ghislaine toiled for hours to perfect every detail with delicate strokes, I felt as if I had fallen backward through time and was watching a younger version of myself. It calmed me to know that when I would no longer be able to paint, I could supervise Ghislaine, who possessed the talents to be recognized one day as a *maitresse* herself.

In the waning days of summer, we completed the last of the illuminations that shimmered in five copies of the *City of Ladies*. One evening, as a bold, orange-hued sunset softened into the pale amber of dusk before fading to night, I felt the long shadows of memory creep across the portal of my *atelier*. My mind traveled back decades to pull a thread from the variegated fabric of my long life. I attached one end to the frame of a dream I'd once had of my daughter, the daughter of my flesh, and tied the other end to the frame of work I'd created with my other daughter, the daughter birthed from imagination's womb. Then this thread found companionship with another and another and another, until I'd woven a tapestry of remembrance. I lay down on the wooden pallet that served as my bed and drifted off to a fitful sleep. In the morning I would rise, and begin a painting I'd too long postponed.

18

THE ROAD TAKEN

VERITY

Verity heard sounds but couldn't make sense of them. She tried to stand, but fell back into a long, dark tunnel. Something cold pressed against her forehead. She forced her eyes open, and a shape slowly emerged from a blurry image, forming itself into the face of Anastasia.

"Where am I?" Verity looked around at the unfamiliar room. It was some kind of office.

"You fainted." Anastasia removed the cold cloth and smoothed back Verity's hair. "I called the librarian and got you on your feet. You took one look at the Poissy breviary and fainted. Luckily, the thoughtful French must have anticipated how shocking revelations from half a millennium ago can be, and affixed caster wheels to the chairs in the manuscript reading room, in case of just such an emergency. So we rolled you back to the staff room to recover."

"We?" Verity couldn't see anyone else besides Anastasia and herself.

"The librarian helped me maneuver you down the hallway. She's gone back to her desk."

"And the breviary?" Verity, now fully conscious, remembered the inciting incident that had sent her swooning.

"Tucked safely back into its coffin and sealed in the vault."

"We found it, haven't we?" Verity sat up, ready to burst.

"It seems so." She rubbed Verity's shoulder and downshifted her emotional gears as smoothly as she'd driven the little green dragon. "And now comes the hard part."

"I know." Verity let out an exasperated sigh, annoyed that Anastasia hadn't allowed her to enjoy her little balloon of a victory a few minutes longer before puncturing it with the sharp spike of reality. "Getting someone besides you to believe in a phantom."

"Don't despair, my darling. The hard part is the best part. The wizardry of phantasmagoria makes the dustbins of scholarly arcana positively explode with hidden beauty, as those medieval illusionists of yours obviously knew." Anastasia pulled Verity into an embrace. "All you have to do is take a chance."

"You make it sound so easy. But it's a tough decision." Verity nuzzled into Anastasia. "One I have to make on my own."

Anastasia pulled away. "You don't want to be with me?" Her voice quavered to the sharp edge of anger. "What about Anastasia, I mean, the medieval artist we've been tracking? Doesn't she matter, either?

"I *do* want to be with you. And you both matter. But I have to decide exactly what that means." She took a deep breath and braced herself for Anastasia's reaction to what she was about to say. "I'm supposed to go back to California in less than two months. I'm scheduled to teach next term."

"And then?" Anastasia asked with a wounded expression, as if expecting the worst.

Verity restrained her urge to disclose the direction she thought she wanted to take. She was still uncertain about making such a drastic decision and knew Anastasia would say it was perfectly fine to be impulsive. And although she loved Anastasia's conviction, loved the euphoria of discovery they shared, she needed time to consider whether where she was heading was where she really wanted to go. She had to weigh the consequences of taking another leap. "That's what I have to figure out," she said, folding her arms. "I need to stay in Paris a few more days. Alone."

Anastasia said nothing at first. Then she lowered her head, raised her eyes, and shaped her lovely lips into a tempting pout. "Without your Cumaean Sybil or me?"

"I'll return to London before the weekend."

"Or I'll come get you."

"I wouldn't put it past you," Verity said, smiling.

They walked back from the library, crossed the Seine at the Pont Royal, and arrived at their hotel. Anastasia checked with reception to switch Verity to a smaller, less expensive single.

"Since it's my last night, I get to choose the restaurant," Anastasia said. "We're going to one of the oldest in the city, Le Procope, a seventeenth-century brasserie in the sixth."

"As long as you're paying," Verity said.

"Thank the British government, not me, though I suppose you'd consider it fair compensation for Henry's capturing Paris during the Hundred Years' War."

"Let's give the fifteenth century a rest for tonight, shall we? I've got a more modern remuneration from a certain British woman in mind."

The next morning, after Verity saw Anastasia off on the Eurostar from Gare du Nord, she wandered the streets of Paris in the direction of Belleville, not exactly sure why, until she found herself an hour later outside the entryway to Père Lachaise, the large cemetery in Paris where so many of the famous and infamous were buried. She entered and walked along cobblestone pathways lined with graves and imposing mausoleums, passing monuments to a constellation of writers, artists, and activists who'd used word, image, gesture, and song to alter the course of history.

"Balzac, Colette, Molière, Wilde, Pissaro, Callas, Bernhardt, Morrison, Piaf . . ." Verity intoned the names of the illustrious dead until she reached the farthest wall of the cemetery, where a nameless group of 147 defenders of the Paris Commune of 1871 had been assassinated and thrown into an unmarked trench. A rugged stone monument commemorated the spot, and Verity stared for a long time at the figure of a woman sculpted as if emerging from the rock, arms outstretched neither in supplication nor surrender, defiantly refusing to be forgotten. The longer she stared, the more sharply other faces and hands, arms and legs came into focus, fragments of the woman's anonymous comrades. It was as if the stone had been porous enough for the dead to return to the present. Just as stars slowly come to light the longer you concentrate on the dark holes in a midnight sky, so whatever can't be seen with the naked eye becomes visible over time through the work of other senses of perception.

It became clearer than ever to Verity what she wanted, what she needed to do. She wanted to bring to light what had too long been concealed—that Christine had chosen another woman to illuminate the miniatures in her *Book of the City of Ladies*, her celebration of women's contributions to the world. She needed to do it, even if it meant jeopardizing her career.

―――――――――――

Two more days in the library convinced Verity that there were no other traces of the existence of her medieval artist in any of the archives. Oddly enough, lacking documentation only emboldened her determination to demonstrate Anastasia's existence by other means. She took an evening train back to London's St. Pancras Station. Anastasia greeted her with a bouquet of gigantic sunflowers, wearing her peacock fascinator. Verity laughed and hugged her.

Anastasia shook her head, making the feathers dance. Then she bent toward Verity and tickled her face with the headpiece.

"What are you doing?" Verity picked feathers out of her mouth. "Have you gone completely mad in just two days?"

"Darling—peacocks?" Anastasia pointed to the ornament.

"I know what they are. But why are you wearing that now?"

"Don't you know what the peacock symbolized to the good folks of the Middle Ages?"

Verity scrunched her face and shook her head slowly. "No."

"Peacocks were the symbols of resurrection, rebirth—ANASTASIA!"

"Oh, my god, the image of a peacock we saw at the bottom of the Poissy breviary! Anastasia must have used that symbol as her signature."

"*Voila!* I didn't even remember seeing it myself until I looked at the photos I'd taken of the folios, and there it was."

"You took photos? I thought photography was prohibited," Verity said, shocked but not altogether surprised by Anastasia's boldness, though she wondered what other tricks her lover had up her sleeve.

"I took them after you fainted." She gave Verity a sheepish look. "I thought you'd need some visual aids for your presentation about Anastasia's illumination of Christine's books."

"You're proposing that I offer a version of your theory of symbols as evidence to support my argument about Anastasia's contributions to Christine's legacy."

"Yes, and you have much more than I had to go on. Add the peacock symbol to what you know about Poissy, about Morris's fascination with the Harley manuscripts, and Siddal's paintings on that jewelry case, and the *Cities of Women*—"

"City of Ladies—"

"Oh, don't be so finicky about malapropisms! It's too late for that now, my dear."

"If I'm going to launch an attack on the established wisdom, I have to be precise at least in some ways."

"All right, then—add all those things to the *City of Ladies* as a latter-day vindication of women and you've got plenty of ingredients for a smashing theory, I'd say."

"I need a drink."

"We're not too far from the Noble Rot Wine Bar I invited you to once."

"*Allons-y*, my beauty!" Verity grabbed Anastasia's hand.

"It's good to have my Verity back," Anastasia said, shaking the feathers on her head into a mad dance.

"I'm changing my name to Vera. I prefer the fiery Russian to the staider Latin, it seems."

During her last month in London, Verity holed up in the basement quarters at Great Percy Street to concentrate on writing her sabbatical research report before heading back stateside. Anastasia had offered to stay with her, but Verity insisted it was better if she was alone. On weekends, she allowed herself to indulge in the fleshly pleasures and conviviality of the living Anastasia, but kept to the more cerebral routines of resurrecting her medieval artist during the week. More than once, she suggested they spend a night at Anastasia's place, but Anastasia always rejected the idea, saying that she was refurbishing her Chelsea flat, and the place was a mess. Verity was too focused on her work to give Anastasia's excuse a second thought.

She'd submitted an abstract of a paper entitled "Whither Anastasia? On the Significance of Absence to Presence" to the Paris meeting of the Medieval Society scheduled for the following June. Her proposal was accepted with an enthusiastic endorsement from the program committee. She planned to go back to California, turn in her research report, and teach one last term. Since she hadn't worked on the Commune book, she expected the tenure committee to reject her promotion application, offer her a terminal year, and she'd surprise them with a rejection of her own—she intended to resign at the end of the semester and chart a new course for herself in London.

Anastasia had assured Verity that she'd help her get a job teaching part-time somewhere in London. It would be enough to secure a work visa and then decide on next steps.

"Naturally, I'd rather get you a position at my university, but we're under a hiring freeze at the moment," she'd said.

"It's better not to be teaching at the same university," Verity said, thinking of her experience with Pauline at Monterey College. It hadn't gone well. "In any case, whether I even continue in academia remains an open question. For now, my goal is to have the world of medieval scholars recognize Anastasia's contributions to Christine's books, one way or the other."

Anastasia nodded, looking relieved.

At their last teary-eyed dinner together, Verity promised to return in five months.

Just after the winter holidays, Verity said goodbye to the birds on the Morris-inspired *Strawberry Thief* wallpaper, tightened a festive red-and-green scarf around Cecil the Crocodile's snout, and took a taxi to Heathrow. Anastasia had offered to drive her to the airport, but Verity couldn't bear another wrenching goodbye. Twelve hours later, she stood at the baggage claim at SFO, jet-lagged and disoriented by the cacophony of American accents chattering around her. Everything and nothing had changed.

The next day, she awoke in her condo to find that the smoke-filled Monterey skies she'd left behind in September had given way to January's torrential downpour. Verity pulled on her slicker, got into her car, and headed for the beach. The waves were spectacles of fury, beating the rocks at the shoreline like timpani into a crescendo of sound. She loved the ocean's implacable repetition. It would be what she'd miss more than anything, except if she stayed in California and had to miss Anastasia's winsome smile, or her ridiculous laugh, or her indifference to whether anyone believed as unimpeachably as she did that you could rewrite history with the magic wand of a new idea. Anyone, that is, except Verity, who'd begun to believe that too. She returned to her apartment and called the real estate agent who'd sold her the place five and a half years ago, and told her to put the condo on the market.

A week later, when the For Sale sign went up and prospective buyers started to come by for viewings, Verity began to have doubts. Everything had happened too quickly. How had she let herself be swept off her feet into an affair with a woman she'd only just met and who wouldn't be making any of the sacrifices Verity would have to make to be with her? Anastasia would still have a secure position at a cushy British university. What would Verity have? No permanent job, no familiar home, and only a hair's breadth of a chance that an outlandish hunch could prove Anastasia's influence in Christine's books. Regina's voice began to rattle around in Verity's head again. *Follow the rules of academic writing. Get published. That's the game.*

Regina was right. It would certainly be easier to make those few changes the Cambridge editor had suggested than to risk everything and fly off to an uncertain European future with nothing more than a verbal reassurance from an enigmatic lover that she could get her a position at some third-rate college. None of that felt as secure as what would happen to her career with her Commune research. She'd get tenure—and, if she still cared about the illuminated manuscripts, could even write an informal essay later. Or not. It didn't matter. If she produced the Commune book, they couldn't deny her promotion. They'd put that in writing already.

Verity hurried back to the safety of her office, turned on her computer, opened the Commune files, and felt her stomach knot into a pretzel. It would be so easy, comfortable even, to fall back into the pattern everyone at the university expected her to resume. But easy and comfortable for whom? Not for Verity, who'd have to ignore what she'd seen and felt in London and Paris—a shimmering image, an unbridled passion, an awakening as monumental as the crash of waves on the rocks. No, she didn't want easy and comfortable anymore. She turned off her computer and spent the rest of the semester teaching her classes and polishing her report on Anastasia (the medieval artist not the lover) and Harley 4431.

Soon after spring break, the Department Chair summoned Verity to her office. "I've read your promotion application," she said with a steely look. Verity prepared herself for what was coming. "I see you opted to use your fellowship on an entirely new project. I must say, I was rather shocked by the audacity of taking on something you've never researched before." The Chair paused to reach for a paper on the side of her desk. "It was such a bold, promising idea, I recommended your project for special funding to the research committee." She handed the paper to Verity. "Congratulations, you've been selected to receive funding. You'll be given another term's leave to complete 'Whither Anastasia.' We've agreed to postpone the promotion decision until next year."

Verity dropped into the seat opposite the Chair's desk like a deflated version of herself. "I don't know what to say."

"'Thank you' wouldn't be inappropriate," the Chair said with a sardonic smile.

"Thank you." Verity barely got the words out of her mouth and left the office in stunned disbelief. She walked down the hall, took the stairs to the ground floor, and exited out of the building into an unexpected quagmire. She'd wanted the decision to leave her position to be made for her. Now, it seemed, she'd have to bear the full brunt of a choice without the excuse of being forced out. The door was left open; she'd have to slam it herself. *So, this is what responsibility feels like. It's like descending a narrow spiral staircase without a banister to hold on to.*

She considered calling Anastasia for moral support, but as soon as that thought came to mind, Verity realized it was the wrong thing to do and suddenly felt more resolved than ever. Holding fast to her conviction, she took a deep breath. It felt like the first breath she'd ever taken must have felt, a delicious, icy sensation coming from deep inside, as if she'd finally been released from a long incubation inside the womb of self-doubt. The next day, she submitted her letter of resignation.

A month later, she sold her condo at a decent profit, bought a ticket to London, and phoned Anastasia to ask her to meet her at the airport, which she did, but without any peacock feathers in her hair and wearing a forlorn expression on her face.

Verity put down her suitcase and moved closer to kiss Anastasia, who offered her cheek instead of her lips.

"Is something the matter?" Verity asked.

Anastasia reached down to pick up Verity's suitcase. "Where are you staying?" she asked, her face hidden from view.

When she stood up, Verity looked at her in disbelief. "I assumed I'd stay with you until I found a place of my own."

"That's not possible," Anastasia said, still not looking directly at Verity. "My cousin lost his job last week. I couldn't say no when he asked if he could stay at my place. He's sleeping on the couch."

"Well, I don't mind. I wasn't planning on sleeping on the couch," Verity said.

"I told you it's not possible for you to stay with me. My place is too small for three people."

Verity stared at Anastasia. "Why didn't you tell me this before? I would have understood. I could have rented Mrs. Fairweather's flat again. Now I have to waste money on a hotel room."

"I was, well . . . surprised to hear you'd decided to come back to London after all," Anastasia said.

"Surprised? You didn't act surprised when I called to tell you I'd sold my condo and made the plane reservation."

"Promises are easy to make, harder to keep."

"I know that. But I've kept my promise." Standing in the middle of the international arrivals hall, surrounded by people embracing and smiling, happy to be reunited, Verity suddenly felt very much alone. "If you didn't want to keep yours, why did you even come to the airport?"

"You wouldn't understand." Anastasia had such a tortured expression on her face, Verity closed her eyes and turned away. "Anyway, where should I drop you?"

"You already have, Anastasia." Verity pulled her suitcase from Anastasia's grip and walked toward the elevator, taking it down to the taxi stand. "Hilton Islington," she said to the driver, choking back angry tears.

A week later, she moved back into the Great Percy Street flat, determined to ignore one Anastasia, while remaining steadily focused on the other one's proving less elusive despite being long dead.

The June date of the Medieval Society's Paris conference was fast approaching when Verity got a message from Anastasia, begging to meet her so she could explain her weird behavior at the airport. She ignored the first one and the next few, until there were so many texts she finally replied.

"Go to hell," she texted.

"Already reached the tenth circle," Anastasia replied.

"There are only nine," Verity texted back.

"Maybe in Dante Alighieri's hell, but not in Anastasia Griffin's," Anastasia wrote back. "I'm sorry. Really, truly sorry. Please meet me at Noble Rot Wine to witness purgation."

Verity agreed and, an hour later, was sitting opposite Anastasia, waiting for an explanation.

Anastasia sipped her wine. Then she took a deep breath. "There's something I have to tell you," she began. "I lied about my cousin."

"Which one?" Verity asked.

"All of them. The one I said lent me the MG, the one I said was staying in my flat, and the other two I mentioned when we were at Lacock. I don't have any cousins—neither of my parents had siblings. In fact, I'm the lone remaining descendant of a long, lonely line of single-child households, extending as far back as I've been able to trace."

"Then why did you tell me you had cousins, much less one living in your flat?"

"Because I didn't want you to see my place. It's ugly." Anastasia covered her face with her hands and began to shake with emotion.

"I wouldn't have cared if you hadn't finished the remodeling," Verity said, reaching over to touch Anastasia's trembling shoulder.

"It's not ugly because of remodeling." She let her hands drop into her lap. Her eyes were red from crying. "I live in a bedsit in public housing in Becontree, far outside central London and about as different from Chelsea as a sow's ear from a silk purse. I don't have a university posting. Not anymore. I lost that position after I failed to publish my paper on the Lacock Abbey nuns. The editor sent the manuscript to a group of readers; most opposed my ideas. Now I teach general humanities courses to fourteen-to-nineteen-year-old aspiring engineers at East London University Technical College, bringing me full circle back to my working-class roots in Swindon. Poetic justice, I suppose, for someone who pretends to be posh."

Verity crossed her arms and sat back in the chair. "So, you've been lying to me all this time. Was the migraine story a lie too?"

Anastasia nodded. "To give me time to rent the MG. I wanted to impress you."

"Are you even a medieval historian?"

"Yes, of course. I lost my post, but not my knowledge. I'm as determined as you to rewrite history, regardless of what my colleagues say." She leaned closer to Verity and reached for her hand. "And I haven't been lying about how much I love you."

"Why should I believe you when you've told so many lies?" Verity asked, not pulling her hand away.

"Remember you asked me why I went to the airport if I didn't want to keep my promise?"

Verity nodded.

"I went thinking you wouldn't show, and it would be a relief because I could go back to my little life and keep feeling sorry for myself. When I saw you appear in the crowd, I was terrified," Anastasia said. "I wanted nothing more than to be with you, but I'd woven such a tight fabric of

pretense to woo you—designer clothes, expensive hotels, fancy restaurants—"

"You were afraid to tell me the truth," Verity said.

"Yes. I knew you'd expect to stay with me, but I was terrified that if
I brought you to my place, instead of a flat in Chelsea, you'd run away
from me like I had the plague. Like Daisy did, after I lost my university
appointment."

"But I wouldn't have run," Verity said, trying not to smile.

"What do you mean?" Anastasia said.

"I already knew the truth. Not about the cousins, but about where
you lived and worked."

Anastasia was stunned speechless, so Verity continued.

"I didn't think much about it until I got back to California. Then
I kept turning over your reluctance to have me stay at your place, or
invite me to your university, and pieced those two bits of information
together with other clues you'd dropped. Like about buying your clothes
in second-hand stores, having a large research grant, but especially about
encouraging me to look below appearances, sniff out hidden stories, touch
what lies underneath the shiny surface of things.

"I began to wonder if you were telling me the truth without actually saying what the truth was. So, I dug around a little and discovered you'd been
terminated but had negotiated a large severance package—the 'research
grant'—because you'd accused them of discrimination for letting you go
while they extended the contract of a male colleague with a less-stellar record
than yours. I found your address in Becontree—the 'public housing' you
mentioned, except it's been converted to private flats. I figured you bought
it because it's near your job at ELUtec—that's the correct acronym, isn't it?"

Anastasia nodded.

"None of those little lies bothered me. I come from a working-class
family too. I understand the pressure to appear posh—we call it wanting
champagne on a beer budget. No, what bothered me was what you said
at the airport."

Anastasia looked sad and confused.

"You said I wouldn't understand why you came to the airport. That
made me angry. It meant you'd given up without giving me a chance

to tell you I'd already discovered the truth about you, the deep truth, not the veneer, and that I loved you despite your little lies. Because I do understand. I understand what it means to make a promise to someone. To say you'll take a leap into the future with her, not knowing what that future will be or even knowing all those old, sad stories she'll drag along with her, put on a shelf in another madwoman's attic, hoping they'll gather dust, until one day those ghosts no longer haunt anyone. Promises are a scary business."

"Oh, Verity. It's probably too late, but I'm so terribly sorry for not trusting you," Anastasia said.

"No, Anastasia, it's not too late. But the one you should apologize to isn't me. It's you." She brushed away a tear rolling down Anastasia's cheek. "Now, let's make a beeline to Becontree. I want to practice my presentation for the conference before the most brilliant historian I know."

The steeply sloped, wood-paneled amphitheater in the Sorbonne quickly filled with sixty scholars of medieval literature and the arts, most of whom appeared to have known each other for years, as evidenced by the triple kisses they pecked on each other's cheeks. After an elegantly dressed member of the organizing committee welcomed the group to the Tenth International Colloquium of the Medieval Society, the first presenter approached the lectern to deliver a talk on the history of sources of patronage for Christine's manuscripts.

Verity leaned over to whisper to Anastasia. "She's talking so fast in French, I'm having a hard time keeping up."

"You shouldn't be listening anyway. Concentrate on your own talk. You're up next."

"From 1399 to 1405, Christine's scriptorium experienced its most productive period, a time when she had the moral and financial support of the queen." The lecturer was coming to her conclusion. "The preparation of the collection now known as Harley 4431 was supervised by Christine herself, who placed her magnificent *Cité des Dames*—her celebration of women's power—at its exact middle, authenticating the queen as the center of the realm while simultaneously highlighting Christine's authority as a legitimating literary force."

A wave of applause rose in the room. The speaker returned to her seat, flushed with pride. Verity walked down the stairs to the podium.

"What a woman's mind can evoke in words, a woman's hands can illuminate in lustrous color. For years, we've known of the artist, Anastasia, from Christine's acknowledgment of her artistic prowess in *The Book of the City of Ladies*. Many have argued that Anastasia may have been more fancy than fact, or contended that, if she did exist, she was skilled only in the lesser crafts of illustration. I wish to disrupt these assumptions, and elaborate Anastasia's existence through lines of filiation between her and Christine, made manifest in recent discoveries I've made." Verity proceeded to weave an elaborate tale with the filaments of association she'd garnered. "I propose we substitute the name Anastasia for the title by which the illuminator of Harley 4431 has previously been known; that we identify the Master of the City of Ladies as the Mistress Anastasia, and give this extraordinary artist her due."

It didn't take long for several hands to shoot up like eager arrows of opposition. "It seems to me that, on the basis of very scant evidence, you are leaping to a conclusion, motivated, perhaps, by an over-eagerness to write women into history," one gentleman in the front row suggested. "As I'm sure you know, there are few extant records from this period that allow us to identify the names of the painters, which is why they've been given titles associated with the works they illuminated rather than their actual names."

"Those names will, however unfortunately, forever remain hidden from history," a woman seated next to him added. "A peacock symbol doesn't seem evidence enough to prove otherwise."

Verity fielded the questions and comments as best she could. Yes, she knew about the lack of records, and yes, she was motivated by the desire to give a woman her due. In fact, if there were no records with which to identify the painters, why assume they were men? In the end, she received a round of faint applause. As the session adjourned for a coffee break, she returned to her seat.

Anastasia squeezed her knee. "I thought you were magnificent."

"It's not you I needed to convince," Verity said, packing her briefcase. "In fact, I think I realized I never really needed to convince anyone except myself."

"Excuse me," a young woman standing next to them interrupted. "But I loved your presentation. It was so inspiring, like, it gave me chills. I mean, you brought Anastasia to life. I want to be able to do that one day. I don't mean Anastasia, of course. I mean, well, you know what I mean. Make something beautiful appear that we haven't seen before."

"Thank you," Verity said. "I hope you will."

The young woman bounded down the stairs. When she reached the bottom, she turned and waved, disappearing into the dispersing crowd.

"I'm so glad we found each other, Anastasia." Verity hugged her lover. "Let's go." She felt so calm, she could hardly believe how easy it was to leave it all behind.

Outside, Paris glistened in the afternoon sun. Down the street from the Sorbonne, they passed a boutique selling beautiful fountain pens and handmade papers and bookbinding materials in silk and leather.

"Care to investigate for your next enterprise?" Anastasia asked. "Book arts, if I'm not mistaken, are where you're headed."

"You read my mind," Verity said, grabbing her hand and pulling her into L'Atelier d'Or. "If I can't bring Anastasia to life through academic prose, I can reproduce her story in the illuminated language in which she excelled."

EPILOGUE

A DISTANT MIRROR

G hislaine found her the next morning in the *atelier*, her fingers curled into a ball, her limbs stiffened, her breath stilled, her silver hair frosted with ice. She wept, her body trembling with grief, and ran from the sight to fetch Christine. There would be time later for mourning. For now, they needed to prepare the body for burial before the earth froze, as if refusing to accept the death of its daughter.

They wrapped her in muslin sheets. Christine placed an amulet around her neck—a gold disk engraved with the initial *A* on one side, and stamped with the feathered eye of a peacock's plume on the other. Jean, Christine's son, and his new bride helped carry the body to a waiting cart led by a white horse.

Christine looked around the room where they'd built the *City of Ladies*. On the workbench, she found a painting of two women—one decorated in her own favorite blue and the other in the madder favored by the artist. She rolled it and tied it with the green satin ribbon she found lying next to it, still bearing a few gray hairs.

The funeral procession snaked its way through the city streets, past the fortified gates of Paris, into the forest, headed for Poissy, where Anastasia would be laid to rest on the abbey grounds.

They read prayers for the dead from the breviary Christine had gifted to the abbey. The Abbess returned the precious memento to Christine, who took it to her bosom, bowed her head, and wept. Later, in the quiet of the night, she would place the last painting Anastasia ever made inside the breviary and lock it in a cabinet in her home, where it remained for the remaining twenty-five years of her life, until becoming an emissary sent back to Poissy to inform Marie of her mother's death.

Perhaps, a century from now, someone will dig in the ruins of an Abbey enclosure and find the remains of a woman's bones and her blued teeth, along with an amulet bearing the mark of her name and the sign of her craft. Perhaps not.

Such are the gossamer threads of filiation, like the intricate patterns Arachne wove on her loom, that have bound and separated women over the centuries, sometimes accidentally, sometimes willfully, sometimes hidden, and sometimes illuminated with the incandescence of beauty's light.

ACKNOWLEDGMENTS

I would like to thank everyone whose friendship and artistic support have sustained me during the years of this novel's development. Thank you to Eugenia Kim, Karen Osborn, Susan Muaddi Darraj, Phil Klay, and Margie Bucheit, early readers of all or parts of the novel whose insights helped improve my craft. Thank you to Carol Ann Davis, whose *Poetry for Prose Writers* workshops sparkled with inspiration. Thank you to Alanna Johnson, Dare Delano, Meghan Muldowney, Jennifer L. Russell, Barb Chintz, Elner Morrell, Celia Bland, Paula Bennett, Gillian Youngs, and H. N. Hirsch for being in my writers' circle and sharing the roller-coaster ride of the writer's life. Thank you to my agent, Katelyn Detweiler of Jill Grinberg Literary, for believing in my work from the beginning. And thanks to my editors, Ryan Smernoff and Amanda Chiu Krohn, and the team at Turner Publishing for bringing it into the world.

Among the scores of books and articles I consulted for this novel, besides de Pizan's published works, I am especially indebted to Tracy Adams's *Christine de Pizan and the Fight for France*; Marilynn Desmond and Pamela Sheingorn's *Myth, Montage, and Visuality in Late Medieval Manuscript Culture: Christine de Pizan's Epistre Othea*; Christopher de Hamel's *Medieval Craftsmen: Scribes and Illuminators*, and his *Meetings with Remarkable Manuscripts: Twelve Journeys into the Medieval World*; Kouky Fianu's *Histoire juridique et sociale des métiers du livre à Paris (1275–1521)*; Ouy, Reno and Villela-Petit's *Album Christine de Pizan*; Richard and Mary Rouse's *Manuscripts and Their Makers: Commercial Book Producers in Paris, 1200–1500*; Barbara Tuchman's *A Distant Trumpet*; and Charity Cannon Willard's, *Christine de Pizan, Her Life and Works: A Biography*. Special thanks to Tracy Adams for reading the manuscript in draft, to Kouky Fianu for pointing me to the GIS project on medieval Paris, Alpage (http://mapd.sig.huma-num.fr/alpage_public/flash/), and to Anita Radini and her colleagues' account of their discovery of lapis lazuli on medieval nuns' teeth.

I am grateful to the librarians in the British Library's manuscript reading room, to Christine Nelson (formerly of the Morgan Library) and to Mara Hofmann (rare books and manuscript curator) for help with background on the illuminated manuscripts. Thanks to the Christine de Pizan Society for their network of support.

Finally, thanks to my family for living with the long process of this book's evolution, especially my spouse, Amy Fraher, without whose love and unfailing support neither I nor this book would have made it this far.

ABOUT THE AUTHOR

KATHLEEN B. JONES was born and educated in New York. After teaching women's studies for two decades at San Diego State University, she resigned to focus on writing, earning an M.F.A. in fiction from Fairfield University. Her scholarly writing includes six books published with academic presses—three monographs and three edited anthologies of critical essays. *Diving for Pearls: A Thinking Journey with Hannah Arendt* won the 2015 Barbara "Penny" Kanner Book Award from the Western Association of Women Historians. Her essays and short fiction have appeared in *Fiction International*, *Mr. Beller's Neighborhood*, the *Briar Cliff Review*, and the *Los Angeles Review of Books*. She lives in Stonington, Connecticut.